TERMS OF BETRAYAL

a novel

T. Milton Mayer

Simon Publishing LLC

T. Milton Mayer

This is a work of fiction. Names, characters, organizations, places, events and incidents are either products of the author's imagination or are used fictionally. Any resemblance to actual events, locals, or persons, living or dead, is entirely coincidental.

Published by Simon Publishing LLC, Naples, FL ®
Simon Publishing LLC logo is a registered trademark
ISBN: 978-9861221-5-1 Trade Paperback
ISBN: 978-8-9861221-6-8 eBook
Library of Congress Number: 2022918827
Cover Design by Robin Ludwig, Robin Ludwig Designs
Printed by Ingram Spark in the United States of America
First Edition
1 9 4 5 2 0 2 2 1 9 4 8

TERMS OF BETRAYAL

T. Milton Mayer

When you see that trading is done, not by consent, but by compulsion —

when you see that in order to produce, you need to obtain permission from men who produce nothing —

when you see that money is flowing to those who deal, not in goods, but favors —

when you see that men get richer by graft and by pull than by work, and your laws don't protect you against them, but protect them against you —

when you see corruption being rewarded and honesty becoming a self-sacrifice — you may know that your society is doomed.

Ayn Rand
Atlas Shrugged, 1957

ONE

Home of Lisa Marie Crawford
Everglades Estates
East Naples, Florida

S leep was a lot like sex. The less you had, the more you needed it, and I hadn't had either for too long. My own fault. After months of insomnia, I had finally drifted into that twilight zone of pre-sleep. A wonderful dream emerged about John and I riding horses in the California surf, laughing and enjoying a romantic afternoon together. Old memories.

A loud noise shook me awake. Startled, I reached for my Sig on the nightstand. Yelling came from the unit next door. *Damn.* Second time this week. Relieved, I put the gun back.

I'd leased the condo for two months. It stood in Everglades Estates, a community east of Naples, Florida where condominiums started at five hundred thousand dollars and houses ranged up to seven million. Those prices bought the owners a trouble-free life and the safety provided by a two-man guardhouse with a wrought-iron security gate, one of the primary reasons why I rented here. Community fees included a membership in two private golf courses, a tennis club, access to three swimming pools, beach transportation, and a long list of what you can or can't do with your own property — emphasis on can't. Apparently, yelling loud enough to keep neighbors awake wasn't on the can't list.

I banged my fist against the wall, so hard I thought I might punch a hole through to the other side. "Enough already," I screamed. The neighbors quieted down but not before I heard the rhythmic sounds of a headboard slamming against the wall. Terrific. Makeup sex. That was all I needed. I covered my ears with a pillow.

It was three in the morning, and my prospects for sleep were nil. What I hated most about nights was lying there, drowning in the brooding blackness of my bedroom ceiling, so dark I couldn't tell if my eyes were opened or closed. Out of habit, I reached over for the reassuring warmth of John's body, his smooth ebony skin, his muscles firm and rippled, hard as though carved from granite. The mere thought of him made me tremble with excitement—but he wasn't there. After three weeks, I still wasn't used to being alone. The headboard banging stopped, and I hugged my pillow, a pathetic substitute for my estranged husband.

Our marriage failed before it had a chance to start. John had insisted I retire from the team, the only family I'd ever known. He said being married to a member of an illegal group was a bad visual for a Deputy Director of the FBI. He forced me to walk away from my life three years ago. I gave up everything I loved—and for what? The promise of a normal life? Of being a Norman Rockwell wife, cuddling on the couch at night with a loving husband, and raising a family of three in our two-story colonial? That illusion of the American dream never happened for me. The sacrifice drained me of my former identity, an independent woman with a purpose, a member of a team of warriors who made a difference in the world, ones who saved our country—twice.

I wanted that feeling of importance again. I wanted to look forward to each new day and all the potential excitement it could bring. I wanted to feel loved again, desired with passion. Only I could make it happen—but how could I while trapped in Washington? I needed a change, and sedate Naples looked like the perfect place for me to regroup and rediscover myself before it was too late.

The alarm buzzed. Five-thirty. I rolled out of bed and put my feet on the hard tile floor, cold and rejecting. I grabbed my Sig and shuffled toward the kitchen, the sounds of loneliness and isolation echoing off the walls. The Keurig awaited, ready for action. I inserted a pod and pushed the selection button for strong. The machine screeched and hissed as the coffee percolated through its tubes, filling the room with the soothing aroma of hazelnut, yielding a cup of magical black liquid that helped fire up my neurons after yet another sleepless night. I took a sip and noticed my chipped, neglected nails. I'd been ignoring myself for months, ever since— I pushed the thought aside. I didn't need any more negativity.

Tropical storm Caroline had stalled just off the gulf coast of southern Florida, ruining everyone's Fourth of July plans. Days of unrelenting downpours forced me to remain inside, deepening my funk. By the third morning, the rain had stopped. I stuck my head out the door to check the weather. The storm had brought with it a cool front, providing a respite from the usual sweltering days of early July. I inhaled a luxurious breath of morning air deep into the bottom of my lungs. Invigorating. I vowed to begin my life anew this morning and I'd allow nothing to stop me.

I pulled on my running shorts and a t-shirt, both tighter than they'd been last year. Too much down time and fast food. I laced up my ASICS and at the last minute, pulled my cellphone armband over my biceps. Before stepping out into the morning, I thought about bringing my Sig, but decided against it. After all, what could possibly happen in sleepy Naples?

After a minute of stretching, I ran along the community's mile-long entrance road, bordered on either side with majestic, tall royal palm trees, their clusters of fruit hanging like red berries. I continued past the resort's guard house, just at the edge of the Everglades. To the east, the sun peeked over the horizon, casting a kaleidoscopic glow of color along the undersurface of Caroline's lingering clouds. Lavish reds, yellows, oranges, and pinks melted together providing a beautiful day to rekindle my spirit. With my legs stiff from months of inactivity, I ran with difficulty, but my muscle memory soon engaged. My legs rippled more with each stride, my body feeling more lithe. *Not there yet.*

I immersed myself in the morning, which wrapped its comforting blanket of serenity around me, leaving behind the demands of Washington—and the disappointing look in John's eyes. When I failed him, I withdrew into my world and he into his career. The distance between us became unbreachable.

Quickening my pace, my stride became more effortless, poetic, almost feral. The rhythmic sounds of my shoes slapping against the pavement was interrupted only by the musical chorus of birds singing their welcome to the new day. My legs churned faster. My blonde hair, pulled back in a ponytail, swung from side to side with each long stride. The clear day hadn't yet alleviated the aching in my soul. Still not there yet. *Need to go faster.*

I followed a path that bordered a large lake on my right, startling a group of white egrets wading in the shallows, their beaks knifing into the water, searching for breakfast. An alligator coasted ten feet away, floating motionless, only its snout and two eyes visible, like a partially-submerged log slowly drifting closer to the birds, hoping to snatch its own meal. Mors tua vita mea. Your death, my life, like the ruthless, dog-eat-dog politicians and bureaucrats I had left behind in Washington. They would lie, cheat, and steal, anything that might help them scale higher up in the political hierarchy of D.C. No price was too great to satisfy their insatiable lust for power and money.

I ran faster, pushing my body beyond its limits, my legs on the brink of collapsing. *Still not there.* Ahead, a thirty-foot incline in the path ushered the way into Seminole Park, a large complex of swampy lakes surrounded by miles of elevated asphalt paths created for walkers and cyclists. I fell into a hypnotic groove, safe from the intrusions and dangers of the outside world. My mind cleared and the anguish began to dissipate.

The serpentine path meandered deeper into the park as another bank of thick clouds rolled by, blocking the sun. Ominous. More rain? I dodged several fallen branches; death left behind in the wake of the storm. To my right, thickets of vines, cypress trees, and gray oaks choked a drainage canal. Their branches dripped with Spanish Moss, swaying in the breeze, creating ghost-like images. On the left, an impenetrable green wall of swamp palms, mangrove trees, and tangled underbrush allowed only intermittent glimpses of the water beyond.

I strained to see something, anything besides the trees. Frustrating. Then, a wide opening appeared, cut out of the brush by the park service to allow visitors a view of the landscape. Acres of untamed swamp spread to the west, a breathtaking sight of an ecological cornucopia providing refuge for wildlife and more species of birds than I could have ever imagined: osprey, diving cormorants, pink spoonbills, great blue herons, and a hundred others. A bald eagle sat majestically on a branch, his keen eyes overlooking his domain, searching for the slightest movement of a potential meal under the water's surface. A cacophony of guttural screeches filled the air. I shivered as I faced a primordial, predatory world. Danger lurked out there, things I couldn't see.

Still, it was a beautiful sight, even more so when the sun peeked out from behind the clouds, making the greens more vibrant. The deep blue water glistened like a sheet of ice, its smooth surface interrupted only by clusters of waterlilies, their delicate white blooms stretching upward in search of the life-giving rays of the sun. Magnificent and serene, but at the same time foreboding, a battle for survival, reminiscent of my childhood home in rural Kentucky. The park's pristine beauty, combined with the sweet taste of the cool air, and the cadence of my stride carried me to a new level, a parallel universe where the cares of my world dissolved into insignificance. Nothing mattered but this moment. The pain in my soul abated. *Finally, there.*

A voice, harsh and heart-stopping like the piercing sound of a weather alert, shredded the mood. "Outta the way, idiot." A blur of yellow-and-black spandex sped past, bumping my left side and knocking me off the path into the brush. The coppery taste of blood filled my mouth. A jolt of adrenaline surged through my body, masking the pain of the fall. I shook with rage. Jacob always told me I should never allow my emotions to control my actions. "Unbridled anger clouds a person's judgment." I was never one to follow my brother's advice.

I jumped up. "Jerk," I yelled at the top of my lungs. "Thanks for the heads up—asshole."

The sound of screeching brakes shouted back. The cyclist came to an abrupt stop and looked back at me. Jacob would have advised me to walk away from this kind of situation. Nothing to be gained by physical confrontation, but walking away from my life is what I did three years ago. Never again.

I held both of my hands up, flashing my middle fingers. "Really?"

The sun again retreated behind a cloud, setting a threatening mood. The cyclist removed his black helmet and stood next to his bike—a jerk, but a young, tall, athletic jerk with arms the size of pythons, and dark hair tipped with blond highlights. The cocky narcissist probably spent hours at the hairdresser for that look. At one time, he might have been a high school quarterback, the kind who talked starry-eyed cheerleaders into meeting him under the bleachers and then bragged about it in the locker room. I hated the arrogant bastard even more than I did when he first knocked me over. He stared at me.

"What?" I screamed, struggling to pull together the fraying threads of my temper.

He took several steps in my direction and glared through squinted eyes.

"Oh, no! He's giving me the evil eye. Whatever will I do?"

He snarled. "Somebody needs to teach you some manners."

"Oh, my God. He's going to teach me a lesson. Won't somebody please help me?" I stood board straight with my chin up, trying to look taller than my five-foot-seven-inch frame suggested. The old Lisa emerged from where she had been hiding for the past several years. "Is this the part where I'm supposed to cower down and pee in my panties?"

He took several more steps toward me. Too close. Five years of intensive training with the team told me what to do next. I bent my knees slightly, centered my weight over the balls of my feet to increase mobility, and assumed a sideways defensive position, left leg in front and the other leg back, prepared to push forward with a kick to his leg at the right time. I cocked my right arm at my side, a loaded weapon ready to fire. All I needed was to take out a knee or crush his windpipe. That would do it. Game over in five seconds. Mr. Spandex didn't stand a chance. He simply hadn't realized it yet. I forced a twisted grin. "Let's see what you've got, cupcake."

The cyclist stopped in his tracks. This entire scenario was not unfolding the way he'd expected. I'd gotten into his head, and could almost see his mind racing, weighing the potential outcomes of this encounter. If he took me on, he faced the prospect of beating a woman a foot smaller and a hundred pounds lighter than him. That might have some serious legal ramifications. On the other hand, if he lost, he'd be forever humiliated.

I took a step toward him. I didn't need to yell anymore. I had his full attention. "I'm going to give you a warning which is more than you deserve. Better quit while you can. If you don't, you'll never walk again—except with a cane."

He blinked several times and scoffed, a show to save what little dignity he had left. He returned to his bike, and peddled away, his ridiculous yellow-and-black spandex disappearing around a bend. Rivulets of sweat trickled between my breasts and my hair matted against my head. Exhausted, I leaned over and placed my hands on my knees, trying to catch my breath.

A flash of blood-red light pierced the periphery of my vision. Another jolt of adrenaline. Now what? It originated from the water's edge, fifty feet away, at the bottom of an embankment. I straightened and searched for the source of the flash just as the sun retreated behind another cloud. Nothing there. What could be shining a red light out here? Impossible. Imagination? I shook my head. No. I saw something, but what? Walking in either direction down the path offered no clue. I stood on a park bench to get a better view and squinted at the water, searching. Still no explanation for the red flash.

The sun again escaped from behind the clouds. Another flash. No doubt about it this time. The source of the red burst was so well hidden in the high weeds, I almost missed it, the rear reflector of a bicycle mostly submerged in the swamp. It looked like a nice one. How did it get down there? Why would anyone abandon a bike like that?

The water around the bike rippled, sending waves radiating across the water. A loud splash. The bike shifted position.

A shiver ran down my spine. Oh, my God, someone's trapped. I rushed down the embankment, thorns and nettles tearing at my legs. I sucked in a lungful of air and pressed on along a thick line of mangrove trees, their spindly roots extending in all directions like the legs of a giant spider. I hated spiders. The ground was slippery from the rain, so I grabbed branches to stabilize myself. That's when a large black bug with yellow stripes and fangs the size of a knife landed on my arm. I screamed and shook it off, losing my grip. I slipped and fell, sliding down the wet grass all the way toward the water. I escaped falling in by digging my heels in the mud at the last minute. The submerged bike sat ten feet to my right, only the rear wheel and seat exposed.

Another splash. The bike shifted like someone tried to tug on it. Someone was drowning! I rushed over, grabbed the wheel, and pulled hard, hoping to rescue the person trapped under the water. No luck. The mangrove roots held the bicycle and its rider captive.

I swallowed hard and reached into the murky water feeling under the surface for the victim. Nothing. Something slimy swam past my hand. I jerked back and shivered. Needed to hurry. I gritted my teeth and again reached into the water and yanked hard. The bike wouldn't budge. Leaning forward, my feet ankle deep, I grabbed the bike's handlebar and rotated it to the left, fully expecting some creature to take a bite out of my leg. Still stuck. One more heave and the cycle dislodged from its woody trap with a deadly sucking sound. The momentum threw me backward onto the ground, the bike landing across my legs, covering me in layers of muck.

The hellish stench of swamp climbed high into my nostrils like it intended to stay there. The odor was the least of my problems. I wiped mud from my eyes and looked at the bike.

"Oh, Jesus." My heart almost exploded out of my chest.

I kicked the bike off my legs and took several deep breaths to fight off the urge to vomit. Something was snared between the bike's chain and the main gear wheel. That something had a French manicure.

The water again rippled directly in front of me. I glanced up to see two large eyes and a snout drifting up amongst the water lilies.

"Shit!" I raced back up the hill on all fours. By the time I reached the path above, I was covered in swamp scum and my legs had become a road map of cuts and scratches, all bleeding. I pulled out my cell phone. My hands shook so severely it took several tries to make a call.

As tremulous as I felt, once forgotten feelings of excitement returned, bringing with them a part of me that had been dormant for the past several years. Exhilarating. I hadn't felt this alive since the team and I destroyed a large terror network in Paris. Nothing like a brush with death to get the juices flowing again.

TWO

Seminole Lakes Park
East Naples, Florida

I paced back and forth along the path, waiting for a response to my call. Time slowed at an agonizing pace as the sun gradually rose in the sky. Seconds became minutes and they bled into an hour. Finally, someone walked down the path toward me. I'd expected a uniformed beat cop to respond, but a woman approached, dressed in black slacks and a white blouse under a linen blazer, its cuffed sleeves rolled up to the elbows. Soft mocha skin complimented straight black hair that cascaded over her shoulders. Her only jewelry was a pair of pearl stud earrings and some silver bracelets. Slender and almost six feet tall, she walked with the grace of a runway model. Not like any cop I had ever seen.

A gold detective's badge hung from a lanyard around her neck. A belt holster with a semi-automatic Glock 19 peeked from beneath her blazer. A look in her eye said she knew how to use it.

Here I stood, covered in dried muck, my hair matted with sweat, and smelling like a swamp rat. I wanted to crawl into a hole.

The detective extended her hand, her grip confident and firm like a person accustomed to being in charge. Her nails were perfectly manicured. I hid mine behind my back.

She dropped her hand. "Detective Cassandra Pierce," she said, checking me from head to toe.

"Detective? I figured a patrolman would come."

"All tied up. I was in the East Precinct office so I took the call." She looked around. "You said something about a possible body?"

"Yes. I found an abandoned bicycle near the water —"

She gazed down the embankment as her smile disappeared. "I don't see a bike."

I looked. "Uh, you can't see it right now. It was in the water, but I pulled it up into the grass."

Detective Pierce shook her head. "You moved the bike?"

"Yes, but —"

"So, you disturbed a potential crime scene? You tampered with evidence?"

I looked to the ground. Why was she being so aggressive and confrontational? Guess I should have known better. "I—I just moved it a little."

The detective pulled a stylus and notepad from her pocket. The earlier smile became a scowl. Her eyes bore into mine. "And you are?" Straight and to the point.

"Lisa Marie Savich." As an afterthought, I added, "Crawford. But —"

Pierce squinted and wrote while saying, "Lisa, Marie, Savich, hyphen, Crawford." Emphasis on the hyphen. "Is that correct?"

"Yes." Forsaking my maiden name had felt like a betrayal of my parents' memory, so I hyphenated. It had been a sticking point in my marriage, especially after my failure to produce children for John.

"Address?"

I gave her my local address. More writing on her notepad. The sun reflected off the two bracelets dangling from her left wrist, a silver one with a heart charm and the other a

Medi-Alert. Strange. She didn't look like someone who'd have a life-threatening illness.

She asked, "Do you live in Everglades Estates fulltime, or are you just seasonal?"

Just seasonal? The question seemed accusatory. "I'm renting a condo. I'm from DC, but —"

"So, you're a visitor from Washington. A politician, I guess."

Pierce didn't wait for a reply. Her look of disapproval told me I had dropped down a few pegs on her scale of respectability. Getting off on the wrong foot here. My concentration already thrown off balance by the weight of her stare, I decided not to challenge the woman.

She checked out my clothes and bloody legs. "So, what happened here and why'd you call the police?"

I struggled to recover and told her my story, starting with Mr. Spandex.

"And this cyclist knocked you over into the brush?"

"Yes, but back to the reason why I called. I was —"

"Must have made you pretty angry."

She wouldn't let me explain. Had I become a suspect? "A little, but —"

Her eyes grew darker, burning into me, probing for any signs of deceit. "Mad enough to push him down the hill and into the water? Maybe injure him? Maybe even kill him. Is that why you called about a body? Is that why you disturbed a potential crime scene?"

Disturbed the crime scene? This conversation was headed in the wrong direction. I held up my hands. "Oh, no, no, no. Nothing like that. The guy was ten yards past me and disappeared around the corner by the time I got up." Not exactly true but I saw no sense in confusing the issue with facts. "That's when I noticed the bike. It began moving, and I was afraid someone was trapped under it. I rushed down the hill, and when I got to it, I pulled the bike out of the water. That's when I found the body part."

Her eyes changed, wide and no longer dark. She stared at the water and tapped her right index finger against her lips. "Body part? That's all? Just a part?" More tapping with her finger. "I need to see it." She stepped off the path and down through the heavy brush.

"I'll follow you."

The detective turned. "No." Her eyes said the matter was not negotiable. "This might be a crime scene, and I don't want you disturbing the evidence any more than you already have."

Another embarrassment. "My husband's the Director of the FBI's Department of Counterterrorism. I know the protocols for a crime scene investigation."

Pierce's eyes softened. "Married to a lawman, eh?" A slight smile transformed her face. She was warming up, but she still studied me through squinting eyes. "Might not be a good idea, Lisa. Poisonous spiders and snakes hide in there. With those running shorts, your legs are going to get torn apart."

I rubbed my hands across the cuts on my thighs. "I think it's a little late for me to be worrying about that." I shrugged and forced a smile. "How much worse can it get? I've already handled most everything this swamp can throw at me. I promise, I'll stay directly behind you and not interfere." I took a few steps. "Careful," I warned. "The hill's slippery."

Pierce held onto a few mangrove branches, just as I had an hour ago to keep from sliding down the hill. She moved slowly and deliberately as she studied the ground in front of her. She stopped. "What's this? The grass is all trampled down. Looks like someone dragged a body through here."

My face flushed. "Like I said, it's slippery. I lost my balance and slid."

Pierce shook her head. A scowl erased her recent smile, turning down the corners of her mouth. "So much for being aware of crime scene protocols. Try not to disturb anything else." Her voice dripped with sarcasm. "Step only where and when I step."

Again, I was on her bad side. She stopped at the water's edge about fifteen feet away from the bike. Her jaw dropped. She stepped back, her eyes wide, almost looking shocked.

"What is it?" I asked.

"Nothing." She regained her composure. "No wonder you called. It's a miracle anything is still there." She walked toward the bike and used her stylus to poke at what was a left hand. It had been severed mid-forearm. "It's trapped in the bike's gear mechanisms. Whatever took her, couldn't get the hand free." A gold band encircled the victim's ring finger. Pierce rotated it and found a large pear-shaped diamond ring.

The diamond flashed in my eyes. Even at that distance, I could tell it must have been at least three carats.

"Looks like a gator attacked her," said Pierce.

I'd been so panicked the first time I saw the hand; I hadn't noticed the make of the bike. It was a Trek Domane, an eight-thousand-dollar model. A different color, but otherwise identical to one I had left behind in Washington. I kept that bit of information to myself. Every time I spoke, I slid further down on the detective's bad side.

Pierce took a dozen pictures with her phone and stepped around the bike. She stood straight and surveyed the surrounding area until her gaze fixated on a spot. "You see that?"

"You mean where I fell on the ground?"

"No, just beyond the bike." She pointed. "An alligator footprint." She squatted for a closer look. "Left front foot." She bent over and spread her fingers out about an inch above the print. "Twelve-footer from the looks of it."

"I think I've already met him," I said. "Up close and personal."

She raised her eyebrows, then set her badge on the ground for a size reference and took a half-dozen photographs with her cell phone. "I'm afraid whoever was riding that bike became this guy's lunch." Her hands started shaking, and she stumbled. "We need to head back up to the path."

I took her by the arm and helped her struggle up the hill. When we reached the path, the detective looked weak, her face drained of all color, like she'd never seen a dead body before. Strange reaction from a detective but this was a special situation with the severed hand and all, but still.

"Are you all right?" I asked. "Want me to call for an ambulance?"

"No. I'll be fine in a minute. She rummaged around in her pocket and pulled out a small box of chocolate-covered raisins and tossed a handful into her mouth. She offered me some. I declined. "Took my insulin this morning just before your call. Rushed out the door and didn't stop to eat breakfast. Foolish mistake on my part." She ate the rest of the raisins. "Should be better soon. Went into insulin shock once in high school. Was in a coma for several days. Probably lost a few million brain cells in the process. Never want to go through that again."

After a minute, the shaking stopped, and the color returned to her face. As though nothing had happened, she looked back down at the swamp, tapping her index finger against her lips. "It wasn't supposed to happen this way."

"Supposed to happen? Wait. What wasn't supposed to happen this way? Your blood sugar."

She slowly shook her head. "No." She pointed to the water. "Her death."

"I thought you said the woman was killed by an alligator."

"What I actually said was that an alligator probably ate her. I believe she was already dead by the time he got to her."

"I don't understand," I said. "What makes you think she was already dead?"

"Alligators rarely attack humans on land. When they do, they grab an arm or a leg and try to pull the victim into the water to drown them. There's usually a battle. The victims fight ferociously, pulling on branches and clawing at the earth, anything to escape. I saw no signs of a struggle down there. No broken branches and the grass was undisturbed, that is until you slid halfway down the hill." She didn't scowl at me this time. It was only an analytical observation. "The woman's nails had no mud or vegetation under them."

I looked down at my dirty nails. "How'd she die, then?"

"Not sure yet, but I believe she might have been murdered."

I thought out loud. "Murdered?"

"Yes. It obviously didn't happen by the water. Someone killed her while she was riding on the path. It certainly didn't happen elsewhere. This site is at least a mile from the nearest parking area. That's too remote for a person to carry a body." Pierce jotted some notes in her pad and took a few more photographs.

"Sounds like someone had to be waiting for her. Had to know her routine," I said.

"Maybe."

"Then how'd she wind up the water?"

"The killer had to have dragged her and the bike down there, hoping the gators would get her, and destroy any evidence."

I looked toward the bike. "So, if she was already dead, how did her hand get caught in the bike's gear system?"

Pierce tapped her finger against her lips. "Haven't figured that out yet." She looked down at the water. "The problem is she's probably been dead since just before Caroline hit. That's not good."

"Why?" I asked.

"If this is in fact a crime scene, it's been at least seventy-two hours since she was killed. The chances of finding any significant evidence are unlikely. Storm probably washed everything away."

"Why do you think someone wanted to murder her?"

"Too soon to tell. There are four primary motives behind every homicide, the four Ls as we call them: Lust, Love, Loathing, and Loot. She still has a fifty-thousand-dollar diamond on her finger, so obviously it wasn't a robbery. Lust is a possibility, though rape doesn't appear to be the killer's intent. That leaves love or loathing. They often go hand in hand. She was married, and in cases like this, the husband is the prime suspect until proven otherwise. He'd certainly be familiar with her routine. Maybe he had financial difficulties and needed the life insurance money. Maybe he hated her? Maybe infidelity? The first thing we must do is establish her identity. That will lead us toward the motive."

I suppressed a smile. *We? Am I part of this now?* My unfocused eyes gazed out over the water. Curiosity and anger about what had happened to the woman consumed my thoughts. Maybe it was because I found her, but on some level, I felt a connection to her, whoever she was. A renewed sense of purpose flowed through my veins.

The detective withdrew a cell phone from her pocket. "This is Cassie from the East Precinct."

I raised my eyebrows.

She looked at me and pressed her phone against her chest. "Short for Cassandra. That's what my friends call me."

Cassie continued speaking into the phone. "I'm at Seminole Park, the rear part of the East path, about two miles from the entrance. Looks like we might have a murder on our hands. I'll need a full forensics team here ASAP. Send the dogs, though I suspect all the rain has washed away any lingering scent." She paused to allow someone on the other end to repeat her instructions. "Roger that. Notify the coroner's office and send for the Gator Guys."

"Gator Guys?" I asked.

"Yes. I need an autopsy to confirm my suspicions. For that I need a corpse. Alligators usually don't eat what they kill all at once. After taking their fill, they hide the rest of the body under a sunken log somewhere to ripen until they're ready for another meal."

"Ugh," I groaned.

"If our victim's body is still out there, the Gator Guys will find it. If they can't, I'll have them trap a few of the largest gators and we can do an autopsy on them to look for human remains." Cassie tapped her index finger against her lower lip as she seemed lost in thought. "There is another reason for a homicide, one not listed in the textbooks. An older detective friend of mine once warned me of a fifth motive."

"Fifth? What is it?"

"No fucking reason at all. Just happens. Some people simply enjoy killing." Cassie stared in the direction of the bike. "Those are the ones that go cold."

"We can't let that happen on this one," I said.

"Hopefully not." She looked down the path. "That was fast."

Following her gaze, I turned to see the forensics team approaching, three men and a woman in white HAZMAT suits. I watched for an hour as Cassie instructed the crime scene techs to approach the bike from along the side of the hill where she and I had walked down. "Be careful not to disturb anything until we obtain full photographic documentation of the scene. Get close ups of the bike, the hand, and that alligator print. Once you're done, wrap the bike and the body part together in cellophane, but don't try to remove the hand before you carry the package up the hill. Inventory that ring. If it goes missing, there'll be hell to pay. Take everything to Dr. Deutschle's office in the morgue. Tell him to start a DNA and fingerprint analysis right away. He should expect more from me in the next several hours."

Not much else was happening, so I ran home. I peeled off my clothes and tossed everything, including my ASICS, in the garbage. They were beyond salvageable. I showered and allowed the hot water to sluice over my body, washing away the stench of the swamp. I rubbed the steam from the bathroom mirror with my hand and studied my blonde hair, a gift from my father. It stood in stark contrast to my perpetual-tan skin, handed down from my grandmother, a full-blooded Cherokee Indian.

I squinted closer at my image. What the hell are those things? Crow's feet? Too much crying over the past year. Enough of that nonsense. I tried to smooth them away with my fingers. No use. A little concealer was the best I could do.

Then, what to wear? I dressed in a long white cotton skirt to cover my scratched-up legs and put on a pink linen blouse. A pair of comfortable tan espadrilles and extra-large sunglasses completed my outfit. I applied a new layer of polish to my nails. They still looked ragged, but it was the best I could do for the moment. Why did I care? It's a girl thing.

I headed back, feeling invigorated, with a new sense of purpose. Excitement coursed through my veins for the first time in years.

THREE

Seminole Lakes Park
East Naples, Florida

By the time I returned to the murder scene, yellow-and-black crime-scene tape cordoned off the area, holding back a dozen or so spectators who had arrived.

"What happened?" asked a woman to my right.

"Some kind of accident," another replied.

"I think it was an alligator attack," offered an older man. "Someone got too close to the water." He shook his head. "Those tourists never learn."

I worked my way through the group until I stood in front of the tape. Five numbered, yellow placards were scattered across the asphalt path. A young, uniformed officer, who looked like a high school student, prevented me from passing. "Sorry, miss. This is a restricted area."

Detective Cassie stood only thirty feet away, giving directions to the crime scene techs as they laid out a grid of three-foot squares to search for evidence along the slope. "Look for anything suspicious, blood droplets, a torn piece of clothing, anything that might constitute trace evidence. Anyone who can find a cell phone gets a day of paid leave, on me."

I called her name. She looked in my direction and scowled like I was a distraction, maybe a reporter. Then a look of recognition developed in her eyes. She walked over. "Lisa? Is that you?" She laughed. It was nice to see her without her all-business look. "Sorry. I didn't recognize you without all the swamp muck." She turned to the officer. "That's all right, Mike. She's with me."

The words made my heart race. I belonged, solidly entrenched in the law enforcement family, part of a team again.

Officer Mike lifted the tape and I ducked under, much to the chagrin of the remaining crowd. One woman in particular sounded angry. She had an ID hanging from her neck saying she was with the Naples Courier Journal. "What about me, Mike?" she asked.

"Sorry, Maddie. No can do this time."

I walked over to Cassie and stared at the yellow placards.

"Evidence Identification Markers," she explained. "The techs found several droplets of blood, but I doubt they're from the victim. Too much rain." She picked up an evidence kit. "Open up."

"What?'

"The blood spatters are probably from your legs. I need your DNA to confirm. I'll also need your prints to compare to any lifted from the bike." She used a cotton swab to paint the inside of my cheek.

After another half-hour, one of the Gator Boys divers surfaced and gave a thumbs-up sign. He removed his mask and spit out his regulator. "Found her. Need a body bag—make it a small one."

They carried the bag up the hill where Cassie awaited. She unzipped the bag, cringed, and turned away. Must have been gruesome, even for a seasoned police detective. "Take her to the coroner's office. Tell Dr. Deutstschle she's a Jane Doe and make the autopsy a top priority."

She turned to me. "Not a pretty sight. Looks like somebody hit her in the right side of the head with something."

I thought about the name Jane Doe, a generic label assigned to an unknown person who had at one time been a wife, a daughter, or maybe a mother. Anger coiled inside my stomach resurrecting feelings that first motivated me to join the team years ago. Our job was to protect the innocent and bring justice for those who had been wronged. I looked down toward the swamp, to the place where someone had murdered Jane Doe. She deserved justice.

There wasn't much left for me to do so I returned to my condo, feeling better about my life and good enough to splurge for the first time in months. A mani-pedi at the nail salon gave a welcomed improvement in my appearance. With this murder investigation it looked like I might be staying in Naples longer than anticipated. I needed more clothes, so I headed to the stores at Venetian Village where I selected a new wardrobe, feminine and trendy.

When I got home, I poured myself a glass of chardonnay, sat on my lanai, and thought about Jane Doe. Who was she? What did she do? Why did she die? Quite a coincidence that Mr. Spandex showed up like he did. The guy was agitated. Could he have been involved in the murder? Maybe he'd come back to the scene of the crime to check it out, to see if the body had been found. Killers did that sometimes. I planned to discuss my thoughts with Cassie in the morning.

T. Milton Mayer

FOUR

The Blue Wisp Jazz Club
Cleveland, Ohio

It had been a tedious four-hour drive from Kentucky to Cleveland, Ishmael's third surveillance trip to the city in the past month. Wearing a black, button-down shirt with khaki pants, Ishmael entered the club and took a seat alone at the far end of the u-shaped, mahogany bar. An air of upper middle-class hipness permeated the room. The subdued lighting offered great cover, and no one noticed him. Ishmael had fashioned himself into the quintessential invisible man, remarkable only in that he was completely unremarkable, the kind of guy his classmates wouldn't remember at high school reunions. At five-foot-eleven, he was neither short nor tall. A traditional haircut framed a face identical to a thousand other faces one might pass on the street. His skin lacked any tattoos or distinguishing characteristics. He appeared approachable, with a non-threatening look others assumed they could dismiss, a potentially fatal mistake on their part.

A script neon sign reading *Blue Wisp* hung on the wall behind a small stage. Overhead lights cast a soft glow over a jazz trio.

"Pretty big crowd," Ishmael said to the bartender.

"It's singles night, or as some of us like to call it, cougar night," the man replied with a chuckle. "What can I get you?"

"Henricks and tonic, with a lime wedge."

"Coming right up, sir."

Ishmael laid a twenty-dollar bill on the bar. "Keep the change." He never used credit cards. Traceable. An unacceptable risk in his line of work. He took a sip of his drink and leaned back to enjoy the seductive sounds of John Coltrane floating through the room. Watching the piano player's fingers dance across the keys brought back the words of his mother. "Practice makes perfect." She mercilessly admonished him every time he complained about sitting for hours in front of the piano. A sharp smack to the back of the head typically followed her words. "Again. From the beginning—until it's perfect." He clenched his fists at the memory. Ishmael loved music, but she had destroyed his passion for it. There was an unexpected benefit, however. He learned how to read her eyes and predict her assaults. He became what she forced him to become, an expert on recognizing the varying patterns of human behavior. The ability to predict how people responded to certain circumstances was what made him so successful at what he did.

He studied the actions of the other customers, their mannerisms, and their body language. Several married couples sat at two-top tables, with little to say to each other. All their stories and secrets had been shared too many times in the past. The excitement of newness had faded, and all that remained was being together. Singles tried to make eye contact with members of the opposite sex, hoping to make some connection to fill the lonely emptiness of their lives. Women wore skirts too short for their age while men sucked in their bellies and hid receding hairlines with ridiculous comb overs. Visual offers were extended, some accepted, some rebuffed. A few lucky singles merged into twos—at least for the evening. Ishmael smirked at the recently paired couples as they tried to impress each other with their wit and charms, men overstating their positions in life, women laughing too loud at inane jokes that weren't funny, all hoping to avoid another night alone.

He scanned the audience but didn't see his next target. A problem. All was in place, and the Client insisted it happen tonight. He kept an eye on the door. By the time he ordered another gin and tonic, she entered, an older woman about twenty years his senior. She sat alone at a table thirty feet to his left. She played with the empty space on her left ring finger and had the wistful look of a widow trying to enjoy life after too many years of mourning and self-imposed isolation. Ishmael had done his homework. Her husband had been the founder and CEO of Rutherford Insurance. Four years ago, the company sold for ninety-five-million dollars. He died shortly after the deal was closed, making Mrs. Rutherford a very wealthy widow.

She dressed tastefully in a tailored, black pencil skirt with a side slit that revealed just the right amount of thigh to garner interest. Black stilettos and a matching black blazer over a coral silk blouse completed her outfit. A large diamond solitaire pendant drew attention to her modest cleavage and said she was ready to re-engage in the game of life. Reserved and poised, she exuded sophistication and a level of sensuality impossible to ignore. Ishmael took a sip of his gin and tried to catch her attention with a smile.

She turned away.

He preferred to remain in the shadows and avoid drawing attention to himself, but he had no choice. Time for plan B. The jazz trio finished their set and were about to take a break, presenting the perfect opportunity. Ishmael approached the leader. "Mind if I use your piano for a few minutes?"

"Knock yourself out, man. I'm sure the owner won't care. Live entertainment keeps the customers drinking and that makes him happy."

Loud conversations and laughter from the crowd resumed as soon as the trio left the stage. The resulting din drowned out the scraping noise as Ishmael pulled the piano bench back and sat down. His fingers performed a ballet across the keyboard as he ran the scales. The old upright was a little tinny but in decent shape and surprisingly well-tuned. He attacked the keys while playing Chopin's Polonaise in A-flat major, a decided break from the jazz the audience had been hearing. All conversations ceased, as the crowd stared at him, their drinks in mid-air. Halfway through the sonata, he seamlessly transitioned into Dave Brubeck's Take Five, then back to Chopin. When he finished, the crowd remained silent for a few seconds before erupting into a standing ovation.

Ishmael returned to the bar, drained his gin and tonic, and focused his attention on the subject. He raised his glass in the woman's direction, and she responded in kind. Nothing like a musical performance to break the ice.

Ishmael ordered a bottle of Sonoma-Cutrer, picked up two wine glasses, and approached her table. "May I join you?"

A smile lit up her face, replacing the look of lonely despondence he'd noticed earlier.

"Certainly." She extended her hand. "I'm Gloria Rutherford."

Ishmael took her hand in his, her skin incredibly soft and cool. "Pleasure to meet you, Gloria. I'm Robert Fenton." The subtle scent of her perfume wafted over him. Enticing.

"I love the way you played, Robert. Chopin and Dave Brubeck together? A work of genius." As he opened the wine, she said, "You're exceptionally talented. Are you a professional?"

"Musician? Oh no. My mother hoped I would become a concert pianist one day. Spent several years at Julliard but dropped out and wound up becoming a systems analyst."

"Systems analyst?"

"I fix difficult problems for other people."

"Difficult problems?"

Ishmael smiled without responding.

"Pity you didn't continue with your studies. I think you would have been successful on the concert circuit." She toyed with her diamond pendant. "My late husband used to play the piano. Chopin was his favorite composer."

"Late husband? You're a widow?" He already knew the answer.

She teared up and turned away, blotting the corners of her eyes with her napkin. "I'm sorry."

"No, I'm sorry. It was none of my business."

"That's okay." Her voice quivered. She took a deep breath. "He passed away several years ago."

Ishmael placed his hand over hers. "It must have been extremely difficult for you."

She didn't pull away.

"Well, your husband sounds like a wonderful person. He had excellent taste in music." He gently squeezed her hand, and looked into her eyes. "And exquisite taste in women."

She blushed.

He liked her. She was demure and kind, nothing like his overbearing mother. He poured Gloria a glass of the wine, and they toasted, "To Chopin."

She tapped the tip of her glass against his. "To Chopin."

Ishmael proceeded to tell her some lies, words every woman enjoyed hearing. After several hours and an empty bottle of wine, he asked, "Would you like to take a walk? It's too lovely a night to remain inside."

They left the bar together, hand in hand. They talked, laughed, and flirted, tentative at first, then more overtly. In a nearby park, they paused and looked into each other's eyes. Ishmael pulled her close, gently kissed her, and hesitated. *Hold on. This isn't part of the plan.*

Gloria's demure façade faded, her face radiant in the glow of the moon. She pulled him closer. "I'm not some fragile, naïve coed, Robert. I'm almost sixty and too old to play the coy act." She kissed him back, hard, opening her mouth and inviting his tongue, melting her body against his. A surprise twist that deviated from the script. Definitely, not part of the plan, but why not? He'd simply have to improvise.

Their kisses became deeper and more passionate.

Her heavy breathing told him she was ready.

Ishmael turned her around and leaned her over the back of a park bench.

Gloria didn't protest.

He lifted her skirt and gave her what she wanted, the sex hot and rough.

When finished, she straightened her skirt and turned to face him, her cheeks flushed and still breathing heavily. Her eyes sparkled with a renewed lust for life. She traced the outline of his lips with her finger. "I haven't felt this way in years. You're a man of many talents, Robert Fenton."

"You have no idea, Gloria." Ishmael took her hand in his. They sat side by side on the bench, gazing at the stars. Leaning over, he kissed her softly on the cheek, his hands gently caressing the sides of her head. With a sudden rotation of his arms, he snapped her neck and sent her off to the hereafter to join her husband, a wide smile still spread across her lovely face. Clean and simple. She didn't even know she was dead. *Perfect enough, Mother?*

The Client had paid a huge amount of money to eliminate Mrs. Gloria Rutherford. She was number nine on the customer's list of thirteen. The only stipulation in the agreement was that he make her death bloodless and appear accidental, a requirement he fulfilled in spades.

Why was Gloria targeted? He wasn't sure, other than she was heavily involved in Ohio politics. For Ishmael, the reason was irrelevant. She was simply another job. Bottom line, it was a successful evening, a good fuck and another several million dollars in his off-shore account, all neatly arranged by his handler, Fedallah. He rested her lifeless head against his shoulder while he decided what to do with the body. *So much for bloodless.*

FIVE

East Precinct Building
Naples PD

The morning after the discovery of Jane Doe's body, Detective Cassandra Pierce entered the Robbery-Homicide Division office pushing open the door with her hip while holding a briefcase full of files in her right hand and a cup of sugar-free latte in her left. She couldn't handle the swill they offered in the break room, brewed in a pot no one had washed since Trump was president. She squinted at the harsh overhead fluorescent lights, several flickering as though they might go out any minute. Police departments were about the same, whether here or in Chicago. Only the sizes of the budgets and the nature of the crimes were different. Naples was a more gentrified city and the extent of its police blotter was generally limited to DUIs, petty theft, and occasional white-collar crimes like fraud.

Cassie's cubicle constituted the entirety of the homicide division. In Chicago, one of the murder capitals of the country, she enjoyed the help of hundreds of detectives working cases. Cassie was it in Naples. No surprise since Collier County averaged only five homicides a year, most of which were drug related and outside the Naples area. This recent Jane Doe case was different. The murder of a wealthy woman was unheard of—until now. It warranted special attention and the level of expertise only Cassie could bring to the table.

She removed the crime scene photographs from her briefcase and carefully arranged them in sequential order atop her standard government-issued gray metal desk. She studied each of them closely, looking for anything she might have missed at the site. Nothing. A yellow legal pad sat to the right, its edges perfectly parallel to the side of the desk. She withdrew a ruler and a black sharpie from her desk drawer and drew a perfectly straight line down the middle of the yellow pad, creating two columns, a ritual she performed at the start of every new homicide case in Chicago. It was her version of the beginning of a murder book. On the top left she printed KNOW. On the right she wrote NEED. Under KNOW, she listed: *female, Caucasian, cyclist, large diamond ring, probably wealthy, must be missed by someone.* The list was sparse. Under NEED she wrote *Identity*, and circled it twice. Under it she scribbled, *Check with Missing Persons.* She also listed the obvious need for DNA studies.

She leaned back in her chair and took a sip of her latte as she held up a photograph of the ring. "Brad, what are you doing today?" Brad Stapleton was her occasional partner — emphasis on occasional.

A voice responded from three cubicles to her right. "Working on that jewelry heist in Port Royal from last week." It had been the seventh one in Southwest Florida in the past year. "Three guys broke in and tied up a Mr. Robert Schoenburg and his wife. They ransacked the house for three hours. Walked off with over a million dollars' worth of jewelry. They were very gentlemanly about it, though. Didn't hurt anyone, plus they offered the victims water and bathroom breaks. Same MO as the others. They always apologize when they leave." He laughed. "Polite criminals. Only in Naples."

"I need to show you something," said Cassie.

"Wow! That's the best offer I've had in months," said Brad. "Never knew you were interested, Cassie. I'm ready for whatever you're offering, but maybe we should wait until after work." He walked over and put his hand on her shoulder.

She cringed and fought the urge to spin around and break his wrist. Brad Stapleton was a good-looking, womanizing boor who wouldn't even have his job without his family connections. Cassie's problem was he was the only asset she had at her disposal, and she needed his help. "I assume you'll be hitting the local jewelers and likely fences for the Port Royal case."

"Waste of time." He rested his butt on top of her papers. She scowled. "The stuff's too hot to fence locally. Probably already in New York, the gold melted down, and the gems reset for sale in legit stores."

She tugged at the papers under him. "Excuse me." He lifted his butt cheek so she could extract them. "That means you have some time on your hands." Cassie gave him a copy of a photograph of Jane Doe's ring. "I want you to canvass the local jewelers and see if someone recognizes this ring."

"Are you kidding? There must be a hundred stores. It'll take me a month."

"Then I guess you'd better get started on it." Cassie outranked him and delighted in letting him know it. As he walked away, grumbling about doing the shit work, she said, "Start with the high-end stores on Fifth Avenue and the Waterside Shops. That'll help narrow the search."

Brad mumbled something under his breath that sounded a lot like "bitch." He stomped away.

Cassie re-straightened the papers on her deck, rolled up her sleeves, and reviewed the preliminary lab reports on the Jane Doe case. The techs were unable to obtain any prints from the hand. No surprise. The skin was too macerated after having been underwater so long. Three days of nibbling by aquatic creatures made it impossible. They extracted some bone marrow from the hand metacarpals for DNA analysis. She hoped to identify the victim by finding a match through CODIS, the FBI's national DNA index system. Unfortunately, it would be another couple days before those results were available

She started to review the toxicology report when the lieutenant yelled out from his glass-enclosed office. "Detective Pierce, would you step in for a minute?"

Around the office, the lieutenant was nicknamed Buford because of his uncanny resemblance to the fat sheriff in the Smokey and the Bandit series. A request for a private discussion in his office usually meant bad news.

Leaving things neatly arranged on her desk, she went into his office where she took a chair opposite his desk.

He closed the door behind her.

Closed door. Very bad news.

His desk chair creaked in protest as Buford stuffed his expansive girth between the arm rests. Looked like the thing might collapse at any minute, and the prospects of him getting back out again seemed unlikely. The job became his due to political schmoozing more than ability. That was how the system worked in almost any city, whether here or Chicago. "How're things progressing with your Jane Doe case from yesterday?"

"We're still in the preliminary stages of the investigation, sir. For right now, I'm working it as a probable homicide."

He leaned back in his chair and played with a paperclip. "That was a quick conclusion, Cassie. The autopsy hasn't even been completed yet. I was under the impression it was a bicycle accident."

"That was my initial thought, sir, but further examination of the crime scene convinced me otherwise."

The lieutenant leaned forward. "And your basis for making this assumption?"

Cassie explained the head injury on the victim.

"That's pretty thin, Cassie. That injury could have resulted from the accident. She probably ran into a tree." He unbent the paperclip. "I assume there are trees in the park."

"Yes, sir."

"I don't know how you did things in Chicago, but here we make decisions based only on hard evidence." He picked up another paperclip and began destroying it. "I spoke to the mayor this morning, and we feel the official story should be that a woman died as the result of an unfortunate cycling accident. Maybe add the possibility that alcohol might have been involved if the press asks."

"But sir, there's no indication of that."

"Is the toxicology report back yet?"

"I haven't finished reviewing it, sir."

"Then, you can't rule out alcohol. You're going to approach this as an accident until you give me definite evidence to the contrary. We can't have the rumor mill grinding out stories of a violent homicide. That leads to speculation about serial killers like the one in Tampa a few years back. The mayor believes the premature mention of a murder could harm the tourist industry and depress home values. Until you have this thing irrefutably documented as a homicide and a suspect in custody, our official story will be it's an accident."

Cassie was about to explode but said, "Yes, sir."

When she got up to leave, the lieutenant added, "And I want you to keep a tight lid on this thing. No talking to anyone, especially reporters. My office will handle any contact with the press, exclusively. Capiche?"

Capiche? Are you kidding me? She returned to her chair and slammed her hand on her desk. *Fucking politicians. Forget the facts and play the misdirection game. That usually comes back to bite you in the ass.* She'd left Chicago precisely because of that. Too many politicians, too focused on nonsensical social issues to address the violence problems staring them right in the face. That and — she picked up a framed picture sitting on the corner of her desk, a photograph of her and another woman, laughing and posing with their arms around each other while standing in front of the famous stainless steel Chicago Bean sculpture.

Cassie outlined the picture with her index finger. Some old wounds never completely heal. *Better times. Miss you.*

Cassie was about to Google the most recent Florida missing persons list when her phone rang. "Homicide Division, Detective Cassandra Pierce speaking."

"Hi, Detective. This is Mary from the coroner's office. Dr. Deutschle wanted me to let you know he's about to start the autopsy on your Jane Doe."

"Tell him to go ahead. I'll be there as soon as I can." Her stomach flipped. Even after ten years of investigating homicides in Chicago, the thought of watching the dissection of another body brought waves of nausea. Especially this particular victim. The procedure distilled a person's life down to its basic organic components. Impersonal, demeaning, violative. The victim was no longer a husband, wife, son, daughter, or lover; just a mass of lifeless flesh on a cold, stainless steel table. Viewing them never got easier. She figured the day it did would be the day she'd look for another career. She busied herself with paperwork, delaying her visit to the morgue as long as possible.

SIX

Collier County Morgue
Naples, Florida

The drive to the coroner's office on Domestic Avenue took fifteen minutes. The secretary said, "I'll let Dr. Deutschle know you're here. Do you want me to show you the way to the autopsy lab?"

"Thanks, but I'm sure I can find it." Just follow the smell. Cassie walked down a hallway, past a bank of small stainless-steel doors, behind which lay bodies waiting for examination. The place reeked of a combination of formaldehyde, disinfectant solutions, and death. The odors always dissected their way into her brain where they remained despite multiple showers and changes of clothes.

Cassie continued through a pair of double doors into the autopsy room. She squinted at the bright fluorescent lights reflecting off three stainless-steel tables. She pushed aside thoughts of her partner in Chicago, lying on a similar table, about to have her dignity and individuality excised, her body violated. Cruel, almost diabolical, but necessary for justice to be served. Jane Doe laid on one of the tables, her face porcelain white, drained of all blood, her body cavities opened, many of the organs already removed for inspection. Swallowing bile rising from her stomach, Cassie looked away.

With a strong German accent, Dr. Deutschle spoke into a microphone. Tortoise shell reading glasses sat perched on the end of his bulbous nose. A white beard hung beneath his clear plastic face shield. "Torso and head are that of a thirty-five to forty-five-year-old Caucasian female. Both legs and much of the left arm are missing. Body is badly mutilated from a presumed alligator attack."

His assistant read out the weight of the left lung.

"Doesn't sound right for a drowning victim." said Deutschle. "Let's take a look." Using a scalpel, he sliced open one of the lungs. "Some water, but not enough to drown her. Something else caused her death."

Deutschle looked up and noticed Cassie standing near the back of the room. His eyes sparkled and a mischievous smile peeked through his long beard. "Now there's a face that can lighten the darkest of days." He turned and wiped his bloody gloves on his white apron. "Welcome, Cassandra. You look stunning, as always."

"Cut the bullshit, Fred. Nobody looks good in here." She smiled. "Except maybe you in your cute little white apron." It stretched tightly across his round belly.

"You're just in time."

"Great," she said with a touch of sarcasm. Cassie avoided looking at the opened corpse.

"You were right, Cassie. This woman was dead before she hit the water. At least she was near death. She must have taken a few agonal breaths after her head submerged. But like I said, there's water in the lungs but not enough to kill her. Fortunately, she was dead before the alligator got there."

"Is there any way you can identify her? Dental records?"

"I can x-ray her teeth, but the NamUs system is only useful in cases where the identity of the corpse is already suspected, such as in a reported missing-person situation. Dental characteristics from the victim can be compared to known dental records in the database. It helps to confirm a victim's identity but that's about it."

"What about clothing or any identifiable markings. Any scars or tattoos?"

"No markings. The only clothing was a torn, pink Lululemon top. Any other clothing is missing for obvious reasons." He lifted a piece of pink fabric. "Oh. She did have this around her neck."

"A sweat band? Was she strangled?" asked Cassie.

"No. Other than a few superficial scratches, there were no neck injuries, and the hyoid bone was intact. I think the sweat band was displaced as the gator pulled her body into the water. They do this death roll thing to separate the appendages and —"

She held up her hand. "That's okay Fred. I get the picture. So, what did her in?"

Deutschle said, "First of all, she wasn't wearing a helmet. If she had been, she might still be alive today. She has a laceration and surrounding contusion along the right side of her head, just above the ear." He dictated into a microphone hanging from his neck, "Blunt object laceration of the right temporal skull." He measured it with a stainless-steel ruler. "Seven point three centimeters in length." His assistant took several closeup photographs.

Cassie asked, "From a branch? Like she hit a tree limb when she fell?"

"Don't believe so. There's no foreign organic material in the wound. That rules out a tree."

"Is it bad enough to kill her?"

"I doubt it. Let's see what's under there." He picked up a scalpel and, with a ripping sound, peeled the scalp from the calvarium. "Ah, here we are. There's a skull fracture just under the laceration." He picked up the stainless-steel ruler and dictated. "Depressed skull fracture of the right parietal bone, five point two centimeters long by three point one centimeters wide. Looks to have been made by a cylindrical object. Based upon the angle of the wound, I'd say the perpetrator was left-handed, facing the victim, and around six feet tall." Deutschle examined the edge of the fracture with a lighted magnifying lens. "Hello. What's this?"

Cassie stepped closer. "What's what?"

He picked up a pair of tweezers and teased away a sliver of something wedged in the fracture line. He examined it under the microscope. "It's paper of some kind, and there's printing on one side."

"What do you think it is?"

"Can't tell. Too much blood, but definitely not from nature. I'll send it to the state forensics lab in Tallahassee. They can do a spectrophotometric analysis."

"So is the fracture what killed her?" pressed Cassie.

"Not exactly." Deutschle was a brilliant pathologist, but he had trouble getting to the bottom line. He loved to play this game of guess-what-I'm-thinking. Cassie checked her watch and tapped her shoe against the linoleum floor. "Okay, Fred, bottom line. What killed her?"

"Not yet. Need to look inside." Using an oscillating saw, Deutschle removed the top skull plate, exposing the brain.

Brutal. It reminded Cassie of a scene from the Hannibal Lector movie. She cringed and plugged her fingers into her ears.

"Ah. Here we go," he said. "When the skull fractured, it tore the right middle meningeal artery. It bled into the skull, rapidly filling the intracranial cavity until the expanding pressure pushed the brainstem down through the bottom, choking off the brain's respiratory center. It's called an epidural hematoma. In car accidents, these people are usually conscious for a short while, but as the bleeding continues, they soon become unconscious and die." He smiled and set down his instrument like a maestro conductor would set down his baton after leading the conclusion of a symphony.

Cassie sighed. "So that's what killed her."

"Ultimately, yes. For all practical purposes, once the killer hit her, it was only a matter of seconds before she was going to die. Made no difference whether she wound up in the water or not."

"So, you think the perp knew what he was doing?"

"Like a professional? Maybe, maybe not. It seems a little too sloppy and uncontrolled for a pro. It might have just been bad luck that an amateur hit her in exactly the right spot. A paid assassin would simply shoot her in the head. No games. And he would've taken the ring."

"Unless he needed to make it look like an accident." Cassie turned to leave and looked back. "Thanks, Fred." She turned around. "By the way, did you happen to find a cell phone on her?"

"No. If she had a phone, it was probably in her shorts pocket. We already know where they wound up."

"Pity. I was hoping to use it to establish the woman's identity. Thanks anyway, Fred. If you come up with anything else, let me know." She didn't have the victim's identity, but at least she now had confirmation of a murder.

On the drive back to the station, Cassie pieced together what she would report as the final few minutes of Jane Doe's life. She had been riding her bike on the asphalt path around Seminole Lakes Park, most likely her routine. Probably happened in the morning, only a few hours prior to the arrival of the tropical storm. The perpetrator waited in the brush along the side of the path and surprised her as she rode past. It was no chance encounter, and that meant he knew her personally, was familiar with her schedule, and knew she didn't wear a helmet. The guy struck her over the right temple with a cylindrical object. Shred of paper? From what? He was facing her when it happened, meaning he was left-handed. The blow didn't kill her immediately, but it was hard enough to stun her. She coasted off the bike path, toward the water, but remained alert enough to maintain control of the bike for a few seconds, long enough for her to career most of the way down the hill. She struggled to remain conscious until she crashed near the bottom, sending herself and the bike tumbling toward the water's edge. That's how her hand got caught in the gear mechanism. She took her final, agonal gasps for air underwater, explaining the water in her lungs. Then, the gator got her. *That'll be the official story.*

Cassie walked into the station with a spring in her step. She had figured everything out. Without being invited in, she walked into the lieutenant's office, and took a seat across from his desk. "Sir, I have incontrovertible evidence that my Jane Doe was murdered. Dr. Deutschle will say so in his official report."

The lieutenant sat forward in his chair and glared. "You don't get it, Cassie. This changes nothing. The mayor's breathing hard down my neck. He wants this Jane Doe situation to be an accident until he can do damage control. That's what he's going to get."

"That's bullshit and you know it. We need to conduct a vigorous homicide investigation. You don't want this to look like a coverup. You could be inviting the Florida State Attorney or FBI to take over. Neither of us want that."

He pointed his finger at her. "I'm warning you, Cassie. If you want to be a part of my team, you'd better keep a tight lid on this one."

Always a fucking politician. Just like in Chicago. Thought things would be better in Naples. I was wrong. What did she expect from a bureaucrat who'd never walked a police beat in his life? *Fuck him.*

Cassie returned to her desk and buried herself in the case. She Googled the up-to-date Florida missing persons list. None of the individuals matched her Jane Doe. Surprising. Surely someone would miss a woman as wealthy as she seemed to be. Maybe no one made a report because of the fourth of July weekend, but what about her husband? Suspicious. She'd check again tomorrow.

She called the Verizon cell company, hoping Jane Doe had made a call before she entered the park. "This is Detective Cassandra Pierce, East Naples PD. I want a list of all cell tower pings in a two-mile radius of Seminole Lakes Park from July first to July fifth."

"I'll need a court order for a search warrant before I can do that, detective," said the person on the other end.

"I'll have one for you this afternoon. I need that information right away. It's part of an ongoing murder investigation." Not the official line, but few people respond to requests for confidential information on a simple accident case.

"It'll be a long list."

"Then get it to me ASAP." As soon as Cassie hung up, the other phone rang. "Detective Cassandra Pierce, Homicide Division."

"Hi Cassie. It's Lisa."

"Lisa?"

"Lisa Crawford. You know. The one who found the bike yesterday."

Cassie sighed. She liked the woman and getting rid of her was going to be difficult. She had no other choice. The lieutenant said to keep a tight lid on things. "Oh, yes. Hi, Mrs. Crawford. How may I help you?"

"I was wondering if you found anything further on our Jane Doe."

"I'm sorry, Mrs. Crawford. We're in the preliminary stages of a confidential investigation. We can't divulge any information to a private citizen."

"Can you at least tell me whether or not you've established the woman's identity?"

"I'm sorry. I realize you've been instrumental in finding the body, but —"

"Instrumental? Without me, you wouldn't even have a body. There'd be no case."

"I realize that and without your help, this accident would not have been uncovered."

"Accident? Yesterday you claimed it was a murder."

"The department's official position is that it was an unfortunate accident."

"But I have a few ideas to discuss."

"Sorry, I can't share any information. Departmental policy."

"So, you haven't identified her yet."

"I didn't say that."

"You didn't have to. If you had, you would have mentioned it. You wouldn't have shared her name, but you definitely would have told me you IDed her. Maybe, I'll let you know when I find her name."

The reply caught Cassie off guard. She leaned forward in her chair. "You? And just how are you going to find out?"

"I have my resources, but we private citizens aren't allowed to divulge our findings to the police. It's policy."

The line went dead. *What did she mean by resources? She's angry and could be an uncontrollable wild card. I don't need her getting her husband and the FBI involved. They might take over my investigation. Maybe I should bring her on board to keep an eye on her.*

Her phone rang again. *Now what.*

"Hi Cassie. It's Fred. I finished the autopsy and found something you need to be aware of." He explained.

"What? Are you sure?"

"I've been a pathologist for thirty-five years, Cassie. I know what I'm talking about."

"Sorry, Fred. It simply caught me by surprise. Thanks. You know what to do."

"Already done."

This complicates everything. Cassie jotted a note on her yellow legal pad in bold letters and circled them. "I'm afraid this thing's about to turn into a political shit storm and neither of us want to find ourselves in the middle of it. Let's keep your findings between you and me. Maybe forget to put it in your official report for a while."

"For you, anything, Cassie."

"Thanks, Fred. I owe you."

"How about us sharing a bottle of fine wine and a few filets at Chops on Fifth?"

"Ouch. That's a little steep for me, Fred. I'm on a detective's salary. Instead, how about a couple of cheap ribeyes and beer at Texas Roadhouse."

Deutschle laughed. "You're on, Cassie. I'm sure it'll be the best steak dinner I've ever had."

SEVEN

Slum Neighborhood
Abuja, Nigeria

The Thirteen project was nearing completion, but LaTrane had more issues to address before reporting to his employer. He walked with three of his personal body guards down several back alleys in the no-man's land between the city of Abuja and the rankest of the Nigerian slums, a magnet area for the worst humanity had to offer. He found what he'd been searching for, a dusty bar that had died years ago but still served as a gathering place for aging prostitutes and men who would kill for the price of a glass of watered-down whiskey. Two of his men stood in the background, scanning the crowd for threats while the third remained at his side.

The dim lights reflected off LaTrane's pale, waxy skin, made all the more bizarre by the contrast against his blood-red lips. His black eyes remained emotionless as he reached into his pocket and wrapped the fingers of his left hand around the butt of a Beretta 9 mm.

The man he was looking for sat alone at a table in the rear corner of the room, his back against the wall as he faced the crowd. LaTrane approached, keeping his eyes on the Colonel's hands. He pulled up a chair, dusted it off with a silk kerchief, and sat down, also facing the crowd. "Colonel Morgan," he said in English with a distinct French accent.

The Colonel nodded. "Mr. LaTrane." He glanced in the direction of the two bodyguards in the background. "You have more work for me?"

Before answering the question, LaTrane removed the Beretta from his pocket and rested it on the table. He leaned back, crossed his legs, and lit a long, slender European cigarette. He held it between the delicate fingers of his right hand. "My employer was impressed by the professionalism of your first two missions and wishes to offer you another." He took a long drag from the cigarette.

The Colonel stared at the Beretta. "Should I assume you want my team to take out another mine?"

Another pull on the cigarette as a long ash hung precariously from the end. "You assume correctly, Colonel. This will be the largest one in the Congo. In fact, it's the biggest cobalt mine in the world."

The Colonel ordered a beer. "Care for one, Mr. LaTrane? Nigerien beer isn't the same quality you're probably used to, but it's better than anything else they serve in this shithole."

With a wave of his hand, LaTrane flicked his cigarette ash on the floor. "No, thank you."

The Colonel drained half his beer. "This'll be my third trip to the Congo in six months. That increases the risk, and it sounds like the target will be substantially larger this time. That means I'll have to deal with more security forces. I expect the compensation package will be increased proportionately."

"Two million."

"That's not going to cut it, Mr. LaTrane, especially since I need to transport more canisters of radioactive material through the jungle. That means more men. I'll need four million."

"My employer has authorized me to increase the offer to three million, max."

The Colonel ordered another beer. "Still not good enough. Make it three and a half."

LaTrane nodded. "Done." He pushed a photograph across the table. "The target is the Liuang Technologies Mine. I'll forward the exact coordinates and specific surveillance details by currier. As usual, my employer will provide all supplies, and munitions. You'll assemble your team members and handle the logistics."

"Terms?"

"My employer wants this to happen as soon as possible."

"Not a problem," said the Colonel. "I'll need a few weeks to put everything together, but it'll be done by the end of the month."

"Excellent. In addition, my employer insists that there be no evidence of any European or American involvement."

"Just like before, the bodies of a few Nigerian mercenaries will be left behind. The government will blame Boko Haram terrorists." He swallowed another mouthful of his beer. "I'll expect the usual fifty-percent deposit into my account by the end of the week."

The deal wasn't sealed with a handshake. LaTrane stood, picked up his Beretta, and left, leaving the Colonel to sit alone and finish his beer.

EIGHT

Ishmael's Home
Lakeside Park, Kentucky

I shmael's two-bedroom single-story home in Lakeside Park, Kentucky was sparsely furnished except for a baby grand that dominated the small living room. Ishmael always insisted his handler, Fedallah provide one every time he moved, which was often in his line of work. He sat in front of the piano and played *Moonlight Sonata*, a dark, moody piece brilliantly composed by Beethoven shortly before he began losing his hearing. It was the piece Ishmael played for his first piano competition when he was nine. A three-judge panel gave him glowing praise as he took first place. His mother's only response was, "You were lucky this time. The competition was weak. You must work harder if you ever expect to measure up." For eleven years, the criticisms continued without a single word of encouragement, relentless, daily, suffocating the passion out of him—until he made the words stop. The thought of that evening and the surprised look in her eyes, still brought a smile to his face.

His cell phone buzzed, interrupting his reverie. A text indicated he should check his email for a new message. No one could contact him except, Fedallah. It wasn't the man's real name and Ishmael had no idea who he was, nor did he care. Ishmael knew only that Fedallah served as a broker between himself and his clients.

Ishmael thought back to seven years ago when he had been functioning as an independent contractor, working directly with customers, and earning less than fifty-thousand dollars a job. It was an uncomfortable arrangement where he was dangerously exposed, with every customer aware of his true identity. If a contract went sideways, one or more of them could easily flip on him in exchange for a lighter sentence.

His situation improved after Fedallah recruited him. The man served as a protective layer of insulation between Ishmael and those who hired him. Fedallah exposed Ishmael to a wealthier class of clientele willing to pay top dollar for his services. After being contracted for the list of thirteen targets, his compensation skyrocketed, and his net worth grew by almost thirty-seven-million dollars.

Ishmael went to his basement office and opened the email. A set of numbers flashed across his laptop screen. They regarded a ghost company, one of many established by Fedallah years ago. The email had been sent via a Virtual Private Network, probably routed through Singapore and a half-dozen other servers around the world. No one, even Homeland Security could figure out who'd sent the message. The screen glowed with columns of various numbers, labeled as sales reports and arranged by regions of the country.

He'd been expecting Fedallah's message ever since the book arrived several days ago. It was a used paperback copy of James Patterson's Kiss the Girls. Fedallah had an identical copy, both purchased at a Half Price Books store. Without the book, the sales numbers on his computer were meaningless and without the numbers, the book was worthless. Together they described the details of his next job offering. The proposed contract came a little sooner than he would have preferred, but it was hard to argue with the burgeoning effect on his bank account.

The last line of numbers in the email read, $107,413. Ishmael opened his paperback and turned to page 107. With a pencil, he marked the fourth line up from the bottom and followed the line over thirteen letters and circled an s. The next number in the sales report was $103,826. He turned the book to page 103 and counted eight lines up from the bottom. The twenty-sixth letter was a t. He continued the process until he had transcribed the entire message: *state senator james torbeson, topeka kansas.* The man was number twelve on the list of thirteen. The most important number in the series was the total sum at the bottom: $2,500,374, indicating the contract value of two and a half million dollars.

Some in Ishmael's profession were ex-military who were excessively concerned with strength and conditioning. Being successful in this line of business didn't depend upon how much weight you could bench press or how far you could run. Those things helped, but keys to the successful completion of any assassination included: thorough research on the target's background, preparation with meticulous attention to detail, and flawless execution of the plan. Any imbecile could kill. Simply put a weapon in their hands and point to a target. It took no imagination to shoot someone in the head or slit their throat. Even an accomplished sniper lacked the innovative skills to become a top-tier assassin.

Ishmael regarded killing as an art form when in the hands of a true professional. The beauty of murder laid not in the taking of a life but in the ability to do so without anyone, including the victim, realizing what had happened. The creation of death took finesse, a skill learned from years of study, personal discipline, and experience. Extinguishing a life wasn't something he enjoyed or felt compelled to do by imagined voices in his head. He derived no pleasure from watching the last flicker of life slowly ebb from his victim's eyes. Unlike serial killers, he took no mementos to relive the events. After the job, the memory meant nothing to him. He concerned himself only with the financial benefits and the knowledge that he fulfilled the terms of each contract to perfection. He had become the

Picasso of assassins, and like the price of any expensive rare painting, he commanded a high fee proportional to his abilities.

He opened a second laptop, began a Google background search on his target, and noticed the same disturbing pattern he first identified after contract number seven on the list. The targets all shared the common thread of being associated with politics. If Ishmael saw this trend, then others might also, specifically those in law enforcement. The similarities could raise questions regarding motivation. Police detectives might unravel the common denominator. Who would benefit from the death of a particular group of victims like the thirteen? Motives could lead back to the man Ishmael knew only as The Client and maybe even to Fedallah. If his plans misfired, Ishmael had no illusions as to the loyalty of either. They would turn on him in an instant.

Another potential problem was the similarities amongst all the victims demonstrated a pattern, leading to an unsatisfactory level of predictability, a dangerous trend in the assassination business. The associated risks of each contract had grown significantly higher and that called for greater compensation. Using his copy of the novel, he sent a return message with his own VPN, opting to route it through Argentina. After decoded, it read, *Final sales totals under-reported. The actual number should be $4,538,000.* Within minutes, his request for four and a half million was accepted. Apparently, The Client had deep pockets and money would not be an issue. He typed, *Corrections accepted.* Two email addresses were destroyed within fifteen seconds, and both Patterson books would be burned.

Ishmael turned off his computer. He'd have to be careful. He'd been lucky with the widow in Cleveland. Having sex with her had been a careless mistake, leaving behind potential clues like DNA and fingerprints. He'd allowed his biological needs to contaminate his perfectly choreographed plan. The mistake constituted an intolerable level of imperfection. Fortunately, the widow's body would never be found, but he'd scrambled to dispose of it. He could not allow that to happen again.

"You stupid fool," said the voice of his mother, percolating up from the dark recesses of his mind. "You must be punished so it doesn't happen again. You know the drill."

As if in a trance, he walked into the kitchen pantry and returned to his workbench with a scented candles from Bath & Body Works. He lit the candle and held the palm of his hand over the flame until he smelled his own flesh incinerating. "Let that be a reminder," the voice snarled. "You're still not good enough."

NINE

Home of Lisa Marie Crawford
Everglades Estates
East Naples, Florida

What a lousy twenty-four hours it had been. After working with Cassie on the murder, I began feeling like my old self again and looking forward to a good night's sleep for once. Didn't happen.

A woman's scream tore through my dreams of John. "No. Please no."

Something hit the wall. A lamp? A body? My heart raced. I pulled my Sig Sauer from the nightstand, a leftover habit from serving five years on an international antiterrorist team. I'd made many enemies, and always kept a weapon nearby.

A slap and another scream, more of a cry. Again, a woman's voice. "Please stop. God help me."

I slammed the palm of my hand against the wall. "I'm calling the police."

Gripping the Sig tightly in my hand, I pressed my ear to the wall. Any more crying or screams for help, and I was ready to run over there. All remained quiet for several minutes — then the cooing sounds of apologies. A marital squabble? I placed my handgun back on the nightstand and tried to sleep, but after a jolt of adrenaline like that, it took several hours.

By morning, I awoke in a dark mood, but figured a call to my new friend Cassie would get me back on track.

She answered, "Detective Cassandra Pierce." Her voice sounded distant and aloof. Strange.

"Hi Cassie. It's Lisa."

"Oh, hi, Mrs. Crawford."

What? Not Lisa? An accident? Now I was just a private citizen, again? Her words crushed me. What happened to our law enforcement family, our new friendship? In less than twenty-four hours I'd gone from being part of an investigative team to a nobody. My mind rioted, and I paced the floor. Good thing it was tile. If it were carpet, I'd have worn a hole through it. Frustrated and angry, I needed to go for a run. John always joked that running was how I burned off my crazies. After no sleep and my call to Cassie, I was full of crazy.

I stretched in the front yard and to my left, I saw a man exit the condo that had been the source of last night's mayhem. He wore a gray suit and a silk shirt with the top two buttons opened, exposing a chest full of dark hair and a heavy gold chain. Really? Stereotypical middle-aged buffoon. He looked like a cast member from The Sopranos. Who dresses like that anymore? He was short and fat but walked with a strut that said he was very much impressed with himself. He flashed a flirtatious smile at me and stared at my breasts.

What an asshole. Second one in two days. I glared back. "Hey," I yelled, pointing to my face. "Eyes up here. I'm not down there."

"Oh, yeah. You must be the loudmouth from next door, the one who keeps pounding on my wall." New York accent.

"And you must be the mindless ass who keeps me up all night with your yelling."

"Honey, if I'd known you looked this good, I'd have invited you over long ago. I'm sure you'd have kept me up all night—if you get my drift." He grinned and blew me a kiss.

I gave him the finger. When he pulled his black BMW out of the driveway, his license plate read TOPDOC. Double asshole. I sprinted away my frustrations until I reached the place where I'd found Jane Doe. A pair of elderly cyclists approached from the opposite direction. "You'd better turn back, honey. The police have blocked off the entire path."

I checked the spot where Mr. Spandex had run me off the path and still couldn't help but wonder if he had something to do with the murder. Everything was quiet, the opposite of yesterday when a team of forensic specialists combed the site looking for evidence. The area had since been abandoned as though Jane Doe had never existed. *Accident? That's what Cassie called it this morning.* Didn't add up. A single patrolman sat in a plastic chair guarding the area. Why a guard if Cassie believed this was an actual accident? It smelled of politics. I looked down and visualized that delicate hand wedged in the bike's gears and shook my head at the obscenity of Jane's murder. . *And now the police want to pass it off as an accident?*

That same attitude led to the police failure to identify the killers who slaughtered my family when I was a girl. I refused to allow that to happen to Jane Doe. Anger percolated up from the depths of my soul. I curled my hands into fists and vowed to find the one who did this, with or without the police. I'd make him pay. Most of my adult life had been devoted to tracking down and destroying international terrorists. How hard could finding one murderer in Naples be? Of course, when hunting terrorists, I had Mr. Winston Hamilton and the entire team backing me up, but the principles were basically the same. Find a thread and pull on it until you uncover a lead. Then, follow that clue wherever it takes me.

First, I needed a name for Jane Doe. *Think, Lisa. You can do this.* I gazed down at the water where I had found her bike. The image planted the seed of an idea in my mind. It grew into an actual plan as I rushed home.

As I approached the driveway of my condo, a petite Asian woman with long, jet-black hair was pulling a garbage can away from the curb. She was headed toward the same garage TOPDOC backed out of earlier. She wore oversized sunglasses, and her lower lip was swollen. The day was already hot, but she wore a long sleeve blouse.

I wanted to offer my help, but as I approached, she winced and took a step back. She stared at the ground, her lips moving without making a sound. Her hands trembled, a pattern of behavior I'd seen before. Spousal abuse came in many forms and from a wide cross section of society. It even affected the wealthy, perhaps them even more so. They were simply able to hide it better.

I introduced myself. "Hi, I'm Lisa. I live next door." I looked her over again. "What happened to you?"

"Uh, I fell. I'm so clumsy sometimes."

I gently removed her glasses and gritted my teeth. Her left eye was swollen shut. I took her hand. "We both know this wasn't from a fall. Is this the first time he's beaten you?"

She bowed her head, tears streaking down her cheeks. "No."

"How long has it been going on?" No reply. Only a slight shrug.

"Any other injuries?" I asked.

She lifted her blouse to reveal a grapefruit-sized bruise on her left side. I placed my hand on her shoulder. "Your husband's license plate says, TOPDOC. Is he a physician?"

"He's a doctor of naturopathy. Got his degree on-line, but he likes for people to think he's an MD."

Figures. "This is never going to stop unless something is done. You must leave him right now. I'll help you pack and give you a ride to wherever you want to go. They have centers to protect women in your situation."

She took a step back. "I can't."

Typical response from a battered spouse. They stay, hoping they can turn the man around. It never happens. The beatings always return, with greater frequency and ferocity until it's too late. "At least let me document your injuries with some photographs."

She looked in all directions. "Not out here."

"Why don't we go inside where it's private?"

"He watches me with cameras."

"Okay. He doesn't have them in my house. It'll take only a minute." She agreed, and I took a dozen pictures with my cell phone. I asked for her phone and entered my contact information under the name of a fake window cleaning company. I was certain her husband checked her phone on a regular basis. Part of the entire control and isolation pattern. "If you need help, call me at any time. I will be there for you."

"If he finds out you've talked to me, he'll hurt you."

"I'd like to see him try. It'd be the worst day of his life." Rage festered inside my heart adding to the anger I already felt because of Jane Doe's death and Cassie's rejection. Mr. double-asshole TOPDOC and I were going to have a serious discussion soon, one he would not enjoy. That would have to wait until I again heard from his wife. I didn't expect it would be long.

I went inside to work on my plan to uncover the identity of Jane Doe. Then I was going to find the spandex cyclist.

62

TEN

Von Hamburg Castle
Brussels, Belgium

The Client's net worth exceeded the gross domestic product of half the European Nations. He gazed down from his fourth-story bedroom window at the thirteen hundred acres of his estate. A shock of uncombed, silver hair wandered in all directions as though he had been struck by lightning. His eyebrows grew into chaotic clusters of gray weeds. Ever since he purchased the castle, his inner circle referred to him as the Baron. Though not an official title, he secretly relished the sobriquet. *An orphaned Jew now part of European aristocracy.* The previous owner had abandoned the Von Hamburg Castle and it had fallen into disrepair over the years. The Baron paid off its thirty-seven-million dollars in delinquent taxes and received title to the wreckage. He invested over a half-billion dollars in extensive repairs of the external shell. Another half-billion went into furnishings, security, and the latest in modern electronics.

The Baron leaned against his cane, its top an apple-sized sphere of polished cobalt-blue stone. He asked his nurse, "Would you have LaTrane come in?"

A minute later, the door to his bedroom opened and a head peaked in, its narrow eyes darting from side to side, checking all corners of the room before stepping inside. He entered with the cautious grace of a large cat, his pale face waxy smooth as though it had been painted on. His red lips held a smile twisted in a permanent sneer. The Baron had discovered LaTrane as a young boy. Filthy and his face badly scarred from burns, he had been living off garbage in the back alleys of Paris. The Baron recognized a fiery determination to survive in the boy's eyes, the same quality that ensured the Baron's own success. He brought LaTrane into his world where he groomed the child in the elegant customs of European aristocracy. He educated him in the arts, sciences, and the complexities of international finance. LaTrane had remained at the Baron's side ever since. As a man, he became as comfortable in the corporate boardroom as in the seediest bars in Gard du Nord. "Yes, sir?"

"What's the status of our project in the Congo?"

"Our people have already neutralized two of the world's three largest cobalt mines. They will destroy the third within the month. It'll be decades until the radioactive contamination can be lowered enough to bring any of them back online. As expected, the price of ore from our own mines has doubled, and our profits are up over two hundred percent. Once we eliminate the third mine, the values will skyrocket. We project a minimum, thirty-billion-dollar annual profit over the next five years.

"Can any of the bombings be traced back to us?"

"No. I've taken all necessary measures to insulate us from any connection to the attacks. Our mercenaries will be eliminated shortly after completing their final mission. Blame has already been placed at the feet of Islamic revolutionaries from Nigeria." LaTrane picked a bloodied tissue off the floor and placed it in his pocket. "Meanwhile, our geologists have mapped out over half of the Congo, and we have purchased all promising lands from local villagers. With what we already own in Australia, over fifty-five percent of the world's reserves are under our control."

The old man hobbled closer to his assistant, his breath that of a man whose body was slowly dying inside. LaTrane took a step back as his boss continued. "Good. That takes care of the supply side. Now we need to focus more on the demand part of the equation. I want another energy bill passed through the US congress. Half must be devoted to the conversion from internal combustion engines to electric vehicles. In addition, I want to increase subsidies and tax credits for all renewable energy sources. Wind and solar power rely on industrial battery storage systems and that leads to even greater demands for cobalt."

The Baron stumbled and LaTrane grabbed him before he fell. "Instruct our brokerage house in the Caymans, to purchase another $50 million of New Dawn Technologies stock. Have them wire the funds into the appropriate numbered Swiss accounts in our Masada Bank. Inform all our people who have steered the necessary bills out of committee, that they will have access to their accounts in a year."

"As you wish, Baron." LaTrane cleared his throat. "The Speaker is meeting resistance from the opposition and even some in his own party. They are concerned that the increased spending might worsen the inflation problem."

The Baron's eyes grew dark. "Tell him to make it happen. It would be very unfortunate if reporters at the L. A. Times received an anonymous packet detailing his financial transactions with us over the past twenty-five years. A federal prison is not a pleasant place to spend the remaining years of his life. While you're at it, keep the pressure on our other political affiliates in Congress. I want the price of oil up over $150 a barrel. That means no drilling, no new pipelines, and no more of that damn fracking."

"Yes sir."

LaTrane shifted his balance from one foot to the other. "There has been one glitch, sir."

The Baron continued to lean against the cobalt topper of his cane as he stared out the window. "Clouds are brewing on the horizon. We're in for a bad storm. Better notify the staff to get the horses in." He turned to face LaTrane. "Glitch?"

"Yes sir, but one so minor, I almost didn't bother mentioning it to you."

"And yet, you did. What is this minor problem?"

"A woman was murdered in Florida, sir."

"A lot of people are killed in the US every day, LaTrane. Why does this particular one pose a problem for us? Was she on our list of thirteen?"

"No sir, but the police investigation into her death might trigger a cascade of events that could upset our plans. If a clever detective were to follow the clues, they could lead him back to our list."

The Baron's face burned bright red. "Then, make sure it doesn't happen. I want this thing nipped in the bud. Turn it over to Fedallah and tell him to make it a priority. I'll not have all my plans destroyed by the death of one insignificant woman." A droplet of blood fell from his nose and ran across his upper lip. He smeared it with the back of his hand. "Get me another damn Kleenex and call for one of those fancy doctors you hired."

ELEVEN

CIA Headquarters
Langley, Virginia

Winston Hamilton's driver headed down Colonial Farm Road until he saw the inauspicious green and white sign that read:

George Bush Center for Intelligence
Next Right

The name had become the butt of endless jokes. Despite that, the center remained the most sophisticated intelligence gathering organization in the world. Beneath the main sign sat a smaller one, warning:

Authorized Vehicles Only

The chauffeur slowed and pulled down the road, stopping at the main gate of the Langley, Virginia complex. Though Winston came here six days a week, the guard still insisted on seeing his ID card. It seemed an unnecessary requirement, but the Agency demanded adherence to strict security protocols at all times since the attempted assassination of President Wagner several years ago. After sliding Hamilton's ID into the facial recognition scanner, the guard raised the gate and waved the car through.

"Drop me off in front, Kingsley." Winston's driver negotiated a series of concrete barricades, placed in such a way that a vehicle with a bomb couldn't accelerate and slam into the entrance.

Kingsley pulled to the curb to let out his passenger. "When shall I pick you up, sir?"

"I have a short day today. I'll call when I'm ready. If you want, there'll be enough time to head to Dupont Circle and pick up a few games of chess. Maybe win a few bucks?"

"Maybe?" Kingsley chuckled and pulled away.

Winston stretched his diminutive five-foot-six-inch frame. Cold, black eyes, and a continuous, horizontal smile gave him the appearance of a reptile. He adjusted his black fedora and entered the building through the double glass doors. Beneath a concrete overhang, the famous emblem of the Central Intelligence Agency was embedded in the gray marble floor. As he did every morning, Winston paused in front of the Memorial Wall and tipped his hat to the one-hundred-thirty-seven gold stars, each representing an agent who had died in defense of their country. Some, he himself had sent on their fateful missions. A leather-bound book, encased in a locked glass box affixed to the wall contained their never-revealed names. He hoped there would be no more stars, but realized more deaths would be a certainty. In this business, loss of life was unavoidable.

After taking the elevator to the third floor, he rushed down the hall to room 319. He was late, but he was the boss, so who would complain? The sign on the door read: *Supplemental Section of the Office of Research and Reports: Winston Hamilton III, Director.* On the surface, his department appeared to be another insignificant piece of the CIA bureaucracy. Very few outside the Oval Office realized it was much more. Even his superiors in the Agency were unaware of the full scope of his activities. His track record and family connections resulted in multiple opportunities for advancement in the agency, but he declined. He didn't need the money, and he already wielded more power than most politicians in D.C. His present position afforded him access to all the information he required and provided the level of anonymity he needed to carry out his mission.

The office, larger than most governmental offices, was furnished like a New York City penthouse. Handmade Victorian walnut bookcases occupied one wall while a matching desk sat in the front of an original oil by Andrew Wyeth. On top of the desk, an assortment of computer screens watched over a bank of secure phones. Tan leather couches guarded either side of a matching antique coffee table. On the walls hung pictures of himself posing with a multitude of influential business and political dignitaries, including two past presidents.

Being incredibly rich had its advantages. Winston was the sole heir to the Hamilton Family Estate. He didn't have to work for a living, but he had a passion for what he did. As a teen, he had achieved the level of a grand chess master. The World Chess Federation ranked him as one of the most promising contenders for the world championship. Many referred to him as the next Bobby Fisher, but by the time he graduated from Yale Law School, Winston became bored with a mere game in which the stakes were meaningless except for the fleeting satisfaction derived from each victory. For him, the game was all too easy. He yearned for a more challenging real-life scenario where the stakes were higher, one in which a win might save lives while a loss could be deadly. Therefore, he used his extensive family connections to secure his present position.

He entered his group of offices and said hello to his secretary, Jeanine.

She looked up from her computer screen and checked the wall clock. "You're late. Sixty-three minutes late to be exact."

Winston held his hands up in surrender. "I know. I know. Traffic was horrible on the parkway. A bad wreck. Kingsley had a difficult time negotiating around everything."

"So, other than that, how's he working out?"

"He's a terrible chauffeur—I guess to be expected from a homeless man who's never had a driver's license until a month ago."

Jeanine raised her eyebrows. "But?" She knew his response.

"But, he's a great chess player. A natural who's never had training. One of the best I've faced, including the Russians."

"There you go, sir. That's what counts." She smirked with her usual morning banter with the boss. After twenty-three years together, she was the only one who could get away with it —she and Lisa Marie Crawford.

Winston set a brown paper bag on her desk. She looked up. "What's this? Your lunch? You brown bagging it now?"

He chuckled, "Oh, no, no." He lifted the bag so she could read the label.

She squinted her eyes. "Kopi Lewak?" she asked. "What's a Kopi Lewak?"

"The most expensive coffee in the world. It comes from one of the Sumatran islands. Asian palm civets select only the finest coffee cherries for their diet."

Jeanine interrupted him. "And exactly what's a civet?"

"I think it's in the cat family. Anyway, they eat only the finest coffee cherries. As they pass through the animal's alimentary canal, the fruit is digested, leaving the beans that take on a unique flavor. Natives spend hours searching the jungle floor looking for the excrement. The undigested beans are washed and toasted to provide a coffee worthy of the gods. I had some once when doing an exhibition chess tournament in Medan. The drink was positively exquisite."

She scrunched her brows together. "You mean that coffee comes from cat poop? Just what do you expect me to do with this stuff?"

"Why brew some fresh coffee for us, of course."

"I'm not putting anything that was scraped from the bottom of a litter box into my coffee maker. You want some of that nonsense, you can make it yourself at home."

"But it cost over four hundred dollars a pound."

She scowled at him. "Let the gods drink it then."

Winston raised his hands in surrender. "Okay, okay, I just thought it might be interesting to expand our gustatorial horizons a little."

"I like my horizons right where they are, thank you very much."

The debate was over. No sense in pursuing it any further. Winston placed his suit jacket on a hanger and set his black fedora on the corner of his desk. "So, what disasters await me this morning?"

"The usual international conflicts, most of which are nothing new. I scanned the morning papers and placed them on the corner of your desk. There's also a cup of coffee, the normal human variety, but it's cold by now. I'll brew a fresh one, not made from cat poop."

Winston's private computer pinged, meaning he had a top-secret message from his close friend. "Ah, first things first." Winston entered his fourteen-character password, and the screen came alive. He opened his email and read the instructions. Winston chuckled and walked over to the chess board sitting on a table in the corner of his office, the worn pieces in midgame arrangement. *Clever move, Mr. President. I wasn't expecting your bishop to attack. Unusually unpredictable and aggressive. Are you being coached behind my back?* His chubby, short fingers moved the President's bishop as instructed. He countered with his own queen. More aggressive. He sent his reply to the White House. *Checkmate in five moves, Mr. President.*

He sat behind his desk. Now for the news.

Jeanine delivered the fresh cup of coffee and waited.

He took a sip and relished the hot liquid as it ran down the back of his throat. "Not my Kopi Lewak, but perfect, as always, Jeanine. Strong, black, and hot." He grinned. "Just like you," he said, ignoring what could be perceived by some as sexual harassment or racism.

"Why, Mr. Hamilton. How you do get on. What in the world did you have for breakfast this morning?" She laughed, slapped his shoulder, and returned to her desk.

He rotated his chair, reached into his humidor, and retrieved a Padron Family Reserve cigar. After lighting up, he took a long pull, allowing the flavor to fill his mouth, and exhaled a plume of white smoke to the ceiling. He was ready for the world. He pulled a copy of The New York Times from the stack of newspapers and scanned the headlines. The President had set a national goal of phasing out all internal combustion engines and transitioning to electric vehicles by the middle of the next decade. That would include all cars, semi-trucks, and buses, bringing America in line with most European nations.

Winston flicked the ash off his cigar. *Noble endeavor, Mr. President, but lithium-ion batteries don't create energy. They can only store it.*

The article then discussed the dilemma:

The country is already experiencing rolling blackouts in some areas during times of peak demand. Many scientists have expressed concerns that wind and solar energy will be unable to cover the shortfall created by the addition of two-hundred million new electric vehicles drawing power. How can we produce the necessary amount of electricity without the use of fossil fuels such as coal and natural gas? Relying on them would defeat the purpose of transitioning to EVs.

Better start making comprehensive plans to supply enough electricity to charge all those vehicles, Mr. President. If you transition from fossil fuels too rapidly, you'll destroy the economy. A minute later, he tossed the paper into the trash.

A framed photograph on the right side of the desk stared at him. It had been sitting in the same spot for fifteen years. Winston picked it up and traced the outline of the images of his wife and two boys with his finger. The picture was a reminder of better days — before his wife packed up the kids and moved to Glendale, a quiet community just north of Cincinnati. She'd demanded he choose between her and his mistress. His choice destroyed their marriage. Another woman hadn't captured his heart. It was the Agency and its attendant intrigue that he couldn't give up. All that remained of those earlier times were old photographs and the knowledge he was protecting the country and the future of his family.

Another pull on the cigar, and another plume of smoke carried the fading memories up to the ceiling. *Enough reminiscing, Winston. Back to the task at hand.* He selected the next paper, *The Wall Street Journal.* The headline on the front page got his attention: Dirty Bomb Explosions in Congo. The article reported that a series of explosions destroyed two of the largest cobalt mines in the world, both owned by Liuang Mining Corporation in China. Several Nigerian rebels were killed in the attack. Local officials stated that the men were part of the Boka Haram terrorist organization. Subsequent inspection of the site revealed high levels of radiation. The IAEA was investigating. They estimated it will take decades to clean the site before workers can return. A year ago, experts projected a 30% increase in the worldwide demand for cobalt, an essential component in the manufacture of lithium-ion batteries for everything from electric cars to storage systems for wind and solar energy. With the loss of two major mines, the price of the mineral was expected to increase exponentially.

Winston opened another computer and typed a message for the CIA Director.

A shortage of cobalt is a serious problem with national security implications. The explosions in Africa are not the work of Nigerian insurgents. Iranians have long supported Boko Haram and could have supplied the plutonium. However, I doubt they would do anything to alienate China, an ally against the US. Boko Haram is a scapegoat. Need to investigate. Primary question: who benefits most by eliminating the world's most productive cobalt mines?

Back to the paper. El Qaeda had made a return from the dead after the Afghanistan fiasco, and now were well-armed with the military weapons left behind by the United States. *Too late to do anything about it.* The next report was on Congress extending a temporary spending measure to keep the government running. The national debt had skyrocketed past thirty-one trillion dollars, an unsustainable situation. The present leaders in the House and Senate were unwilling to tackle the problem head on. *Too interested in their political careers to make the tough decisions needed to avoid the country's collapse.* He created his team to protect the country from its enemies, abroad and domestic. But how could they protect the country from itself?

Attached to the article were two related reports: one by the Federal Reserve about the threat of continued inflation. Not surprising after the unprecedented amount of cash Congress infused into the economy with the COVID relief and infrastructure bills. *Too much pork. Markets are going to be hit hard.* The other article described the progress of a new organization. He read the report in its entirety. *Interesting. Finally, someone's doing something concrete to get America back on track. Their efforts are a long shot, but well-worth the cost.*

Winston set his cigar in the ashtray. "Jeanine, get Jason Hartford on the line." The man was vice-president of Preston-Simons, a Wall Street investment bank. Now, his sole job was to serve as the personal manager of the twenty-seven-billion-dollar Hamilton Family Trust.

A minute later Jeanine replied, "Mr. Hartford is on line three."

Winston picked up the phone. "Jason. What do you know about the TBA organization?"

Hartford explained what little he knew.

"You think they're legit?"

"They certainly appear to be, Mr. Hamilton."

Winston picked up his Padron, relit it, and leaned back in his chair. He called Jeanine back into his office.

"More coffee?"

"That would be nice, but first I want you to have the research section investigate this Take Back America organization." He showed her the article. "I want a full report within the week."

76

TWELVE

Ishmael's Home
Lakeside Park, Kentucky

Ishmael sat at a workbench in the basement of his home. Purchased by Fedallah through an offshore corporation, Ishmael's name wasn't on the deed. In fact, he didn't even exist as an individual. Neither did his present identity, Roger Wembley. He couldn't be found on any official governmental records. He had no DNA profile or fingerprints on file in the FBI's IAFIS data bank. His social security number and passport were perfect fakes, created by Fedallah. The name Ishmael was a code name given to him seven years and a dozen aliases ago. His only record of factual identification was a retinal scan and a fifteen-digit numbered account used exclusively to identify him at his multiple off-shore banks.

He just returned from spending a week in Topeka, surveilling his next target, Senator James Torbeson. Having already outlined the basics of a plan in his mind, Ishmael spread several dozen photographs of the man's home and office building across his workbench. Torbeson was divorced and lived in a modest two-story home, twenty miles south of the Kansas State Capitol. All targets had at least one point of vulnerability. It was simply a matter of identifying it and taking advantage at the right moment. Other than his preference for the comforts of male companionship, Torbeson led an uneventful life with only two passions: Kansas politics and his house which he kept in immaculate condition with professionally designed landscaping, and a perfectly manicured lawn. Torbeson's gay lifestyle offered potential, but his home provided the best opportunity.

Ishmael pinned several key photographs on a bulletin board above the workbench. In them lay the basis for his plan. He'd obtained two bags of crushed white marble at the local Home Depot store. He emptied the stones onto the bench and sorted through them, selecting several dozen pieces that would suit his purposes. After studying each under a magnifying glass, he set aside the majority due to the presence of small cracks or fissures. Securing one of the stones in a jeweler's lathe, Ishmael polished it to the desired dimensions. He repeated the process until he successfully sculpted ten of the stones to the precise requirements.

He picked up a rifle and used an eighteen-inch drill bit to destroy the barrel's rifling. The process would affect accuracy but failure to do so would result in projectile fragmentation. He'd need several days of testing before he could be certain everything would work according to plan.

THIRTEEN

Home of Lisa Marie Crawford
Everglades Estates
East Naples, Florida

My plan to identify Jane Doe was simple. The bike was a Trek Domane, an expensive model. Naples was a high-end community. Some joked that even God owned a condo here. Just the same, I doubted many people had acquired a specialty bike like the Domane. I opened my laptop and called up the last several issues of the Naples Daily Courier. I found what I wanted: articles written by a reporter about my age with blonde hair. Her name was Maddie Carmichael. A slight change in my hair style and a pair of glasses did the trick. I put on a pair of espadrilles, a new khaki skirt and a silk avocado-green blouse I'd bought the day before. A linen jacket added a sexy but professional look. I flipped my hair from under the collar and let it fall across my shoulders.

The only Trek Cyclery store, located on Tamiami Trail, was about four miles away. I spoke to the owner and he agreed to meet me in an hour.

The building was new and much larger than I expected. Several dozen new bikes sat on display in racks along one wall. About the same number of used cycles, still in pristine condition, rested on kickstands along the other side. In the center, shelves held items like custom seats, helmets, water bottles, and multiple other accessories cyclists needed. A man wearing a purple polo shirt with the name Trek Cyclery embroidered over the left breast walked around the counter and extended his hand. "Mrs. Carmichael? Hi. I'm Todd Maultry."

I shook his hand and looked him directly in the eye. "Miss," I replied, "But my friends call me Maddie."

His eyes twinkled with enthusiasm, and a wide smile spread across his face, a look that said he was interested. "How may I help you, Maddie?" he asked with extra emphasis on my name.

"As I said on the phone, the paper wants me to do a report on local businesses and how they survived the COVID era. Your store came to mind." I leaned against the counter, crossed my legs at the ankle, and gazed around. "Your place is beautiful."

His smile beamed with pride. He puffed out his chest. "My father started it in a small strip mall in Bonita just over thirty years ago. COVID was an unexpected boon for us. With normal socializing restricted, people looked to the outdoors to entertain themselves. Purchases of bicycles soared, and we were unable to keep up with the demand. When I took over the business, I moved it to our present location. It's allowed us to double our inventory and sales."

He showed me the individual bikes. I played along and took a multitude of photographs until we stopped in front of the model I was interested in. "My, this is a beautiful bike."

Todd removed it from the rack so I could check it more closely. "It's a Trek Domane. One of our finest bikes."

I ran my newly manicured fingers over the crossbar of the bike, stroking its sleek surface. I wrapped my fingers around the metal tubing and squeezed. "Firm and solid," I said with the sultriest voice I could muster, forcing away a laugh. Todd studied my hand closely and grinned.

"It looks very expensive."

"This one runs about twelve thousand, but we've been known to negotiate substantial discounts for our special customers." He stressed the word special. "That is, if you're interested."

I flashed my most flirtatious grin. "Oh, I'm definitely interested, Todd." I had him. "Speaking of which, you know what would make my article better? An interview with several of your satisfied customers. You know, to get a few testimonials."

He shook his head. "I don't know, Maddie. We don't like to share personal information about our clientele."

I conjured up a sexy pout. "But it would help so much. Our paper enjoys a daily distribution to over a hundred thousand homes around Naples, more when you consider internet viewing. Personal recommendations have the greatest impact. It's like getting ten thousand dollars of free advertising. I'll check with my editor. If the piece is good enough, with some human-interest angles, I might be able to get it on the front page."

His eyes widened. "A hundred-thousand homes?"

I batted my eyes at him, knowing I'd closed the deal.

"Exactly what do you need, Maddie?"

"How about a list of all the Domane purchases over the past three years."

His smile faltered a little, but he produced the list. After spending another thirty minutes at the store and taking notes, I thanked him. On my way out I said, "Look for the article next week." I regretted the lie, but it wouldn't hurt him—except maybe his pride when he realized he'd been conned.

<hr>

When I returned to my condo, I changed into a pair of jean shorts and a t-shirt, poured myself a glass of Kim Crawford chardonnay, and sat on the lanai. Todd's list of Domane purchasers held just over thirty names. After weeding out any addresses outside a ten-mile radius of the park, I excluded neighborhoods where I felt the residents didn't have the financial capacity to buy expensive bikes or fifty-thousand-dollar wedding rings. Granted, this approach relied on a few assumptions that might not have been valid, but it was a start.

I whittled the original list down to seventeen customers. I called the phone numbers and crossed off most of them because they had already sold their homes, or were seasonal snowbirds, unlikely to be in Florida during the summer. That left me with five prospects, a workable number. Unfortunately, none were women, and I was afraid I'd have to find Jane Doe's identity another way.

Frustrated, I poured another glass of wine, and decided to Google the five men. I was surprised to find what I wanted on the second one. His name was Preston Wellington, owner of Wellington Investments, a financial advisor company managing over twenty-five billion dollars in assets. I Googled his company and found a picture of him at a fundraiser for the Naples Philharmonic Orchestra. Posing next to him was a tall, blue-eyed blonde in a full-length rose-colored gown, poised and beautiful, with a smile that was accustomed to being photographed. Her right hand curled around her husband's waist while her left hand rested on her hip. I zoomed in on the ring finger. Bingo! She wore a huge pear-shaped diamond ring. The caption under the photograph said her name was Savannah.

I leaned back in my chair and finished the rest of my wine. Jane Doe was Mrs. Savannah Wellington. I Googled her and was shocked to find she had been the House Speaker for Florida's State Legislature.

FOURTEEN

Wellington Building
Naples, Florida

D etective Pierce said the primary suspect in any murder is the spouse. I knew interviewing Preston Wellington would be challenging, but doable if a reporter offered to do an article on his Wellington Investments company in the Naples Courier Journal. I had to be careful. It wouldn't be as easy as with Todd at the Cyclery Store. Savannah's husband was smart and bound to see through my act if I slipped up. I called his secretary and identified myself as Maddie Carmichael.

"Mr. Wellington has been out of town on the West Coast for several weeks. Just got back yesterday."

Three thousand miles away until yesterday? So much for him being the killer. I was about to give up on that angle, but he still could have hired someone to do it. He was certainly wealthy enough. "I understand," I told his secretary. Needed an angle that might get me in. "I'll keep my interview brief, and focus mainly on his charity work in Naples." I could hear her fingers working the keypad on her computer.

"He does have a small opening." She gave me an appointment for the following afternoon.

The Wellington Building was a new four-story structure on East Tenth Avenue. The secretary escorted me into Preston's plush, fourth-floor office, decorated with modern furniture. One wall of floor-to-ceiling glass offered a panoramic view of Naples Bay. Multiple photographs and original oil paintings hung on the other walls. I recognized one by Salvador Dali. As I studied it, Preston entered with the look of a member of the privileged upper class: tall, slender, aristocratic nose, and a light dusting of gray along the temples. I half expected to see photographs of him on a horse at the Naples Polo Club.

"Miss Carmichael?"

"Yes." I extended my hand.

"Sorry to keep you waiting. I was on a conference call with some investors." His smile was engaging and genuine as he received my handshake, his grip confident but gentle. "I'm Preston Wellington." He was handsome and not at all stuffy as I expected. "It's a pleasure to meet you." He motioned to a leather chair opposite his desk. "Have a seat." He waited for me to sit before doing so himself. A gentleman—like John. "Would you care for something to drink? Coffee? Water? A soft drink?"

"Water would be great."

He called over the intercom to his secretary. "Maria, would you please bring in two glasses of San Pellegrino, one for Miss Carmichael and one for me?"

The guy didn't act much like a killer—whatever that meant. Still, the most successful killers were probably the ones who appeared least capable of murder. As I took a sip of the water, I observed several back issues of the Naples Courier Journal on his desk. I held my breath. Maddie Carmichael's photo was included at the top of each of her articles. Would my disguise hold up?

He smiled. "I've taken the liberty of reading some of your work. Very impressive, but I noticed that most of your reporting deals with criminal activity. I hope that's not an indication of why you're here today."

Relief. He hadn't noticed. "Oh, no, Mr. Wellington, —"

He smiled and interrupted. "Please, call me Preston."

Smooth. "Okay, Preston, and you may call me Maddie." I took another drink of water and pulled a coaster close before setting the glass down. "I thought it would be nice to do a positive article about one of our city's most successful businessmen. I'd like to focus on your philanthropic efforts."

He leaned back in his chair. "There are many successful businessmen here in Naples, most of whom are involved in charities. I'm honored you selected me. Where would you like to start."

"As they always say, let's start at the beginning. Why don't you tell me about yourself and how you got into the financial advisor business?" I set my recorder on his desk. "May I?"

"Of course." He stared at a portrait of an elderly man hanging on the wall behind his desk. "It was my father." Over the next ten minutes, he gave me some background. He was born and raised in a middle-class neighborhood in Naples. His father had been a frustrated loan officer at one of the local banks. He wanted more for Preston than just a job that put a roof over his family's head and food on their table.

"Once I graduated from college, Dad gave me a loan to start my own financial advisor business. With the grace of God, and some help from Lady Luck, the business grew well beyond my expectations. We now manage over twenty-five billion dollars in assets. We recently started our own SPAC division."

"SPAC?" I asked. "What is it?" I leaned in closer, honestly interested.

"A special purpose acquisition company. We raise capital from investors and search for companies to buy. SPACs have great profit potential. That's where I've been for the past several weeks. I flew out to the West Coast to recruit investors. We need people willing to take the necessary risks."

"The greater the risks, the greater the rewards," I said.

A slight twinkle in his eye. "Very insightful for a crime reporter. Maybe you should transfer to the financial desk."

I laughed. "I think my editor might have some issues with that. I have trouble figuring out my monthly bank statements." We talked about his interest in the local arts and his activities as a fundraiser. I gazed around the room at the collage of framed pictures hanging on the wall. One was an award certificate from the Naples Museum of Fine Arts. Next to it hung a picture of Savannah, taken with two men.

"Is that your wife? She's a beautiful woman."

"Savannah? Yes, she is."

Present tense? "Is she also interested in the arts?"

"She'd like to be, but she's very busy. That photograph was taken with the governor a few years back."

"She's a friend of Governor Cartwright's?"

His smile beamed with pride. "Savannah is the Speaker of the Florida House. The only woman to ever serve in that capacity."

Again, present tense. Savannah is, not was?

"I'm surprised you didn't know that being a reporter and all. Politics not your schtick?"

My mind froze. Almost blew my cover. I recovered with a slight head shake and stared at the picture, taken on the steps of the Florida Capitol Building. Governor Cartwright's left arm wrapped around Savannah's waist, his hand a little too low, nearly resting on her buttocks. Interesting. Another Andrew Cuomo? "Who's the gentleman on her other side? Opposite the governor."

Preston got up to take a closer look. "As I remember, his name is Masterson." He paused and ran his hands through his hair. "No, wait, that's not it." He snapped his fingers. "It's Matheson, Scott Matheson. He's with an organization called TBA. I'm not sure exactly what they do but it has something to do with passing resolutions in the various states."

"That was a couple years ago?"

"Yes. Two or three."

"So, Savannah must have been good friends with the governor for quite a while."

"They worked closely on a number of issues together."

"Is she working on anything important right now?"

His proud smile faded. "I don't know. I haven't spoken to Savannah for almost a year now. We've been separated."

That explained why he hadn't reported her missing.

He continued, "I'd been preoccupied, traveling and building up the business. Savannah was busy with her political career in Tallahassee. We drifted apart." His eyes appeared unfocused as though he were in deep thought. "I returned from an extended business trip last year, and when I got home, she was gone." Preston smiled slightly, the kind that covers up an inner sadness.

That's what I did to John. No warning. I simply left. I changed the subject to more comfortable areas like his philanthropic work. His demeanor improved and after another fifteen minutes, I thanked him for his time and left. I couldn't say for sure whether or not he murdered Savannah but my gut told me he was innocent. I'd gone about as far as I could on my own. I needed to know if Cassie had she made any progress, but how could I find out? I came up with another plan.

FIFTEEN

Home of Rachael Morris
Tallahassee, Florida

Rachael paced the floor of her condominium. "Where's Savannah?" She asked the empty room. Her phone rang. She cringed and hesitated to answer, but she had no choice. The chief of staff for House Speaker Savannah Wellington didn't ignore a call from the governor's office. "This is Rachael Morris."

The voice on the other end sounded irate. No surprise. Rachael was angry herself. "We're expecting her to arrive any minute." A lie. Rachael had no idea where her boss was. They hadn't spoken to each other for a week. Not unusual. Savannah was prone to disappearing for days at a time, especially with a new boyfriend. Rachael held the phone away from her ear. More impatient words from the caller. "Yes, I'll let you know as soon as she walks in the door."

Savannah had always been an ambitious woman who admittedly broke a lot of rules to get where she was. Rachael could hardly blame her. Politics remained predominantly a man's game, and Savannah had learned to use their weaknesses against them whenever the opportunity arose. That included flagrant flirting and more—like sleeping with anyone who might be able to help her career. Rachael had tried to rein her in, but it was like trying to put a leash on the wind.

Rachael called her assistant. "Have you heard from Savannah?"

"Me? She barely knows I exist. You're the only one she'll speak to."

Rachael and Savannah Wellington had been best friends since high school. She'd been Savannah's roommate in college and maid-of-honor at her wedding to Preston. Savannah had always been glamorous and engaging while Rachael was intellectual and introspective. Together they made a perfect team. For the past fifteen years, Rachael had followed Savannah up through the Florida political system, serving as Savannah's campaign manager, political advisor, and personal confidant. Rachael had introduced her to Scott Matheson, founder and director of the Take Back America organization. Savannah used that association and its goals as a platform to gain national attention and became a regular guest commentator on Fox News.

Despite her occasional tendency to be irresponsible, Savannah would never miss an event like this. Tomorrow was a special day. She had a joint press conference scheduled with Governor Cartwright. He planned to appoint Savannah as Florida's next United States Senator, replacing Senator Roberts who died unexpectedly from a heart attack last year. It was a once-in-a-lifetime opportunity that meant Rachael would be traveling to Washington with Savannah. Translation: a much higher salary and standard of living. More importantly Rachael would have opportunities to network with A-list individuals, but Savannah had made one major mistake that could derail all their plans. She fell in love; a problem Rachael had been trying to cover up for the past six months. It could ruin everything.

So where was she? Rachael tried calling Savannah's cell phone again. No answer and her voicemail was full.

SIXTEEN

The Blue Line Bar
Naples, Florida

I'd identified the victim as Mrs. Savannah Wellington and hadn't needed Cassie to do it. However, I still wanted her help. The investigation would make better headway if we worked together as a team. To make that happen, I needed leverage and the knowledge of what information the police already had thus far. Cassie wasn't willing to share, but I had an idea on how to get it. John once told me that all cops, including FBI agents, were about the same. They liked to hang out together and share war stories, especially after a hard day of work. Smaller departments like those in Collier County and Naples were no exception. After a bit of digging, I learned the name of their favorite watering hole, Buddy's Blue Line, a small bar off Airport Pulling Road.

Choosing the right outfit was critical—sexy, but not slutty. Didn't want to look desperate. My new purchases from yesterday hung in the closet. I selected a black skirt, not too short, and a silver-sequined blouse. I slipped into my new Christian Louboutin black stilettos and looked in the mirror. Perfect. A pair of large silver hoop earrings and matching bracelets completed the outfit. A soft pink lipstick, a final check in the mirror, and I was ready, all except for the wedding ring. Before heading to the bike store, I had taken it off and set it on the dresser. My finger felt naked without it. Yes, John and I were separated, but we were still married. I put the ring back on my finger. Better. After stuffing my Sig Sauer into my purse, I headed out. Never can be too careful. After all, a woman had just been murdered in Naples.

Buddy's Blue Line Bar was twenty minutes away from my condo. I gripped the steering wheel tightly, worried about how I should handle the evening. With too many variables to consider, I'd have to play it by ear.

Vehicles packed the parking lot and places like this didn't offer a valet service. It took a while, but I finally found a spot on a deserted side street three blocks away. It was going to be a long walk, especially in four-inch heels. When I finally got to the front door, my feet hurt so much, I didn't think I could handle another step. Next time I'd put some comfortable flats in my purse.

Buddy's was dark and seedy, with the obligatory neon beer signs hanging on the walls: Budweiser, Amstel, and Corona. A pool table sat in the rear, the balls clacking together loudly as a young man in a patrolman's uniform did the break. The sounds of two balls falling in pockets brought a smile to his face as he chalked his cue stick and lined up his next shot. The random collision of the balls against each other paralleled the arbitrary interactions of people in life, many resulting in long-lasting, meaningful relationships—others ending in murder.

Waylon Jennings' *Luckenbach, Texas* played in the background. One of John's favorites. It brought back fond memories from better times. I pushed them aside.

I coughed. A no-smoking sign peeked through clouds of smoke. Apparently, tobacco regulations didn't apply to law enforcement officers. Laughter filled the room and bravado oozed from every corner. I chose a seat at the bar with an empty stool on either side of me, feeling a bit like a lamb in a roomful of wolves. However, for a woman with the right attitude and motivation, it constituted a target rich environment. I put on my game face, smiled, and ordered a vodka with a splash of cranberry juice. Turning around on my stool, I faced the crowd and took a sip of my drink, my lipstick marking the edge of the glass. I crossed my legs, allowing my skirt to ride high, exposing just enough thigh, and cast my feminine charms into the sea of testosterone spread out before me. It was like chumming the waters before fishing. In a few minutes, I got a nibble. All I needed to do was set the hook and reel him in.

A tall detective, wearing a sport coat over a blue button-down shirt approached. He was thirtyish, handsome, and had his hair parted down the middle, with blond highlights in the tips. Looked like a surfer. A girl could easily get lost in those dreamy blue eyes. *Careful, Lisa. Remember, you're married.* He walked closer—actually, more of a strut. Something was familiar about that gait. Cocky and arrogant. *Shit.* Mr. Spandex from the park. *A cop? He's a fucking cop?* So much for my theory of him being a murder suspect. I looked at the floor, hiding my face. *What if he recognizes me?* I wanted to run, but he didn't act as though we had met before. Of course, he'd only seen me as a bloodied, sweaty mess at the park. Good.

"Do you mind?" Not waiting for my reply, he sat down next to me, and flashed a disarming boyish grin. It looked fake and predatory like that of a used car salesman. His cologne smelled cheap and too strong.

"Suit yourself," I said, not wanting to seem too anxious to start up a conversation. Milking information from him would be a slow process. Didn't want to spook him.

"We don't see many beautiful girls like you here at Buddy's."

Gimme a break. I played the game. "Drove by. It looked interesting, so I decided to stop in."

"Well, I'm glad you did. You made my evening." He looked at himself in the mirror hanging behind the bar and smiled at his image.

What an ass. Mr. Spandex extended his hand. "I'm Brad Stapleton."

Of course, his name was Brad. Figures. The quintessential high school football star still basking in the glory of his younger years. I accepted his hand. "And I'm Lisa."

"A pleasure, Lisa." He motioned to the bartender. "Another one for my new friend, Lisa and a bottle of Stella for me."

He winked, and the bartender responded with a subtle nod. Brad clinked his bottle against my fresh glass. "To a wonderful evening."

A woman stepped up and touched Brad's left arm. "Hi Brad," she cooed. "You have anything for me tonight?" She probed me with cold eyes, hardened with the cynicism of a squandered past.

He cut her off. "Not now, Maddie. I'm busy."

Maddie? She's Maddie Carmichael? The reporter whose identity I stole for the Cyclery Store? She looked nothing like the pretty, wide-eyed young reporter in her newspaper photo. She smelled of stale tobacco and alcohol. Bad habits and the years had taken their toll. That and spending too many nights in places like this, doing whatever she needed to get a story.

I scrunched down on my bar stool, trying to make myself less visible.

"I need to talk to you, Brad," she pleaded.

"I said I was busy," he repeated. Cold and harsh.

I felt sorry for her. Another crushed cheerleader.

She pouted and took a seat on the other side of Brad, who turned his back to her while she glared at me like she wanted to stab icicles in my eyes. She ordered a Makers Mark, neat.

"So, Lisa. Do you live in Naples full time?" Brad asked.

"Just here for a few weeks of vacation."

"What do you do when not vacationing?"

I grinned and set the hook deeper. "I enjoy life."

Brad's smile widened, exposing a mouthful of perfectly white teeth, probably hoping for a quick roll in the hay and then sayonara. He raised his glass. "Here's to enjoying life."

"To life." I took a small sip of my new drink. Burned my throat all the way down. Whew, it was strong—more than strong. I cleared my throat. Time for business. "What do you do, Brad?"

He puffed out his chest. "I'm with the Naples police. NPD we call it."

I allowed my left leg to touch his. "That sounds exciting, and maybe even a little dangerous." I put my hand over his. From the look in his eyes, I could tell I had him. "Are you a dangerous man, Brad?"

"Some might say so." He winked and took a mouthful of beer.

"Are you working on anything exciting right now, Mr. Dangerous?"

He glanced from side to side, leaned closer to me, and lowered his voice to a whisper. "Looks like we have a murder on our hands."

So, Cassie had lied about it being an accident. I faked a gasp. "Oh, my God. Here in Naples?"

"Yep, a woman." He drained his beer and ordered another. "Happens more often than you might think. Local tourism industry doesn't like to talk about it. The department's trying to pass this one off as an accident." He took another mouthful of Stella. "The chief made me the lead investigator on the case, so I know better."

"Lead investigator? That's impressive" Another squeeze of his hand. "So, what happened to her?"

He couldn't tell me fast enough. It was like turning on a faucet.

"In my opinion, Jane Doe —"

"Jane Doe?" I interrupted, trying to look naive.

He chuckled in a condescending manner. "A term we detectives use to call an unidentified female murder victim."

"So, you don't actually know her identity?"

"Not yet, but I will soon." Another smile in the mirror. He ran a hand through his hair, clearly enjoying the image. "Anyway, she was riding her bike in Seminole Lakes Park." He looked at me. "Ever heard of it?"

"I believe so."

"Well, that's where I found her body. It was well-hidden in some weeds, but I knew it had to be there. I have an instinct for these things."

So full of himself.

"Anyway, the autopsy shows she was hit in the head and killed with some blunt object. I'm thinking a crowbar. The murderer left her for the alligators."

I faked a shiver. "That's horrible."

"That's not all. She was knocked up."

"Pregnant?"

"Yeah, the pathologist told me around four or five months based upon the size of the fetus."

Pregnant! The word ripped through my insides, my mind racing so hard I could barely focus my eyes. I struggled to suck in my next breath. Tears threatened, but I pushed them back. John and I had tried for years to get pregnant. Dozens of lab tests, x-rays, and insemination procedures, and nothing to show for it except three miscarriages. The fertility specialist said another try would be futile. My uterus couldn't carry a baby to term. It wasn't fair. Most likely, this Savannah Wellington wasn't even trying to get pregnant, but she did. Now, that baby was dead, murdered along with its mother.

The asshole grabbed my arm and shook me. "Hello. Is anybody home inside there?"

I dug my nails into the palms of my hands, hoping the pain would help me regain my composure. Now I really wanted to nail the bastard who had killed them.

I struggled to piece some words together. "How frightening. It sounds like one of those gruesome stories on TV crime programs. If you solve this case, you might wind up being a television star." I batted my eyelashes. "You're certainly handsome enough." *Slow down, Lisa. Don't overdo it.* I tried to milk some more information from him, but he was tapped out.

He looked at me with his bedroom-blue eyes. "Let's finish these drinks and maybe go somewhere more intimate so we can discuss the case in detail."

Time to get out of there. I looked at my phone and pushed the message button. It buzzed. "Oops. I gotta go."

"But you haven't finished your drink yet. At least stay long enough for that."

"Can't. I'm sorry, but it's my husband. He expected me over an hour ago."

"Husband?"

I showed him my ring, and pouted. "Yes. One of the biggest mistakes of my life. He watches me like a hawk. I'm supposed to be out with girlfriends tonight. I'd better go." I took a final sip of my vodka. "Thanks for the drink, Brad."

When I stood, his smile transformed into a snarl, the same look I had seen in the park. He slammed his hand down over mine and squeezed hard. "What kind of game are you playing here? Is this how you get your jollies, Blondie? Being a little tease?" He squeezed harder. It hurt. Thought he might break my fingers.

"No, I ..."

"You have no idea who you're messing with, girlie. Someone should teach you a lesson."

In his face, I saw the cold, dark eyes of a killer. Who better to get away with murder than a cop. I hated to fall back on John, but I had few options. "No, I'm not playing any games. My husband's an agent with the FBI. He's suspicious and can be ruthless."

"FBI?" Brad loosened his grip.

I jerked my hand away and rushed toward the door, not looking back.

———————————•———————————

When I staggered out into the night, my head felt fuzzy from the vodka. What was in that anyway? Glad I didn't drink any more than I did. The parking lot lights were out, and everything around me was darker than I expected. I knew I'd left my car somewhere on a side street, but I had a hard time focusing. Was it to the right or the left? I walked for a few hundred yards and searched in all directions, but nothing looked familiar. I was lost. The swimming in my head worsened. Did that bartender spike my drink? Rohypnol?

The small amount of light from a full moon created a penumbra of shadows on the sidewalk, each one looking like a threat. That's when I heard them—footsteps behind me. Probably nothing, but I decided to walk a little faster. *Damn.* Shouldn't have worn the stilettos.

The steps grew louder.

My heart raced.

I quickened my pace, but the stalker's stride matched mine, with no apparent attempt to conceal the sounds of his steps. If it was a maneuver designed to frighten me, it was working. I reached into my purse, wrapped my fingers around the Sig, and withdrew it. After racking the slide, I rushed as fast as my high heels would allow. Thought about kicking them off and running barefoot, but I had no idea where I was going. It was too dark to see glass or any other hazards on the sidewalk. The guy kept getting closer, but who was it? Spandex Brad was pissed enough to do this. Or did TOPDOC follow me here? Maybe his wife confessed that she had talked to me, after he beat it out of her. Either man was capable of violence.

I turned down another street, hoping the stalker would continue straight. I didn't want to shoot anyone unless I had to. It might only be a coincidence, him heading in the same direction as me. *Damn.* The footsteps continued to follow and were gaining.

I stopped and spun around, pointing my gun. The flash of metal must have given my stalker second thoughts. He broke off the chase.

I continued walking as fast as I could, fully expecting him to jump out of the bushes and take me by surprise. Finally, I recognized the street and found my car. I fumbled my keys, almost dropping them. I jiggled the key into the lock, jumped in and sped away, my heart pounding inside my chest.

I didn't know how or when I made it home from Buddy's Bar last night, but I woke up on top of my bedspread with all my clothes still on, except my heels. One sat outside the bedroom door in the hallway and the other in the bathtub. My mouth felt like the Sahara Desert. Bright sunlight assaulted me through the windows, and I squinted through a throbbing headache. I massaged my temples for a minute, hoping to squeeze away the relentless pounding. I hadn't had a hangover like this since college. It even hurt to blink. *What the heck was in that drink?* I stared at the white ceiling, seeing a swarm of black floaters drift through my eyes. When did those things happen?

I tried to get up but felt like I needed a crane to help me out of bed. Made it and stood still for several seconds ensuring my balance before trying to move. *Need Coffee.* I shuffled to the kitchen where I swallowed a couple ibuprofens and chased them down with two cups of coffee, black and strong enough to burn the cobwebs out of my brain. I jumped in the shower to wash away the smell of Buddy's Bar and the lingering creepy sensation of dealing with Spandex Brad. My body protested against the thought of food, but a handful of TUMS helped to douse the brushfire raging in my stomach.

That's when Cassie called, her voice frantic, the sound drilling into my brain.

SEVENTEEN

East Naples Police Precinct
Naples, Florida

Cassie entered the precinct office the following morning. As soon as she sat at her desk, the lieutenant's voice exploded across the room. "Pierce. My office." A half second later. "Now!"

She took a seat in a chair opposite his desk. He didn't bother to close the door behind her. Instead, he threw a copy of the morning's Naples Daily Courier on her lap. On the front page, in large bold letters, the headline read:

BRUTAL MURDER IN NAPLES
Police Coverup?

The article was partially speculative and somewhat cryptic but contained too much accurate information to be dismissed, including the fact that her Jane Doe was pregnant.

"Is this your doing, Cassie?"

"Sir?"

"This report by Maddie Carmichael. I thought we had an understanding about this case. We weren't going to talk to the press."

"I didn't, sir."

"Well, someone did, and the mayor is pissed. A police coverup? For Christ's sake, Cassie. What the fuck were you thinking? My phone's been blowing up all morning. The city council's demanding blood, and it's going to be yours. You have the lead on this."

Cassie met his stare with her own. "I haven't talked to anyone about anything."

The lieutenant smacked the paper with the back of his hand. "She was pregnant? For God's sake. How in the hell does some reporter know more about this case than me?"

He threw a pen against the wall. It ricocheted back, almost hitting him in the head. It was almost funny. Would've served him right, the little prick. She suppressed a laugh. No sense in making the situation worse.

"Did you ever think it might be a good idea to let your lieutenant know about this pregnancy?"

"I wanted to keep it low profile, sir, per your wishes. Nobody but me—and maybe the killer—would know about the pregnancy. Figured it might constitute a motive and help identify the perp."

"Well, it's not a damn secret anymore. The whole fucking city knows about it." He balled up the paper and threw it in the trash, then pointed his finger at Cassie. "You'd better find the source of this leak, or you're headed back to Chicago."

Cassie refused to be bullied. She sat straight in her chair and smirked. "Am I to assume you now want me to work this case as a homicide—in my free time—while I search for your leak?"

The lieutenant's face turned bright crimson, his cheeks as red as a pair of ripe tomatoes. She could almost see the steam rising up from under his shirt collar. "That mouth of yours is going to get you into trouble someday, Pierce." He stood. "Now get out of my sight and don't come back until you've figured out what happened. I'm not taking the fall for your stupidity."

Cassie returned to her desk and stared at the phone for a few seconds before she made a call.

"This is Lisa Crawford."

"Have you seen today's paper?" asked Cassie.

"Yes. Pretty nasty article. Guess it shook things up there."

"That's a monumental understatement. Now, I'm in hot water. Was it you?" That moment of regret about letting Lisa get involved in the case bored into her brain.

"Me what?"

Was she really going to play innocent? Cassie's regret quickly turned to anger. "You know what. Did you leak this story to the press?"

"No, I'd never do that to a friend, Cassie. But I know who did."

Cassie tapped her fingers on the desk pad. "And?"

"Do you know of a detective by the name of Brad?"

Cassie groaned as Lisa relayed the story about how Brad was at the Blue Line Bar and boasting about the case. "A reporter by the name of Maddie Carmichael was sitting next to him and must have overheard everything."

"And why in the hell were you at that bar last night?" The pot was about to boil over. This was why she shouldn't ever let a civilian get close to a case. Before Lisa could answer, Cassie said, "Never mind. I think I know." *But I wish I didn't.*

"I do have some information that might help get you out of the jam you're in."

Cassie sat up straight. "What?" This had better be good.

"I know the identity of Jane Doe."

"How did —?"

"Like I said on the phone yesterday, I have my own resources."

"I need a name."

"Not that easy, Cassie. I want to help, but this is a two-way street. We need to meet in person. How about lunch at Brambles. Do you know where it is?"

"Sure."

"I'll see you there at noon."

Cassie looked up at the ceiling. *How did Brad know the woman was pregnant?* Only she and Deutschle were privy to that information. She remembered writing the word down on her yellow legal pad but she'd locked it in her drawer. That drawer was now unlocked and the pad was sitting right where she had left it, but it was upside down. *That moron.*

EIGHTEEN

Brambles English Tea Room
Naples, Florida

I arrived fifteen minutes early. Brambles was a tiny English Tea Room restaurant along a sidewalk of terracotta pavers off Fifth Avenue. The entrances at either end were framed in arches of natural ivy while a series of planters, filled with an assortment of flowers hung on either side of a tile grotto. I selected a table outdoors under a small green and white striped awning. Behind me, a splashing fountain sounded like a hammer smashing into my skull. The ibuprofen hadn't helped the hangover. *Maybe a little bit of the hair of the dog?* I ordered a bottle of Pinot Grigio and waited for Cassie. She arrived several minutes later, looking a little frazzled, but still stunning.

"I took the liberty of ordering some wine." I filled two glasses before noticing the bracelets on her wrist. "I'm sorry. I forgot about your diabetes."

"No problem. I need this. I can always give myself an extra boost of insulin if necessary." She drank most of the glass before sitting. "Sorry for brushing you off on the phone yesterday. My lieutenant ordered me to keep a tight lid on the investigation. It wasn't fair to you, though. He and I argued about it."

I refilled her glass. "Bad morning, I guess."

She took another mouthful. "You have no idea. That newspaper article almost cost me my job." She explained what happened at the station. "You said you could help." She stared into my eyes. "So, who is she, our Jane Doe?"

"First, let's eat." I signaled the waitress to bring a couple menus. She had a Russian accent, common in Naples but unexpected at an English Tea Room. We each ordered a crab salad tower with aioli on the side. Cassie's bracelets kept clinking against her plate. Hard not to notice. "That's a cute bracelet," I said. "May I?"

She raised her wrist for me to see. In addition to the Med Alert bracelet, she wore a second one that was silver with two interlocking hearts. Between them sat a diamond solitaire. "Beautiful," I said and released her hand.

"A gift from a good friend. She gave it to me to help hide the Med Alert one. We each have one."

"Nice friend."

Cassie stared at the wall fountain and took a sip of wine. "She was."

Was? I didn't pursue it. Didn't want to seem nosey. After some small talk about jewelry and clothes, we got down to business.

"Cassie, I realize you represent official law enforcement on this murder and I'm only a civilian, but I think we can solve this case more rapidly if we work together." I leaned forward and tapped my fingernails on the table. "I want in."

She sipped her wine and raised her eyebrows in a look of skepticism.

I continued, "I can bring a lot to the table. I've had extensive experience in tracking down international terrorists and bringing them to justice."

Her eyes widened. "Justice, eh. I don't even want to know what that might have entailed." She pushed several cranberries around on her plate with a fork. "You work for the CIA?"

"Not exactly. Our team functioned more as independent contractors."

"So, who'd you work for? Officially, that is?"

"I'm not at liberty to say. It's important to note that as part of my training, I've learned to cut through the red tape that hampers traditional law enforcement agencies—like Naples PD."

Cassie squinted at me. "Translation is you did illegal things. How does that work with you being married to an FBI agent? A director of counterterrorism at that?"

I met her gaze, then looked away. "It's a delicate situation. That's why I retired."

Cassie rested a finger against her lips. "I'm not saying that it could work, but if we do investigate this case together, am I going to wind up having to arrest you when it's all over?"

I tried to suppress a smile. Unsuccessfully. "You could try, but it would be a bad idea." She smiled back. I liked her. "Bottom line is, if we combine our resources, you officially, and me off the books, we can find our murderer and save your job."

Cassie frowned. "I'm not so sure I still want this damn job. Too much politics."

"Be that as it may, I'm sure you want to bring Jane Doe's killer to justice."

She tipped her wine glass against mine. "Agreed." After taking a mouthful, she said, "You've kept me waiting long enough. Who is she?"

I looked around to be sure no one could overhear. "Her full name is Savannah Wellington."

Cassie choked on her wine. "The Speaker of the Florida House? I'm shocked no one has reported her missing."

I nodded. "Seems strange, but now that we know her identity, we can focus on why someone would want her dead. I spoke to the husband."

"You what? You contacted the primary suspect in a murder investigation? Do you realize how dangerous that could have been?"

"I'm used to dealing with dangerous terrorists. I can handle myself. As you said a few days ago, the prime suspect would normally be the husband, so I decided to talk to him. I pretended to be a reporter doing an article on his work with charities."

"And?"

"He appeared to be a pretty decent guy, and he was in California at the time of her death. He also talked about her in the present tense. I don't think he did it. He doesn't even seem to know she's dead."

"You didn't tell him she was murdered?"

"While I was impersonating a reporter for the Naples Courier Journal? Of course not. I'm afraid telling him will be your job."

"Thanks a lot. It's the part of this job I hate the most. I'll make arrangements to meet with him first thing in the morning."

"While you're there, check out a photograph of Savannah on the wall of her husband's office. It was taken with Governor Cartwright a few years ago. Let me know what you think."

"Why?"

"You'll see." I took a mouthful of wine. "I don't think he knew she was pregnant."

Cassie waved a fork in my direction. "Maybe, the baby wasn't his and he knew. That alone would constitute a motive for murder. I'll need to push him about it. Meanwhile, I'm waiting for a DNA analysis on the fetus. We can compare it to potential suspects and that might give us the answers we need. We find the father and we'll likely have the killer."

"At least, it might lead us in the right direction," I said. "Another thing to consider is that this entire situation might be politically motivated somehow. She was the Florida Speaker."

"That's true. Politics is a nasty business and I'm sure she stepped on a lot of toes to get where she was."

"Enough for someone to kill her?"

"It's been known to happen." Cassie pulled out her iPad and made a few notes. "I'll check into her background to see what enemies she might have made. However, in the meantime, the husband should be our primary focus." She pulled up a to-do list. "I've been in contact with Verizon about screening all calls routed through cell towers within several miles of the park. I was afraid it would take weeks to receive it. Now that we have a name, I can narrow the search to her specific phone and expand the time frame to the past six months. I should be able to get the list by tomorrow."

The Russian waitress returned carrying a silver tray with an antique teapot and matching cups with clusters of pink flowers painted along the sides. She had spread an assortment of exotic teas across the tray. We hesitated.

"It's complimentary," said the waitress.

After finishing our tea, Cassie blotted her lips with a napkin, folded it several times into a perfect square, and centered it in the middle of her plate. She was almost out of her chair, when I asked, "Before you leave, there's one other matter I'd like to discuss with you. How much do you know about detective Brad Stapleton?"

Her brows furrowed, and she sat back in her chair. "You mean other than the fact that he's a chauvinist idiot? Not much. Rumor around the station is he went to some fancy Ivy-League College, but you'd never know it. Obviously, it wasn't because of his exceptional mental prowess. Apparently, he was recruited by a few alumni for some kind of athletic scholarship." She stared at me. "Why do you ask?"

I told her about how the guy in the park who ran over me with his bike was Brad. "It was quite a coincidence, him being there at the crime scene, and I don't believe in coincidences. Do you think he might be involved somehow?"

"In a murder? Maybe, I guess, but I've never known him to be violent."

"I've seen a side of him that you might not have." I told her how aggressive Brad had been when I rejected his advances and tried to leave Buddy's bar. "He almost broke my hand. When I pulled away, he said someone needed to teach me a lesson. Those are the exact same words he used after he ran over me in the park. Then, I think he followed me out to my car. It was scary."

"Did you actually see him following you?"

"No."

"Hmm. I guess he could be involved in this. He's a womanizing moron, but I can't believe he'd be stupid enough to think he could get away with murder. What could be his motivation?"

"I don't know," I said. "Maybe he was somehow romantically involved with Savannah. She broke it off and he was pissed. He obviously doesn't take rejection well. You might want to dig into his background some more."

"I'll see what I can do."

"I can do some things from my end."

"You? How?"

"As I mentioned before, I have resources."

"Like your husband?"

"No. He and I are separated and don't speak. My resources are even better than the Bureau's. If Brad Stapleton has any skeletons in his closet, I'll find them."

Cassie held up her hands. "Say no more. I don't want to hear about it. I need plausible deniability if the proverbial shit hits the fan."

NINETEEN

Topeka, Kansas

Ishmael used a micrometer to ensure all the stone measurements conformed to the precise specifications required for a standard NATO round. He then removed the lead tip from ten active shells while preserving the gunpowder and primer. Using a reloader, he inserted each of the sculpted stones into its new casing.

As Ishmael approached the Kansas State border, he chugged down the last of his third can of Red Bull. He stretched his back, sore and stiff after eleven hours behind the wheel. These long drives were getting to be too much, but he had no other choice. He couldn't fly. Making a plane reservation meant creating a paper trail. He couldn't afford that. Though he didn't exist, he didn't want any airport surveillance cameras recording his image. Repeated trips near the time of any target's death allowed for facial recognition software comparisons and might provide law enforcement with the means to track him.

He headed toward the south side of Topeka until he found what he needed. Every major city had one, the kind of neighborhood that fostered the WOKE movement and gave politicians a sense of purpose, though they seldom did anything about problems other than giving lip service and throwing money at them. He arrived just before dusk. The partially lit sign said River View Motel though the nearest body of water had to be at least ten miles away. He pulled into the parking lot where used syringes, broken whiskey bottles, and discarded pieces of clothing were strewn about. Tall dying weeds sprouted up intermittently like tufts of hair in a bad transplant. A "Vacancy" sign hung precariously by one screw. Of course, there was a vacancy. He doubted the motel had been full in decades. The surrounding area looked like a rough neighborhood where everybody minded their own business. No stray eyes to notice his comings and goings.

Ishmael entered the lobby, a small room with a rusted metal chair in the corner. From behind a thick Plexiglas window a Hispanic woman said in a heavy accent, "$18.00 a night, in advance."

"I'll need a room for several days."

"ID?"

He pushed five one-hundred-dollar bills through the metal slot in the window. "Will this suffice?"

She held each bill under the light and smiled. "Of course, Mr. Benjamin Franklin. We always welcome celebrities here," she said in perfect English. The accent disappeared.

"The money is also payment for your short-term memory issues."

"Goes without saying, Mr. Franklin. You were never here." She handed him the key.

His room was at the far end of the building, hidden behind some tall bushes. Ishmael unloaded two duffel bags from the trunk of his car. The key worked, and the door creaked as he slowly opened it and looked around. The damp musty smell of prior occupants immediately hit him. A film of haze from decades of smoking covered the windows. The room held one double bed with a stained bedspread that looked like it hadn't yet received its annual wash. There was a single, flat pillow sans a pillowcase. The carpeting was torn, and the towels were so thin you could almost see through them. A through-the-wall air conditioner clanged and groaned as it blew out warm air. A dump—exactly what Ishmael wanted, unimpressive to the point of being invisible.

Laying a plastic tarp over the bed, he unloaded the contents of one of the duffle bags, taking inventory to be sure everything was there and in working order. Pulling out another plastic sheet and a sleeping bag, he arranged a bed area on the floor. A few preparations needed completion prior to retiring for the evening.

He retrieved a bag containing the leftover marble stones and headed to the target site. The set up was always as important as the execution. An hour later, he returned to the River View Motel, crawled into the sleeping bag, and reviewed his schedule for tomorrow morning. Any potential, last-minute surprises had already been factored into his plan. All was ready. It wouldn't be one of his finest works, but it would be pretty damn good, more than worthy of the four and a half million-dollar price tag. He fell asleep within minutes.

Thanks to Fedallah, an empty Topeka Energy van sat waiting in a nearby Walmart parking lot. After checking to be sure he was out of view of any security cameras, Ishmael transferred his equipment to the van and headed to the senator's home. He parked on the opposite side of the street, about thirty feet beyond the man's driveway. Divorced, Torbeson led a simple life in his small home. The crown jewels of his yard were his prize roses, so remarkable, the Topeka Capital-Journal featured his garden in the paper's Sunday Home Section. Over three dozen varieties of roses filled a flower bed running along his property line. The garden was meticulously mulched and bordered by a rim of crushed white marble on all sides.

Most individuals preferred a certain amount of routine in their lives. That level of predictability made Ishmael's job possible. Fortunately for him, the senator was a compulsively-organized man with a rigid schedule. After an early Saturday morning walk through the neighborhood, he regularly devoted three hours to tending the roses: weeding, fertilizing, and deadheading spent flowers. Not to be outdone, his neighbor spent a sizable part of his Saturday morning taking care of his own yard.

The garage door opened and Torbeson exited dressed in jeans, a long-sleeve denim shirt, and canvas gardening gloves. He pushed a garden cart toward his prize roses just as his neighbor started his John Deere riding mower. They waved.

"Great day, Senator," said the neighbor.

"No doubt about it. Going to be a good one. Why don't you stop by when you're finished? I just got a box of fresh Montecristo Classics yesterday. We can light up and have a beer on my patio."

The neighbor gave him a thumbs-up and placed his noise-canceling earphones over his head. As was his habit, he started on the right side of his yard and worked his way to the left toward Torbeson's.

Ishmael studied the two closely. *So far, so good.*

After thirty minutes a loud clang shattered the Saturday morning peace. The neighbor shrugged his shoulders, got off his mower, and shut down the motor to see what had happened. He bent over, picked up a marble stone, and raised it in the air. It was one of the stones Ishmael had scattered across the man's lawn last night. "Squirrels must have knocked it into the grass." He searched the ground, found five more stones and tossed them into the rose garden border. "Busy little fuckers." He restarted the mower and continued cutting, still several feet from the property line.

Ishmael lowered a small window on the rear of his Topeka Energy van. After attaching a sound suppressor, he chambered one of his special bullets into his modified rifle. Eliminating the rifling grooves could affect accuracy but was essential to keep the marble projectile from shattering too soon. He waited until the neighbor rode his John Deere close to the senator's garden. *Perfect.* As Torbeson leaned over to prune away some dead flowers, Ishmael centered the crosshairs of his rifle on the side of the man's skull, the temple area where the bone was the weakest. At the right moment, he squeezed the trigger. *Pfft.* The shot dropped Torbeson instantly, blood pulsating from the side of his head. The stone fragmented as soon as it pierced the bone, the pieces shredding his brain. While riding his loud mower, the neighbor failed to notice the senator toppling over in the roses, providing precious time for Ishmael to pull away without arousing any attention.

The police report would describe it as a freak accident, occurring when his neighbor's lawn mower threw out a stone, killing Torbeson instantly. Ishmael smiled. *Another four and a half million dollars deposited into my offshore account. One final contract on the Client's list and I can retire to my home overlooking the Cote D'Azur.*

In the Walmart lot, Ishmael switched back to his car and began the return trip to Kentucky. An hour east of Kansas, his cell phone buzzed. A message from Fedallah. Ishmael shook his head. Number thirteen? *Already? Too soon — and much too dangerous.*

TWENTY

Wellington Building
Naples, Florida.

The following morning, Cassie met with Preston Wellington in his office. His secretary didn't want to grant an appointment, stating that his schedule was fully booked. She relented when Cassie mentioned it concerned urgent police business.

Wellington seemed genuinely surprised by her visit. She took a seat opposite his desk and skipped the small-talk pleasantries. She had always found that it was best to address the issue of a family member's death right away rather than beating around the bush. The abruptness of the words threw any potential suspect off balance, preventing them from organizing their thoughts and lies if they were the perpetrator.

"I have some unpleasant news for you, Mr. Wellington. Your wife's body was found in a pond at Seminole Lakes Park a few days ago."

"Body?" He stared at Cassie, his eyes swimming in disbelief. "You think Savannah's dead?" He shook his head. "Impossible. It can't be true."

"I'm sorry, sir."

"Are you saying Savannah was the woman mentioned in the paper?"

"Yes, sir. I suspect she was murdered."

His shoulders dropped. Cassie had interviewed a lot of murder suspects during her career in Chicago, and this guy appeared truly shocked. He looked like all the life had been sucked out of him. His eyes fixated on the picture of his wife and Governor Cartwright for several seconds.

"Could you please give me a second?"

"Certainly." Cassie gazed down at her notes for a minute. When she looked up, he was composed, but his eyes were red.

"I don't understand. Are you sure it's Savannah?"

"We're positive, sir. We have DNA confirmation."

"And you think she was murdered?"

"That's what we believe, Mr. Wellington."

"I—I just don't understand. Who would want to hurt her? Everybody loves Savannah."

"That's what we're trying to figure out. Can you think of anyone who might have had a grudge against her?"

"I can't think of anyone." He fiddled with some pens on his desk, lining them up by height. He used his right hand to do so. Dr. Deutschle reported that the killer was probably left-handed. "But I must confess, she and I have been separated for almost a year now. I can't speak about anything that might have happened since then. Like I said, everyone seems—or seemed to be genuinely fond of Savannah."

Cassie interviewed Preston for another hour, looking for inconsistencies in his story or any indications he was hiding something. Though he appeared innocent, he could simply be a good liar. She needed to interrogate him in a less friendly environment than his office. "We'd like you to come down to the station this afternoon to make an official statement."

"I'll do anything to help identify who did this to her. I'd like to bring my attorney, though."

Cassie leaned forward. "You think you need an attorney?"

"I know it looks bad for someone to have legal representation present, but I've seen enough television crime shows to realize that the husband of the victim is always the primary suspect in a wife's murder."

"It's your right to have legal counsel present." Cassie looked at the calendar on her iPad. "Would three o'clock work?"

"Yes." He looked down at the floor and his eyes moistened. "Would it be possible for me to see Savannah?"

Cassie knew he'd never recover from the sight of his wife's mutilated body. They might have been separated, but apparently, he still loved her. "I'm afraid not, Mr. Wellington."

Cassie returned to the station and waited for her computer screen to come to life. There were more emails than she had time to review. A message from Verizon caught her eye. They had sent the report about Savannah Wellington's cell phone activity. Too complicated to review on a screen so she printed it, twenty-seven pages in all. In Chicago she'd have several others to help her comb through the list. After what Lisa had told her about Brad, it wouldn't have been appropriate to bring him into the investigation. It had to be up to Cassie. She began poring through the numbers. Savannah's last call was logged on the morning of July 2. That matched the coroner's approximate day of her death. No calls to or from her husband in over six months. That corroborated his story that they had not been in contact. It still didn't rule out the possibility of a murder-for-hire scenario. Cassie checked the list on her yellow legal pad and wrote down: *Husband. Hired a pro???* Beneath it she added: *Secret Lover???*

A multitude of calls were made from two separate numbers to Savannah's phone but none in return. Cassie called the numbers, but they were throw-away phones and no longer active. All the calls originated from the Naples area. She wrote on her legal pad, *Check back. Any way they can identify the caller?* Most of the remaining calls were either to or from three different phones: the Florida governor's office, Savannah's own office in Tallahassee, and some organization in Washington called TBA.

A few were to Topeka, Kansas, and a half dozen other cities around the country. She scoured the list looking for any calls to or from Brad Stapleton. There were none. Looked like he wasn't a part of this mess after all. Then again— "Brad?" she called out.

No answer. Someone from one of the other cubicles yelled, "He's out working on that jewelry case in Port Royal. The perps bypassed the security cameras and alarm systems. He's checking to see if it could have been an inside job."

She walked over to his desk. It was a mess, with papers scattered all over the top and a half-consumed Styrofoam cup of cold coffee left for someone else to clean up. Figures. She'd never paid any attention before, but she noticed he didn't have any pictures of his wife or kids like everyone else in the office did. Strange. His only photograph was of a college baseball team. *That must have been the athletic scholarship.* The caption along the bottom read: *Princeton Tigers: 2003 Ivy League Baseball Champions.* She picked up the photograph and found Brad standing in the second row, holding a baseball bat and flashing his same cocky smile. She picked up the coffee cup with a paper towel. "Don't any of you guys ever clean up after yourselves?" She walked to the break room and poured the coffee down the sink. She was about to throw the cup away, but paused. Instead, she retrieved a plastic evidence bag from her desk and inserted the cup. She called the forensics lab. "I'm sending over a Styrofoam cup. I want you to see if you can get a DNA profile from the edge and compare it to the DNA from the Jane Doe fetus. By the way, she's been identified. Her name is Savannah Wellington. You might want to make the changes on her record." She was about to hang up when she said, "Keep this confidential, just between you and me."

Cassie returned to Savannah's cell phone list. She'd start with the woman's office in Tallahassee. She dialed the number and a woman answered on the second ring.

"Savannah Wellington's office, Rachael Morris speaking. How may I help you?"

"This is Detective Cassandra Pierce from the Naples police department."

"Naples Police? Is there a problem, Detective?"

"I have a few questions regarding Mrs. Wellington's schedule over the past several weeks. I need to speak to her personally."

"I'm sorry," said Rachael. "She's not in the office at this time, and I'm not sure when she'll be back. I'm her chief of staff. Perhaps I can help."

The woman doesn't seem to know. Pretending? Need to knock her off stride a little. "I'm sorry to inform you that Mrs. Wellington is dead. We're investigating her death as a potential homicide." Short and to the point. Classic murder investigation 101. When you're trying to identify a suspect, keep people off balance. That was the best way to get information, before the individual can organize a cover story.

Rachael gasped. "Savannah's dead? How can that be? Governor Cartwright was about to appoint her to the United States Senate."

Cassie jotted that information down on her legal pad.

Rachael broke down and sobbed. She cried during the beginning of the conversation, but when Cassie asked specifics about Savannah's schedule, the crying stopped. "When did you last speak to Savannah?"

"Let me think for a second. It was before the Fourth of July weekend." She paused. "It was about the time Tropical Storm Caroline hit. As I recall, it was the morning of July second. She planned to go cycling and wanted to clear up a few issues she had in regards to the governor's announcement this week."

She knew about the cycling. "Do you know where she planned to ride her bike?"

"When in Naples, she generally rides the trails in Seminole Lakes Park. Not sure exactly where it is."

Cassie asked, "Can you think of anyone who might have had a reason to kill her?"

Rachael's voice changed, guarded, almost defensive. She denied any history of conflicts with others outside the usual political battles. She claimed she couldn't think of anyone who might have had a serious grudge against Savannah.

"Was anyone strongly opposed to her appointment to the senate?"

"Of course, the opposing party would have protested if they knew, but nobody was aware of it. The governor wanted everything kept a secret until their press conference."

Cassie tapped at her lips with her pen. "Just off the record, Miss Morris. Was Savannah involved with any legislation that might directly or indirectly help her husband's company? Or hurt a competitor to the point it might place her life in jeopardy?"

"Wellington Investments? Never. That's an ethical line Savannah would never cross. Besides being wrong, it would be political suicide if discovered."

The remaining fifteen minutes of the conversation were non-productive, but something had rattled the woman and it wasn't just Savannah's death. After leading a hundred murder investigations, Cassie could tell when someone was holding out. There was a lead here somewhere. She'd have to arrange a face-to-face visit with Miss Morris in the near future. Maybe summon her down to Naples for an official statement. That would loosen her tongue. Cassie added a note on her yellow pad: *Rachael Morris – hiding something?*

Her next call was to Governor Cartwright's office. He was busy, but when Cassie identified herself, the secretary transferred the call to the governor's press secretary. He expressed the expected level of shock and proceeded to praise Savannah's long history of service to the people of Florida. "She will be missed by all." Standard, impersonal political response.

Cassie thanked him and disconnected the call. No help there. Cassie had noted the photograph hanging in Preston's office, the picture of the governor's hand around Savannah's waist, almost on her ass. She made another note on her pad: *Need DNA from Governor Cartwright. Father of Savannah's baby?*

Next was the Washington DC number. She dialed it.

"Take Back America, Jeremy speaking," The voice was soft, almost feminine.

"This is Detective Cassandra Pierce from the Naples Police Department. I'm calling about Savannah Wellington."

"The police? I hope she's not in any trouble."

"What was the nature of your association with her?"

"She worked for us as a political consultant."

Worked? Past tense? Cassie hadn't yet mentioned she was dead, and there had been multiple calls between this office and her only a few days before her death. "What did she do, exactly?'

"She worked closely with our organization to pass a resolution in the Florida legislature calling for a Convention of the States."

"I'm not sure I understand," said Cassie.

"Our country faces some serious challenges, financially and socially. It's been headed in the wrong direction for too many years and the present legislators in both political parties refuse to address the problems. We need to provide for new leadership not beholden to special interest groups. The only solution is to change the constitution to establish term limits to get rid of the entrenched old guard and their special interest backers. But it's no easy task. The process requires two-thirds of the state legislatures to pass a resolution calling for a constitutional convention where amendments may be presented. That's a lot of states."

Sounded like he was reading talking points from a fund-raising brochure. "And how was Speaker Wellington involved?"

"Without her efforts, I don't think it would have happened in Florida."

"How long ago was that?"

"Let me think. Uhm, it must have been two or three years ago."

The time frame ruled out any relationship between TBA and Savannah's murder. The line went silent for a few seconds as Cassie was about to scratch TBA from her list of areas to pursue.

Jeremy said, "Why do you ask?"

She set down her pen. "I'm sorry to inform you that Savannah Wellington is dead."

"Dead? But that's impossible."

He didn't ask when or how she died.

"Why?" asked Cassie.

"Why what?" asked the man on the other end, his voice sounding irritated.

"Why do you think it's impossible?"

The man hesitated. *Here we go again. This guy's searching for the right words. He's going to try to stonewall me.* Finally, he said, "We talked to her less than a week ago."

"We?"

"TBA's executive director, Scott Matheson and I, but mostly me. I've handled the majority of conversations with her."

"About what?"

"She finished our project in Florida, but Savannah continued to work with us as a political consultant. She met with other state legislative leaders across the country trying to pass resolutions similar to Florida's. As I mentioned, we need a two thirds majority of the states to sign on, and we're getting close. It was Savannah's job to push the ball over the goal line."

"Like a lobbyist? Was she compensated for her services?"

"You mean financially? No, of course not," said Jeremy, clearly indignant. Too much of an act? "That could be construed as a conflict of interest and would be illegal in almost every state. Savannah simply believed strongly in our quest to provide the framework for term limits."

Cassie leaned forward in her chair. She was close to something. She could feel it. Could her work be a reason for murder? "Who has she been in contact with most recently?"

"She'd been working with a number of state legislators. Let me check my records." Sounds of typing on a computer keypad. "Ah, here it is. State Senator Torbeson from Kansas. She's also been in contact with a half-dozen other state leaders including Governor Murray of Ohio." He gave Cassie Torbeson's phone number, then asked. "Why is the Naples Police Department involved in Savannah's death?"

"She was murdered." Cassie disconnected the call. She wanted that information to percolate in Jeremy's mind for a while. She would soon travel to DC to meet with him.

Cassie placed a call to State Senator Torbeson's office in Topeka. A woman answered. Cassie introduced herself. "I need to talk to the senator right away."

The woman started weeping. "I'm sorry, b—but he passed away last week."

"Died?" An ominous feeling coiled inside Cassie's chest. "What happened?"

"The police said it was a freak accident. His neighbor's tractor mower threw out a stone as the senator was working in his garden. It hit Senator Torbeson in the head. The coroner said the stone shattered inside his brain. He died instantly." The weeping turned to sobbing. After several seconds and multiple tissues, she asked, "Can anyone else help you?"

"No. Thank you for your help. I'm sorry to hear about the senator." Cassie hung up and wrote three names on her yellow pad: *Savannah, Torbeson, TBA. Connected??*

Cassie folded her list from Verizon and ran it through the shredder.

TWENTY-ONE

Rachael Morris Home
Tallahassee, Florida

Rachael sat in her condo and looked at her phone's blank screen, her mouth opened in disbelief. *Savannah is dead? Murdered? That can't be.* She poured two fingers of Woodford Reserve into a glass and tossed it down her throat. No surprise. Savannah led that kind of life, one that led to problems, the kind Rachael was tasked to keep out of the news. That lifestyle finally caught up to her. *But murdered?*

Rachael filled her glass with more bourbon and drank half. The promising new career she'd anticipated only a few days ago had been destroyed. There would be no living in Washington after Savannah became a United States Senator. There'd be no rubbing elbows with the country's elite and powerful. Rachael's hopes for a career as a political consultant and campaign manager for a national office holder were dashed. Savannah could have run for President one day, the first woman to successfully do so. With Rachael at her side, anything was possible.

Now Rachael had nothing. Gone was her job for which she was admittedly overpaid, better than anyone else in a similar position. Being Savannah's best friend had its advantages, but that was all gone. She could no longer afford her luxury condo in Tallahassee. She'd have to sell her Porsche.

She drained the rest of her glass of Woodford Reserve and stood in front of the window overlooking the Florida State Capitol building. She had to do something. She'd been Savannah's closest friend and was privy to information few others knew — valuable information — incriminating information. Another glass of bourbon and an idea took shape. Many individuals would benefit from Savannah's demise, but who could want her dead enough to murder her? Rachael tapped her fingers against the glass and made a mental list of the likely candidates. She picked up her cell phone and made the first call.

She recognized the voice on the other end. She didn't allow him to speak. "This is Rachael Morris, Savannah Wellington's chief of staff and close friend. Don't pretend like you don't know me. I was her personal confidant, and she told me everything."

"Exactly what do you think you know, Rachael?"

"I know about it all. I have information that could be devastating for certain careers."

"What do you want?"

"When someone killed her, they stole my entire future. I'm entitled to some compensation so I can get on with my life."

"Blackmail?"

"Harsh word, but yes. Blackmail. You should be familiar with it. It's a dirty business, but a common one in Washington. It's how things are done there. You know, quid pro quo."

"How much?"

"Two million."

"Are you insane? That's an impossible amount of money."

"You have that much and more. Don't try to fuck with me on this. If you don't come up with the money, I'll host a press conference, and you will not enjoy what I have to say."

The line remained quiet for a few seconds. "When?"

"I'm a reasonable person. I'll expect to receive a suitcase with the full amount in five days. I'll give you further instructions regarding where and when the transfer is to occur." She terminated the call and made four others, demanding similar amounts.

Blackmail was a dangerous business. She contacted someone for protection. A man answered on the fourth ring. "Spyder, it's Rachael. How soon can you drive from Naples to Tallahassee?"

"I can be there tomorrow. Why? What's up?"

"I need to have my security system upgraded to the best available. I want one even better than the one you installed for Savannah. Cost is no object." He agreed to be there the following afternoon.

Rachael checked her nightstand to confirm the revolver was there. She sat in her chair, poured another drink, leaned back, and smiled. *Two million bucks, at least. That'll only be the first installment. I didn't need Savannah after all. She looked out at the Capitol building and grinned. Time to celebrate.*

TWENTY-TWO

Ishmael's Home
Lakeside Park, Kentucky

It had been several days since Ishmael received the numbers offering another job. All he needed was the corresponding book to decipher the code. When the postman left a package in his mailbox, he walked down his driveway to retrieve it. As usual, the book was wrapped in plain brown paper. No return address. He tucked it under his arm as the little girl from next door raced down her driveway on a new purple and pink tricycle. Pink bows in her hair matched the streamers blowing back from the shiny chrome handlebars. Ding, ding. She rang her bell to get his attention. "Good morning, Mr. Wembley." She coasted to a stop.

"Good morning, Allison." Ishmael reached into his pocket just as he did each time he made a trip to the mailbox. "Let me see if I have anything for you today." He withdrew a pack of Skittles. "Well, look what we have here."

Her eyes lit up, and she turned to her mother who was standing on the porch. The woman nodded her approval and walked down the driveway. "Good morning, Mr. Wembley."

"Good morning, Mrs. Fenton." Ishmael handed Allison the candy. "Don't eat it all at once or you'll get a tummy ache." He stepped back and studied her tricycle. "That's a beautiful bike, Allison. Is it new?"

"I just got it yesterday. My daddy sent it to me from heaven." Her mother mouthed the words, "Thank you."

Ishmael smiled in response.

"Will you be joining us again for dinner this Sunday, Mr. Wembley?"

"Absolutely. I'd never miss an opportunity to enjoy your home cooking." Allison and her mother were the only real family Ishmael had ever known. They'd treated him kindly since he moved into the neighborhood a year ago. The mother was distraught because her husband had died unexpectedly and left his family with a heavy mortgage and no means to pay for it. Ishmael planned to have Fedallah retire the debt in its entirety, the money coming out of his own personal accounts.

"Don't expect too much. I'm making meatloaf." Mrs. Fenton seemed interested in a closer relationship with him. Tempting. He'd been looking forward to a normal life someday, one with his own family, but it would remain nothing more than a mere fantasy. His involvement with Fedallah and the Client made any attempt to leave the business impossible for the foreseeable future. Such action would merit harsh consequences — for himself and anyone he cared for. He needed to separate himself from little Allison and her mother as soon as possible.

"Meatloaf is my favorite. I'll see you Sunday." He turned to Allison and patted her on the head. "Maybe I'll bring another treat for you."

A wide grin spread across the girl's face as Ishmael walked back to his front porch. When inside the living room, he removed the paper wrapping from the book, a used copy of Moby Dick. He smiled at the irony. *Call me Ishmael.* Fedallah was usually all business, but it appeared the man had a sense of humor. Ishmael set about decoding the message. When finished, he leaned back in his chair, stunned. He rechecked to make sure he hadn't made a mistake. His previous contracts from the list of thirteen involved local state politicians and a few civilians. Number thirteen was a sitting governor. That took Ishmael to an entirely different level, one bound to attract attention, especially when the target was a popular national figure. A governor would be surrounded by a large contingent of bodyguards wherever he went. A job like this would normally require months of planning and preparation. The demanded timeline was too short, and he was tempted to decline the contract. It would be a dangerous proposition to deny a customer as rich and powerful as this one. It could trigger a contract on himself. Despite that risk, he prepared to type the word *rejected*—until he saw the fee. He blinked several times to be certain he read the number correctly. Fifteen million dollars? His most lucrative contract by far. The list of thirteen was almost complete, and he'd never again have the opportunity to earn such an amount.

The key to a successful career as a professional assassin was knowing when to quit and disappear. Do something once and it will go unnoticed; twice might garner attention in a few circles; three times constituted a definite pattern. If you stayed in the business too long, jail—or worse—was an inevitability. The fifteen million made the possibility of a retirement in luxury a reality. He thought about his home in the south of France and accepted the contract. Number thirteen would be his last.

After the recent job in Topeka, another freak accident this soon would draw unwanted attention. There had been too many in the past several years. At some point, a hungry young reporter was certain to notice. He had successfully used poisons like cyanide before his association with Fedallah, but death was immediate and the cause too obvious. The Client had insisted upon more subtle approaches. The man insisted on avoiding any appearances of foul play. A single drop of dimethyl mercury on a target's skin led to multiple organ failure in several months. Without a history of exposure, the cause of death was seldom identified. However, the Client wanted the governor neutralized within the week. To complicate matters, delivering any toxin to a man continually surrounded by State Troopers would be impossible.

Ishmael sat at his computer and spent hours reviewing every videotape and news report he could find on the governor. *Bingo.* He discovered a routine the man followed almost religiously. It was his point of vulnerability. He checked the governor's calendar of events. *Perfect.* Even with short notice, it was doable. He ordered the supplies he needed through Amazon and headed to his workstation in the basement to design the delivery system.

This is where my artistry will shine.

TWENTY-THREE

Von Hamberg Estate
Brussels, Belgium

The Baron stood before a large glass vault, recessed into a wall of his bedroom. Its one-inch transparent walls and temperature-controlled environment protected his collection of priceless relics, rare paintings, and family heirlooms, all confiscated by the Nazis after they invaded Austria. Many of the items had been hidden or lost over the years. It had taken most of the Baron's adult life and hundreds of million dollars to recover them. He purchased some back from private collectors and seized others from former Nazi officials when his reprisal team neutralized them.

He punched in his electronic password, and the lock disengaged, the door opening with a hiss. He walked in, sat in the room's only chair, and gazed at what remained of his family history, reliving the precious memories of his childhood, before the Nazis murdered his parents. Resting on one shelf in a velvet-lined cradle was his mother's violin, a Stradivarius, worth in excess of fifteen million dollars today. She played it while serving as concertmaster for the Vienna Symphony Orchestra.

He put on a pair of cotton gloves and lifted the violin, remembering how her soft hand caressed his cheek the same way she caressed the violin against her neck. He stroked the same strings his mother's delicate fingers once played. The vision of her smile warmed his heart, but he also remembered the terror in her eyes as the Nazis chased his family across the Austrian countryside. He carefully replaced the instrument in its cradle. Next to it sat an old photograph of him and his parents standing in front of the Hofburg Palace in Vienna. He traced his finger over the surface of the picture, faded over the years, and spotted with stains. Blood? Perhaps his parents'? The picture was found in the possession of a former commandant at Dachau. He had a collection of multiple photographs of executed Jews, some hanged or gassed, others shot. When the Baron's reprisal team found the commandant hiding in Argentina, they tortured and then executed him.

One of his most coveted items was an oil lamp, uncovered by his father during an archeological dig in the desert valleys east of Jerusalem over eighty years ago. It dated back to the first century BC. His father gave it to him as a parting gift before hiding him in a wooden crate and transporting him to Switzerland by wagon. The country was not the safe haven his parents had expected for their son. Despite their claims of neutrality, the Swiss were complicit with the Holocaust. He survived only by posing as a German youth, orphaned by the war. He had kept the oil lamp at his side ever since, all the while comprising a mental list of his enemies. *Never again.*

He learned the only way to survive another holocaust was to become so powerful and incredibly wealthy he could stop any threat. He spent the most of his life becoming one of the richest men in the world. His elderly eyes still glowed with the embers of hatred as he left the vault and called to his nurse to get LaTrane.

The man slithered into the room, checking all corners, his waxy face shining in the lights.

The Baron asked, "What are the latest financials?"

"I ran a report yesterday, sir. Your direct assets total two hundred eighty-seven billion. That number doesn't include at least another two hundred billion in industries where you have a substantial interest under different subsidiaries. The pandemic situation is fading, and I believe we've made as much as we can on it. I've instructed our team to decrease our interests in the health sector. Our banking systems are performing adequately, but less than optimal. This is due to the disappointing balance sheet of our Masada Bank in Geneva."

"We have no options there. We need the bank in order to transfer securities and sanitize cash equivalents before making them available to our allies."

"Understood, sir. On the positive side, our military weapons divisions are thriving, thanks to increased international conflicts and the embargo on Russian products. The push to increase NATO members financial commitments to defense spending will bolster our bottom line, and as always, revolutions abound. Telecommunications and technology divisions are steady. Overall, I expect our annual revenues to grow by twelve percent and that doesn't include the windfall from cobalt sales."

"Good. Have the securities department double our position in the microchip industry."

"I'll do it today sir."

"How are things progressing with our Retribution Project and the acquisitions?"

"Every individual on our list has been hanged, killed by the Mossad, or shot by your own teams. We found the last one a year ago hiding in a small South American village. I don't believe there are any remaining alive, but we're still searching. If any show up, our men will handle them per your instructions." He plucked a piece of lint from the lapel of his suit coat and placed it in his pocket. "A few isolated areas of neo-Nazi activity have erupted."

"Destroy them."

"Sir?"

"Can you imagine how many lives might have been spared if that priest had let Hitler drown when he was a boy? Six million Jews wiped out by that maniac. Kill them all before their evil seeds of antisemitism can germinate."

"I'll have them begin immediately, Baron."

The Baron turned to the large picture window overlooking his gardens. "Contact the speaker and our other associates in Congress. Tell them to stop that nonsense about denying funds for Israel's Iron Dome. It's essential for the country's protection. The same goes for that BDS talk. I want it stopped."

"I've been working on it, Baron. I've also been organizing our efforts in the next set of elections.

"Good. How are we looking?"

"I canvassed most of our regional directors in the United States and Europe. Combined, they have secured primary victories for over three-fourths of the candidates we support."

"And what of our other project?"

LaTrane smiled. "We're on schedule, sir. The list of thirteen is almost complete. The Kansas problem has been eliminated and passage of the resolution there has stalled out. I was in contact with Fedallah yesterday. He has his best man working on the list and expects no setbacks. We have removed most of TBA's major political and financial supporters. Without their backing, the organization will wither away. I can assure you the movement will be little more than a footnote in the annals of political history."

"And that messy situation in Florida?"

"Fedallah promises it's being taken care of."

The Baron stared out the window, gazing vacantly, lost in thought. "That damn oak tree."

"Sir?"

"The one struck by lightning a few years back."

"Yes, Baron. Shall I have the landscaper cut it down?"

"No. I want to watch it die. I'm determined to outlast the damn thing."

"I'm sure you will, sir. By next month, you will have your own personal hospital just down the hall. Work is almost complete on the operating room and Intensive Care Unit. It's already fully staffed with some of the finest nurses, physicians, and surgeons in Europe. We are well-prepared to handle anything that might happen to you."

"I hope so, considering all the money I spent on them." The old man had a paroxysm of coughing. He wiped the blood from his mouth and leaned on his cane. "I'm running out of time, LaTrane. I've spent decades and a small fortune buying politicians in the United States and Europe. I won't allow that TBA organization to dismantle everything I've built with their damn term limits. I don't have the time to develop new people."

"We will prevail, sir. Fedallah is almost finished. Elimination of the thirteen individuals on your list will ensure our continued success."

TWENTY-FOUR

East Naples Precinct
Naples, Florida.

At three o'clock, Cassie watched from her office as Preston Wellington walked into the Naples station accompanied by his lawyer, a stocky man with a thin mustache. With his chest puffed out and carrying a briefcase as large as a duffel bag in his left hand, the man looked like he was prepared for a major battle. He approached the front desk and in a loud voice said, "Mr. Wellington here to see Detective Pierce." Too much bluster and show.

The receptionist smiled and looked into his eyes. "Of course, Mr. Wellington. She's been expecting you."

The lawyer huffed. "I'm not Mr. Wellington. I'm Daryl Pfister, his attorney of record. Mr. Wellington is standing to my right." He handed her his business card, embossed in gold.

Cassie chuckled under her breath. The receptionist knew exactly who Preston was. She simply wanted to throw his arrogant lawyer off balance. Bullying tactics wouldn't work here. She escorted them into a tiny interrogation room with a steel table in the middle and two metal chairs on either side. The gray cinder block walls oozed a sense of futility, meant to intimidate.

Cassie turned off the A/C, and let them stew for a while to soften Preston and to irritate his attorney. She turned on the audio-video systems. Sometimes suspects would unknowingly share incriminating information with their attorney when they thought no one was watching. After the interrogation room door closed, Preston leaned over to say something to his lawyer, but the man held up his hand. "Not now," he whispered and pointed to the camera in the ceiling. The guy was a pompous ass but knew his stuff.

After fifteen minutes, Cassie walked in. "Hello, Mr. Wellington."

Preston stood. *Still a gentleman despite his pain.* With his shoulders stooped, and his face drawn, he looked twenty years older than he had this morning. A look of despondency shadowed his sunken eyes.

Cassie shook his hand. "Thank you for agreeing to meet with me again. I realize this is an unfortunate situation."

The attorney stood; his face frozen in a perpetual scowl. "And I'm his personal attorney, Mr. Daryl —"

She cut him off with a dismissive wave of the back of her hand. "Of course, you are." She nodded to Preston. "Have a seat. Can I get you anything? Water? Coffee? Soft drink? I must warn you; the coffee here is almost undrinkable."

"Water would be fine."

"I'll have the same, please," said the lawyer, his voice less confrontational.

Cassie called out to the receptionist and asked for three bottled waters. The woman returned a minute later and set a bottle, dripping with condensation, in front of each of them. Cassie and the lawyer took a mouthful. Preston left his unopened.

Cassie began, "Though we already spoke early this morning, there are a few matters I'd like to clear up, Mr. Wellington." Suspects tended to be comfortable in familiar surroundings like their home or office. It was a bit like home-field advantage in sports. In a more hostile environment like an interrogation room, they became distracted and, if untruthful, were more likely to slip up.

The attorney spoke. "I want the record to reflect that Mr. Wellington is here today of his own volition. He is not required to submit to further interrogation other than what you already put him through this morning—unless of course you have a warrant. If you do, this interview is over."

"No warrant." Cassie, folded her hands in front of her and stared at Preston. No telltale droplets of perspiration clung to his upper lip, and his hands weren't fidgety. He didn't look like a person guilty of any crime. Rather he appeared broken, something to be expected from a grieving widower, the same impression she'd had this morning. *Could be an act, though.* If so, her questions should rattle and expose him.

The attorney looked at her. "You and I both know why you wanted him here. He came against my advice because he has nothing to hide."

The hired pit bull was doing his job, a show mostly for the benefit of his client. The usual level of posturing she'd seen hundreds of times in Chicago.

"Duly noted counselor," she said, keeping her focus on Preston. "Mr. Wellington, this morning, you told me you and your wife have been separated for the past year."

He looked up and met her stare. "That's correct."

"And why did that happen?"

"We grew apart. Savannah and I started living separate lives several years ago, but our marriage began slowly dying before that. She spent most of her time in Tallahassee, while I stayed in Naples. The only time she came to our house was when I left town for business—which was too often."

"And who might know about her schedule and when she would be in town?"

"I can't say for sure. I guess the people in my office, our house staff, and maybe her people in Tallahassee. It's hard to be certain."

"So, you two never saw each other. Is that it?"

"Unfortunately."

Cassie leaned forward in her chair, her palms flat on the table. "Can you account for your whereabouts between July first and July third of this year?"

"Yes. I was in California recruiting investors for some products we've launched."

"Involving?"

"Several areas including establishment of stronger microchip manufacturing in the United States and improved consumption-based business model programs."

His answers seemed legitimate. "Do you have proof you were there?"

"Yes. My secretary can provide you with records of transportation, lodging receipts, and my schedule of meetings."

Cassie made a note to check on those activities. So much for the easy questions. Time to play hardball. "When were you last intimate with your wife?"

The lawyer jumped out of his chair and yelled, "What kind of a question is that, detective? This man is a grieving husband who just learned of his wife's death this morning— and you decide to play this ambush game?"

"I'm simply trying to get a feel for the status of their relationship and to establish some timelines, counselor. Both legitimate areas of interest." Most attorneys protested and objected during questioning to disrupt the rhythm of the interrogation. Cassie was too experienced to allow that to happen and ignored him. She needed to figure out whether or not Preston was the father of Savannah's baby. If he denied contact with his wife and the DNA test confirmed he was the father, it would prove he was a liar and a legitimate suspect in her death.

"This conversation is over." The attorney placed his hand on Preston's shoulder. "We're leaving."

Preston held up his hand. "That's all right. I have no problem answering the question. I have nothing to hide, and I'll do whatever it takes to clear me as a suspect as quickly as possible so the police can focus on finding the real killer."

Cassie knew many killers said the same thing after murdering their spouses. It was a tactic used to portray an air of innocence, deflecting suspicion away from themselves. She didn't believe that was the situation in this case, but since the husband was always the most likely suspect, she had to push the issue to Wellington's limits.

Preston turned to Cassie. "Savannah and I haven't been intimate in years."

Cassie leaned back in her chair. "That's a long time to go without a sexual relationship, Mr. Wellington. Have you ever sought the comfort of another woman? One who might have wanted to get Savannah out of the way?"

"No, never. It wouldn't have been right to see other women. We were still married, and I didn't want to do anything that might jeopardize the chances of us getting back together again."

Cassie tapped her fingers against her upper lip. "What about Savannah? Is it conceivable she had other relationships?"

Preston lowered his head. "I'm not a stupid man, detective. Savannah demanded attention and she always received it. Anytime we attended a function together, all eyes in the room, male and female, remained fixated on her. They couldn't help staring. In a way, I felt proud she was mine, but Savannah didn't belong to anyone, not even me. She was a complex woman who needed more than any one man could give her."

Cassie squeezed her hands together until her knuckles turned white. Complex woman? A euphemism for a whore without a conscience.

Preston continued. "Have I had my suspicions about other relationships? Of course. I think anyone would. She was very secretive about her personal life, even before we separated. There were frequent hushed cell phone conversations, unexplained absences from the house, and too many late nights out with her friend, Rachael. But I saw no concrete evidence of an affair."

"Was there anyone specific you might have been concerned about?"

"Several possibilities, but I thought there might be something going on between her and the guy who managed our security and internet systems. She spent a great deal of time with him. Again, I didn't have any hard evidence, but I wasn't looking."

Cassandra picked up her pen and pulled her legal pad closer. "Do you have a name?"

"Spyder something. Never met the guy but remembered the name because it was so unusual. Savannah initially hired him to install security systems in her office in Tallahassee. I think he did her condo there also."

"And your home in Naples?"

"I believe so, yes."

"Do you have a last name?"

Preston scrolled through his cell phone. "No, but my secretary can probably get it for you. If not her, then Savannah's chief of staff, Rachael Morris should have it."

"How about with a woman? Is it possible she had a relationship with a woman?"

The attorney exploded out of his chair, knocking it over. "That's enough, detective. This man is in mourning. How dare you besmirch his wife's good name?"

"Just trying to explore all possibilities, counselor."

Preston's cheeks flushed. "Not possible. She was definitely heterosexual."

Cassie set down her pen, stared into Preston's eyes, and flashed her most intimidating detective look. "I assume you were pretty angry about Savannah's possible affairs."

He looked down at his hands for a few seconds before replying. "Angry? No." His eyes glistened. "Disappointed and hurt? Yes, of course. I loved her, but I knew what I was getting into when I married someone fifteen years younger than me. I hoped that as we both matured, she would become more content with our life together."

"Did you ever consider the possibility of monitoring her activities?"

He looked up, his eyes blank. "You mean like having her followed?"

"Yes. Or checking her Verizon phone records."

Preston gave a shake of his head, a lock of his hair falling down his forehead. "No, I didn't."

"Why not? You certainly have the financial resources to do so."

Preston pushed his hair back in place. "One reason I've been successful in business is my ability to identify unfavorable situations and being willing to confront them before they became bigger problems. Unfortunately, I was unable to apply those policies to my personal life."

Cassie leaned in and rested her elbows on the table. "I'm not sure I understand."

"I didn't want to know. Suspicion of infidelity is one thing, but proof of an affair is an entirely different matter. Once that stone is unturned, all is lost. It can never be placed back. I always hoped that Savannah would eventually get through this stage in her life and return to me." A tear ran down his right cheek. He made no attempt to wipe it away.

Together again? Was this guy for real? Despite everything, he still loved her. Why? Who the hell knew? She didn't deserve his love. Savannah was a serial cheater who cared only about herself. She was unworthy of anyone's love, especially Preston. *This poor guy wasn't culpable in this murder. He's as much a victim as Savannah.*

Cassie started her last set of questions. "Can you think of anyone who might have wanted to harm her?"

"No. As I told you this morning, everyone seemed to be genuinely fond of Savannah."

Cassie was convinced Lisa was right. Nobody could ever see this guy as anything but a grieving, innocent widower. She had no further questions except to request a buccal sample for DNA analysis, and a polygraph. His attorney demanded the name of the person administering the test. "If your man tries any shenanigans, I'll have my own person do one."

"Agreed, counselor." Cassie knew the results were little more than a physiological measurement of pulse, respiratory rate, and perspiration, all of which increase during times of stress related to lying. The test was scientifically subjective and inadmissible in court, but it could help narrow down a list of suspects or guide the investigation in a different direction. She believed Preston would pass. "Just wait here. One of our forensics techs will be out in a few minutes to take the buccal sample."

Forty-five minutes later, Cassie had confirmation of her suspicions when the polygraph expert pulled her aside. "The guys telling the truth, Cassie. He had nothing to do with it. He wasn't even aware she was dead until you told him this morning."

"How about the pregnancy?"

"It was a delicate situation. I didn't want to spring it on him out of the blue. That would have been pretty dirty. I danced around the issue and approached the subject indirectly, but I'm convinced he's totally unaware of her maternal status."

Cassie went back to her desk and scratched the name *Preston Wellington* off her yellow legal pad list of suspects. A secretary had delivered an envelope from the forensics lab. It contained the report on Brad's coffee cup. His DNA profile excluded him as a potential father of the fetus. She crossed his name off. The list of suspects was dwindling.

The lieutenant's voice exploded from his office. "Pierce, my office."

Now what? When she walked in, Cassie stood and looked down at him. A pile of mangled paperclips sat on the desk in front of him. He skipped the niceties. "What's the status of Preston Wellington?"

"I'm releasing him, sir. He's innocent. He passed the polygraph."

"That means nothing. Some people can cheat the machine. I'm told you gave him a copy of the questions in advance. Are you crazy?"

"Standard procedure, sir. Any surprise questions are worthless because they artificially distort the examinee's physiological responses." *Something you would already realize if you'd ever done any actual police work.*

"I've been watching your interview on the closed-circuit monitor," he said. "I'm convinced. He's as guilty as hell."

Cassie crossed her arms over her chest and resisted an eye roll. "You're wrong, lieutenant. He's not a good suspect. No DA with half a brain would take him before a Grand Jury. The case would be thrown out of court, and we'd be a laughingstock. You remember the headlines in the paper about a potential police coverup? Preston's arrest will look exactly like that. The public will insist the FBI take over."

"He lawyered up for God's sake. That should tell you something."

"It was his constitutional right."

"You can see it in his body language. He killed his wife. I know it for a fact."

"Is that opinion based upon your extensive experience as a homicide detective?" Cassie smirked, took two steps closer, and loomed over him. "Tell me, lieutenant, how many murder cases have you worked in your career?" She held up her right hand and closed her index finger against her thumb, creating a zero.

His jaw twitched. A large vein in the center of his forehead looked like it might explode any minute. "Book him, now."

"What?"

"You heard me. Put him in cuffs."

"No. I'm not going to do that. I'm not going to destroy the credibility of this investigation and the reputation of a good man because you need a scapegoat."

The man's face turned bright red. "That does it. You're off the case, detective."

Cassie scoffed. "Are you kidding me? You're taking me off it? Exactly who's going to run the investigation then?"

"Detective Stapleton."

"Brad? You've got to be joking. He's the moron who was the source of the leak you wanted me to find." The lieutenant's eyes widened with this information. "That's right. Brad leaked the case to the reporter. The guy couldn't find his way out of his own bathroom, much less find Savannah's killer. Surely you can't be stupid enough to put him in charge — then again, I guess you could."

The lieutenant stood and slammed his fist on the desk. "That's enough, Pierce. Turn in your badge. You're fired."

Cassie pushed her nose an inch from his. "No, I'm not, you idiot. If you do that, I'll hire Preston Wellington's lawyer and file a discrimination suit against the city of Naples, the department in general, and you personally. Then I'll file a sexual harassment claim against Brad, and it'll stick. I'll claim that you covered up my complaints."

"That's preposterous. I did no such thing." The lieutenant's eyes widened in fear.

"I assume you've heard of the Me-Too movement. By the time the news media finishes with you, the mayor, city council, and the public will all be in my corner. They'll need their own scapegoat. How long do you think it'll take before they throw you under the bus? They might even give me your job to smooth things over."

"I ... I ..." He choked on a few words, but said nothing intelligible.

She headed for the door. "Now stay the hell out of my way so I can work my case."

152

TWENTY-FIVE

Sands Bar and Grille
Naples, Florida

Cassie and I needed to meet in person to compare notes. She suggested dinner and drinks at an inconspicuous bar on Central Avenue. Since I was not officially participating in the investigation, we needed to be discreet. Sands Restaurant was away from the busy tourist areas, and primarily catered to the local population. The parking lot reminded me of the dark one behind Buddy's where someone had stalked me several nights ago. Keeping an eye over my shoulder, I rushed through a small alley toward the door.

On my right, a panhandler, a rarity in Naples, sat on the curb, a small dog at his side. He wore a tattered army jacket and had a paper cup on the ground in front of him. Veteran? If so, he deserved better. I pulled a twenty out of my wallet and stuffed it into the cup. Not enough to turn his life around but maybe enough for a decent meal tonight. He nodded his thanks.

I entered the restaurant and walked past a long bar, where a gauntlet of singles and pretend singles searched for a connection. An older man with a huge diamond ring on his right pinkie stepped in my way. He wore a shirt unbuttoned halfway down his chest. All he needed was a few pounds of gold chain around his neck to complete the stereotype. To cap things off, a gold wedding band strangled his sausage shaped ring finger. "Can I have your autograph?" he asked.

"Excuse me?"

"Your autograph. Aren't you Blake Lively?"

Another cheating asshole. My eyes bore into his and I snarled. "Wow! Is this where I'm supposed to get all gushy and blush? Go back to your wife, creep."

He shrugged his shoulders and turned his attention to the girl walking in behind me. "Can I get your autograph?"

"Fuck off, jerk," she said.

I chuckled as she and I exchanged eye rolls. I found Cassie already sitting at a table in front of a large picture window in the rear. It overlooked a small courtyard with a fountain in the middle. She waved me over and I sat down. "Do you think I look like Blake Lively?"

"The movie star?" She tilted her head and studied my face. "Now that you mention it, you do." She giggled. "Let me guess. Some toad with lots of chest hair asked you for your autograph."

"How'd you know?"

"He told me I looked like Gal Gadot."

"Wonder Woman?" I smiled. "He's not far off, but you're much prettier."

She laughed out loud and brushed aside the compliment. "I can say the same about you and Blake."

The waiter came over with a wine list.

We ordered Conundrum.

He asked, "Would you like to share a bottle?"

I looked at Cassie and she nodded. "A bottle would be great, and I think we're ready to order. What's good?"

"We're known for our steaks. Tonight's special is a twenty-four-ounce Tomahawk served with grilled asparagus and our special mashed potatoes."

"I'm famished, but that's a bit much for me," I said. "I'll have the petite filet, medium well, and the blue cheese lettuce wedge. Dressing on the side, please."

Cassie closed her menu. "That sounds good. I'll have the same, but make mine medium rare."

While we waited, we discussed our backgrounds. She'd been orphaned after her parents were killed during a robbery in their small convenience store just outside of Chicago. She had no living family members, so she was placed in the foster care system. "That didn't work out very well. I never lived in one home more than six months at a time. I was an out-of-control rebel and ran away a lot."

"You were probably angry about being left alone with no one to care for you."

"At eleven years old, I felt like my parents abandoned me, though in my mind I knew it wasn't true. Teens aren't exactly known for their rational behavior. In retrospect, some of the foster parents were actually decent people, but too many were horrible and used me as a maid or babysitter for their own kids. Several pervs tried to sexually assault me. I broke one's jaw with a bottle of Jack Daniels." She attempted a chuckle but failed. It obviously bothered her.

I reached over and squeezed her hand. "He deserved to be hit."

"Yes, but I nearly killed him. It earned me nine months in juvie."

"Is that why you became a cop?"

"That's what the psychiatrist thought."

"Then why Naples?"

"I left Chicago because of the police defunding policies instituted by the mayor. After a few years of understaffing, my partner was killed trying to break up a domestic dispute. No backup. Simply another typical day in the south side of Chicago, but a devastating one for me."

"Your partner? How terrible," I said. "Was he another detective?'

"No, she was working a patrol when she was shot." Cassie paused and stroked the stem of her wine glass. "I still miss her terribly."

"It's hard to lose someone you worked with closely. I lost a friend several years ago."

Cassie swirled her wine glass and took a large mouthful. "She was more than just a friend, Lisa. We lived together."

Lived together? It took a while before the words registered. Cassie was such a beautiful head-turner, I never imagined …

She continued, "It was difficult being gay on the police force. The snide remarks were painful, but in time, we got used to them. Gail and I never planned to be gay. It's how we were wired. We didn't flaunt it or have a political agenda. We simply wanted to be happy together, but life took it all away from us."

"Gail? Is she the one who gave you the bracelet?"

She didn't answer, just shook her wrist causing the hearts to sparkle. "I never take mine off."

"Losing her must have been very difficult."

"It was. I've tried to move on, but so far, I haven't found anyone who could replace her. She was honest and loyal, a rarity in today's world. We kept no secrets from each other. Can't say as much for the other relationships I've tried since."

"It's impossible to replace someone you lost. You might not be able to find another love exactly like her, but I believe there must be someone else who is just as good for you, but in different ways."

"Maybe, but it's difficult when you're gay. Even in today's more inclusive society, you still must be careful. You never know who to trust and I don't want to be betrayed again."

Again? Another sip of wine and I allowed the conversation to settle for several seconds. "We have much in common. My history is similar to yours, but I was never in a foster home." I told her how my parents had also been murdered when I was a child. "At least I still had my brother, Jacob, and our grandmother who raised us. It happened in south-eastern Kentucky."

A smile almost turned up the corner of her lips. "Like Hatfield and McCoy country?"

"Nearby," I said. "Same type of family-first, protect-your-own, Appalachian culture."

"Is there any room in that culture for friends?"

"Especially friends."

We clinked our glasses in a toast. "Here's to good friends," she said.

"To great friends." I took a sip of the wine.

"Who killed them?" she asked.

"A corrupt county sheriff."

"And?"

I smiled. "Mountain justice. Translation—we took care of things ourselves. The pursuit of justice has driven me ever since. I wound up fighting terrorists, a job beyond the fringes of traditional law enforcement. It didn't gel with a husband married to his job at the FBI. The situation led to us having severe marital problems." I swallowed a mouthful of wine. "We separated over a month ago. He's still in Washington."

"Has to be difficult. We do seem to have a great deal in common," Cassie said and again clinked her glass against mine. We each took a mouthful. The more we talked, the more I liked her.

"I came to Naples to rediscover myself," I said.

"That's why you're so committed to this case?"

"Yes, and the fact Savannah was pregnant when she was killed." I told her about my own fertility issues. "When John and I finally became pregnant through artificial insemination, I was elated, the happiest I'd been in my life. I was so afraid of losing the baby, I remained inactive, at home, all day, every day. I carried it for almost six months, until one morning I woke up with horrible cramping, and the sheets covered with blood.

Afterwards, John wanted to try again, but the obstetrician told us it was no use." Tears built up. I fought them back, but a few escaped down my cheek. "I hated the world. Most of all, I hated God for teasing me with the baby, only to snatch it away."

Cassie placed her hand on mine. "You must have been devastated."

"I was. It made me feel worthless."

She squeezed my hand. "That's not true at all, Lisa. Your level of fertility isn't what defines you as a woman. You're beautiful, caring, and intelligent." She pointed to my heart. "It's what's in there that counts."

By the time our order arrived, we'd gone through the entire bottle of Conundrum and were getting pretty tipsy. The waiter asked, "Another bottle?"

"Maybe just one more glass," I said. "We both have to drive home." I gazed up at him. "Do you have any suggestions?"

"We have a nice Opus One."

"Oh, that's a pricey one," said Cassie. "How much is a glass?"

"Normally it's forty-nine a glass, but we have an opened bottle from yesterday. I can make it twenty dollars for a couple of lovely ladies like you."

Cassie smiled. "We'll take two."

"That's still a lot of money for a glass of wine," I said. "I doubt I'll be able to taste the difference."

"You will," she said. "It'll be the best wine you've ever had. It was Savannah's favorite."

I furrowed my brow, thinking I had missed something earlier. "Wait a minute. You knew Savannah?"

"Oh, no. Her husband told me she liked the finer things in life and one of them was the Opus."

The waiter interrupted our conversation when he brought our food. Cassie cut into the steak to see if the center was to her liking. I was too hungry to care. I cut off a piece and shoved it into my mouth. Delicious.

After eating, we got down to business.

"You were right about Preston Wellington," said Cassie. "He's not involved. I crossed his name off my suspect list. I checked Savannah's cell phone records and Brad's never made a call to her. His DNA results rule him out as a father of her baby. Bottom line, he has no motive. He's not a good suspect."

I shook my head. "Damn, I was almost sure it was him." I took a sip of my Opus One and swirled it in my mouth. Cassie was right. It was the smoothest wine I'd ever tasted. I looked at her. "I think it could be premature to dismiss Brad just yet. It might not be a bad idea for you to dig deeper into his past. If you can gain access to his personnel file, you might find some connection between him and Savannah."

"Not possible. The only one with authorization to review those files is the lieutenant, but he and I aren't on the best of terms right now." She gave a rueful smile. "I kind of called him an idiot."

We both laughed so hard my wine almost came out of my nose.

Cassie finished her glass. "From what I've discovered, Savannah had several love interests. Any of them might have had a motive to kill her, especially if one fathered her baby. Problem is, I don't have any specific names."

"Terrific. Back to square one."

"There's still the possibility that the killing was politically motivated. Savannah was involved with voter integrity laws. She pushed hard for passage of a photo ID requirement at the polls. However, this has been the substance of a nationwide debate involving hundreds of legislators in every state, and no one else has been targeted."

"To the best of our knowledge," I said.

The waiter picked up our plates. "Would either of you ladies like to order dessert? We have a delicious New York cheesecake."

I looked at Cassie and we both said no.

"I'd like a cup of coffee," I said. I needed some caffeine to offset the effects of the wine.

"One or two?" asked the waiter.

"Make it two," said Cassie.

When he left, Cassie said, "Savannah had been working with a political group called Take Back America. TBA, they call themselves. She was instrumental in pushing a resolution calling for a constitutional convention through the Florida legislature."

"Her husband talked about that. Their leader's some guy called Scott Matheson."

"That's not all. Savannah continued to work with other state legislators lobbying to push similar bills. I called her most recent contact, but —"

"Don't tell me. He's dead."

"Yep. Hit in the head with a stone thrown out by a neighbor's lawn mower. It was ruled an accident."

I leaned back in my chair. "Wow! That's too improbable to be true. An accident is what someone wanted us to believe about Savannah. What are the odds against two politicians dying from a bizarre head injury within a few weeks of each other?"

"Pretty damn high," said Cassie. "It would take a pro to pull it off."

"Savannah's death might have nothing at all to do with her unborn baby or a rejected lover. This might be all about that TBA organization."

"It's possible, but I believe the pregnancy is still the most likely lead. When I questioned Savannah's secretary about things, she started to clam up. I think she's hiding something."

"Maybe I should visit the secretary while you keep looking into things here."

"No, I'll take care of it." She sounded insistent.

"You already have too much on your plate. She might be more relaxed with someone not wearing a badge."

"How could you pull that off?"

I tried to suppress a smile. Didn't work. "The same way I discovered Savannah's identity and got in to interview Preston. Lie, but I might need a little help from you."

When the waiter delivered our coffee, I heard a loud obnoxious laugh coming from the bar, followed by the same words I heard outside my condo several days ago. "Get my gist?" I looked over and almost choked. *TOPDOC! What the hell is that bastard doing here?* Next to him stood a girl, barely legal and with so much dark eye makeup she looked like she was headed to a Halloween Party. Her miniskirt, fishnet hose, and dangerously high platform stiletto heels said she was a working girl.

"Who's that?" asked Cassie.

"Who?"

"The asshole who keeps squeezing that young girl's ass."

"Nobody."

"And yet, he caught your interest. What's going on, Lisa?"

"Remember that night I was stalked —" I didn't finish my sentence. My phone rang. It was TOPDOC's wife. "Excuse me, Cassie. I need to take this. It's urgent." I stood and walked a few feet away. "This is Lisa," I whispered, pressing the phone against my ear. "What's wrong?"

"He beat me again."

My heart raced and I felt like grabbing the guy by the back of his collar, and pummeling him. "What happened?"

"He was dressed up and headed out the door. He'd been drinking, and I knew what he was up to. I begged him to stay home. Told him we needed to work on our marriage." She started sobbing. "He punched me in the face and knocked me to the ground. I was mad and told him to get the hell out, go see his whore, and don't bother coming back. That's when he started kicking me. Over and over. Thought he was going to kill me."

"Where are you now?"

"Hospital emergency room. They say I have a concussion and internal injuries. There's blood in my urine. They're about to take x-rays. I'm so afraid. I don't know what to do."

"You stay there until I arrive. I'm going to take care of this so you'll never have to be afraid again."

How would John handle the situation? Probably arrest him and let the courts sort it out. Not good enough. The guy would be out on bail in a day. A restraining order would be of no use. That's when most abused spouses were beaten to death. What was needed here was some good old fashioned Savich family mountain justice. When I returned to the table, Cassie probed me with her detective eyes. "Okay, Lisa. What's going on here? You look like you're about to explode."

I watched TOPDOC pay his bill, put his arm around his little honey, and head for the door. I turned to Cassie. "I'll be back in a minute."

"Where are you going, Lisa? Don't do anything stupid."

"Me? Not a chance."

She raised her hands. "Never mind. Don't want to know. Think I'll head to the ladies' room and check my blood sugar. All that wine probably jacked it up."

After I was sure she was out of sight, I followed TOPDOC to the parking lot. He and his girlfriend were staggering. My own heels clicked on the pavement, and I made no attempt to be quiet. Two could play at this stalking game.

He whirled around to face me.

I glared at him. "Looks like you're drunk, TOPDOC."

"Do I know you?"

"Naples Vice," I said and looked at the girl. "You'd better run home to your mommy, little girl. This John you picked up likes to beat women. Probably the only way he can get it up."

The girl hesitated.

"Hurry on now, before I decide to arrest you."

The girl ran as fast as her ridiculous high heels would allow. Thought she might trip and hurt herself. I turned to face him. "Isn't that right, TOPDOC? That's the only way you can get it up? Is that why you beat your wife?"

"You," he screamed. "The loudmouth bitch from next door. I'm going to teach you to stop meddling in other people's private business."

I kicked off my shoes. "What is it with all you Neanderthals? Always wanting to teach me a lesson."

He got into my face and drew his hand back to punch me. "Okay, cutie. You've been asking for this."

What happened next was pure instinct, a reflex imprinted on me from years of training. Before he could strike, I slammed the heel of my right hand into the middle of his face.

His nose crunched, and blood poured over his mouth. He wiped the back of his hand across his face, smearing wide patches of red. When he saw it, his face transformed into that of a madman. "Now you're going to die."

He lunged at me.

I responded with an elbow to his left jaw, knocking him to the ground. Something cracked, and he howled as his jaw twisted at an impossible angle.

I stood over him. "That's how your wife feels every time you hit her."

"I never —"

Before he could finish, I kicked him in the ribs and heard more cracking.

He gasped for air.

I squatted down until my face was inches from his. "Here's what's going to happen from now on, cupcake. If your wife decides to take your sorry ass back, and I pray she doesn't, you're going to be a model husband. If you so much as lay a pinkie on her, I'll know. I'll find you and when I do, I'm going to do a Lorena Bobbitt procedure on you." I made a snipping gesture with my fingers. "You'll be singing soprano for the rest of your life. You get my gist?"

I looked down at him. "I'm going to call for an ambulance to take you to the ER. If anyone asks you what happened, tell them someone mugged you." I pushed my foot against his broken ribs. More howling. "Don't even think about calling the police. I am the police, and I'll find out. If that happens, I'll release photographs of your wife's injuries. Your pathetic career will be over, and you'll go to jail. Might even wind up getting married to a cellmate called Bubba."

I turned to leave and saw the panhandler still sitting on the curb. He'd seen everything, but gave me a thumbs up. I looked over my shoulder at TOPDOC. "By the way, don't try stalking me again like you did at Buddy's."

"Wh—what are you talking about?"

Didn't sound like he was lying. If it wasn't him, it must have been Spandex Brad. Or was it someone else?

TWENTY-SIX

Home of Lisa Marie Crawford
Everglades Estates
East Naples, Florida

In the morning, I called Savannah's office and identified myself as a representative from the Naples police department. Not an actual lie. I made an appointment to meet with her chief of staff, Rachael Morris the next day. It would be a seven-hour drive up I-75, so I planned to leave before noon and spend the night in Tallahassee.

On the way, I stopped at the hospital to check on TOPDOC's wife. She was stable but had sustained two broken ribs, a concussion, and a bruised kidney. I recommended that she move to a woman's shelter, but she insisted on giving him another chance. I told her it was a bad idea but doubted he'd ever attack her again, especially after our discussion in Sand's parking lot. He'd be in bed, sucking his meals through a straw for at least a month.

On my way out, I ran into Cassie and asked her to look in on the woman so she could file an official report.

"Does this have anything to do with the guy who kept squeezing that young girl's ass last night? We received a call about a man matching his description getting mugged by three men right behind Sands. They worked him over pretty well. He was admitted with multiple injuries. I just finished interviewing him." She studied me with her detective eyes. "Please tell me you weren't involved."

I didn't want to lie to her, so I simply responded with my own question. "Was one of the attackers a blonde wearing a skirt and black stilettos?"

"No, and his story was corroborated by a nearby panhandler."

"There you have it, then."

Cassie stared down the hall. "Still, it seems strange that it happened outside the same restaurant where we were eating and about the time you excused yourself from the table."

I shrugged. "Another one of those coincidences, I guess."

Cassie shook her head. "Coincidence? Those same kinds of things you don't believe in? Jesus, Lisa. Would you try to remember I'm a cop?"

***

I arrived in Tallahassee at nine that evening, found a room at the Marriott, and ordered room service. The following morning, I drove to the capitol complex. The stately original building stood in the shadows of a modern twenty-three story tower that served as the center of Florida's government. The legislators' offices were in a building to the right. I followed the signs and rode the elevator up to Speaker Wellington's office on the fourth floor. The elderly receptionist wore black, probably in honor of Savannah's death. She said that Rachael Morris was aware of our appointment, but wasn't in yet. I asked the receptionist to call, but Rachael didn't answer her phone. I mentioned that I was with the Naples Police and needed her home address. It was in an upscale condominium complex only five minutes away.

Security cameras monitored the front door and lobby of the building. I pressed the buzzer for her unit but received no reply. As an elderly couple exited, I took the opportunity to enter through the opened door. When they looked at me with suspicious eyes, I identified myself as the police. "Someone reported a prowler."

The elevator took me to the third floor and I headed down the hall to unit 307. The door was slightly ajar. Bad sign. I pulled out my Sig, and nudged the door open with the tip of the barrel. The coppery smell of blood assaulted my nose. A worse sign. I stepped back, shocked by the sight of two bodies lying side by side, their open eyes staring into the endless abyss of eternity. The killer had carved a pentagram in each victim's forehead. *Bizarre.*

Rachael Morris had been shot in both knees and finally through the left eye. A wide pool of clotted blood surrounded her head. The man next to her appeared to be in his mid-thirties. A trail of bloody smears followed him from the front door to his current position. I saw no bullet holes in the front of his chest, suggesting he'd been shot in the back.

Keeping my Sig pointed forward, I checked the rest of the condo, being careful to avoid disturbing the crime scene. In Rachael's bedroom, the mattress had been flipped, and all the dresser drawers pulled out with clothing scattered across the floor. A second bedroom clearly served as an office and was also ransacked. Desk drawers had been opened and a mouse sat on top, but the laptop was missing. Must have contained some serious information someone wanted badly enough to kill two people. Without muddling the scene, I searched for a cell phone. Couldn't find it.

Using the tip of my pen, I pushed around some papers on the desk. One was a receipt from the Guardian Security Company for over seven thousand dollars. According to the date on the paper, the new system had been installed just the day before. *How'd the killer get past it?* So much for expensive alarm systems. It was still on, but somehow had been disabled. I suspected any internal surveillance cameras had been bypassed. I took a photograph of the alarm control panel and the receipt with my cell phone.

From the looks of things, the assassin must have been waiting in the dark for the couple to return. I could only imagine the terror they felt when they turned the lights on. They probably froze in position, shocked by seeing someone pointing a gun at them. *Did they recognize him?* When the young man turned to the door to escape, the intruder shot him in the back. The lack of exit wounds meant the killer used a 22 caliber, likely silenced, the favorite weapon of professional assassins. I noticed a bullet hole in the door frame where Rachael must have turned to run but stopped when the warning shot was fired. The intruder didn't want to kill her. He needed information, like computer and phone passwords, things he couldn't find when he ransacked the place. After she failed to provide what he wanted, he started working on her knees until she talked. The final shot through the eye ended her misery.

I was about to leave when I realized the perpetrator might not have disabled the cameras in the lobby. If not, they would have recorded me entering. I couldn't take a chance on leaving now because I would become a prime suspect. I was in a sticky situation and I had two options—both bad. I could leave hoping my presence wasn't documented on camera, or I could stay and try to bluff my way out of things.

I called the police.

While I waited, I called Cassie to let her know what had happened and that she'd probably be receiving a call to confirm that I was with the Naples Police Department investigating the murder of Savannah Wellington.

"Good God, Lisa. What have you gotten yourself into now?"

I explained briefly. "I'm up to my neck in alligators here, Cassie, and I need you to bail me out. I'll fill you in on the drive home." That was if the police were inclined to let me leave.

When the Tallahassee police arrived, I had to do some serious selling. I explained what had happened. Since I didn't have a detective's shield, I referred them to Detective Cassandra

Pierce in Naples. Much to my relief, she confirmed my status. I owed her. Within the hour, a homicide detective and full forensics team arrived. I pulled the detective aside and relayed why I was there and my take on the situation. He agreed. The target was Rachael Morris and the boyfriend had simply been in the wrong place at the wrong time. "Poor sap looks like he was another Ron Goldman when O.J. murdered his wife, Nicole."

One of the crime scene techs said, "She had a damn sophisticated security system. Only someone who knew what they were doing could bypass it without triggering an alarm."

"What about all the surveillance cameras she had in here? Did they record anything?" I hoped I was right in assuming they'd been disabled.

"Looks like the perp created a loop so there's nothing on them except a recording of empty rooms from before the entry," said the tech. "We can check the lobby cameras, but I suspect they've also been looped." Using latex gloves, he picked up Rachael's purse and searched it. "Her phone's missing. We could put a tracer on it."

The detective said, "Give it a try, but based upon the way the bodies look, they've been dead at least twelve hours. The killer probably already downloaded everything he wanted and destroyed it." He scanned the room. "No shell casings. The perp was a pro and smart enough to pick them up. We can dig that bullet out of the door frame and check it for ballistics. Other than that, and the slugs we retrieve from the bodies, I doubt this guy left any other evidence behind. Sweep the place for prints and DNA anyway."

He looked at me. "Do we need to print you for exclusions?"

That would have created a major problem for me since I wouldn't be found in any databases. Winston Hamilton had any history of his team members erased years ago. "No, I didn't touch anything." The detective accepted my word, and I quietly exhaled in relief. I watched as he called the coroner.

"What do think those pentagrams are about," I asked

"Done with a knife from the kitchen. There's no blood around the wounds so the cuts were made post-mortem. I think they were added as an afterthought to give the impression of a serial killer. I'm not buying into it. The killer probably used the symbols to send us on a wild goose chase, looking for a Night Stalker wannabe. Can't tell for sure, but we'll have to waste a lot of man hours checking into the possibility."

I gave him an official statement and hoped he wouldn't look further into my background. Then, I thanked him for his time and let him know how to get ahold of me or Detective Pierce in Naples if he needed more information.

An hour south of Tallahassee, I called Cassie and filled her in on what had happened.

"This isn't some simple murder investigation anymore, Lisa."

"I know. Four people are dead: Savannah, that Torbeson guy, and now, Rachael and her boyfriend. "

"The common denominator on the first two seems to be that TBA organization, but I don't see how Rachael Morris fits in," said Cassie. "The circumstances of her death are different. Hers was an obvious execution, made to look like the work of a serial killer. Why not make it look like another accident?

The killer must have been in a hurry and didn't have the time to plan everything. He needed to get his hands on whatever information was stored on Rachael's computer and cell phone. He wanted to erase the records before anyone else got access to them."

Cassie said nothing for several long seconds. "You say she had an alarm system?"

"Yes, but it was bypassed," I said.

"Do you have a name for the security company that installed it?"

"Just a minute. I took some photographs of her place." I pulled down an exit ramp so I could stop and check my camera's photo files. "It's called Guardian Security."

"Is there a name on it?"

"Someone signed it, but I can't make out his name. Looks like the first letter might be an S. I do have a phone number for the company. Why?"

"Savannah's husband told me he believed she might have been having an affair with a security expert. The guy put a system in their home and her office. His name was Spyder."

I enlarged the photo. "That's it." I thought for several seconds. "Push him to see if he has an alibi for last night. Find out where he was on the July Fourth weekend. Maybe get a DNA sample to see if he's the baby's father." I was about to head back onto I-75 but stopped. "He doesn't have any connection to Torbeson, though. We still need to check into that TBA Organization."

"I already spoke to a Jeremy there, but I'll call back again and rattle his cage. Something might shake out. What about you?"

"I have an idea I need to pursue."

"It's not going to be one of your little illegal escapades again, is it?"

"Moi? Of course not."

It was another six-hour drive home, and the sun was settling lower in the sky. I wouldn't get to Naples until late. I missed the days when I could fly on Winston Hamilton's private jet for missions. No ID requirement and no waiting in line to board, and none of those damn COVID masks. Speaking of Mr. Hamilton, I needed to call him. I checked my watch. It was past eight and he'd be out of the office. I'd try in the morning. My mind drifted to my brother, and my friends on Mr. Hamilton's team and all we had accomplished. Then I thought of John and the way we used to be. The good memories made the rest of the drive more tolerable.

TWENTY-SEVEN

Ishmael's Home
Lakeside Park, Kentucky

I shmael used a Dremel saw to expose the inner workings of an insulin autoinjector. His first attempts destroyed three of the devices. It was simply a matter of sawing along the correct seams which allowed safe removal of the injector mechanism. He extracted the medication from its small class containment cylinder and replaced it with the oil by inserting a tiny tuberculin syringe into the rubber end cap. The greatest challenge he faced was the rate of injection. The normal cylinder took almost three seconds. He only needed several drops, but the oil was three times more viscous than insulin, resulting in an unacceptably long injection time. He'd have a second at the most to complete his task. He couldn't increase the gauge of the needle for fear it might cause a noticeable deformity at the site of penetration. His solution consisted of adjusting the spring coils to increase the force and speed of the injection. That cut the delivery time to a half second. *Perfect.* The entire system fit nicely into a widebody BIC pen, though it did rattle around a little too much. *Might attract attention.* He solved that problem with some clear silicone caulk to stabilize everything. If discovered, his device looked no more threatening than a ballpoint pen.

Satisfied with his creation, Ishmael stood, stretched his back, and climbed the steps to his bedroom for some much-needed rest.

A cell phone rang, the sound coming from his top nightstand drawer. *Not good.* Fedallah had given him the phone when they first started doing business together; to be used only for emergencies. It contained Threema, a protective app that provided end to end encrypted conversation ability. No third party, including servers, the FBI, or Homeland Security could decrypt or eavesdrop on content of messages or calls. This was the first time the phone ever rang. He entered his eight-digit randomly generated ID number, and pressed the answer button.

Fedallah's voice sounded mechanical. "Delay the upcoming acquisition for several weeks. The situation has changed."

"Why?"

"The buyer has another property he's interested in, and we must make an offer this week. Further information will be forthcoming. Use the same protocols. You will be compensated for the extra work."

The call disconnected. *Delayed? They want a new contract executed this week?* No time to prepare. You can't put an artist on a deadline. *Did the Pope tell Michelangelo to finish painting the Sistine Chapel in a month? Of course not. It's a ridiculous proposition.*

Ishmael opened his computer, and a series of numbers flashed across the screen. He picked up his copy of Moby Dick, decoded the message, and sat back after reading the name. *Who is this?* He Googled the individual. The information was sparse. *A nobody. This week? Why the urgency?* He had no time for proper reconnaissance and the necessary planning to make it look like another accidental death. The contract would have to be up close and personal. Knife? Gun? Messy options that increased the risk of exposure by leaving behind trace evidence. Such an obvious hit would draw the attention of law enforcement and might eventually lead them toward the Client. It made no sense, but the compensation softened his disappointment. Five million dollars for the inconvenience, a great deal of money for a nobody. Acceptance was a forgone conclusion. The Client hadn't offered the contract. It was a command that couldn't be rejected—not if he wanted to live long enough to enjoy his retirement in France.

After several hours of searching for some area of vulnerability, he found it. He could do the kill within the necessary time frame and still make it look like an unfortunate accident. No problem. Afterwards he'd refocus his talents on the governor, number thirteen. He made a note to stop at the store and buy a dozen Red Bulls. It was a long drive to Florida.

176

TWENTY-EIGHT

CIA Headquarters
Langley, Virginia

The screen on Winston Hamilton's computer flashed an interdepartmental memo. Antifa and other radical extremists were in their fourth week of rioting in Portland and Detroit. No surprise. Rather than being against fascism, the group embraced the fascist strategies of Hitler's Sturmabteilung, a paramilitary group used for violent suppression of free speech. With a wink and a nod, too many current politicians have given tacit approval of the group's activities. *The team can do it. They could infiltrate Antifa and cripple them. Time to call Jacob Savich back from France. Wedding or no wedding, we need him now.*

His secretary, Jeanine, walked in with a fresh cup of coffee and set a notebook on his desk. He looked up and raised his eyebrows. "What's this?"

"It's that report you requested on the Take Back America organization."

He lifted it in his right hand. "Heavy."

"Fifty-seven pages, sir, back and front. I told them to be thorough."

He leafed through the manuscript. "This'll take me hours to review. Is there an executive summary?"

Jeanine smiled, a glint in her eye. "There wasn't, but I typed one up for you last night. It's the first page."

"Excellent as always, Jeanine."

She put both hands on her slender hips and smirked. "Nice words but they'd be better if they came with a pay raise."

He sipped his coffee and gave his standard response. "You know it's out of my hands. Salaries are determined by the standardized government tables." Winston knew she was kidding. Every Christmas, he gave her a hefty bonus, one that more than matched her annual salary, one he paid personally. After she left the room, he lit up a cigar, and leaned back in his chair while reading the report.

"Article V in the United States Constitution, provides two processes whereby the Constitution can be altered: by Congress, or by a convention of the States. For the latter, two-thirds of the state legislatures must pass a resolution calling for the convention. At such a convention, amendments to the constitution can be proposed and, if ratified by three fourths of the individual state legislatures, they become law.

"The dilemma is that there is nothing written to limit a constitutional convention to specified proposed amendments. Many legal scholars believe that such a convention could open a Pandora's box, creating a runaway convention leaving the most cherished sections of the constitution, like the First and Second Amendments, vulnerable to attack. For this reason, there has been strong opposition to a convention from both sides of the political aisle. In 2015, an attempt was made to call for such a convention of the states, but fell short due to a lack of interest and funding. Three years ago, the movement was resurrected through the efforts of Mr. Scott Matheson and the financial backing of Mrs. Gloria Rutherford, a wealthy widow from Ohio. They formed an organization called Take Back America with offices on Connecticut

Avenue in DC. The group claims to be on the brink of getting enough states to sign on, but they are running short on the cash needed to finish the job."

Winston signaled for Jeanine to come in.

She stuck her head around the door jamb, and asked, "Need more coffee?"

"That would be nice, but first, I want you to contact Jason Hartley and have him send a million dollars to the Take Back America organization, care of a Mr. Scott Matheson. Tell them that if I see significant progress, I'll increase it to fifty million."

"Yes, sir." She returned to her desk just as her phone rang. A few seconds later, she said, "You have a call on line three. It's Lisa Savich."

Winston almost knocked over his coffee cup reaching for the phone. He hadn't heard from her since she retired from the team. She was sorely missed. "Lisa? What a pleasure to hear from you. It's been a while."

"Just over three years, Mr. Hamilton."

"Far too long, my dear. We've all missed you." He took a puff from his cigar. "Well, how are you and John doing? I imagine he's pretty busy at the Bureau."

There was an uncomfortable silence on the other end before Lisa responded. "Probably so, but I can't say for sure right now. I haven't seen him in over a month. We're separated."

Winston lowered his voice. "I'm so sorry to hear, Lisa." He looked at the photograph of his estranged wife and two boys. "I understand all too well how the rigors of life in Washington can impact one's personal life. How are you doing? Personally, I mean."

"Trying to work through it."

"Well, I don't know what I can do, but if you need anything, please let me know."

"That's why I called. First of all, is this a secure line?"

"All my phones are secure, but that doesn't mean they're the same on your end. Why the caution?"

"I'd rather not say right now. How's Norman doing?" Norman Deets was the team's IT expert and was responsible for much of their success over the years.

"He's moved into my home in Washington. He has his own computer lab with all the most sophisticated equipment available. Unfortunately, his muscular dystrophy has worsened and he's been confined to a wheelchair. I hired a full-time physical therapist who works with him daily in the hopes he can get back to using his crutches. I'm not optimistic."

"I'm so sorry to hear. I should have stayed in touch with him."

"He seems happy as long as he has access to the internet." Winston relit his cigar. "Why do you ask about him?"

"I wanted your permission to talk to him about a special project I'm working on."

"You don't need my permission to speak to him, Lisa. I'm sure he'd look forward to hearing from you." He gave Lisa the phone number. "Maybe you can explain what's going on."

"Someday, but not yet. Thank you, Mr. Hamilton. I'll fill you in later."

Winston took a long puff from his cigar and exhaled to the ceiling. *What the heck was that all about? I pity whoever's in her crosshairs. The girl's relentless. Once she gets her teeth into something, there's no letting go.*

TWENTY-NINE

Return from Tallahassee

I reminisced for a second before making the call. Norman was a genius, a child prodigy who had been accepted into MIT at the age of fourteen. During his freshman year in college, he was arrested for hacking into several major bank credit card systems and deleting hundreds of millions of dollars-worth of balances. He got into the most trouble when he penetrated the data banks at the National Security Agency. It took them six months before they realized their systems had been compromised. Norman claimed he meant no harm. He just wanted to see if he could do it. The government decided to send a message to all future wannabe hackers. The result was a loss of Norman's scholarship to MIT and a ten-year jail sentence. Winston Hamilton decided the boy's mind was too valuable an asset to wither away behind bars. After some intense, behind-closed-doors negotiations, Winston had the boy released into his custody.

"Hello, Norman. It's Lisa."

"No way. You mean, the Lisa? The former bad-ass-from-the-team, Lisa?"

I'd last spoken to him in Paris where we'd destroyed a major terrorist cell. His voice was deeper now, more mature, something to be expected after three years, though he still talked like a kid. "What's going on?"

"Before we speak, is your line secure?"

"Afraid someone's listening in?"

"Never can be too careful, Norman. Someone's always listening."

"All my systems are secure, but I doubt your phone is. Hold on a second." I heard him typing on a keypad and then a static humming filled my phone.

"Okay. We're good. I just scrambled your transmission so it's encrypted. It'll take eavesdroppers a year to decode. Not even Homeland Security can hear us. Now, what's up."

"I have a project for you if you're interested."

"Hell yeah, I'm interested. Not much has been happening since we killed the Scorpion. I'm tired of playing video games. I've updated my Looking Glass program, but Mr. Hamilton won't let me do any hacking with it. Been so bored I've been trying to prove the Reimann Hypothesis."

"Reimann what?"

"It's a classic mathematical problem people have been trying to solve for over a hundred years. Someone postulated a solution in 2016, but it didn't stand up to scrutiny. A million-dollar prize is at stake. Had to familiarize myself with theoretical mathematics first, but I might be close to solving it." He lowered his voice. "Got to keep a little quiet. Mr. Hamilton's chauffeur, Kingsley just came in. Trying to teach me chess, but I suck at it. B-o-r-i-n-g. Once he leaves, I'm going to have a go at the FBI and Homeland Security systems."

"Jesus, Norman. Don't get caught. They'll send you back to jail."

"It'll never happen, especially with my new Looking Glass program." He paused for a few seconds to tell Kingsley he needed some alone time. Said it was a private conversation with a girl. After a few seconds he returned to the phone. "So, what do you want?"

"It's a little complicated. I need to find out how many state and national politicians have died over the past three years. I'm mostly interested in sudden, unexpected deaths like from accidents or acute illnesses. Can you do that?"

"Sure, I can, but it'll take a while. I doubt there's any central record of such information, so I'll have to draw from a multitude of sources in each state, maybe even every legislative district. There must be thousands of files to review."

"I was hoping to get the information in a few days."

"Few days? That'll be a challenge. If you give me an idea as to what's going on, maybe I can streamline the search."

"Okay. I'm looking for deaths of any individuals who might have had some affiliation with a Florida state congresswoman."

"Name?"

"Savannah Wellington."

"Sounds radical. This'll be fun. I can hack into Mrs. Wellington's personal computers at home and work. Hopefully, they can lead me in the right direction."

"That might be a problem," I said. "Mrs. Wellington is dead."

"Makes no difference. I can still access her systems."

"You might start with the death of her assistant, Rachael Morris. She was murdered and the killer stole her computer."

"This is getting a little hairy, but I'll see what I can uncover. I can even search the FBI's systems to see if they have anything."

"Hold on, Norman. The Bureau and any other governmental agencies are off limits."

"Got it, but I might wander into some off-limits systems — purely by accident, of course."

I could almost see him grinning. "Just one more thing."

"Sure."

"See if you can find any recent homicides where pentagrams were carved into the victim's forehead."

Norman exhaled through the phone. "You mean like the Night Stalker? Richard Ramirez died in prison a decade ago."

"I know, but I'm looking to see if there might be a copycat killer. Maybe someone he spent time with in prison."

"You're investigating serial killers now? Better be careful Lisa. I'll call when I have something."

I mulled the case over in my mind, afraid I might be missing something and headed off on a wild goose chase. There had to be a connection between Savannah's murder and the deaths of Torbeson and Rachael. Savannah's pregnancy was hard to ignore, but I couldn't tie it in with the other two. I still wasn't convinced of Brad Stapleton's innocence, but he had no clear motive to kill Savannah and had no ties to the other two. I remembered sitting in Preston Wellington's office and looking at the photograph of his wife standing next to Governor Cartwright of Florida. He was too chummy with Savannah, his hand a little too close to her ass. It was a long shot, but I decided to check it out. I picked up my cell phone.

Winston Hamilton answered at once. "Lisa? No contact in over three years and now a second call within the hour. Do you miss me? Want to rejoin the team? We'd love to have you back."

"A tempting offer, Mr. Hamilton, but I wanted to see if you have any contacts with Governor Cartwright."

"From Florida? Certainly. I've been a major contributor to his last several campaigns. Cartwright's been a favorite amongst his party's conservatives. I think he has aspirations to be president after Jack Wagner finishes his second term. Why do you ask?"

"Is there any way you could arrange for me to meet him? Without it looking too contrived?"

"Exactly what are you up to, Lisa?"

"Can't say just yet."

"Does this have something to do with needing to talk to Norman?"

"In a way. Can you help me?"

Winston called out to his secretary. "Jeanine when is that fund raiser for Governor Cartwright?" I couldn't hear her reply, but Winston said, "Really? That soon?" He got back on the phone with me. "Looks like the Governor is having a fundraiser dinner this Saturday in Naples. I can get you a ticket if you want. Is that convenient enough for you?"

"Very. Where's it being held?"

"At the Ritz-Carlton. I'm sure he'd be more than happy to welcome my personal representative, especially if she's carrying a check from me for fifty-thousand dollars."

"That's a lot of money, Mr. Hamilton. I don't need to see him that badly."

"I was going to send him the money anyway. It's a formal dinner. You'll need a nice dress. Can you get one in time?"

"In Naples? Never a problem. Thank you, Mr. Hamilton."

"If you ever decide to rejoin the team, let me know. I'll make it happen. Good luck, Lisa."

After disconnecting the call, I punched in Cassie's number. "Do you have a dress? We're going to a fundraiser for Governor Cartwright."

THIRTY

Ritz-Carlton Hotel
Naples, Florida

Early Saturday evening, I picked Cassie up in front of her condo in Pelican Village, a small, gated complex north of the city. I waited for ten minutes before she opened the passenger door.

"Sorry I'm late. Checked my blood sugar, and it was high. Had to give myself an extra dose of insulin to cover this dinner." She looked stunning in an off-the-shoulder ruffled black gown and strappy black heels. I was never one to second guess the way I looked, but it was hard to feel adequate, knowing I'd be standing next to her all night. I chuckled at the thought of the men who would be tripping all over each other vying for her attention. *Sorry boys. She's not interested.*

She looked up at her condo and turned to me. "Damn, I forgot to leave the hall light on."

"You want to head back upstairs to take care of it?"

"No, we're late enough as it is." She fastened her seatbelt. "And why exactly are we going to a fundraiser for Governor Cartwright?"

I exited through the security gate. "He's been too close and a little too handsy with Savannah over the years. We need to find out if he could be the father of her baby, though

I seriously doubt it. He goes to church every Sunday and is happily married with a bunch of kids."

"He has a penis, doesn't he?"

I chuckled. "I assume so, if he really fathered all those children."

"If he has a penis, he can have an affair, married or not." Cassie stared through the windshield at the oncoming traffic. "You've probably never had someone cheat on you."

I turned to her. "No." The question sent a sting of pain through my conscience. John would never have an affair even though I abandoned him.

"Betrayal by someone you trusted down to the soul of your being is something that affects you forever. Anybody can do it, even a governor."

"I realize that, and it's why I want to check him out. We need a sample of his DNA."

"DNA? And exactly how are we going to do that?" asked Cassie. "Walk up and say, 'Excuse me, Governor, but we suspect you've been diddling Savannah Wellington and fathered her illegitimate baby. We'd like a sample of your DNA to prove it. You don't mind, do you?' I'm sure that'll go over well."

I outlined my plan which wasn't much of a plan. We'd be improvising most of the evening.

The Ritz-Carlton sat in the middle of the Tiberon Resort, north of Naples. I pulled into the entrance, garnished with a fountain as large as most people's homes. I continued around the fountain and drove up a slight elevation on an avenue bordered on both sides by stately royal palm trees. At the end, the Ritz stood, as luxurious as I expected. A line of cars backed up from under the large portico as drivers waited for the valet service. Cassie said, "I don't think I've ever seen so many Porsches, Bentleys, Ferraris, and limousines in one place."

"I know. My little KIA looks out of place. It's a bit like wearing flip flops to the Academy Awards." A young man in a white jacket took my car keys and my KIA disappeared around a corner. Probably hid it in the back where no one could see it.

We entered the ballroom together. It was as grand as anything I'd ever seen, even in DC. Multiple crystal chandeliers hung from the high ceiling, and the room featured ornate silk wall coverings with mirrored backdrops. At least five hundred of southwest Florida's most wealthy and influential citizens mingled about, all dressed in formal attire. At a minimum of ten-thousand dollars a plate, it would constitute a sizable haul for Governor Cartwright's campaign coffers.

"Wow," said Cassie.

Trying to move my lips as little as possible, I said, "For a woman as stunning as you, all this is well within your grasp — if you play your cards right." I winked at her. "Of course, you'd have to pretend to be straight."

"No thank you. That's not me."

All eyes — even those accompanied by spouses — fell upon Cassie. No surprise. At six feet in heels, she was impossible to ignore. We waited in the reception line to meet the governor. He was tall, tan, and fit, with an engaging Hollywood smile, the perfect political candidate for any office. I introduced myself as Mrs. Lisa Crawford. He shook my hand for a brief moment and was about to turn to greet the next individual in line. His assistant leaned over and whispered in his ear. He must have said something about the check I'd just handed him. Governor Cartwright ignored the next person and placed both his hands over mine. "Mrs. Crawford. What an absolute pleasure it is to meet you. I understand you're with Winston Hamilton."

"Yes. A wonderful man, and a fan of yours." I waved Cassie over to me. "And this is my good friend, Cassandra Pierce."

The governor's mouth opened, but he remained speechless for several seconds, unusual for a politician. "And what a delight it is to meet you, Mrs. Pierce."

Cassie smiled. "It's Miss."

That did it. She had him hooked and dominated his time for the next thirty minutes. For all practical purposes, the rest of the reception line faded into insignificance. I became little more than a potted plant in the corner. He was looking more like a man who could have had an affair with Savannah and fathered her child.

A waiter in a black jacket stopped by with a tray of red wine and offered us a glass.

Cassie tipped hers against the governor's. "To your successful re-election, Bill." They each took a sip.

Oh, it's Bill now? I was surprised she didn't say successful erection by the look in his eyes. They sipped their wine. That was my cue. I tripped and fell against him, knocking the glass out of his hand and spilling my red wine all over his tuxedo. His glass shattered when it hit the floor.

"Oh, my God. I'm so sorry, Governor."

Cassie used a napkin to wipe off the front of his tux while I scrambled to pick the pieces of broken glass from the floor.

"That's not necessary, Mrs. Crawford. The staff will get it."

"No, Governor," I said. "It's my fault, and I'll clean it up." I noticed he didn't bother to tell Cassie to stop cleaning the front of his tux. I picked up the most important pieces of his wine glass and wrapped them in the napkin I'd been using. Then, I dashed off to the ladies' room to hide them in my purse. When I returned, embarrassed at having spilt some wine on my dress, I excused myself for the evening. Much to the governor's clear disappointment, Cassie left with me. We scrambled away like Cinderella running from the ball, except Cassie didn't lose her shoe on the way out.

"Do you think he's onto us?" asked Cassie.

"Are you kidding? Did you see the look in his eyes when you were wiping the wine off the front of his pants? He looked like his brain cells shorted out. I doubt he could even tell what day of the week it was." We laughed so hard I could barely drive down the Tiberon exit.

Cassie said, "I haven't had this much fun since a bunch of us girls snuck a case of beer into the local drive-in movie in high school."

After a couple miles, I said, "Damn. A ten-thousand dollar a plate dinner, and I didn't get so much as an appetizer."

"Me neither," said Cassie. "I'm famished, and I don't want all that insulin to go to waste."

"There's a McDonald's straight ahead on the right."

"Sounds perfect."

We each ordered a Big Mac, fries, and a Diet Coke. We were the only women in the place wearing formal gowns and heels, something that earned us a number of stares. Cassie bit into her burger. "Oh, my God. I forgot how good these things taste. It's better than sex."

"I can't remember," I said. We both laughed, garnering us more stares. We toasted with our Cokes. "To the simple pleasures in life."

"Ditto," she replied.

We ordered two more burgers to go and ate them in the car during our drive back to her condo.

"Did you get a chance to check into that Guardian Security company?" I asked.

"They look legit. I Googled the company and found they averaged a four-star rating. The only significant negative review came from an elderly couple in Port Royal, a high-end community just south of Naples. It seemed they had the most expensive security system installed in their thirteen-thousand square foot, waterfront mansion. Burglars had bypassed the alarms and stolen a million dollars' worth of the wife's jewelry."

"Same type of bypass used at Rachael's place. How about the owner, that Spyder guy?"

"Didn't speak to him personally, but I checked with his secretary. His name is Spyder Tomlinson, but he's not our man. He has a solid alibi. He was in Key West at the time of Savannah's murder."

"He could still be the father," I argued between bites of my Big Mac, the sauce running down my chin. I wiped it off with a napkin.

"Nope," said Cassie. "He was in the Keys with his boyfriend. Spyder is gay."

"According to his secretary, but you didn't confirm it with him?"

"Didn't need to. His alibi was airtight."

"Just the same, it's certainly suspicious, him being the one who installed the security systems for Savannah and then Rachael."

"I think it's Governor Cartwright."

I turned to face her. "What?"

"Did you see the way he was all over me? All I had to do was give him a little bit of an opening, and he jumped right in." She laughed. "Sorry. Bad choice of words."

"But every other man at the reception would have done the same."

"No, there was something creepy about him." Cassie stared straight forward, her eyes boring through the windshield, focusing on nothing. "Did you notice the way he had his hands groping all over Savannah's ass in that photograph? He had an affair with Savannah. I just know it. Then he got her pregnant. He's the culprit. We should go after him."

"But don't you think we should wait for the DNA results first?"

"Makes no difference," she said. "Even if he's not the father, that wouldn't mean he's not responsible for her death. He's a man with political ambitions. His affair with Savannah would've destroyed his political career. She was probably blackmailing him. That explains why he was about to appoint her as a US Senator."

"A speaker of the house blackmailing the governor sounds pretty far-fetched, Cassie. You're making assumptions that aren't backed by any hard evidence. Just for the sake of argument, let's say he did. Why would he be involved in Rachael's murder?"

Cassie stopped before shoving a couple french-fries in her mouth. "She and Savannah were close friends. She had to have known about the affair. He probably killed Rachael after she threatened to expose him."

Sounded crazy to me. "What about the guy from Kansas, Senator Torbeson? Cartwright had no interaction with him."

"I don't know, but there must be something there," said Cassie. "Maybe we're too fixated on the Torbeson thing. Maybe his death was simply an accident after all."

Cassie was adamant about Governor Cartwright being the killer. We argued about the case until we pulled in front of her condo. We finished our burgers in the car.

Cassie burst out laughing. "I'll never forget the look on the governor's face when you spilled wine all over him."

"Not as funny as the look he had when you wiped it off the front of his pants. I think he'd be more than happy to invite you to his next fundraiser."

We laughed again until tears came to our eyes. Despite our disagreement about Cartwright, it was a fun night, one that cemented our friendship. Cassie unbuckled her seatbelt and looked up at her condo. "Oh, look. I left the hall light on after all."

I drove several miles before noticing the headlights behind me, close, but far enough away I couldn't tell the make of the car. *Not this again. Another stalker?* I prayed I was wrong. I turned onto Davis Boulevard, hoping the car would continue straight. It didn't. *Damn.* Was it the same guy as outside Buddy's Bar? I knew it couldn't be TOPDOC. He was in no condition to do much of anything. Brad was a moron, but was he that stupid? My heart pounded. Whoever it was, I didn't want him following me home.

I took a hard right onto Airport-Pulling Road.

The car followed.

I had to lose the guy. I ran a red light and pulled onto Tamiami Trail in the wrong direction. Probably gave dozens of senior citizens a heart attack. Then, it was a sudden left into a Walmart parking lot where I hid my car between two pickup trucks. I got out and crouched behind a dark van, my Sig in my right hand, loaded and cocked. *Control your breathing, Lisa.*

It looked like I lost him, but I waited another thirty minutes before returning to my car and heading home. I kept my eyes glued to the rearview mirror. When I got home, I slept with my loaded Sig under the pillow.

THIRTY-ONE

NCH Baker Hospital
Naples, Florida

I didn't sleep well, even with my gun nearby. I rolled out of bed and peeked through the window's plantation shutters, checking the street in all directions. No suspicious looking cars. I made coffee and scanned the emails on my laptop. A message from my brother, Jacob said he was getting married in Paris soon. I responded, "Great news. Raphael's a lovely lady and I know you'll both be happy together. When and where?"

I had several messages from John asking me how I was doing. "Fine," I replied. "Missing you, JC. Maybe we can get together and talk soon." When in public we referred to each other as Lisa or John. Privately, I called him JC for John Crawford, and he called me L for... well, that's obvious. I was telling the truth. I missed him terribly. A part of me wanted to tell him about the murders, but it didn't feel right. He might see it as a request for help, and I couldn't realistically ask him to help me after I hadn't been there for him for the past six weeks.

I spent an hour doing research on Florida Governor William Cartwright and came up with a blank. Nothing in his history suggested he was anything but a faithful husband and devoted father. He did fawn over Cassie at the fundraiser, but given the opportunity, every other man there would have done the same. She was remarkably stunning, but that didn't mean any of them would have acted inappropriately or agreed to a clandestine affair. Even I might have flirted with her if I were so inclined. I had reached a brick wall with nothing to do but wait on Governor Cartwright's DNA report.

Before jumping in the shower, I made the mistake of stepping on the scale. Shit. I'd gained ten pounds since arriving in Florida. Too much wining and dining in fine restaurants, an endemic problem in Naples. Of course, the two Big Macs and fries last night didn't help. I vowed to eat better and start running on a regular schedule again. I'd been neglecting my fitness program since finding Savannah. After dressing, I headed to the grocery to buy some healthy food. While in the produce department at Publix, my phone rang. I didn't recognize the number and assumed it was a SPAM call regarding the warranty on my car. I disconnected, but my phone rang again seconds later.

"Mrs. Lisa ... Marie ... Crawford?" Though her voice sounded urgent, the woman dwelt on each word as if reading my name from a paper.

"This is she. Who's calling?"

"This is the NCH Baker Hospital. We found your name and number in a patient's purse."

Chills ran down my spine. This couldn't be good. NCH was the same hospital where TOPDOC's wife had been admitted. Somehow, the bastard must have gotten to her. "What's this regarding?"

"A Miss Cassandra Pierce was admitted early this morning."

My heart dropped five inches in my chest. "Cassie? Oh, my God. What happened? Is she okay?" The words almost stuck in my throat. I feared the worst.

"Before I give you any information, are you related to Miss Pierce?"

My instincts told me to lie. "Yes, of course. She's my stepsister."

"Are there any other family relatives available?"

"Cassie and I are the only ones left. What happened to her?"

"She was involved in an auto accident early this morning. She's been in a coma ever since."

"I'll be there right away." I left my grocery cart where it was and raced to the hospital. The elderly receptionist in the lobby told me Cassie was in stable condition and presently in a monitored room. She gave me a temporary ID badge and directions. When I got to the floor, I spoke to one of the nurses. "What happened?"

"The doctors said she had a sudden hypoglycemic episode and lost consciousness while driving her car to work. She ran into a utility pole hard enough to knock it off its base. Destroyed the car."

"Oh my God. Is she okay?"

"Fortunately, the EMTs were nearby and stopped to help her. They noticed on her Medic Alert bracelet that she was a diabetic. A quick fingerstick blood glucose gave a reading of below 20."

The number meant nothing to me. "How bad is that?"

"Critical. They gave her a bolus of IV glucose which saved her life. She must have known what was happening because there were several empty candy wrappers on the passenger seat. Without those she might not have survived long enough for the EMTs to arrive."

She almost died? My mind raced. "Can I see her?"

"Not right now. She's still in a coma, so they ordered an MRI scan of her head. The doctor's with her down in radiology right now. Should return in about an hour."

There was nothing for me to do but wait. I was too agitated to sit, so I went down to the cafeteria. A display of pastries was tempting but the ten pounds loomed heavily over my head. I selected a cup of black coffee and low-cal, vanilla Greek yogurt instead and sat at a small table while I watched Fox News. I almost choked on a mouthful of my coffee when I saw a picture of Savannah filling the television screen. I'd never seen a close-up of her before, just Preston's small photograph of her standing next to Governor Cartwright on the state capitol steps. If I were prettier and had a hair stylist and makeup artist like her, I could almost pass as her sister. The caption under the photograph said, "In Memoriam, Savannah Wellington, Fox News contributor." Savannah was the quintessential Fox News girl: blonde, beautiful, and bright. I wondered if any of the station's executives could have been the father of her baby. Doubtful after what happened to Roger Ailes, but that didn't stop CNN's Chris Cuomo from grabbing his producer's ass or Don Lemon from grabbing some guy's crotch in a bar. Anything was possible. The list of potential suspects in Savannah's murder was growing exponentially.

I checked my watch. I'd only killed thirty minutes, so I headed to the first-floor gift shop. On a table near the entrance, I saw a display featuring some best-selling books. One of them was *Where the Crawdads Sing,* the story of a young girl abandoned in the lowland marshes of North Carolina. It reminded me of my own life in the Appalachian coal country of southeast Kentucky, where my family was killed when I was only five. I was almost an orphan, but at least I had my brother, Jacob to protect me. I bought *Crawdads* and three magazines.

Cassie was already back in her room by the time I returned. After fighting international terrorists for five years, I was accustomed to seeing the horrors of combat, but I wasn't ready for this. My beautiful friend lay unconscious in her bed, an IV line in each arm, an oxygen cannula in her nose, and a catheter hanging from the side of the bed. Her once-beautiful, dark complexion had faded to alabaster and her black hair was caked with dried blood. My legs buckled and I grabbed the edge of her bed railing so I wouldn't collapse.

The cardiac monitor mounted on the wall next to her bed recorded a strong, regular heartbeat, but when I held her hand, her skin felt cold and clammy. "Cassie, it's Lisa."

No response.

A different nurse walked into the room. She was older, her white uniform crisply starched, and her hair pulled back in a tight bun.

"Does she know I'm here?"

"Her blood sugar's been normal for several hours now, but she's still in a coma. The doctor said she suffered a brain contusion."

"Like a concussion?"

"Yes, but a little worse. The MRI scan showed bruising of her brain. That means blood. They don't know how much of the coma is attributable to the head injury and how much is from the severe hypoglycemia. Her blood sugar dropped to potentially fatal levels. The brain's neurons can't survive for long without glucose."

My head swung back and forth between the nurse and Cassie. I was afraid to take my eyes off my friend. "Do you think she'll recover?"

She rolled her eyes and clicked her tongue. "Completely? Who knows? Only time will tell, but I have to warn you, she's in pretty bad shape."

I didn't like this nurse. I had the uneasy feeling she was almost enjoying the conversation. "Shouldn't she be in the intensive care unit?" I asked.

She smiled, condescending, more of a horizontal smirk, like Nurse Ratched from the Cuckoo's Nest movie. "It's full of people with pneumonia on ventilators. This is a monitored floor so we can give her the best of care here." The nurse shifted her weight and looked out through the glass window separating Cassie's room from the nurses' desk. "I do need to discuss something with you."

I raised my eyebrows and waited.

"Does Miss Pierce have a living will?" She smirked again.

I glared into her eyes. "No, but I want to make one thing perfectly clear. There is to be none of that 'No Code' nonsense. You are to take any and all aggressive measures to insure her complete recovery. Do you understand?"

"Well, we always do what we can." The nurse huffed and retreated to the safety of the nurses' station and whispered something to the other nurses sitting nearby. They didn't like patients' families telling them what to do in their own little kingdom. I could only imagine what she said about me, but I didn't care. I would remain at Cassie's side full time to be sure she was being monitored properly. I sat in a chair next to her bed, my hand firmly holding hers, hoping she could feel my presence.

Nurse Ratched returned to inject something into one of Cassie's IV bottles. I didn't like or trust the woman. "What's that?"

She sighed deeply. "Hyperglycemia can be as lethal as the hypoglycemia she experienced. We put insulin into each IV to keep her blood sugar from getting too high. Is that all right with you?"

Sarcasm. I squeezed the edge of my chair to keep me from slapping that never-ending smirk off her face.

———————◆———————

The sun was setting outside, and the skies grew darker. The nursing shifts changed, and a fresh set of white uniforms arrived, younger and less rigid in their ways than Ratched. Cassie's new nurse came into the room, introduced herself, and asked, "Are there any other family members we should contact?"

"Just me," I said. She was a sweet girl who appeared to know her stuff. What a refreshing change. I told her I'd like to spend the night, and she said it was all right with her. She even brought in a blanket and pillow for me. I asked for a comb, a towel, and a bowl of warm soapy water. I draped the towel around Cassie's shoulders and spent the next two hours trying to comb the dried blood out of her hair. I found over a dozen staples in her scalp.

When finished, I sat in a chair and pushed a few loose strands of hair behind my ear. I read my new book and listened to Cassie's cardiac monitor, its regular beeping sound mesmerizing. Hypnotic.

I didn't know how long I slept, but it was still dark when I awoke to someone calling my name, weak and breathy. Cassie squeezed my hand. "Not an accident. Someone tried to kill me." Her head rolled to the side, and before she lapsed back into a coma, she whispered, "The Governor."

THIRTY-TWO

NCH Baker Hospital
Naples, Florida

I stretched my back and groaned. It's hard enough to sleep in a hospital chair, but Cassie's words ricocheted through my mind, keeping me awake. "Someone tried to kill me." Then she said the word "governor." Seemed preposterous, but the question remained. Who would try to kill a cop? Had to be someone powerful. Governor Cartwright would fit the bill, but he didn't strike me as someone capable of murder. Brad? Maybe he was afraid Cassie was getting too close to the truth about Savannah's murder, but there had been no prior connection between him and Savannah. Was the investigation of Savannah's death leading us to someone else? Another politician? Someone at TBA or Fox News? One thing was for sure. We'd shaken a hornet's nest and the game had changed dramatically.

Cassie opened her right eye, stole a glance around the room, and whispered, "Are they gone?"

I was shocked that she was awake and alert enough to ask about who might be eavesdropping. I checked the door. Nurse Ratched was at the nurses' station, reviewing charts. "We're alone for now. How long have you been awake?"

"Several hours now. I had to wait until we were alone before talking."

"I don't understand. Why do you think someone tried to kill you? It looked like you simply gave yourself too much insulin. What happened?"

"What happened to me was no more of an accident than what happened to Savannah or Torbeson."

Nurse Ratched came in to check the IV, and Cassie went back into her coma mode. After the nurse left, Cassie reopened her eyes. "I took my usual dose of insulin yesterday morning, just as I have done every day for the past twenty years. I made sure I ate breakfast so I wouldn't repeat what happened to me that afternoon at Seminole Park. While driving to work, I felt the symptoms of hypoglycemia developing, so I popped a couple pieces of candy in my mouth. The next thing I knew, I was in the hospital."

"So, what happened?" I whispered, keeping an eye on the door.

"Somebody must have tampered with my insulin vial. Remember when we were leaving for the governor's reception and I mentioned how I forgot to turn on the hall light? When we got back, the light was on. An intruder must have done it."

"That kind of rules out Governor Cartwright."

Cassie shook her head. "He figured out that we were after a sample of his DNA and sent someone to do it."

"That doesn't make any sense. The person who tampered with your insulin had to have done it while we were at the reception. Cartwright didn't even know we existed until then, and he had no time to set up something as complex as this."

Cassie stared at the ceiling. "I guess you're right."

I saw disappointment in her eyes and didn't understand why she was so convinced Cartwright was involved. "The only one who makes sense in this is Brad," I said.

"A possibility." Cassie repositioned her arm. "Anyway, I had to pretend to still be in a coma until you and I could talk."

"Once they find out you're still alive, they'll come back to finish the job."

"That's what I'm afraid of, but you can't remain here twenty-four hours a day to protect me."

"I'll do whatever's necessary, Cassie. In only a week, you've become my closest friend."

Nurse Ratched walked in, again with her forced smile. "Are you talking with someone?" she asked, her hands on her hips.

Cassie closed her eyes and resumed her coma act.

"Just reading to Cassie. I've done some research and found that reading to a comatose patient might help them recover. The belief is that on some level, they're still able to understand that a loved one is with them."

She huffed. "Whatever you think might help. You know what's best."

More of that damn smirking. *Sarcastic bitch.*

"What a peach," said Cassie after she left. "What should we do now?"

"One thing's for sure, you're still in danger, Cassie. I can't leave." I feared my presence might be the only thing keeping her alive. My mind raced as I searched for a plan. I needed help and knew only one place where I could get it. get it. I pulled out my cell phone and punched in the number.

"Winston Hamilton's office, Jeanine speaking."

"Hello Jeanine. Is he busy?"

"Never too busy to talk to you, Lisa. Hold on."

I heard her call out to Winston. They rarely used an intercom.

"Lisa, my dear." He always treated me like a daughter. "Another surprise call." He gave a snort. "You just made my morning. What can I do for you?"

I explained the situation and how someone tried to kill Cassie.

"Is this related to your recent conversations with Norman?"

"Probably."

"Sounds like you're in a dangerous predicament."

"Very. When the killer or killers find out they failed, they'll try again, and I won't be able to protect her on my own."

"There's something else to consider, Lisa. If someone wants your friend dead, they might have plans for you also."

The car that had been tailing me several nights ago after the governor's reception?

Winston asked, "Have you thought about asking John? I'm sure he'd help."

"He would, but after leaving him, I can't exactly run back when I need help. Besides, I don't have enough specifics about what's happening. I can't go to him with suspicions and sketchy circumstantial evidence. The only one who can help me is you, Mr. Hamilton." I explained what I needed.

"Say no more. I'll send one of the team members down to lend you a hand. I'm thinking of using Carla. I can fly her down on my jet."

"Is that the Carla who took my place?"

"Nobody can take your place, dear, but she's smart and almost as tough as you are. If there is an impending attempt on your friend's life, Carla will take care of it. No one will get past her."

"She'll need a nurse's uniform and maybe a Florida license."

"Not a problem. I'll have her at your side in less than four hours."

"There are several other things, Mr. Hamilton."

THIRTY-THREE

NCH Baker Hospital
Naples, Florida

By two that afternoon, Carla arrived wearing the traditional white nurse's uniform. I almost didn't recognize her with her new magenta-colored hair. Striking. Because of her diminutive size some have underestimated her abilities, a huge mistake on their part. She personally killed five terrorists and saved my life in Paris.

Carla was a warrior and one of only a few women accepted into the Army's grueling Special Forces training program. She excelled in all aspects of combat skills, creating an air of resentment with some of the male trainees. Her commanding officer tried to convince her to quit, saying combat was no place for a woman. When she refused, he decided to take her down a few pegs. He raped her. She went to the base commander to report the incident but they drummed her out of the military due to alleged "Psychiatric delusions." She only obtained justice by taking matters into her own hands. Her rapist spent the rest of his life as a eunuch.

"Thanks for coming, Carla."

She responded with a slight nod of her head. "Mr. Hamilton filled me in on your situation." She handed me a bag of things I'd requested from Winston. "You believe your friend's life is at risk?"

I checked before responding. Nurse Ratched sat at the nurses' station, completing more chart work. She looked up long enough to see me talking to the private duty nurse I had hired. She scowled at the magenta hair and I turned to face Carla, speaking softly. "Yes, someone or some group already tried to kill her yesterday, and if they find out she's still alive, they're bound to return to finish the job. They're professionals and very good at what they do."

Cassie opened one eye and winked. Carla noticed and smiled. "I understand. No harm will come to her. I guarantee it. I'm a professional also, and I'm better at what I do."

With that she set two duffel bags on a chair and looked at me.

I unzipped one and found a short-barreled, tactical shotgun.

"It has a shell in the chamber and sixteen in the magazine." She patted the other duffel. "I have one also. Like I said, no harm will come to your friend." She set one of the duffels on the floor, next to a chair.

"If anyone tries to mess with you at home, a few blasts from this puppy will warn them to back off." She tipped her fingers in a salute. "We take care of our own. Now get out of here and get some rest."

I slipped the bag over my shoulder and turned to leave. Carla handed me Cassie's purse. "Better take this with you. Wallets and valuables tend to disappear from hospitals."

I left the hospital confident Cassie was in good hands for now, but Carla couldn't remain at Cassie's side indefinitely either. I needed a plan to get her to a safe place.

On the drive back to my condo, I couldn't shake the feeling someone was following me again. No surprise after all that had happened over the past several days. My eyes remained glued on my rearview mirror but didn't see anyone. I was probably being excessively paranoid, but as my brother always told me, "A little paranoia is a good thing. Keeps you on your toes, ready for the unexpected while you hope for the best-case scenario." To be on the safe side, I took evasive maneuvers, and arrived at my home an hour later, exhausted.

No time for rest yet. During the drive, I came up with a plan. The chances for success were slim, but it was the best I could come up with. I made my first call.

A woman answered. "Collier County Coroner's Office. How may I help you?"

"I need to speak to Dr. Deutschle. It's urgent," I said.

"I'm afraid he's in the middle of an autopsy," she replied. "He won't be available until tomorrow afternoon at the earliest."

Too late for me. "Tell Dr. Deutschle it's about Cassandra Pierce. I know he'll want to talk to me."

A minute later, he picked up the phone and spoke in a heavy German accent. "This is Fred Deutschle. You're calling about Cassie?" Before I could respond, he fumbled the phone. I heard him say, "No. Weigh the heart first, and then open the coronary arteries to see how much plaque he had." He returned his attention to me. "I'm sorry. New autopsy tech. Now what about Cassie?"

"My name is Lisa Crawford, and I'm a close friend of hers. We need your help." I explained the situation and he agreed to do whatever was necessary.

The next call was to Mr. Hamilton. I told him about my plan and what I needed.

"Are you sure about this, Lisa? If John gets wind of what you're doing, he'll —"

I interrupted, "He's not going to find out."

He chuckled. "Figures. Always the hard way. When there's an explosion, most people run in the other direction. You and your brother always feel compelled to run toward it, but you'll be putting yourself in serious danger this time."

"And when have I not been in danger while on the team?"

"Touché. I'll do whatever you need. I only hope you know what you're doing. Keep your eyes open and stay safe."

Thank you, Mr. Hamilton. I owe you—in more ways than one."

Everything was falling into place. My most difficult call was to the Naples Courier Journal. I needed to talk to Madeline Carmichael, the reporter I'd been impersonating for the past week.

THIRTY-FOUR

NCH Baker Hospital
Naples, Florida

I hadn't slept in over thirty-six hours and was exhausted. After completing my calls and eating an apple, I took a four-hour nap before heading back to the hospital. When I returned, I noticed the smell, a combination of alcohol and death. I always hated hospitals. They were home to the deadliest germs and the place where people went to die. *Not Cassie. Not on my watch.*

When I returned to the floor, I was met with the symphonic sounds of cardiac monitors, all chiming in different pitches and rates, some noticeably irregular. The lights were low, and a different shift of nurses was working. Nurse Ratched was gone for the day. Good.

Carla sat, alert, in the same chair where I had left her, the duffel back with her equipment at her side. She gave me a subtle thumbs up. Cassie was still on the cardiac monitor, her heart beating strong and regular. I held her hand and she squeezed it twice, telling me she was still pulling off the fake coma. Unfortunately, the sweet nurse from the day before wasn't working.

Cassie's nurse that evening was even younger. She had a personality that said she wanted to please, her eyes as innocent as a newborn fawn's. I pulled her aside for a little chat. As I spun my story, those eyes widened in disbelief at a world she believed only existed in the movies, the dark side of reality. I flashed a fake badge provided by Winston and introduced myself as FBI Special Agent Lisa Marie Crawford. "The patient who you know as Cassandra Pierce does not exist. For the past five years, she has been the girlfriend of a prominent Chicago mob boss, and knows everything about his illicit business transactions from drug distribution to human trafficking. More importantly, she knows where all the bodies are buried and who ordered the hits. She's agreed to testify against him in court."

The poor nurse turned as pale as her uniform.

"Obviously, this mobster can't allow her to make it to court. He placed a ten-million-dollar bounty on her head. They missed a few days ago, but they'll be back. They won't stop until she's dead. That's why she's in protective custody as we speak. It's my job to see that she makes it out of this hospital alive."

I'd become alarmingly adept at lying, and John would be shocked to see this side of me. He never lied, no matter the situation, one of the many reasons I fell in love with him.

The nurse trembled as I pulled her closer and whispered, "You're going to see some strange things happening here in the next few hours, events that might shock you. You'll be tempted to call security, but I need you to follow my directions to the letter. This woman's life is in your hands. Do you understand?"

She gave a vigorous nod. Nothing was more important to a nurse than saving a life. It's the reason most entered the profession in the first place. By the time I finished the story, I could tell she was on board, but you never know for sure until the action starts. I handed her a sheet of paper to put in Cassie's chart. It was a "No Code" form.

I pulled up a chair and sat next to Carla. For the next hour, we waited for Dr. Deutschle to arrive. That's when Nurse Ratched walked into the nurses' station. What the hell was she doing there? She could ruin everything. She looked at me and flashed her usual smirk. I doubted she had any other facial expression.

"The hospital lawyers held a meeting tonight with the head nurses to discuss the new litigation prevention procedures being implemented next month. Thought I'd stop by to see how everything was going."

She spoke to my young nurse and whispered in her ear. *Damn. Stay cool, sweety. Don't spill the beans.* She smiled and nodded as Ratched spoke. When Ratched turned to leave, the young nurse gave me a thumbs up. We were still good. I exhaled slowly and checked Carla. She was unfazed, her hand positioned inside her duffel. I thought of the shotgun. Thank God, Ratched hadn't decided to come into the room to confront Carla. The encounter might have been messy.

Around eleven o'clock, a crescendo of new voices gathered around the nurse's station. Shit! I hadn't factored a change of shifts into my plans. My new doe-eyed friend disappeared through the door with a fantastic story she could tell her grandkids one day. Everything was turning sideways. Deutschle was due to arrive soon, and I didn't have the time to groom another nurse. I pinched the bridge of my nose, and came up with a backup plan.

I nodded to Carla. "Almost time." That was her cue to begin removing Cassie's IVs and the nasal oxygen.

A bearded man with a heavy German accent entered the unit, barking orders to those around him. He and his assistant wore official Collier County Coroner jackets. "Someone called the coroner's office?"

"What are you doing here?" one nurse asked.

This was about to get ugly fast. While Deutschle tried to bluff his way in, I picked up a bottle of rubbing alcohol from a cart and headed out into the hall toward the restroom. I stuffed a dozen paper towels into the stainless-steel trash can and poured in a little of the alcohol to get things started. Not too much. I wanted a diversion, not a full-fledged inferno. I ran toward the nurse's desk yelling, "Fire! My God, there's a fire!"

The ward clerk pushed a button, and a piercing alarm filled the hospital. "Code red, fifth floor transitional care."

One nurse grabbed a fire extinguisher and followed the smoke to its source. Others scurried about replacing wall oxygen with portable tanks and began moving patients.

Carla removed cardiac monitor leads from Cassie's chest signaling an absence of cardiac activity.

"Arrest in room three!" yelled one nurse.

"She's a no code," yelled another after checking the chart.

"Are you sure? No one mentioned it in the report."

"Yes, the family must have signed it earlier this evening. Keep moving the other patients."

Deutschle used his stethoscope and listened to Cassie's chest. "Yep, no heartbeat. She's definitely dead." He looked at the clock. "We'll call it 12:08 a.m." During the chaos, he and his assistant loaded Cassie's body onto the coroner's gurney and headed toward the elevator, joining the others in the fire evacuation. Carla threw her duffle bag over her shoulder and followed Deutschle.

On the way outside, a voice blared over the ceiling speakers. "Cancel code red."

Needed to hurry. Carla and I rushed ahead and escorted everyone to the ambulance bay. We helped Deutschle load Cassie into the Coroner's van which would transport her to the Naples Airport where Winston Hamilton's jet waited to fly her to Washington.

Just before placing Cassie on the plane, Dr. Deutschle handed me a manila envelope. "Would you give this to Cassie when she's better?"

It felt light. "What is it?"

"When I did the postmortem on Savannah Wellington, I found a small sliver of paper lodged in her skull fracture. I sent it to the state's forensic lab for identification. This is their final report. I included a copy of her official autopsy report."

"And?"

"It's in the report." He looked around. "I'd better get out of here before someone notices the coroner's van. I'll have enough explaining to do as it is."

He drove off just as Winston's Citation taxied toward the runway. At least Cassie was safe. On the drive back home, I took the usual counter-surveillance measures and got home later than I'd hoped. I crashed as soon as I hit the bed. I slept soundly with my Sig under my pillow and my new best friend, the tactical shotgun at my side, a round in the chamber, ready for action.

THIRTY-FIVE

Naples, Florida

I woke up late the following morning with my clothes still on, but at least I didn't have a hangover this time. I read the morning paper with my cup of coffee. The article by Madeline Carmichael was on the second page.

> **Homicide Detective Cassandra Pierce died last night due to severe brain injuries sustained in an auto accident. She had long suffered from complications related to diabetes mellitus. She came to Naples from Chicago ...**

I smiled. Maddie had done her job. I still had to deliver on my promise of a blockbuster scoop that would change her career. Problem was, I didn't have one for her yet.

As I sipped my coffee, I read the autopsy report Deutschle had handed me last night. He believed the attacker was around six feet tall and left-handed. Brad was at least four inches taller, but the report was a guestimate at best. I couldn't recall whether he was left-handed or not. Didn't pay attention, though he had used his left hand to crush mine against the bar at Buddy's. A second report was from the analysis of a paper fragment found in Savannah's head wound. It was a piece of a label, but they couldn't identify a specific product. The sample was too tiny and distorted by the victim's blood.

The autopsy report further described the weapon as cylindrical. Maybe a baseball bat? If the killer brought a bat to Seminole Park, it meant he had planned the murder in advance. Premeditated murder translated into a potential death sentence. He had nothing to lose and that might have explained the attempt on Cassie's life. Could I be next? Had to be cautious.

I hoped to resume my conditioning program, but by the time I stepped outside, the heat and humidity were already suffocating. So much for running. Maybe later in the evening, when it cooled off.

The only thing left for me to do was work on the case, but without Cassie and her police resources, how was I going to do that? *The same way you always do things, Lisa. Just start pulling on threads until something begins to unravel.*

Cassie hadn't interviewed Spyder Tomlinson from the Guardian Security Company. Her information came second hand from his secretary. I needed to talk to him in person, so I called the company to make arrangements to meet with Tomlinson that afternoon. I dressed in the same outfit I wore to Buddy's police bar, except this time, I traded the stilettos for a pair of sensible low business heels. Never knew when you might have to run again. Looking in the mirror, I hiked my skirt up a few inches. There's nothing as effective at loosening a man's tongue as showing a little leg. It had worked well with Spandex Brad.

I had time to drop off the wine glass fragments from Governor Cartwright at Dr. Deutschle's office for DNA retrieval. He asked how Cassie was doing and I reassured him she was safe.

He chuckled. "Tell her she still owes me a steak dinner at Texas Roadhouse."

"It might be a while, but I'm sure she'll remember." I advised him against any discussion regarding her situation with anyone. "It's essential that everyone thinks she's dead.

"Understood."

Dick's Sporting Goods was less than a mile from the Guardian Security office. I went to the counter, flashed my forged FBI badge and identified myself as an agent involved in a murder investigation, another of the many lies I hoped would never make their way back to John. The young man was eager to help and gave me a history of baseball bats. Aluminum bats were used in knot-hole leagues, high school, and college. The major leagues used wooden bats, prohibiting the use of aluminum because of what he called the "trampoline effect." A baseball exploded off the aluminum bat. It resulted in more power and hits for the batter, but created a dangerous situation for pitchers and infielders. That meant they were also probably more destructive when used to smash in someone's skull. He said it would be impossible to track down the purchase of a particular bat since they are sold by the thousands in hundreds of stores around the country every year. Another dead end, except the killer might have some association with baseball.

My next stop was the Guardian Security office on Industrial Boulevard. A tall, athletic man unlocked the door. He wore his long sandy-colored hair pulled back into a ponytail. A tight, black t-shirt stretched across his muscular chest and displayed a logo with the staggered letters G S over the left breast area. His green eyes looked directly into mine, his eyelashes black and long. Mascara? Cassie said he might be gay.

Confident, but cordial, he asked, "Miss Crawford?" His disarming boyish smile conveyed an image of pure innocence.

I flashed my badge. "That's Special Agent Crawford. I'm working with Detective Pierce."

He scrunched his eyebrows together in a confused look. "Pierce? That name doesn't ring a bell."

"She spoke to your secretary a few days ago." I reached into my purse and pretended to read from a small notebook. "You took a small trip to Key West recently? I believe it was the Fourth of July weekend."

"Oh, yeah. I was on a fishing trip with friends. We were shut out by the tropical storm."

"Can you give me the names of your friends?"

He dodged my question and pointed to the back of the store. "Let me show you to my office."

We walked past rows of display shelves offering a wide array of security merchandise from camera systems and alarms to cans of personal pepper spray, in a variety of colors, including pink for women. No guns. A combination of old dust and vague chemical smells hit my senses. His small office held a desk and only a single chair, worn and stained with black streaks. I sat in it anyway and crossed my legs, tastefully exposing some thigh. The guy didn't so much as steal a brief look. *Damn!* I once read that as a woman gets older, she becomes invisible to men — but I was only thirty-seven. *Must be gay.*

"Thank you for your time, Mr. Tomlinson."

"Just call me Spyder." Wide grin.

"Okay, Spyder, this shouldn't take long." I studied my blank notepad. "Before we start, have you ever played baseball?"

The question caught him off guard. He stammered for a second as if trying to process the significance of the question. "Well, of course. What young American boy hasn't?"

"How about in high school or college?"

"A little." He scrunched his brows together, creating furrows where there hadn't been any. "I'm sorry, but what does this have to do with why you're here?"

The baseball reference didn't seem to faze him. "We're investigating the death of Cassandra Pierce." I looked for a small change in his expression, anything that might suggest I made him uncomfortable. Nothing.

"Wait a minute. You said you worked with a Detective Pierce. Is she the same Pierce I read about in the paper this morning? The article said she died from diabetes."

I leaned toward him, trying to intimidate. "Yes, but the circumstances of her death are a little confusing." Still no sign of discomfort. "She was investigating the murder of Savannah Wellington." He blinked. He corrected the change in his expression, but I saw it. He recognized the name.

"She was also investigating the death of Savannah's assistant." I pretended to read from my notes. "A Miss Rachael Morris." More blinking. I'd definitely hit a nerve, so I pushed on it. "I understand your company provided security systems for both women."

He shifted in his chair. "Yes, we installed several systems for Mrs. Wellington in her home in Naples and a condo in Tallahassee. Must have been a few years ago. As I recall, she was a bigwig in the state capitol."

"Speaker of the House to be exact. How about Miss Morris?"

He tried to act nonchalant, but it wasn't working for him. His voice was unsteady. "She had one installed only last week."

"Anything irregular about the installation?"

"No. Just that she said it was urgent."

"Urgent. Hmm." I smoothed out my skirt, uncrossed my legs and recrossed them. Still no attention. "She's lived in Tallahassee for over ten years. Why now?"

"She sounded like she was afraid. Didn't give me any specifics."

His expression didn't change. Not even a blink. Needed to push harder. "Doesn't it strike you as being strange, two of your customers being murdered? Someone disabled Rachael's alarm system and cameras just prior to the crime. How could that happen?"

He crossed his arms. "Unfortunately, no system is perfect. A professional criminal with the necessary skills can bypass even the most sophisticated set up by looping the circuits and the camera image. Of course, they'd have to know what they were doing to avoid raising suspicions in the central monitor station."

"Has anything like this ever happened to any of your other customers?"

"Never. We pride ourselves in the quality of our installations." Perspiration beaded along his upper lip.

I stared into his eyes. "And yet, you failed at Rachael's home. Maybe it's happened before, and you aren't aware of it."

"Impossible."

"Like what happened at Rachael's was impossible?"

No reply.

"Did you happen to install an alarm for Detective Pierce?"

"Not that I recall. Hold on a second." He opened a laptop computer and scrolled for a minute. "No, she's not in our files." He closed the computer. "Why do you ask?"

"Someone might have disarmed hers. Who might have the skills necessary to circumvent your alarms?"

"As I said, professionals."

"What about the police?" I'm not sure why I asked the question, but it hit him like a jolt of electricity. Another rapid recovery, but I'd uncovered something. I pressed on. "Could they bypass your systems?"

His pupils dilated. "If a man is well-trained and determined to enter a home, nothing can stop him."

He didn't answer my question. "And was Miss Rachael Morris' system sophisticated?"

"Top of the line. She told me money was no object."

"Rachael's cameras had been disabled. Is that something you or one of your employees could do."

"I guess, but why would we do that? Unless you're accusing me of some criminal activity. If so, I want my lawyer here."

I raised my hands. "No, not at all. I'm simply trying to understand what happened." I made a fake entry into my blank notepad. "You mentioned a central monitoring system. Where is that located?"

"Here, in our office. When an alarm is triggered, the home owner is immediately notified and the police are automatically dispatched."

"Do your surveillance camera systems store any activities that occurred before the cameras were disabled?"

"Like catching Rachael's killer on tape?"

"Yes."

"Let me check." He opened his laptop, punched a few keys, and studied the screen. "Nothing unusual here. If someone entered her home, we would have an image of them. Her system had only been in place a few days and I had checked the cameras and alarm thoroughly before I left, so I'm positive they were working."

"Except they apparently weren't." I let the comment sink in. "What about Savannah Wellington's system? Could her security cameras have recorded home activities, and picked up the image of a suspect? Or have her systems malfunctioned like Rachael's?"

"We conduct random quality control reviews of all our customers' alarm and camera systems from time to time. Sometimes they go offline. If a unit is malfunctioning, we immediately replace it."

"Are those reviews conducted on site or peripherally from your office?"

"If a camera or alarm pad stops working, we schedule an appointment with the customer to replace it. Most often, we don't have to enter a customer's home. I can simply review their systems from here."

I was certain many of these security guys took a quick peek at their unsuspecting customers, especially beautiful ones like Savannah. I tried to look shocked and allowed my mouth to drop. "You violate their privacy?"

He raised his hands. "No. No. Not really. We always notify them by email a few days in advance, so we don't catch them at the wrong time."

"Like being undressed and such?"

"Yes, but sometimes customers forget or miss our email entirely."

Yeah, right. I stared, chewing over his story. Something was amiss. Bet he had an entire file of private videos on his computer. "Have you seen anything suspicious on Savannah's systems here in Naples or at her condo in Tallahassee?"

He shifted position in his chair. "I'm afraid I can't divulge anything private about our customers. It's privileged information." His jaw muscles fasciculated.

I was onto something and needed to bluff my way through it. Like Winston once told me. "Facts are irrelevant, my dear. What matters is the perception." I leaned forward in my chair and tapped on his desk with my finger. "This particular customer of yours is dead. I'm not some lowly gossip columnist looking to publish dirt in the local paper. I'm the FBI and this is a murder investigation. Two of the victims have a direct connection to you. Now, if you don't want a half dozen agents crawling through your office tomorrow morning, you'd better start talking. My people are exceptionally good at what they do, and they'll search every square inch of this place, beginning with the financial records and personal communications on your computer. Believe me, our forensics accountants always uncover interesting material, the kind you probably don't want anyone like the IRS or my agency to see."

Spyder fidgeted and looked down at his desk, weighing how much he should share. One thing was for sure, he didn't want anyone combing through his records. Why? A collection of private videos?

"Okay. There was an incident around six months ago. Savannah mustn't have read my email about checking her cameras. It was late morning, and she was sitting at a kitchen table enjoying coffee. That's when another person appeared."

This caught my attention. I leaned toward him. "She had a guest over for breakfast?"

"It didn't look that way to me. The individual was wearing a robe. They kissed."

I almost jumped out of my chair. Six months ago? It had to be around the time her baby was conceived. The visitor might have been her killer. "Are you telling me someone spent the night with her?"

"It appeared that way."

"Did you get a good look at his face?"

"No, just the back of the head. I can't even say for sure it was a man."

"Are you trying to tell me it might have been a woman?" I couldn't imagine Savannah being bisexual.

"No. All I'm saying is I couldn't tell anything about the person."

"Height? Weight? Anything that might help me?"

"Nothing besides the way they acted."

"Can I see a copy of the video?"

More shifting in his chair. "Sorry. I erased it as soon as I realized what was happening. This type of information could be ammunition for blackmail if it fell into the wrong hands. I wanted nothing to do with that. If word got out that I recorded personal situations, it would destroy my business."

Blackmail? A motive? I leaned back in my chair and looked at the ceiling. This guy was hiding something, but what? A bad feeling tickled at the back of my mind. I doubted he had erased

Savannah's video, and I needed to push more buttons. "Things erased are seldom gone forever, Mr. Tomlinson. My people at Quantico can review your hard drives and easily retrieve any videos you might have deleted."

The color drained from his face. Not so innocent looking any more. He checked his watch, stood, and opened the door. "I have an important meeting in a few minutes. I'm afraid we'll have to continue this conversation later. I can't turn over any more information without a warrant."

"I'll have one by tomorrow morning. Just be sure you don't try anything funny with your computers before then."

His eyes bore holes into mine. "I'd like to see that badge of yours again."

My act was wearing thin. Time to get out of there. "You can see it again tomorrow when I come back with a search warrant and my team of experts. Better make sure you and your computer are here, or I'll charge you with obstruction of justice." I stood and headed toward the front door. I rushed out of his office, my goal being the door I had entered an hour earlier. It seemed farther away than when I first arrived. I kept expecting a blow to the back of my head with a baseball bat. With each stride, the door seemed farther and farther away, like in one of those horror movies.

THIRTY-SIX

Coastland Mall
Naples, Florida

I walked out with as much confidence as I could muster, jumped in my car, and drove out of the lot. Fifty yards down the road, I pulled to the side, retrieved my Sig from my purse and set in on the passenger seat. I scrunched down, and watched the store through my rearview mirror.

Less than five minutes later, Spyder exited, clutching his laptop under his left arm and holding a cell phone tight against his right ear. The conversation looked animated. I must have rattled him hard. He fumbled with his keys, locked the front door, and hopped into a black Porsche Boxster. *Security business must be pretty good.* He revved the engine and turned right, his tires squealing away from my direction. Good. I completed a U-turn and followed a safe distance behind him. He took standard counter surveillance precautions similar to what I was trained to do while on the team.

He took a left onto Tamiami Trail. Not wanting to be seen, I risked turning onto a parallel street a block down and caught up with him a couple minutes later. When he turned into the Coastland Shopping Mall, I lost him for a few seconds but picked him up again just as he pulled into a parking garage opposite the Macy's department store.

Leaving my car fifty yards to the east, I approached the garage on foot, staying low, and using the parked cars for cover. The Porsche sat in the dark shadows of a far corner of the garage. Spyder remained inside. What was he doing? I found a position where I could keep an eye on him by looking through the tinted windows of a Ford SUV. A silver-gray Bronco pulled into the space next to him. A customer? A tall driver got out and scanned the area surrounding him. The image sucked the air out of my lungs for several seconds. Spandex Brad? What the hell? Apparently satisfied he wasn't under scrutiny, he climbed into Spyder's Porsche.

The men engaged in a heated discussion. After several minutes, Brad handed him a thick envelope. Spyder withdrew a great deal of money and started counting the cash. Brad pushed his hands down out of sight, and jerked his head to the right and left, looking to see if anyone was watching. Blackmail? Had Spyder seen Brad on one of his security cameras? Maybe with Savannah? This was the proof I wanted, some potential connection between her and Spandex Brad. I needed documentation of this meeting. I pulled my cell phone out of my purse to take a picture. No good. It was too dark in the garage and the tinting of the Ford's windows made taking a photo through them impossible. I stepped from behind the SUV for a clear shot, zoomed in, and pressed the button.

The camera flashed. Damn.

Both men snapped their heads in my direction. The look in their wide eyes said they recognized me. Brad jumped out of the car and ran toward me while Spyder peeled out in his car, probably to block my escape on the other side of the mall. I reached into my purse for my Sig. Shit. I'd left it on the car seat, and my car was too far away. I'd never make it. I was in trouble with few options.

I made a dash for the front door of the mall and into the side of Macy's, with Brad only a few hundred feet behind me. My eyes darted across the large store, searching for a place to hide. Nothing. I was cornered in there. I raced down the mall's main corridor passing a dozen stores on either side: Victoria's Secret, Guess, and Kay Jewelers. No help. Too small to offer any cover. I made it to the food court with a play area for little kids. No place to hide there. A dozen Goth teens in stereotypical black clothing and piercings milled about, talking to each other with no apparent interest in shopping. No way I could blend in with that group.

I hoped Brad wouldn't try anything in public, but he was a cop, and he could make it appear as though I were a fugitive. Even if I screamed and put up a fight, all he had to do was flash his badge. Who would people believe? The cop, of course. I was screwed anyway I looked at it.

Toward the other end of the mall, Spyder made his way in my direction, ducking into and out of small stores, searching with a stride that said he wasn't interested in having a polite conversation. The two men had me sandwiched and I had nowhere to go. I could take either one alone but both at the same time? Probably not. I searched for something, anything that might help me. Between Chick-fil-a and Chipotle's, I spotted a sign directing me to the final bastion of safety for any woman in distress—the ladies' room.

I ran down a narrow hallway and into the bathroom. All the cubicles were empty. Good, but I couldn't stay in there forever, and the only exit was the long hall that emptied back into the food court, exactly where those guys would be waiting for me. I searched for a window, but those escape opportunities only occurred in movies. I was trapped, with no way out. *Should've taken my chances out in the mall. Think Lisa.*

A young girl with a silver ring hanging from her nose walked in and stared at me. One of the Goth teens I passed a few minutes ago. She wore tattered black jeans, a matching knit hat, and a loose top emblazoned with the words, THE CURE. Thick, black eye makeup made her look like a vampire. She scowled at me.

She had an attitude. It gave me an idea. I stared back.

"What's your problem lady?" the girl asked.

"What size are you?"

"Size four, not that it's any of your fuckin' business."

Real nice girl. "I'd like to buy your clothes and use your makeup."

She took several steps back and held up her hands. "Okay. Here we go. You some kind of a nut job? Maybe a dyke, cruising the ladies' room looking for young girls?"

"Neither. I need your help. A couple men are after me. They're waiting outside."

"Who?"

"My ex-boyfriend and his buddy." I described them. "He's crazy jealous and I'm afraid he might try to kill me. If I can switch clothes with you, I just might be able to make it out of here alive."

She squinted with the eyes of a snake just before it strikes. The girl had street smarts. She leaned her butt against one of the sinks and looked me over. "How much?"

I pulled out my wallet and counted the cash. "I have one hundred seventy-two dollars. You can have it and my clothes which cost me over three hundred a few days ago."

She grabbed my hand and checked out my Apple Watch. Strong grip. John had given me the watch on our first anniversary. "I want that too."

"Don't get greedy." I pulled my arm back. "That's not included."

She took a step forward, into my space. "What's to keep me from taking it?"

I bored my eyes into hers. "My fist when it hits your neck and crushes your windpipe."

She blinked. That changed the dynamics of the conversation. She retreated several steps and started undressing. I put on her jeans and top. They were a little tight but passable. I cringed and wondered when they were washed last. I checked the hat for any crawly things, tucked my long blonde hair underneath, and pulled it low on my forehead. I emptied her beaded crossbody purse on the counter and retrieved her eye shadow and black mascara, both of which I applied liberally. It went on in clumps. I looked like a member of the Adams Family, but hoped it'd be enough to make it past the two guys waiting for me.

She had three tiny plastic bags of white powder. I looked at her. "Really?"

She shrugged her shoulders. "A girl's gotta make a living."

"There are better ways." I didn't have the time to straighten this girl out. I stuffed my phone, wallet and car keys into my new purse. I almost forgot to include my FBI badge. The girl's cell phone sat on the counter. "You have friends out in the mall?"

"Of course. They're my business partners."

I groaned. "Ask them to start shouting."

"Shouting?"

"I need a distraction. As soon as they start, I'm going to walk out of here and try to make it to my car. A minute after I leave, I want you to walk out in the opposite direction." I hoped Brad and Spyder would follow her.

The girl smiled. She looked pretty in my outfit, better if she'd lose the heavy black makeup and nose ring. "Sure thing. We girls have to stick together." She made the call and the commotion erupted outside.

I waited, held my breath, and walked out keeping my head down. Brad and Spyder had moved to see what the ruckus was in the mall. I made it out of the food court and headed back toward Macy's and the exit to my car. I looked back.

Big mistake. My girl stood in front of Brad while he pulled a wad of bills out of his wallet, and handed them to her.

She pointed in my direction. *Shit. So much for us girls sticking together.*

I ran, but wasn't going to make it. I exploded through the Macy's exit toward the parking lot.

Brad was only a few-dozen steps behind me, a Glock in his right hand. I couldn't outrun a bullet.

An old Mercedes convertible approached, and I jumped in front of it, slamming my hand on the hood as hard as I could. Falling to the ground hurt more than I expected, but it served its purpose. Within several seconds, a crowd of people gathered around to help me.

"Call 911," a woman yelled.

"I saw some guy chasing her. Poor thing," said an older gentleman. He removed his sport coat, folded it, and placed it under my head.

I allowed my eyes to flutter open, and grabbed my fake FBI badge. I groaned. "Help me.... Drug dealers."

Brad and Spyder melted into the background. Too many sympathetic witnesses with too many questions.

An elderly female struggled to exit the Mercedes, looking like she was on the verge of a heart attack. Her hands trembled, and I felt bad about what I had done. "I'm so sorry, dear. I didn't see you."

"I'm fine." I must have looked like Lazarus as I jumped up, grabbed my beaded purse, and ran to my car.

I didn't see Brad or Spyder, but I needed to hurry. They were obviously desperate to wipe me out. It wouldn't take long for them to uncover my identity and find out where I lived.

THIRTY-SEVEN

I-75, North
Florida

I raced back to my condo, washed the makeup off my face and changed clothes. Threw everything I owned into a couple suitcases and tossed them into the trunk of my car. Anything that wouldn't fit, including the shotgun, wound up in garbage bags on the back seat. Fifteen minutes later I was on the road, my purse and Sig on the front passenger seat.

Which way should I go? If I headed south, I'd be trapped in the Keys. To the west was the ocean. That left me with the only options of driving East or North. Brad would likely put out an APB for Collier County Police to look for my car, but he wouldn't want them to apprehend me because he needed to eliminate me before I could talk about what I'd seen. What was their scam that made killing me so important? *Is that what happened to Savannah? Had she discovered something?* I headed north on I-75, racing to get as far away from Collier County as possible—to where, I hadn't figured out yet.

I kept my eyes glued to the rearview mirror, searching for any familiar vehicles. It wasn't until I reached Tampa that I allowed myself to relax my guard. What was the connection between Brad and Spyder? Was Spyder using videos of Brad and Savannah together to blackmail him? Why would the two of them work together to kill me? Why kill Savannah? Nothing made sense. I needed more information. I called Norman Deets.

"Hi, Lisa. I don't have much on those deaths you asked me about. It's more complicated than I expected. I did check into the pentagram and came up with a blank."

"That's kind of what I expected, but worth a try." My phone battery was low and I looked down to plug it into my charger. "Oh, Christ!" A car cut in front of me and forced me hard to the right. I wound up on the shoulder and struggled to get the car back on the road before it flipped upside down into a drainage canal. I accelerated back onto the expressway, my back tires fishtailing as I pursued the car. It wasn't the Bronco I'd seen at Macy's parking garage, but it had to be Brad and Spyder. Who else could it be? Problem was, they were now driving a large white Cadillac.

I raced to catch up to them. When I pulled abreast of the car, I picked my Sig up off the seat and looked over at the driver, ready to fire. It was neither Spyder nor Spandex Brad.

Clenching the steering wheel with both hands, a bespectacled, elderly lady leaned forward, straining to see the road ahead.

I sighed in relief. The woman never realized how close she came to taking her last breath. She pulled over and I followed right behind her.

She rolled down her window. "I'm sorry dear. Are you all right?"

"Yes," I said, "but you gave me quite a scare running me off the road like that. What happened?"

"I'm so sorry. A car pulled over and hit the front of my car. When I tried to avoid him, I must have done the same to you. Afraid my eyesight and reflexes aren't what they used to be."

I walked to the front of the woman's car and along the driver's left front bumper I found streaks of gray paint. Brad's

Bronco? I checked the road but the car was long gone. I reassured the woman that I was fine and advised her to contact the police.

I got back in my car, still a bit shaken, and picked up the phone. "What just happened?" asked Norman.

"Almost had a tango with another car. I'm fine now." I put my gun back onto the passenger seat but kept a round in the chamber, convinced the entire incident was aimed at me. "Put that present project on hold for now. I want you to check into the student files of Princeton University. Look into a Brad Stapleton who attended there on a sports scholarship about fifteen years ago. See what you can dig up. He's presently works as a detective in the East Naples Police Department."

"Naples?"

"Yes. I also need you to hack into the department's personnel files. See if he's been the subject of any disciplinary action. Will that be a problem?"

"I'm insulted you'd even ask that question, Lisa. The Naples PD will be easy. Law enforcement is so focused on getting information about others, they don't spend the resources to protect their own systems. This is getting to be fun. What else?"

"Guardian Security. It's a company that installs alarm and monitoring systems for homes and small businesses in southwest Florida. I think the owner might have some sensitive information on his laptop. I don't think he wants anyone to know what's on it."

"Name?"

"Spyder Tomlinson."

"And he has the laptop on him?"

"I'm sure he does. Can you still get into it?"

"If his company has a website. I can access the site and backtrack through it to his computer. Even if he's trashed it, he probably has everything stored on the Cloud."

"Great. I think he's involved in something illegal."

"Along with that Naples cop? This sounds dangerous, Lisa. You want me to notify Mr. Hamilton?"

"Let's just keep this between us for now. Hold on a minute." I gazed at the road in front of me. Brad and Spyder were sure to be waiting ahead on I-75. I turned off the interstate and onto route 301 toward I-95. "I need one other thing, Norman. Would you book a hotel reservation for me in DC? I'll be there late tomorrow, and I expect to need it for at least a week. Use another name."

"Intrigue. I love it. This is like old times. Are these two guys terrorists?"

"No, just bad guys and they're probably after me. See if you can have something on them for me by the time I get to Washington." I found a sign for I-95 North. Eighty miles ahead.

"How's my friend Cassie doing?"

"Taking a nap right now, but she seems to have recovered from her head injuries. Mr. Hamilton has arranged for a nurse to stop by and remove the staples from her scalp in a few days." He remained quiet for an uncomfortable length of time, like he was trying to figure out something in his head.

"What is it, Norman?"

"That friend of yours — she's annoying."

"Why do you say that?"

"Don't get me wrong. She's smoking hot. The hottest woman I've ever seen. Uh, except for you of course, but you're like a sister."

"Get to it, Norman."

"At first, I kind of enjoyed her looking over my shoulder, leaning against my back, you know, pushing her —"

"Enough, Norman. I get the picture. So, what's the problem?"

"She's a strange bird and that's coming from me, who's a pretty strange guy. She's too nosey and keeps asking me about why I need crutches. She always wants to know what I'm working on."

"She's a cop. Asking questions is what she does."

"Maybe, but she constantly bugs me for personal information about you and John and how you're doing with the murder investigation."

"She's pretty much a control freak, but that's what makes her such a good detective. This was her case until someone tried to kill her. So, it wouldn't be surprising for her to want updates."

"I guess. Just saying, she's a little strange. Carla doesn't trust her."

"Carla doesn't trust anybody. I gotta go. Talk to you tomorrow."

<hr>

I placed a call to Maddie Carpenter, the reporter at the Naples Courier Journal and told her what had happened between myself, Spyder, and Brad.

"That misogynist asshole. I knew he had to be dirty. What do you need?"

"This isn't the big bombshell I promised you for doing the obit article on Cassandra, but I think it might be something good for your career. Could even make the wire services and get you noticed by the national media."

"You have my attention."

"I can't figure out the connection between Brad Stapleton and Guardian Security. Something about them doesn't add up. I initially thought they might be involved in some kind of a blackmail scheme but now I'm not so sure. Whatever they're up to might have something to do with the murder of Savannah Wellington and her assistant, Racheal Morris. They're probably the ones who tried to kill Casandra Pierce. I have my IT guy working on some background information on them, but I need someone like you who has a better feel for what's happening in Naples. See if you can find any prior relationship between Guardian, Brad, and Savannah. There must be more to this than what I've seen so far."

"I'll get on it. The newspaper has extensive files of all past stories, and I can search for any thread connecting them. I'll get back to you tomorrow."

"Thanks Maddie. I owe you."

"I'm going to hold you to that, Lisa."

I followed route 301 East for a couple hours, doubling back intermittently, checking for tails, especially a gray Bronco. I didn't know what resources a cop like Brad might have at his disposal, but he seemed desperate enough to pull out all the stops. Why? I didn't know for sure, but if he found me, I knew I'd never be seen again. In Ocala, I picked up I-95 which would take me north to Washington. And back to John?

By the time I reached the Georgia state line, I relaxed a little. Brad had no jurisdiction outside of Florida. Darkness had fallen and the full moon cast a silvery glow across the landscape. Too tired to stay awake, I pulled down an exit labeled Kingsland, wherever that was. Turned out to be a bigger town than I expected. I passed a few national chain motels but didn't stop. If Brad did happen to pick up my trail, searching those would be too obvious.

My stomach growled, threatening to digest itself. As hungry as I was, I couldn't bring myself to eat the typical gas station offerings of heart attack food. A half-mile down a quiet road, a sign saying The Pink Pig invited me in. The waitress, a gray-haired lady with a pink bow in her hair and matching eyeshadow, recommended the barbecued ribs with green beans and hush puppies. "They're our specialty. Best in Georgia."

She was right. It might have been because I was so hungry, but they were the best ribs I'd ever tasted. I asked the waitress about a nice out of the way place to spend the night.

"There's a bed and breakfast just up the road a little. Been there forever. Used to be a small motel. The original owner died a ways back but his daughter fixed it up and turned it into a nice B and B." She leaned over and whispered, "It's still just a motel, but with a fancy name."

I took a left at what turned out to be the town's final traffic light. A mile later I saw the illuminated sign, *Kingsland B&B – Vacancy*. To the left of the sign a large southern magnolia with white blooms the size of dinner plates, glowed in the light of the full moon. I pulled in, my tires crunching across the motel's gravel parking lot. I stood next to my car and stretched, breathing in the clean natural scents of freshly cut grass and newly plowed soil, familiar smells only a small rural town could provide. Fireflies danced across the evening sky, and the night filled with the summer sounds of an innocent world: crickets, frogs, and an occasional howl. Coyote maybe. Most noticeable was the welcomed absence of traffic noise. I felt isolated and secure.

The B&B's lobby reminded me of the old Bates Motel from the movie, *Psycho*. At least no stuffed animal heads lined the wall, just a faded Confederate flag. A matronly woman in a denim house dress stood behind an old wooden reception desk, her gray hair pulled back in a loose bun. A pair of reading glasses hung from a silver chain around her neck. Behind her, a television played what sounded like reruns of an old horror movie. Kind of creepy.

"Good evening, dearie." Her voice was a little too sweet. More creepy. "Need a room for a while?"

"Just tonight. I'll be leaving in the morning," After thinking about that Psycho movie, I added, "My husband's expecting me home early tomorrow."

When I registered, I showed her my DC driver's license with my photograph on the left and a star in the upper right-hand corner proving it was Real ID compliant.

She grabbed her glasses and perched them on the tip of her bulbous nose. "Lisa Marie Savich Crawford? My word, that's a lot of names, dear."

"Yes, ma'am." What else could I say?

"Shall I put the room charge on your credit card?"

"I'd prefer to use cash. My husband keeps me on a tight budget." More importantly, it kept people like Brad and Spyder from being able to track me down.

She squinted her eyes as though she suspected something unsavory. However, I knew in a small-town, family-owned businesses like this one, cash was king. No paper trail for the IRS.

"Of course, Mrs. Crawford. Cash it is — in advance. I'll put you in the Blue Room. It's the last unit on the left, our nicest one. I'll show you the way." The woman's slippers shuffled along the wooden walkway and stopped in front of the Blue Room. She turned to leave and said, "We serve breakfast at six thirty."

The only blue in the "Blue Room" was the bedspread. Otherwise, it looked like any other motel room where I'd ever slept. The scent of a lavender plug-in didn't mask the inevitable musty smell of an old building in which smoking was once common. A night stand with an alarm clock and a small lamp separated two queen beds. Matching prints of Civil War battles hung over each bed. Opposite them was a dresser with a small desk at one end. A wide screen TV dominated the wall above it. In the corner sat a cozy armchair with a floor lamp next to it.

The room was nicer than expected and appeared clean. I was relieved it wasn't next to the lobby where a Norman Bates clone could watch through a peephole as I undressed. Just the same, I decided to wait until morning to shower. I pulled the curtains shut, wedged the easy chair against the door, and climbed into bed, my tactical shotgun at my side and the Sig on the nightstand. After tossing and turning for a while, I picked up my cell phone and called Cassie. She answered on the first ring. "It's Lisa. How are you feeling, girl?"

"Hi, Lisa. It's good to hear your voice." She sounded a little groggy and her speech slurred. Did I wake her, or had she just taken a pain pill? "I'm fine. Still have bad headaches from the concussion, but at least my blood sugar's under control." Her voice brightened up. "Who is this friend of yours who flew me to Washington?"

"Winston Hamilton."

"He must be the richest person I've ever met. Have you seen his home?"

"Never had the opportunity. We always conducted team business at our compound in Kentucky."

"The place is like a luxury hotel. Must be worth at least thirty million. I haven't seen most of it, but my bedroom alone is bigger than my entire condo in Naples. The staff treat me like a princess."

"The most important thing is that you're doing well."

"I am. Carla and Norman have been taking good care of me. I think he likes me."

I saw no sense of telling her what Norman said to me on the phone earlier. "What's not to like? You're every young man's fantasy, a beautiful woman with a great body."

"He's incredibly intelligent and kinda cute—in a nerdy kind of way."

"I know what you mean, but I thought you didn't like men."

"I prefer women, but sometimes they can be so heartless and mean."

I didn't know what to say. Cassie was right, but the same went for some men I'd known. Of course, not my brother, not Winston, and certainly not John.

She said, "Thank you for what you did. You saved my life. I won't ever forget it."

"That's what friends are for." I told her what happened with Brad and Spyder. They might have been involved in Savannah's murder and probably the attempt on your life." I mentioned the car incident on the expressway.

"Wow. At first, I didn't think Brad was capable of something like that. Looks like I was wrong. What're you going to do?"

"Nothing for me to do. I suspect the State of Florida might have to get involved, or maybe even the FBI."

"That would be unfortunate. We don't want the state or the FBI snooping around. This is our case."

"You're right. Guess I'll keep working it, but I need to investigate a few things first. Meanwhile, my primary focus is not letting those guys kill me. I'll keep you posted."

"I'm getting pretty tired. Hard to keep my eyes open. Percocet."

"I understand. Sleep well."

"Thanks for saving my life. Love you, Lisa."

"Love you too, my friend."

By the time I disconnected the call, my eyes had grown heavy. I'd started dozing off, but the sounds of tires slowly crunching on the parking lot stones shook me awake. The car stopped outside my door. No headlights. Not good. My nerves twisted like a rubber band on the brink of snapping. I held my breath and sat up in bed, trying to avoid making any noise. Did that gray car follow me here? Didn't see how it could have.

When I heard footsteps on the walkway, I rolled onto the floor behind the bed, my arms resting on the mattress, my finger on the shotgun's trigger. I quietly pumped a round into the chamber and aimed it at the door. *Maybe it's nothing. Or maybe it's Brad. Could be a creepy guy wearing his grandmother's dress and carrying a butcher knife. No matter. If anyone tries to break in, the last thing they'll see is the blast from my barrel.*

I waited for what seemed like an hour. *Why don't they simply break down the door and come get me?* In my mind, I answered my own question. There was only one way in and they had no idea whether or not I was armed. My eyes remained wide open, staring into the blackness, ready to fire the instant the room's door handle moved.

The sun woke me the following morning. I was back in bed but with the shotgun still in my hands, and pointed at the door. *Lucky, I didn't shoot myself in my sleep.* I got up, tiptoed to the curtain, and peeked out, looking for any suspicious vehicles, specifically a gray SUV. All was clear. In fact, there were no cars at all, which was worse. Who pulled up last night?

After showering and dressing, I tucked the Sig in the back of my waistband and loaded my bags into the trunk of my car. I returned to the lobby where I enjoyed a home-cooked breakfast of bacon, eggs, cheese grits, and black coffee—lots of coffee, while keeping the Sig under a napkin on my lap. Then it was back to I-95. Eight hours to go. I still kept an eye on the rearview mirror, looking out for suspicious gray vehicles.

T. Milton Mayer

THIRTY-EIGHT

Muirfield Village Golf Club
Dublin, Ohio

I shmael arrived in Dublin, Ohio by mid-afternoon, three days prior to the event, enough time to complete several days of on-site reconnaissance. Governor Murray's schedule presented a perfect opportunity to complete the contract. Like most people, the man was a creature of habit, especially when it came to his golf game. By the time he finished with the governor, Ishmael would have over fifty-five million dollars in the bank, more than enough to retire in luxury on the Cote d'Azur.

His first stop was the Jack Nicholas, Muirfield Village Golf Club in Dublin, Ohio, the site of Governor Robinson Murray's annual celebrity golf outing benefiting Ohio's five Children's Hospitals. Guests paid handsomely for the opportunity to play with the many sports celebrities expected to attend. Outside the pro shop, the club's personnel scurried about preparing for the event. When one of them left his sport coat draped over a chair, Ishmael walked past and lifted the man's ID badge. Afterward, he drove thirty miles down the 270 loop around Columbus and checked into a Marriott Courtyard motel where he logged onto the website of the Cincinnati Children's Hospital. Focusing on the hospital's list of staff members, he found a photograph of Dr. Walter Eisenberg, a man close enough in appearance to himself. *Simply need some gray hair coloring and a pair of reading glasses.* He printed a copy of the doctor's photograph in the hotel's business center, and used it to create his own badge. *Won't stand up to close scrutiny, but good enough.* After picking up the glasses and a bottle of the hair dye at a Walgreens, he made his way to the nearest grocery store where he bought a jar of natural peanut butter.

On the day of the tournament, Ishmael presented himself to the event organizer who was manning a post inside a large reception tent. He extended his hand. "Good morning. I'm Dr. Eisenberg from Cincinnati Children's. The Chief of Staff sent me to help in any way I can."

The man was busy and didn't even look at his badge. With the wave of a hand, he sent Ishmael to the pro shop where the assistant said, "We don't have much left to do, but you can put a couple bottles of water and a few sleeves of balls in each cart."

The electric golf carts were all lined up with the names of the players listed on the back of each so the caddies would know where to place the individual golf bags. Ishmael began dispensing the water bottles and the sleeves of golf balls, saving the cart labeled Governor Murray for last. A commotion arose when Joe Burrow, the star quarterback for the Bengals arrived. Then it was the Red Sox pitching legend Roger Clemens, The Ohio State Buckeyes football coach Ryan Day, and Johnny Bench, former Cincinnati Reds Hall of Famer. Activity increased exponentially with the arrival of each celebrity. The scenario was the perfect distraction.

A black limousine escorted by several police cars pulled in front of the club house. Governor Robinson Murray, a man much larger than Ishmael expected, emerged from the back seat and was immediately surrounded by a bevy of hungry reporters. His entourage of state troopers tried to keep them at bay, but ever the politician, the Governor said, "That's all right, boys. Let em through." He withdrew a few things from his shirt pocket and handed them to his assistant.

After the aide withdrew Murray's clubs from the limo's trunk, he looked around for the governor's cart.

"Over here," said Ishmael, directing him to the cart where the young man strapped in the golf bag and dropped two cellophane-wrapped cigars on the cart's dashboard.

Cameras flashed as reporters bombarded Murray with questions. "When are you going to declare your candidacy for the presidential election, Governor?"

He flashed his trademark wide grin. "That's a long way off, boys. I haven't even thought about it. I'm too busy serving the citizens of Ohio. We have a great number of challenges facing us, the most important of which is the state's budget."

"There are rumors you've been supporting a resolution calling for a convention of the states. The goal is to establish term limits. Can you comment on that?"

Murray smiled. "That's a constitutional issue that must be addressed on a national platform. I think it would eventually be a good idea, but other pressing matters require my full attention."

While the news media surrounded Governor Murray, Ishmael removed his pen injector and selected one of the two cigars. It only took him a second to inject it through the cellophane and the cigar band. When finished he inspected his work to be sure the injection site was undetectable.

Another reporter yelled, "Is it true that your supporters have already established an exploratory committee to begin fundraising for a presidential run?"

Murray grinned. "Looks like it's about time for me to tee off, boys. I'd better go. Thank you." He headed for his cart.

***

Ishmael followed the Governor's foursome. On the first tee, Murray lit up one of his ceremonial cigars and threw it on the ground. He placed his ball on the tee, and after a practice swing, drove the ball over two hundred-fifty yards down the middle. He picked up his lucky cigar and headed down the fairway. His partner, a long-time friend and federal judge, drove the cart. Each subsequent shot was the same: a couple of long puffs on the cigar, toss it onto the grass, then make the shot. Afterwards he'd pick it up and take another puff.

On the seventh hole, the judge said, "You know, Rob, it's probably not a good idea to throw your cigar on the ground like that and then put it in your mouth. These courses spray all kinds of weed killers and insecticides on the grass. Some of those chemicals might get into your bloodstream. I assume you've heard about lymphoma and that Roundup lawsuit?"

The Governor laughed and slapped his friend on the shoulder. "Judge, I've been playing golf like this for forty years, one lucky cigar on the front nine and one on the back nine. Without them, I couldn't play worth a damn. That's one reason I've won so much money from you." He laughed and took another long puff.

After the turn, the governor had the honors on the tenth tee, a short par three. He removed his back-nine cigar from its cellophane sleeve, used a cutter to nip off the end, and lit up, taking a long pull to let the taste fill his mouth before exhaling. "I'm up two strokes on you Judge. Wanna press?"

The judge laughed. "No thanks, Governor. I know when I'm being hustled."

Murray birdied the hole with a ten-foot putt, followed by a couple more puffs on the cigar. He cleared his throat, and headed for the eleventh tee box. Another pull on the cigar and he sliced his drive into a lake. He rubbed his hands. "Fingers are swelling. Damn arthritis." He dropped a ball behind the water hazard and hit it close to the green.

"Great recovery, Rob," said the judge.

Governor Murray rubbed his fingers and coughed. "Lucky shot." He picked up his cigar, took a long drag, and started wheezing.

"That doesn't sound good, Governor. You really should stop smoking those things," said his friend. "You ought to get a chest x-ray."

Murray waved him off and continued playing. The wheezing worsened.

By the thirteenth hole his face had turned blue. "Can't breathe." He fell to his knees, tore open his shirt collar, and grabbed his throat. Seconds later he was on the ground and foaming at the mouth, his cigar in the grass at his side.

"Call 911," yelled Ishmael. When a crowd surrounded the man, Ishmael picked up the cigar and tossed it into the lake.

"I told him not to smoke those damn things," said the Judge as he performed CPR.

Chaos ensued as several ambulances arrived.

An EMT yelled something about anaphylactic shock, adrenaline, and cardiac arrest. Ishmael smiled. Too late. He quietly made his way to the parking lot, and drove away. An hour up the road, he stopped at a gas station and tossed the jar of peanut butter and the drug injector system into a dumpster. *Ironic. Number thirteen on my list finished on the thirteenth hole. Ready for some sunny days on the Mediterranean.* He drove north toward Philadelphia where Fedallah arranged to have travel documents ready for his new identity.

THIRTY-NINE

I-95, North
North Carolina

Norman called me late-morning, as I crossed into North Carolina. "You were right about that Brad Stapleton guy. He definitely has a dark side. Seems your boy has a violent streak. There have been five official complaints filed over the past three years about his use of excessive force."

"In Naples? It has to be the octogenarian capital of the country. Hardly the place where any force would be needed."

"Yep, but one tourist wound up in the emergency room with a skull laceration after Stapleton hit the guy in the head."

"Hit in the head?" I almost swerved into the next lane. "Sounds like my murder victim, Savannah Wellington. That's too much of a coincidence. What happened to him?"

"His personnel record states he received an official reprimand and a one-day suspension without pay. Then, the report was buried. He must have some powerful friends in his corner."

"He should've been arrested and fired. Maybe Savannah and her baby would still be alive." My foot pushed hard against the accelerator. *Settle down, Lisa. You're going to kill someone.* I slowed and exited the expressway. Needed gas anyway. "What else?"

"I checked his history at Princeton University. Their system was more challenging than the Naples police. Had a rigorous firewall, but I got in. He attended three years on a baseball scholarship and was good enough for the Red Sox to draft him."

"And?"

"He never finished college. He was expelled halfway through his senior year after two complaints of sexual assault."

"Two at once?"

"Separate incidents. The second occurred a month after the University began investigating the first."

"Moron. What happened to the girls?"

"Brad's family is wealthy. Looks like his rich daddy paid the girls off to keep the family name out of the news. From what I can tell, the father disowned him afterwards."

When the gas pump clicked, I returned the nozzle and went inside for a coffee, the phone cradled against my neck. *I need to get some of those wireless earbuds.* "Is that when he moved to Naples?"

"No. I checked the Princeton Community Newspaper. He was drafted as a power-hitting first baseman and spent three years in the Boston minor league system. Then he flamed out. Looked like he couldn't make the transition from aluminum bats to wood."

Bats? I pulled back onto the interstate. "Anything else?"

"No, but I can keep digging if you'd like."

"No. That's all I need for now. Thanks, Norman. Maybe you can solve that Reiman thing you were working on and win a million bucks."

With the photographs I'd taken at the mall and the info Norman uncovered, I had a lot of what I needed to pin Savannah's death on Spandex Brad. It probably wouldn't take much to tie him to the Rachael Morris murder and the attempt on Cassie's life. I checked my rearview mirror and saw a gray SUV, about five cars behind me.

My phone rang. It was Maddie Carmichael calling back. "Hi Maddie."

"I owe you, girl."

"What?"

"You just gave me that blockbuster you promised."

"I don't understand."

"I dug into Guardian Security and asshole Brad Stapleton's background."

I pulled over onto the shoulder to talk. The gray SUV passed me but was going too fast for me to get a license number. It looked like a Florida plate.

I switched my phone to the other ear. "And?"

"Are you aware of the rash of jewelry heists along southwest Florida over the past several years."

"Kind of." Where was she going with this?

"Over five million dollars of jewelry and cash were taken. Guess what security company supplied alarm and monitoring services in each case?"

I turned off my engine and leaned back. "Guardian Security? No way."

"It gets better. The company was in Chapter Eleven bankruptcy. Then, they suddenly withdrew their petition and paid off all their debts. Spyder Tomlinson even had enough money left over to buy a new home and a Porsche Boxster. His new-found financial stability began soon after the second jewelry heist."

My head was spinning. "How does Brad fit into the picture?"

"Guess who was the only investigator for all seven robberies?"

"Oh, my God. Brad. The two were working together. I bet the crimes were never solved."

"You got it. Insurance covered the losses, and everyone was happy."

I was really confused by then. How did any of this fit in with Savannah's case?

"Now for the best," she said. "Both Brad and Spyder have disappeared."

"You're kidding. I guess nothing says I'm guilty more than running."

"I need to tie up a few loose ends on this thing, but my editor gave me the go ahead to run the story tomorrow. A lot of people are going to start popping antidepressants on this one. Thanks again. Gotta go."

The phone disconnected. Brad and Spyder missing? Not good. They could be on their way to Washington to get me. Maybe in a gray SUV?

I pulled back on the road and turned on the radio to clear my mind. Selected a Hits of the Sixties station on Sirius Radio. I always enjoyed the innocence of the older music. That's when they played the Sam Cooke classic, *Bring It on Home to Me*, a song about a woman leaving her lover and him begging her to bring her love back to him.

The guilt bore down to the depths of my soul. The song pointed directly at me, telling me to bring my love back to John. Regret already ate through me like a cancer. Didn't need any more reminders. I changed the station to the Fox News channel where anchor Bret Baier was giving a special report. "Governor Robinson Murray of Ohio died suddenly today while playing in his annual Children's Hospital Golf Tournament. Witnesses said he looked fine until he collapsed on the thirteenth hole with a seizure. He died while in transport to the hospital. Preliminary reports state he suffered a fatal anaphylactic reaction due to peanut exposure. Governor Murray was the consensus front runner for his party's nomination for president of the United States. While this appears to be a sudden medical catastrophe, state police say are investigating the matter to figure out how he could have been exposed to peanuts since he had religiously avoided them since his teen years. We have Marsha Vehr, local Fox reporter for WJW News in Dublin, Ohio …"

Another politician dead? What the fuck was going on? No way could Brad and Spyder be involved. I called Norman.

"That project I had you working on, the one about the dead politicians? Give it your full attention. I need something by tomorrow morning at the latest."

FORTY

JW Marriott Hotel
Washington, DC

I entered the address for my hotel into the Google Maps app on my phone and followed the directions across the Potomac River, entering Washington from the south. I had driven past the US Capitol many times before, but the sight of its huge dome never failed to instill in me a sense of awe. Here sat the most recognizable symbol of democracy in the free world, the center for the creation of laws and policies that affected the entire globe. It was also a breeding ground of monumental egos with an unparalleled potential for corruption and abuse of power. The country's concept of the system of checks and balances was the only thing holding the democracy together.

The sight of the Capitol steps reminded me of the day Jacob and our team thwarted an assassination attempt on President Jack Wagner four years ago. I missed those times when I felt relevant. I missed my friends, I missed my brother, but most of all I missed John.

The city hummed with energy and the inexorable vibrations of power. Waves of tourists of varying nationalities followed guides, each holding color-coded flags high in the air, trying to herd their groups toward the historical sights of the National Mall. Sounds of traffic assaulted my ears. Organized chaos. A far cry from the peaceful tranquility of our family farm in Kentucky. The noise was only one of many reasons I hated living in DC.

After driving down Pennsylvania Avenue for a mile, I pulled under the portico of the JW Marriott Hotel, a huge structure only minutes from the White House. The porter took my bags, and the valet parked my car, reminding me it was sixty dollars a night. I stared at him. "You're kidding, right?"

He shrugged his shoulders. "It's Washington, ma'am. Parking is limited."

I scowled. I was too young to be called ma'am.

My shoes clicked on the spacious lobby's marble floor as I passed under a series of huge crystal chandeliers. A man, sitting on a leather couch and reading The Wall Street Journal, checked me out as I passed. I should have seen the attention as a compliment, but it annoyed the hell out of me.

The receptionist at the front desk wore a burgundy blazer over a white shirt and tie. His gold name tag read, Brad. I cringed, hoping it wasn't an omen. "Hi, Brad," I said, feeling the need to wash the word out my mouth with soap. "I believe I have a room reserved by Winston Hamilton."

He checked the computer screen and a wide grin spread across his face. "Of course, Miss Hamilton. Your father made the arrangements. All fees have been paid in advance. Gratuities and incidental charges will be automatically debited to the credit card Mr. Hamilton has on file."

So, it looked like my name here was to be Lisa Hamilton. How creative of Norman. Could have been worse. The porter took my room card, inserted it into a slot in the elevator, and pressed number twelve. "Access to your floor is restricted to individuals with a specially coded room key card. For your protection, security is strictly enforced at all times. Cameras monitor the hallway outside your room twenty-four hours a day."

Hope they're better than the ones Spyder installed for Rachael Morris.

He opened the door to what he referred to as the Presidential Suite. The floral scent from a huge vase of pink roses permeated the air. An embossed card, signed by the hotel manager read, "Welcome to the Marriott, Miss Hamilton." Next to it sat a fruit and cheese platter wrapped in cellophane. The suite had a huge living area and two separate bedrooms. It was larger than the entire condo where John and I lived near DuPont Circle, much more than one person needed. In fact, a family of four could easily live in comfort here. I turned to the porter, "This is a bit much. Are you sure this is the correct room?"

"Certainly, ma'am."

Ma'am again? Annoying. I pulled out my wallet to hand him a tip.

"It's already taken care of, ma'am."

If he called me that one more time, I vowed to break his nose. After placing my bags in the bedroom, he showed me the suite's features: climate control, the television and stereo systems, and a fully-stocked complimentary bar. He pushed a remote control and walls of curtains along one side opened, offering an expansive view down Pennsylvania Avenue, past the Old Post Office Tower, and toward the dome of the Capitol Building. The Washington Monument stood proudly straight ahead. He opened a glass door to a private terrace overlooking the city. Must have cost Winston a fortune. "The view is even more spectacular at night," said the porter. With that, he bowed and walked away.

My phone rang. Looked like I wasn't going to get any rest. It was Maddie again. "Just found out. They picked up Spyder in San Antonio this morning trying to hire a coyote to smuggle him across the border into Mexico." She chuckled. "That's a switch, sneaking into Mexico. Anyway, turns out the guy he hired was an ICE agent and put him in cuffs. Spyder had a duffel bag with almost a half million dollars."

"Good thing for him it wasn't a real coyote," I said. "If it had been, Spyder would have had his cash stolen and been left for dead in the desert."

"Preliminary reports are that he threw Brad under the bus and blamed him for everything. Claimed the jewelry robberies were all Brad's idea. Spyder insisted his only involvement was to disarm the security systems. I'm thinking he's negotiating for a reduced sentence, knowing the DA will set his sights on the corrupt cop angle. Said he knows nothing about Savannah or Cassie, though."

"Thanks, Maddie. Keep me posted." I wasn't surprised Spyder would deny any involvement in Savannah's death. Robbery was one thing, but a murder charge took his situation to an entirely different level. But what about Brad? Where was he if he wasn't with Spyder? Here in DC? I'd have to keep a watch out for him.

I hadn't eaten since breakfast at the B&B. After the porter left, I gorged on the fruit and cheese. The bar looked inviting, but after two days alone on the road, I needed people around me. I showered, dressed, and headed down to the lobby bar. In the corner sat a baby grand where a piano player floated the sounds of soft jazz across the room and into the lobby. The guy was talented. A patron tried to tip him but he refused. Apparently, he wasn't an employee of the bar, just a business traveler. I ordered a Vodka gimlet and took a mouthful, savoring the citrusy taste before swallowing. Just what I needed to calm what remained of my nerves after two days on the interstate, being tailed by some gray car. Ten minutes later, I ordered a second one.

A man near the opposite end of the bar stared at me, the same guy who checked me out in the lobby earlier. The hairs on my arms stood up. Did he drive a gray SUV? He wore a nice suit and a club tie, his hair perfectly coiffed. I lifted my drink with my left hand, letting him see my wedding ring. He tried to act disinterested but kept stealing glances out of the corner of his eye.

My cell phone rang. "Lisa, it's Norman."

"Hi. Thanks for the room, but it's too much."

"Mr. Hamilton insisted. You've always been his pet. Anyway, I wanted to let you know I finished that research project of yours."

I leaned forward in my chair. "And?"

"I found thirteen unexplained, suspicious, or accidental deaths among state politicians over the past two years. The last one was that Ohio Governor Robinson Murray. I compared the deaths to similar death rates in the general population. I controlled each group for age, economic status, and gender. Unfortunately, there was no significant difference between the groups."

His words deflated any optimism I might have had about solving Savannah's murder. I had eliminated Savannah's husband. Florida Governor Cartwright wasn't looking promising. The probability of Spyder or Brad being involved was dwindling. The political angle was all I had left.

Norman continued. "Obviously, that was disappointing, so I refined my search by focusing only on those who had been supportive of state resolutions calling for a constitutional convention. Listen to this. There was a statistically significant difference between that group of thirteen and the general population."

"Wow. Now we're getting somewhere. How much difference?"

"Not much, but enough to suggest something was awry. So, I narrowed my study parameters further to include only those who had an affiliation with the Take Back America organization you mentioned. Hold on to your seat on this. That relationship increased the chance of death tenfold. I did a regression analysis and chi square test on the results."

"Too technical, Norman. Bottom line?"

"There is almost a zero percent chance that the deaths I found were random. Though they were reported as accidental or illness related, it appears the people were murdered."

"Like the attempt on my friend Cassie?"

"Yes, like crazy Cassie. Definitely a pro and he had to be extremely clever in order to keep law enforcement from recognizing the pattern. I checked the FBI databases and there's no indication they're aware of what's happening. I'm e-mailing you a map of the states, color-coded to show which ones had already passed resolutions and those where the resolution bills were proposed but not yet voted upon. I placed stars in the states where the thirteen were killed and all are in the states where resolutions are proposed. It's incredible no one has noticed this before. Congratulations, Lisa. Without you, these murders would've never have been uncovered."

That was interesting, but it didn't answer my original question. Who killed Savannah Wellington and why? Her involvement with TBA preceded her death by several years. What was to be gained by killing her now? Florida had already passed the constitutional convention resolution. Made no sense to me, but I had an idea.

"Is Mr. Hamilton available?"

"He's in Boston, but he's expected to fly back in the morning."

"Great. Please tell him to call me when he returns. I need his help on something."

I finished my second drink and was too tired to head to the restaurant for dinner. Another snack from the fruit tray would have to do. On the way to the elevator, I stepped into the hotel's business room and sat in front of one of their computers. I needed access to a printer. After pulling up my G-mail, I opened Norman's message and printed the map. It was more impressive than I imagined. I put it in my purse and headed toward the elevator, joining two other people already there. They were holding hands and pushed the button for the tenth floor. *Married? Maybe. To each other? Maybe not.* I entered my Presidential Suite room card, pressed twelve, and stepped to the rear corner of the elevator, behind the couple. Anti-terrorism 101, never allow someone to stand behind you.

Just before the doors closed, Mr. Perfect Hair from the bar stepped in. He stood in a rear corner just opposite me and checked me through the corner of his eyes. Probably drove a gray SUV. I'd been at this espionage game long enough to know when someone was stalking me. Once we were alone, he'd probably stick a knife between my ribs. He made a mistake though. He didn't push a floor button. Brad was still out there somewhere. Did he send this guy to get even with me? I centered my weight over the balls of my feet and waited until the couple exited. Once the door closed, I spun around, slammed my elbow into the guy's neck, and pulled my Sig, aiming it at his left eye. "Who the hell are you and who sent you?"

He struggled to talk. I released some pressure from his neck. "I—I'm with Mr. Hamilton."

I removed my elbow but kept the Sig on his eye.

He grabbed his throat and took a deep breath. "Mr. Hamilton told me to be careful. Said you were more than able to take care of yourself. I believe him." He coughed a few times. "He sent me to keep an eye on you."

"Keep an eye on me? Why?"

"Norman Deets told him what you were up to and the deaths you've uncovered. Mr. Hamilton's afraid you might be upsetting some powerful people. He has a feel for these kinds of things, so he assigned me and three others to your protection detail. I assume you haven't IDed them yet because they're all still able to walk. If you do notice them, it would be in your best interest if you didn't shoot them."

I removed my Sig from his eye but kept it at my side as he escorted me to my room. He waited outside my door until I locked it behind me. After I heard him return to the elevator, I took a hot bath and went to bed, my Sig under the pillow. Sleep came reluctantly.

FORTY-ONE

JW Marriott Hotel
Washington, DC

The following morning. I ordered breakfast from the room service menu and ate on the terrace. My thoughts revolved around John and myself, those times before life got so complicated between us. Initially, he'd been understanding and attentive to my needs. At the same time, he was a man driven by the demands of his job at the bureau. Because he was black, he believed he had to work harder than those around him in order to succeed. His concerns weren't based on reality, but that's the way he saw it, so it was his reality. His job became his identity, and our marriage suffered. It wasn't all John, though. I was equally to blame. I withdrew into my own world after the miscarriages. We became the proverbial islands in a stream, forever paired but separated by our lives. I missed sharing coffee with him in the morning, hearing his voice, strong and reassuring, yet soft when necessary. It lingered in my mind as I called his direct phone line.

"Director Crawford speaking."

He answered the phone personally. Usually, his calls were screened by his secretary and she was unhappy if calls were not about official FBI business. John must have recognized my number on the caller ID. "Hello, JC. Are you busy?"

"L? Is that you? It's great to hear your voice. I've been so worried about you." He yelled to his secretary to hold all calls. "How are you? Where are you?"

"I'm in Washington. Had to come here on business."

"Business? What kind of business? Are you coming home? When can I see you? I have a lot to tell you." His words raced faster than I could think. It wasn't like him.

"I'm staying at the JW Marriott. I'll be there for a week."

"Oh, a week?" The excitement in his voice faltered.

"I'd like to see you, JC," I said. "We need to talk."

"Talk? About what?"

I should have been more specific. The concern in his voice was palpable. "About us. I miss you, JC. I'd like to discuss what we need to do to get our marriage back on track." I heard him sigh.

"I'd like that, L. I'd like that very much. How about tonight?"

"Can't. I have some meetings. Maybe dinner tomorrow?"

"Sounds great. The Old Ebbitt Grill.? It's just up the street from your hotel. Seven?"

"Perfect." Same place where he proposed. " Can't wait to see you."

"Why don't I pick you up?" he asked.

"I think I'd prefer to walk. Helps me clear my mind. I'll see you tomorrow."

"Sure, I understand." More disappointment in his voice, but I had to handle the situation carefully lest I fall back into the same rabbit hole I had recently escaped. As soon as I disconnected, I punched in the number for Winston Hamilton. "Hello, Mr. Hamilton."

"Hi, Lisa. I think I already know why you're wanting to talk to me."

"You do?" He had an uncanny way of knowing what people were thinking before they knew themselves. Guess that's why he was so successful in the CIA.

"Norman filled me in on the project he's working on for you. Impressive. You'd like to get in to see the people at Take Back America."

"Yes. I think they might help me solve a murder I stumbled across in Naples."

"Does this have anything to do with the attack on your friend, Cassandra?"

"Maybe, but I can't say with any certainty yet. There are several possibilities. We've uncovered a great deal of information relating my Naples murder victim to a string of deaths involving state legislators around the country. They all have one thing in common—an affiliation with the TBA organization. I need to talk to their CEO."

"Norman gave me some background information, and I'm afraid you may be wandering into some dangerous territory. I realize you and John have separated, but perhaps you should discuss what you found with him. Let the FBI handle this."

"Right now, I don't have anything concrete, only speculation based on a statistical analysis. I can't go to John with that. Besides, I must handle this on my own. Once I've been able to corroborate a few things, I can discuss the case with him in detail."

I heard Winston light up a cigar and take repeated puffs. It sounded much like a fish out of water, gasping for air. "If you proceed along this path, I must insist you allow my people to continue shadowing you—without harassing them."

"I met one last night. He wasn't very impressive."

"He's actually rather good, but you're a tough assignment. I'll add some of your former teammates. You might notice them, but nobody else will. Those are my terms and they are not negotiable."

"Deal," I said. "I'll try not to hurt any of them."

Winston chortled into the phone. "The head of TBA is a man named Scott Matheson. He's one of the good guys and has a perfect plan to change the course of our country. I've already pledged a million dollars to his organization and have promised more depending upon their performance. You can interview him as my personal representative. I'll set something up for tomorrow morning."

"Perfect. Thank you, Mr. Hamilton."

It was noon by the time I hung up. I had enough time to shop for a new dress and get my hair and nails done for my dinner with John the next evening.

FORTY-TWO

DuPont Circle
Washington, DC

I slept late the following morning, but the chimes of my cell phone awakened me. Winston again. His voice sounded tense, and he got right to the point. "We must meet as soon as possible."

His abruptness caught me off guard. I hadn't had my morning coffee, and my brain hadn't kicked into gear yet. "Why? What's this about?"

"Norman showed me a copy of the map he sent you. I double-checked his results and I'm surprised I never noticed the trend before. It's my job to uncover such things. You are in grave danger."

"From whom?"

"Difficult to say with any certainty. This call for a constitutional convention is a controversial subject. Notable legal scholars have warned about the dangers of meddling with the constitution. Resistance is strong from both sides of the political spectrum all the way from The Proud Boys on the right to the Anarcho-Socialists on the left. . All are exceedingly passionate in their opposition."

"Enough to murder?"

Apparently so, based upon the thirteen killings thus far. Suffice it to say that you have upset some powerful and dangerous people. I know you're opposed to sharing your information with John, but maybe it's time for you to get your brother involved. Nobody has ever protected you as well as Jacob."

"Absolutely not!"

"He's already coming back to the US. I need him to return because of domestic terrorism issues."

"Sorry Mr. Hamilton, but no. For the first time since he was a child, Jacob has a chance to live a normal life. I'm not about to ruin that for him. I will handle this problem myself."

"I thought you might say that. I want you to meet me at the DuPont Circle chess area? Are you familiar with it?"

"Sure. John and I had a condo a few steps away. Why? What's the urgency?"

"You need to be aware of some serious new developments. Be ready at noon. Do not travel alone. I'll send a driver. You'll recognize him."

After he gave me detailed instructions, I showered and dressed. I considered getting breakfast, but my watch told me I was short on time. A black Chevy Suburban with heavily tinted windows pulled up to the hotel's front door. *Typical CIA.* The driver still had a bruise on his neck from when I slammed him into the elevator wall a few nights ago. He said nothing.

The man dropped me off ten minutes later. Dupont Circle had been the site of an old slaughterhouse. In 1871, the US Army Corps of Engineers used the land to create a park surrounded by a large traffic circle formed by the convergence of five major roads in DC. The iconic Dupont Fountain, a marble landmark dedicated to Civil War Hero, Admiral Samuel Francis DuPont, dominated the center of the park. Canopies of mature oak and maple trees sheltered the walkways. Lush patches of green grass, bordered by flower beds and boxwoods, created an arboretum atmosphere. Along the north periphery, rows of aggregate concrete chess tables sat in front of players, some standing, others sitting. An eclectic mix of individuals from across the social spectrum of Washington and the entire

East Coast, came here to test their abilities. They ranged from businessmen carrying obscenely expensive leather briefcases to the homeless.

In the background, peaceful sounds of chirping birds and water splashing in the fountain filled the air. I overheard a half-dozen different languages and accents as I made my way around the park, searching for the man Winston had described: a tall black man, wearing a frayed Washington Redskins cap and a Chicago Bulls t-shirt. I found him sitting alone at one of the tables, a chessboard in front of him, white and black pieces arranged in preparation for a game.

Per Winston's instructions, I stood across from him. "Care to play?"

He looked up at me with gentle dark brown eyes and smiled. "Ah, my first challenge of the day, and such a beautiful one at that," he said with an accent. Jamaican? "Put twenty dollars on the table."

"Twenty dollars?"

He laughed. "It normally costs fifty to play me. You're getting a discount." He leaned across the table and whispered. "My name is Kingsley. I'm Mr. Hamilton's driver, and I'm proud to say, his close friend."

I must have looked surprised that Winston would be friends with a homeless man.

Kingsley grinned. "I'm sure it seems strange that a multibillionaire would be associated with the likes of me, but chess is a great equalizer that ignores all pretense of socioeconomic status."

I already liked the guy. I pulled a twenty from my purse and sat down. "I don't know a thing about chess."

He centered his pieces in the squares. "No problem. Just duplicate the same moves I make. If you're about to do something wrong, I'll tap my finger on the table."

Soon a crowd of a half dozen spectators surrounded our table.

"Don't worry," he said. "I'm a bit of a celebrity here and it's not unusual for patzers to gather round and watch me play."

"Patzers?"

"Poor chess players who think they're good. Can't complain, though. At fifty dollars a pop, many of them used to help pay my bills. Some of the observers around us are with Mr. Hamilton. They're here to protect you from anyone who might want to hurt you. Remain calm and don't look around, but someone is watching you."

At what I estimated to be about six four, Kingsley would be an imposing bodyguard. I felt safe, but asked, "Should I be afraid?"

No response. He moved one of the little white pieces I knew to be a pawn. I did the same with my black pawn and leaned in. "Why all the intrigue?"

He laughed. "Mr. Hamilton is with the CIA. Everything he does involves intrigue. For him, all of life is a chess game—a deadly one. I'm kind of a protector, his knight if you will. I make sure it's safe for him to be here."

I moved a piece Kingsley called a bishop. "How did you come to be associated with Winston?"

He tapped his finger on the table.

Wrong move. Too late. I'd already removed my hand from the piece.

"I met Mr. Hamilton in this very park a few years ago. He's a grand master who had been invited to play for the world championship in Russia. He lost interest in the international competitive aspects of the game, but still enjoys playing. I've faced him at this very table dozens of times. Beat him only twice. Mostly we played to a draw. We soon became friends and he eventually said I was too great a player to be hustling fifty-dollar games from patzers. Said I deserved better, so he hired me to be his driver and moved me into his mansion. He pays me handsomely, so I no longer need to hustle games. Now, I play mostly for fun."

"And the occasional fifty dollars, tax free."

He laughed aloud, drawing the attention of the other players. He moved his knight. "Your good friend, Miss Pierce is doing well."

"Cassie?" I copied his knight move.

"Yes. She's recovering nicely from her wounds, but Mr. Hamilton believes she should remain in the mansion considering she's supposed to be dead. I'm afraid Carla doesn't trust her very much."

"Carla doesn't trust most people."

"She's part of the group watching over you today. She's pushing a guy in a wheelchair."

"Wheelchair? Norman's working in the field?"

"He's been pressing Mr. Hamilton for a chance to be more active. The boss finally yielded but paired him up with Carla so she can watch his back. Norman's one of the few people she likes." Kingsley moved his queen across the board. "Just so you're aware, we have five more people stationed around the park."

Kingsley looked over my shoulder and nodded. "Turn your king over onto its side."

"What?"

"Turn your king over, Lisa. You're in checkmate." Kingsley put my twenty in his pocket and stood.

Winston approached the table, wearing a pinstripe gray suit and his black fedora. His mischievous eyes twinkled. "Care for another game?" His narrow, colorless lips smiled.

"I don't know. Is it going to cost me another twenty?"

Winston winked. "No, my dear. We'll play for fun. Do you know the basics?"

"I've learned a little from Kingsley, but the game ended so quickly, I didn't get much."

Winston took Kingsley's spot across from me and his chubby fingers arranged his pieces with the grace of a concert pianist, caressing each as though it were a priceless treasure. I still played black and centered my pieces on the squares. He advanced his knight.

"Why are we meeting like this?" I asked.

He answered by placing a paper bag on the table. It had a logo of the United States Capitol building on one side and the words Capitol Coffee Bistro on the other. I removed a Styrofoam cup of café latte and a blueberry scone.

"I figured you might not have had time to eat."

"Thank you." I sipped my coffee and took a bite of my scone. Delicious. I copied Winston's maneuver with my knight. "So why are we here?"

"Someone has been following you. Been doing it ever since you arrived in DC." He moved the pawn diagonal to his queen. "My people have kept you safe thus far, but you're still vulnerable. We needed to start taking some aggressive measures. I had you come here where I could keep a close eye on you while I flushed out your stalker."

I scanned the park out of the corner of my eye. "How does anyone even know where I am?"

"Your phone, my dear."

I about slapped myself on the forehead. Of course. How could I have been so stupid? Someone was tracking my I-phone.

Winston moved his queen across the board just as Kingsley had. "Look in the bag again."

I did and pulled out a new phone.

"Norman disabled the tracking feature and installed all your important numbers. He also downloaded his customized version of the Threema app."

"Threema?"

"It's the most protective phone security program available. No-one, including Homeland Security, can monitor your communications or track your location. Hand me your old phone and I'll destroy it." He placed it in his coat pocket.

I tried to move my queen, but it was blocked in. I had to settle for a pawn.

"Check the bag once more," he said.

I fished around under some napkins and found a small black metal box about half the size of a pack of cigarettes. "What's this?"

"A GPS tracking device. My people found it under the rear wheel well when they searched your car."

Must have been that night at the Kingsland B&B when I heard someone outside my room. "Who put it there? Who's following me?"

"We don't know for sure yet. I was hoping you could tell me. He's tall, athletic, jet-black hair and a matching scruffy beard. He's the guy in the sunglasses, standing next to the fountain. He's pretending to take photographs of the park, but he's mostly been focused on you."

I moved my second knight and looked around the park, trying to appear bored. The guy was there, just as Winston described. He'd changed his hair color and the beard was new, but I recognized his cocky attitude and that affectatious part down the middle of his hair. "His name is Brad Stapleton. He's a cop from Naples."

Winston squinted his eyes. "Doesn't sound like someone who would care about a constitutional convention. Why's he so interested in you?"

"While I was looking into that murder in Naples, he became my primary suspect. As part of the investigation, I uncovered a string of home invasions he orchestrated, and I leaked the information to the local Naples newspaper. He's been on the run ever since. He'd like to get some payback."

Winston's eyes turned dark. "He threatened you? I'll make him disappear."

Brad likely killed Savannah Wellington and her assistant Rachael. I was fairly sure he tried to kill Cassie because of our investigation. It would serve the bastard well if Winston's boys erased him, but I said, "No. Can we somehow turn him over to the Naples police department? They've been searching for him, and they have enough to put him behind bars for years, maybe even life."

Winston pulled a cigar from his pocket, nipped off the end, and lit up. He puffed at it repeatedly, again creating those gasping fish sounds. He took in a large pull and blew the smoke into the air. "I can do that." He waved his hand slightly. Within seconds, Carla and the guy I slammed into the wall at the Marriott, book-ended Brad. He flinched when Carla pressed a gun barrel against his ribs. He had no chance to run. They led him away without a problem.

"What'll happen to him now?"

Another puff on his cigar and Winston moved his queen across the board. "He'll be blindfolded, put in a van, and transported to Naples. By this time tomorrow, the police will find him handcuffed to a utility pole outside their headquarters."

That put a smile on my face. I moved my knight.

Winston moved his queen again. "Checkmate in two more moves, my dear."

"But we've only made a half dozen moves each."

Winston shrugged. "I've been doing this most of my life, Lisa. I'll have Kingsley teach you how to play.

Winston's smile turned serious. "From what you and Norman have told me, that police buffoon from Naples may have killed Savannah Wellington and her secretary, but I seriously doubt he has the mental capacity to pull off the series of mysterious murders you've uncovered. He's definitely not clever enough to have tampered with Cassie's insulin. Stay vigilant, Lisa. This isn't over yet. There are still those out there who might wish to do you harm. Could even be someone inside this park right now. I will continue to have my team provide a bubble of protection around you." He stood and adjusted his fedora. "Promise me you won't hurt any more of my people."

He turned and disappeared down the street, the fingers of his right hand locked around his cigar and Kingsley towering at his side.

FORTY-THREE

Old Ebbitt Grill
Washington, DC

I tried on several outfits before deciding on a simple black dress showing just enough cleavage to be interesting. How sexy should I look? Didn't want to start up something that was destined to fail again. I slipped on a pair of slingback pumps, and checked myself in the mirror one last time. Not too much makeup. John preferred a more natural look, but would it be good enough?

The Old Ebbitt Grill was the oldest bar in DC and a favorite meeting place for some of the most powerful movers and shakers in the country. Though it was only a short walk from my hotel, it felt like miles. A part of me dreaded this dinner. What should I say? Would John be angry? Almost turned back until I passed a couple walking in the opposite direction, arm in arm, love in their eyes, and laughing. Could that ever be John and me again?

As I reached the front door, I stopped, took a deep breath, and exhaled away all my anxieties. When I entered, John was already in the same booth we sat in the night he proposed. The memory overwhelmed me for a minute. After dinner, John and I had walked to the National Mall. It was a beautiful evening. Washington glowed under the soft lights of the monuments and the star-filled night sky. With the Lincoln Memorial behind us, he got down on one knee and asked the question. Warm memories with so much promise. I pushed them aside, not wanting to allow myself to fall back into the pit. *Take it slowly, Lisa.*

A single pink rose lay on the middle of the table in front of him. *My favorite color.* His normal contingent of FBI bodyguards was nowhere to be seen, unusual for the Director of Counterterrorism.

He stood, wearing his favorite gray suit that no longer looked tailored. The collar of his white shirt bunched up under a red tie. His shoulders slumped and I noticed a new dusting of gray at his temples. He hugged me. Old desires resurrected that familiar fluttering in my heart, but something was wrong. My once tall, muscular husband felt smaller. He'd lost weight. His eyes were wide and he looked happy to see me, but his smile now appeared tentative, forced, hiding an underlying sadness.

It hit me with a jolt. I had done this to him. I destroyed the man I loved just as our marriage had destroyed me. Maybe this meeting was a bad idea after all. Maybe we were destined to be apart. A voice inside my head told me to turn and run, jump into my car, and drive until I couldn't anymore. But that would have been the same as running away to Naples a few months ago. I couldn't escape my problems that way. They would have followed me relentlessly, the guilt slowly devouring my soul. Determined to see this through, I stood on my toes and kissed him on the cheek. I swooned at his touch and the subtle scent of his cologne. My heart soared in a way it hadn't in a year.

He stepped back. "You look beautiful, L."

"It's good to see you, JC." My words sounded stiff and formal, like I might say after shaking a friend's hand at a class reunion. I couldn't say, "You look great." He would've seen right through the lie. We sat on opposite sides of the booth.

A waiter, dressed in a crisp white coat, approached our table. "Welcome back Mrs. Crawford. You look stunning as always." He asked if we wanted a drink.

John raised his eyebrows. "Conundrum?"

"Perfect."

He ordered a bottle. The waiter poured a glass, and I took a sip, then a mouthful. It was exactly what I needed to calm my nerves. We tried some small talk, dancing around our obvious issues, but we'd been emotionally separated for so long, any discussion seemed too contrived. I needed to face the problem head on.

I reached over the table and held his hands. "I'm sorry, JC. I had no right leaving the way I did. I should have stayed so we could discuss our problems."

"You have nothing to apologize for, L. I'm the one who's sorry. I got so wrapped up in my career, I ignored what was happening to you. After..." he stopped mid-sentence and swallowed hard, "after the miscarriages, I buried myself deeper in my work, and wasn't there for you when you needed me most. I had my priorities upside down."

Tears threatened my eyes. "Still, I shouldn't have run away." I wished we'd had this discussion before I left, but I didn't give it a chance.

John stared down at the table. "I guess we both could have done some things differently, but past mistakes are just that—in the past." His eyes locked onto mine. "What's most important is what happens from here on. I'm hoping we still have enough to build upon. I know only this. I love you deeply, L. My career and everything else are incidental. Without you, my life is meaningless, so I will do whatever it takes to make our marriage work. Simply tell me what you want."

"I love you too, JC, but I need more in my life. I miss my team."

"I understand that now, and I should have never insisted you retire. It was selfish and self-centered on my part. I don't care anymore if you want to resume your career. You've already accomplished more to protect the country than I could in ten years as the Deputy Director."

The waiter returned to take our order.

I set my menu down. "I'm not very hungry. How about you, JC?"

"Me neither, but there is somewhere I'd like to take you."

The disappointed waiter gave us our check, and John left a huge tip to soften the man's loss. He took my arm in his and escorted me outside. Four members of his protection detail waited by his car. John dismissed them for the evening and opened the door for me.

"You think that's a good idea — to send your men home?"

He looked around. "Sure. I'm an FBI Deputy Director. No one's going to try anything in Washington. Besides, I want you all to myself. I'd like to show you something."

"Mysterious." For a half-hour, we headed northwest along a parkway until we reached the exit for Rockville, a small, upscale community in Maryland. "Where are we headed?" I asked.

"Almost there," he said with a wry smile. Five minutes later, we pulled down a quiet suburban street and into the driveway of a quaint, two-story colonial with a wide front porch, reminiscent of my family home in Kentucky, only much larger. When we got out of his car, he handed me a small box wrapped in gold paper and a white bow.

"What's this?"

"Open it."

Inside was a keychain with several keys. "I don't understand, John."

"For our new home. That is, if you like it."

I stood there dumbstruck, my mouth gaping open. When I could finally speak, I said, "Our new home?"

"I finally realized how much you hated living in DC. It was great for me since it was so close to the Hoover Building, but our condo must have seemed like a jail cell to you. No wonder you had to leave." He faced the house. "I closed on this last week."

"Seriously?" After we married, a house was all I wanted—that and maybe a few children. "What about our condo by Dupont Circle?"

"Put on the market and it sold in a day, way above list price. It's how we could afford this."

John led me up the brick walkway. He unlocked the front door and followed me inside. "The furniture came with the house, so it's just about turnkey." He looked around. "You can change whatever you like, new furniture, paint, drapes, whatever. Make it your home."

It was perfect. The entrance foyer had a high ceiling with a chandelier suspended in the middle. On the left, a stairway with a wooden spindle railing led to the second floor. Straight ahead, a short hallway opened into a spacious kitchen with cream-colored cabinets and dark granite countertops. Pendant lights hung over an island with three stools on one side. Along the back of the kitchen, a large bay window afforded a view of a rear deck and a beautifully manicured backyard. Behind that a heavily wooded area provided privacy. The kitchen opened into a cozy family room with an L-shaped sectional couch sitting in front of a stone fireplace.

"It's gas, so we don't have to worry about firewood," said John. It was a little warm for a fire, but John grinned and pushed an app on his cell phone. The fire came to life. "Just showing off my new toy."

A warm smile spread across my face as I imagined us sitting together on the couch on a cold winter's afternoon, snuggling under a blanket, and sipping hot chocolate. It was one of those Norman Rockwell moments I thought we could never enjoy. I threw my arms around him and hugged him hard. I missed that.

John pushed a few more buttons on his phone and soft music filled the room. "Sonus System. It controls music in every room of the house. I'll set up the app for your phone later." He walked over to a small bar in the family room and pulled out a bottle of chardonnay. "Sonoma-Cutrer. Still your favorite?"

"Perfect."

He poured two glasses and handed me one. "To our future," he toasted.

"And to our new home."

"Come on, I'll show you the rest of the house." He grabbed my hand and led me up the stairs, his touch as soft as a whisper. "It has three bedrooms. Straight ahead is the master."

The bedroom was spacious, with a large king-sized bed in the middle and soft cream-colored carpeting on the floor. The more he talked, the more I felt the cadence of his confident, masculine voice wash over me, reassuring, hypnotic, erasing any resistance I might have had. I leaned into him, allowing myself to be wrapped in his arms. John's touch sent an electric jolt through my body. I trembled. It had been a long time since we'd enjoyed each other like this. John wanted to start a family soon after our wedding, and sex became a mechanical exercise. We abandoned all fun and spontaneity, relying on timing and the correct positions to ensure a successful pregnancy. Tonight was different. No rules. No agendas.

We kissed, tentatively at first, then hard and deep. I felt passion I hadn't experienced in years. His lips burned against mine, and I was beyond caring about the consequences of what we were about to do. My singular thought was that I wanted every part of him to be a part of me, the two of us melting together as one again, dissolving all that might have separated us.

We were like two teenagers, lost in a blur of passion. I took the lead. He didn't protest. I pulled at his belt and undid his pants, allowing them to fall to his ankles. He lifted my dress and tore off my panties. Now was not the time for finesse. We fell back onto the bed. I pulled him inside me and looked into his eyes as they penetrated deep into my soul.

It ended as quickly as it started. Still breathing heavily, I rested my head on his shoulder. God, how I missed those moments like this when time seemed to stand still and all else became irrelevant. Gone was the FBI. Gone were thoughts of Savannah. Gone were my concerns about my self-worth. All that mattered was John and I being together. We'd both yearned so hard for what we thought was a normal life that we forgot the reason why we married in the first place. It wasn't about raising a family in a quiet neighborhood. We wanted to spend the rest of our lives with each other, because the mere thought of being apart was incomprehensible. It took a hard journey through a great deal of pain before we finally realized that being together was all that mattered.

The rhythmic sounds of John's deep breathing lulled me to sleep. I didn't know how long I was out, but when I awoke in the morning, my watch read six-thirty. I still had six hours until my meeting at TBA, and I wasn't tired. I snuggled against John from behind, molding myself against him and enjoying the warmth radiating from his body. My heart ached for him, and I reached around his side, racking my nails across the ripples of his abs.

Though still asleep, he groaned.

My hand explored lower until I found him ready for more love. I squeezed gently until he was fully awake and rolled over onto me. We took our time, immersing ourselves in each other's touch, fighting to make the moment last. Last night we fucked, the sex raw and unbridled. This morning we allowed ourselves to be intimate, our love making unrestricted and as free as two lovers, stepping off a cloud hand in hand, floating weightlessly, unafraid, knowing the falling would never end as long as we remained together.

I got up an hour later, and the worries of real life slowly wormed their way back into my mind. Our time together was unforgettable. I knew he'd want me to move in with him as soon as possible, but I needed to resolve some issues first. I still had people out there who wanted to do me harm and, by extension, those I loved. I turned to John who was still lying in bed, smiling.

"Do you have an alarm system?"

A confused look replaced the smile on his face. "We live in a gated community. Besides, no one would try to rob the FBI Director of Counterterrorism."

"I think you should have one."

John raised up on his elbow, looking irresistibly handsome. "The old alarm is outdated and doesn't work, but I can have a new one installed next week. Why the urgency?"

I walked over and kissed him goodbye. "I think it'd be a good idea to do it as soon as possible."

"I'll call them this morning." He studied me as I dressed and got ready to leave. "Sure you can't stay for breakfast? I've learned to cook a mean omelet."

"Sounds tempting, but I have a few meetings this morning."

"Anything you want to talk about?"

"Maybe later. Love you, JC."

"Love you too, L."

I called for an Uber and walked out the front door, checking the street in all directions.

FORTY-FOUR

TBA Offices
The Atlantic Building
Washington, DC

Last night was exquisite, the best evening of my life, and I looked forward to seeing John again soon. I loved our new home. The words "our home" warmed my heart and seemed so right. Things between us had changed, but I wasn't ready to return full time. We weren't quite there yet, but we were definitely headed in the right direction.

The Uber took me back to the Marriott where I showered and dressed in a sensible tan pencil skirt, a pink, floral button-down blouse, and business heels. The Take Back America group had its offices on the fourth floor of the Atlantic Building on F Street, less than a mile from my hotel. It was a beautiful day, so I decided to walk. What could happen to me in broad daylight on the sidewalks of Pennsylvania Avenue? I checked for my protection detail but only found the guy from the bar at Marriott. If I hadn't already met him, I would've never noticed. The rest would be spaced a hundred feet from me in a four-quadrant pattern, but I couldn't make any of them. If they were still on me, they were good. I relaxed and allowed my mind to drift, reliving every delicious moment of last night.

After walking a few blocks, my stomach growled. *Can't live on love alone, Lisa.* I walked into the Capitol Coffee Bistro, the same place where Winston bought me a coffee and scone. My sunglasses made it too dark to see inside so I pushed them up onto my head, forcing my hair behind my ears. The walls of the shop were painted a soft mocha brown color and decorated with photographs of what looked to be South American coffee plantations. Three blackboard signs displayed tea and coffee drink offerings that would be the envy of any Starbucks. A large lady stood behind the counter. Her frizzy orange hair struggled to escape from under one of those ridiculous looking white bouffant surgical caps. Her body said she enjoyed too many of the shop's glazed donuts and caramel macchiatos. She scowled at me, a look I suspected was perpetual for her. I ordered a latte and blueberry scone like Winston gave me at Dupont Circle yesterday.

"You're too late," she sneered. "We're out of scones."

I pointed to several sitting in the glass cabinet under the counter. "How about one of those?"

"They're reserved. All I can give you is a plain bagel or a donut." She had all the social skills of a rabid pit bull.

"Reserved? A scone?" I wanted to ask her for whom but decided against it. I scanned the menu board on the wall looking for other options. "I really don't want a bagel or donut."

She smirked. "Then I guess you're just out of luck, honey." She turned her eyes to the man standing behind me. "Next." She was enjoying her little power trip.

She reminded me of Cassie's Nurse Ratched at the hospital. I was about to go full bore Beth Sutton on her and wipe that smirk off her face, but I took a deep breath. It could lead to a serious confrontation. I didn't care personally, but it wouldn't bode well for John's career, and being thrown in jail wouldn't help me with my ultimate goal of solving Savannah's murder. I forced a smile. "That's all right, honey." Emphasis on honey. "I'll just have the coffee." More scowling, but I paid for my drink and sat at a table in the corner, knowing I had won that little battle anyway.

While I sipped on my coffee, I opened my phone and checked my emails. The first was from Dr. Deutschle. The DNA from Governor Cartwright's glass fragment didn't match Savannah's baby. He wasn't the father. No surprise. It had been a long shot anyway. The second email was from Jacob regarding his wedding plans. It would have been nice to have him at my side the past few weeks. He'd have this murder solved in a few days. His methods were unconventional, but extremely effective. Maybe Winston was right. Maybe I should ask Jacob for help.

I finished my coffee and headed past the Old Ford Theater building where John Wilkes Booth shot Lincoln. It always looked smaller than I expected. Around the corner sat the Atlantic Building, old but impressive. The two-story lobby had been updated with light-gray granite floors and original oils depicting battles of the Revolutionary War on the walls. I took the elevator to the fourth floor where I encountered a long wall with the letters "TBA" painted across the backdrop of an unfurled American flag.

Every organization had its own unique personality, usually formed by its leaders. TBA was no exception. The cultish smiles and hyper-energetic look in their eyes said the staff was unconditionally dedicated to the TBA cause. After I walked through a set of double doors, a woman with short black hair met me. She wore a black blazer, a red skirt with black tights, and red pumps. Pinched lips, painted bright red, demanded attention. She was the person in charge, the gatekeeper who decided who may and who may not enter the sacred, inner confines of the executive offices. Nothing happened in the organization that she didn't know about.

She looked down her narrow nose at me. "May I help you?"

When I introduced myself as Miss Hamilton, her demeanor softened. Amazing, the effect money had. "Of course, Miss Hamilton, we've been expecting you. Mr. Matheson asked me to apologize for being late but he's stuck in a meeting at the Hart Senate Office Building. I expect him back shortly. Meanwhile, let me introduce you to his assistant."

She escorted me to an office where an impeccably dressed man stood and extended his hand. The hint of expensive cologne hung in the air. "Miss Hamilton? It's a pleasure to meet you. I'm Jeremy Mumford."

The tall slender man in front of me wore a gray, perfectly tailored suit over a light blue button-down shirt and a pastel pink tie. He had a patrician nose, and his hair was perfectly coiffed, every strand in place. His nails looked like he had recently spent time in a salon. On the wall opposite his desk hung a map almost identical to the one Norman had sent me, but without the stars indicating the murders. Next to it was a blackboard with a running tally: *34 states needed, 29 resolutions passed, 7 resolutions pending.* Someone added in quotations, "Five More To Go!"

I accepted Mumford's handshake, his skin soft and delicate. "I appreciate you taking the time to meet with me. I'll get to the point of my visit today. The Hamilton Family Trust has already invested a million dollars in the Take Back America organization."

"We certainly appreciate Mr. Hamilton's interest in what we're doing."

"My father plans to increase his investment. He's thinking of another fifty million. Before he authorizes any more cash transfers, he wanted me to get a better feel for what you're trying to accomplish."

Jeremy's eyes dilated and excitement danced across his face. "Let me ask you a question, Miss Hamilton."

"Sure."

He leaned forward, placing his hands flat on his desk.. "What do you believe is the greatest threat to the United States today?"

He caught me off guard. I searched my mind for an intelligent answer. "I'm not sure. There are so many. There's the pandemic that never seems to disappear. It's caused untold emotional and financial hardships for many of our citizens. Then there are the ongoing geopolitical problems associated with the continuous threats from the Chinese Communist Party. Of course, there's Putin's quest to expand the Soviet influence across Eastern Europe."

"Certainly, all legitimate concerns, Miss Hamilton, but there is one overriding risk to the future stability of our country, one that most politicians and the media choose to ignore. It's not the Russians, the Chinese, or even middle east terrorists. The biggest threat to the country is us. We have an uncontrolled addiction to spending and it's getting worse every year. We spend over a trillion dollars more than we collect in taxes. At present, the national debt has blown past thirty-one trillion dollars. Our debt to gross domestic product ratio exceeds 130%. That's a staggering amount, and one that's not sustainable."

"I'm not sure I understand, Mr. Mumford."

"Can you imagine what would happen if any individual or business spent that much more than they earned?"

Enthusiasm shined in his eyes. He didn't wait for me to reply. "They'd go bankrupt. Our country is on the precipice of an unprecedented financial disaster, especially as interest rates continue to increase. None of our leaders want to deal with the issue because it's a political third rail. Addressing it would demand some belt tightening and that runs contrary to the way most of congress gets elected. The result is overwhelming debt and its cousin, paralyzing inflation."

The guy was making me nervous. "So, what does TBA propose?"

"A two-pronged attack. The first is to provide the framework for a balanced budget amendment. Elected legislators won't support this because it threatens their electability. Can't buy votes. That makes the second prong essential, an amendment providing for term limits. Present legislators are firmly entrenched in their positions and too many have made tens of millions of dollars through sweetheart deals and insider stock trading, things for which you and I would go to jail. A culture of corruption has infected every level of our government. Elected officials have betrayed the public's trust."

The lady with the pinched red lips and black blazer stuck her head in the door. "I'm sorry, Mr. Mumford, but Richard from Ohio is on the line."

Jeremy snapped his head toward her. "Not now, Penny."

"He says it's urgent," she said. "It's about the lieutenant governor who took office after Governor Murray died. Richard says he's back peddling and threatens to withdraw his support for the resolution."

Jeremy's eyes glared. "I said not now. Tell him to take care of it. If he can't, I'll find someone who can."

The sudden, Jekyll and Hyde transformation in his demeanor startled me.

When pinched-lips Penny left, he again smiled and returned to his sales pitch. "That's why Scott founded TBA. We've been supporting a movement in the states calling for a constitutional convention where the necessary amendments can be enacted. It's a process opposed by a number of extremely powerful people, so we've been struggling to get the message out to the voters."

His level of enthusiasm seemed over the top, but he made some compelling arguments and was obviously passionate about what he did. I leaned back in my chair. "And that's why you're desperate for more funding."

"Desperate?" His cheeks flushed. "A harsh word, Miss Hamilton, but you're right. We are in need of further financial support to get more states to pass the necessary resolutions."

"And what's your function, Mr. Mumford?"

"My job is fundraising and putting out brush fires."

"Brush fires? Like in Ohio?"

His eyes narrowed. "Yes. Our organization has ruffled the feathers of the political establishment and we've encountered some intense pushback. Both liberal and conservative groups attack us on a regular basis. It's my job to squelch any threat to the organization and keep the movement on track."

Would Savannah Wellington have constituted such a threat?

His phone buzzed. "It looks like Mr. Matheson is back and ready to meet with you. I'll have his secretary show you the way."

FORTY-FIVE

TBA Offices
The Atlantic Building
Washington DC

Scott Matheson hadn't yet entered his office, so I took a chair opposite his desk and waited. The room smelled of stale tobacco smoke. Unlike the pristine look of Jeremy Mumford's office, Matheson's was a mass of clutter, his desk piled with empty cans of Diet Coke, newspapers, and stacks of reports. To the right sat an ashtray that hadn't been emptied in a week. On the left corner of the desk stood a framed family portrait of Scott and his beautiful wife, young looking and fit despite having given birth to five daughters, each as lovely as their mother. Next to the photograph rested a dysmorphic mass of clay sculpture, painted pink. Looked like it was supposed to be a dog, but I couldn't tell for sure. Probably a school project by one of his younger girls. Behind his chair hung a painting of the signing of the Declaration of Independence. On the walls were photographs of himself and multiple congressional leaders, including one of him fly fishing in Wyoming with President Wagner.

A minute later, I stood as Matheson charged in, removing his suit coat, and loosening his tie. His disheveled brown hair gave him the look of a young boy who just got off the monkey bars at the playground. Looked more like a cross between Cool

Hand Luke and a high school football coach than the founder of a national movement. I was struck by the clarity and intensity of his deep blue eyes, half expecting him to give a thunderous pregame pep talk. He extended his hand. "Sorry for being late, Miss Hamilton."

His voice was soft and almost lyrical, his smile engaging. I accepted his handshake, his grip confident but gentle. If Jeremy Wembley was the poster face of TBA, Scott was clearly the force behind it, the man who made things happen.

"Would you like something to drink?" he asked.

"Water would be nice."

He called over the intercom. "Penny, would you please bring in some Dasani for Miss Hamilton and me?"

A minute later, the pinched-lips Penny carried in a tray with two bottles of water and two glasses. She poured one for me. Scott twisted off the cap of his and guzzled half of it. He wiped a drop from his lower lip and smiled. "Two hours of meetings with a group of pompous senators drained me dry." He rolled up the sleeves of his white shirt revealing tan, muscular forearms.

I had hoped that Matheson might be a good candidate for the father of Savannah's baby, but the guy didn't seem to be her type. He was the polar opposite of her husband, Preston. Still, there was something appealing about him, a rugged sensuality that was hard to ignore, the kind of man who could make a woman glad she was a woman. If I hadn't been married, he'd be undeniably tempting, in a feral kind of way, like the shirtless men on the covers of romance novels. My mind wandered. Somehow, the room seemed warmer, and my face flushed. *Oh no! Was I blushing? Does he notice? Get this under control, Lisa.* I dug my nails into the palms of my hand to keep me focused.

He flashed a sheepish grin as he gathered up the empty Coke cans and tossed them in a trash can that was already overflowing. "Diet sodas are my feeble attempt at being healthy. I'm hoping the avoidance of sugar drinks will offset the negatives of my eating habits."

I shrugged. "Does your physician buy into that?"

He laughed. "Don't think so. He's pretty much given up on me." He got right to the point. "I understand you're here to follow up on Mr. Winston Hamilton's investment."

"Yes. Before pledging any more money to your cause, he wanted me to meet with you personally to find out more about your organization."

He smiled. "I understand you've already spoken to Jeremy."

"He gave me what I must assume is the organization's standard sales pitch. He was extremely thorough, but I had a few questions for you. I understand your quest is to get enough states to sign up for a constitutional convention. How well is that progressing?"

He put a cigarette between his lips and hesitated just a second before lighting it. "You mind if I smoke? A bad habit I haven't been able to shake. My wife has been pushing me to quit for years."

"No problem," I said. "We all have our vices."

He squinted at me through a cloud of smoke. "I guess we do. To your question, we've been highly successful thus far, but still need resolutions passed in five more states to ensure a convention. The hardest part in most games is that final push to put the ball over the goal line. That's why we're in need of additional financial support."

"So, what was the impetus behind you starting TBA?"

"I was the campaign manager and senior advisor for Senator Cranston Barnes of South Carolina. Started with him right out of law school. Wanted to make a difference, which we did. After two six-year terms, the Senator's approval numbers exceeded sixty percent and winning any election became a forgone conclusion. The process ran on autopilot. One of my daughters could have probably organized his campaign, so in all honesty, I became bored. At the same time, I witnessed a gradual but persistent decline in the culture of our government. The key to success in politics was no longer doing what was best for the country but more about catering to special interest groups and buying votes with expensive programs. That has led us down the path toward the brink of fiscal insolvency. We've become a snake devouring itself. The only way to turn things around is to take control of the country away from the powerful elite and transfer it back to the people. At TBA, our primary goals are to seek a balanced budget amendment and term limits. When we cut out the career politicians, we eliminate the potential for corruption and fiscal irresponsibility."

"But don't elections accomplish that?"

"In theory, they should, but incumbency brings with it the assurance of re-electability. Too many people tend to vote for the familiar names who promise the most handouts. In 1787, Alexander Tytler warned that a democracy can only exist until voters discover they can vote themselves generous payouts from the public treasury. He warned that, because of this, every democracy is destined to collapse within two hundred years. The United States has existed well beyond that time. We want to reverse that trend. If we can, it will constitute a watershed moment in the history of American politics."

All of this was interesting, and I agreed with most of what he had to say, but my purpose for being here was to gather information about Savannah and the murdered thirteen politicians. "Jeremy told me you've met some resistance from present power brokers."

"Certainly. We've been a serious threat to the established political hierarchy in Washington. There are financial rewards for being senior members of Congress and that has led to incestuous corruption.. Despite laws prohibiting it, insider trading in the financial markets runs rampant. As evidence of that, congressional leaders' portfolios outperform the average citizen by a factor of up to five times. Term limits erase those activities by removing politicians from their positions before they become corrupted."

I had him off guard. It was time to push my reasons for being there. "Do you think resentment about what you're doing might be the reason why Savannah Wellington was killed? I understand she was instrumental in your early successes."

He shifted in his chair, the way a person with a bad back might do, trying to find a more comfortable position. His pupils dilated and he crushed out his cigarette in the ashtray. I caught a slight tremor in his voice. "What a tragedy. She was an exceptional woman. We miss her terribly. You're correct in saying she was an integral part in our early successes. Without her help, I don't know if we could have gotten to where we are. All of us at TBA were deeply saddened to hear about Savannah, and we pray her killers will be found and brought to justice."

His secretary called in. "Mr. Matheson, Jeremy needs to see you in his office immediately."

He stood. "I'm sorry. I'll be back in a few minutes."

I'd struck a nerve. Matheson was obviously upset about discussing Savannah's death. Maybe, too upset. I reached into his ashtray, snatched up a cigarette butt, wrapped it in a Kleenex, and dropped it into my purse. I had all I needed. On my way out the door, I stopped to face the pinched-lips Penny. "Tell Mr. Matheson I said thanks for his time. The next installment of Mr. Hamilton's investment in TBA should arrive within the week."

On the way out I overheard Matheson and Jeremy involved in a heated discussion about Savannah. Had Jeremy been listening in on my conversation with his boss?

T. Milton Mayer

FORTY-SIX

Von Hamberg Estate
Brussels, Belgium

The Baron struggled toward the glass display vault, pushing his IV pole as he shuffled, its line extending into his left arm. He turned, and the IV tubing became snagged on his chair, almost tripping him and pulling the needle through his skin. "La Trane. Get in here and get me out of this mess."

LaTrane rushed through the door. "Yes sir?" He untangled the line. "You're supposed to remain in bed, Baron."

"Nonsense. I'm not an invalid. I don't know why I need these damn blood transfusions anyway."

"You have a form of chronic leukemia sir. They call it CML. It's made you anemic and that's why you've been so tired."

"Everybody my age is tired."

"The doctors want to make you stronger before starting chemotherapy. They believe there's an excellent chance they can cure you."

"Doctors. They all lie." He grumbled and struggled over to sit in a chair. "I need some positive news. Tell me about the demand for cobalt?"

"We've strangled the supply, sir. Since the destruction of the third Chinese mine, prices have exploded."

"Speaking of explosions, I'm concerned about our using the dirty bomb materials. It was a bad idea. Attracted too much international attention."

"We had no choice, sir. Without them, the Chinese mines would have been up and running again within a year."

"But the INRC might track the nuclear signature back to us."

"That won't happen, sir. It can only be traced to an Iranian nuclear waste site. It would be no surprise since they are known financial supporters of the Nigerian insurgents."

"And no one suspects us?"

"No, sir. The news media is buying into the entire Boko Haram story. Profits from our own mines have increased another three hundred percent and continue to rise."

"What about our people in Congress?"

"Per your instructions, the US Speaker has pushed hard to shut down the fossil fuel industry. New oil leases and fracking have been halted. Projections are that oil could soon increase to over $150 a barrel. That translates into higher costs at the gas pump and should drive the auto market away from internal combustion engines."

"What else?"

"He's backing legislation to support significant federal tax write offs for the purchase of all new electric vehicles. He's also pushed through a $10 billion bill to supply charging stations across the US. Once the programs have been fully implemented, sales of electric vehicles will increase exponentially. Cars aren't our only area of interest, though. The push for renewable energy will mean an increased need for large-capacity storage battery systems for solar and wind energy. That means even higher demands for cobalt."

"Good. Let the Speaker know we are pleased. Tell our people to purchase another hundred thousand shares of New Dawn Technologies and place them in his account at our

Masada Bank. He and his wife may have access to the shares after he retires next year."

"Retires?"

"Yes. I've already selected his successor."

LaTrane raised an eyebrow. "As you wish sir."

"What's going on with that murder investigation in Florida?"

"Fedallah's man successfully removed the detective who had been working the case. We have a newspaper report confirming her death. We still have a problem, however. Penny, our source at the Take Back America offices, reports another woman has been snooping around the case."

"Another homicide detective?"

"I don't know for sure, but she's a thorough and relentless investigator. She's been asking questions about deaths of the thirteen politicians associated with TBA. She's also been facilitating a significant influx of cash into TBA's accounts."

"Name?" asked the Baron.

"She presents herself as Lisa Hamilton, but Penny was suspicious, so she did a background search on her. The woman's real name is Lisa Marie Crawford. Apparently, she's married to the FBI's director of counterterrorism.

"She's getting too damn close and could ruin everything. I don't care who her husband is, LaTrane. Get rid of her. Tell Fedallah I want that woman dead by the end of the week. Money is not an issue. While you're at it, send some of our own men to be sure he gets the job done right."

"Already taken care of, sir. I made the necessary arrangements a few days ago. Since the list of thirteen is complete, perhaps it's time to sever ties with Fedallah."

"After he's eliminated the woman."

"Of course, sir."

FORTY-SEVEN

National Mall
Washington, DC

Walking back from the TBA offices, I headed toward the Marriott with as many questions as I had before my meeting. After what Winston told me about the possibility of others pursuing me, I felt vulnerable. I scanned my surroundings to see if Winston's people were on me. I hoped they were.

My new cell phone rang. It was John's office. Normally, if he needed to get ahold of me, his secretary left a message for me to call back. She never introduced herself or said, "Hi Mrs. Crawford." At most, the woman would leave a curt message to call John. "John?" She always referred to him as John rather than Director Crawford. *What's with that? Seemed a little too chummy to me.* When I'd call back, she'd sound annoyed. I'd hear her icy voice over the intercom, "The wife is on line three." I'd never met the woman in person, but I hated her. I pushed the answer button on my phone, expecting to hear the witch's voice. Instead, it was John. "Good afternoon sweetheart."

Sweetheart? For as long as I had ever known John, he had never called me sweetheart. I liked it. "Hi," I answered. Not very clever or romantic but it was all I could think of.

"Where are you right now?"

I'd been in such deep thought about my meeting, I hadn't been paying attention. I raised my sunglasses to look. "Walking down Pennsylvania Avenue. I'm about to pass in front of the Hoover Building."

"Great," he said. "I'll tell my secretary to cancel my appointments for the rest of the afternoon. It's too nice a day to be cooped up inside. I'm going to take you out to lunch. Wait by the front doors. I'll be down in a minute."

"Will do." Another first. The old John would never take an afternoon off. Bet his secretary didn't approve. That put a smile on my face. I waited under the J Edgar Hoover logo outside the glass doors.

He sauntered out, smiling wide, his suit jacket slung over his shoulder. His eyes danced with excitement. *Because of me? Who was this man?* I hugged him and gave him a hard kiss.

He looked surprised. "What was that for?"

"My way of thanking you for loving me." I grabbed his hand. "What did you have in mind for lunch?"

"Let's head over to the National Mall. It's just a block away. Neither of us have seen it since the night I proposed."

He led the way, but I wasn't aware of any restaurants along the mall. We headed toward the Smithsonian Museum of Natural History and took a right on Constitution Avenue. The Washington Monument towered directly ahead, much larger than I remembered. We passed a half-dozen street vendors parked along the streets. They created an olfactory stew of tantalizing scents.

"I've always wanted to do this," John said. "You like hot dogs?" He didn't wait for me to answer. He walked up to one of the food trucks and studied the menu. "I'd like two of your Jersey Dawgs, two orders of fries, and two Diet Cokes."

"Boy, are you living dangerously," I said.

"You only go around once in this life. Time to have fun."

The Pakistani guy behind the counter handed John our order in a brown paper bag and we walked the rest of the way toward the monument. It was a marvelous afternoon with whimsical white clouds floating across a clear blue sky. A circle of fifty American flags surrounding the giant obelisk flapped in the gentle breeze. We walked past the World War II Memorial until we found a stone bench by the reflecting pool, the Washington Monument towering over one end and the Lincoln Memorial at the other. It was the same place where John had proposed. Seemed like a lifetime ago. John and I talked and laughed for hours, discussing what each of us needed in life. I mentioned how I had become depressed after having lost my identity.

"I realize that now," he said. "I was so wrapped up in what I was doing, I failed to notice what you were going through." He held my hand. "I want you to do whatever you must to make yourself feel fulfilled. I don't care what it is, even if it means returning to the team. If it's important to you, it's important to me."

His words nourished my soul and I felt whole again. We kissed several times and watched squirrels chase each other, waging war over their turf. Flocks of pigeons patrolled the sidewalks searching for stray morsels of food that might have dropped to the ground.

"I'll qualify for a pension soon, and I've been thinking about leaving the Bureau."

My mouth dropped. "You can't do that, John. You love the FBI."

"Not so much anymore. It's become too politicized over the past several years. Directors pursue political agendas beyond their mission of fighting crime. The bureau was originally created to protect citizens from criminal elements, but in the past several years it's become weaponized into an organization more focused on targeting innocent civilians." He stared across the water. "Maybe we can move back to Cincinnati and I can set up a small private law practice."

Several mallards, with their babies following closely behind, swam past, hoping for a free meal. I pinched off a small piece from the edge of my bun and threw it in the water, but I wasn't about to give up any of my hotdog. More swam over, looking for handouts. John tossed them a few fries which they attacked. A man walked behind us, wearing one of those souvenir caps with the Capitol Dome emblazoned on the front, the kind tourists purchased at the roadside stands. He sat on a bench twenty feet to the right of ours and threw some bread into the water. The more he fed the ducks, the more they gathered around him looking for more. He turned in our direction and smiled. I smiled back and said, "Beautiful day."

"That it is," he said and got up to leave.

It was one of the most glorious days of my life. We kissed again and John said, "The sun's getting lower in the sky. Let's head home."

Home. I liked the sound of it.

<hr>

Once we got to the house, John tried to hug me.

I pulled back. "No way. I need a shower first. Where are the towels?"

John grinned. "That's right. I didn't get around to showing you the entire house last night. Seems we got distracted somehow and never made it past the bedroom."

"Funny how distractions like that happen. Looking forward to more of those."

He grinned and looked up the stairway. "Shower's to the left, just off the bedroom. Linen closet's behind the bathroom door."

On the way up the steps, I turned. "Maybe you can whip up something for us to eat? That hotdog didn't stay with me very long, and I'm starving."

"Will do."

After a long hot shower, I found a pair of my skinny jeans in the closet and put on a red sweatshirt of John's over my bare breasts. The words *Cornell Law School* were emblazoned in white across the chest. It was too big, but I loved feeling something of John's against my skin. When I came back downstairs and entered the kitchen, multiple containers of Chinese food covered the kitchen table.

"I have Moo Goo Gai Pan, Chicken Chow Mein, crab Rangoon, sweet and sour pork, fried rice, and egg rolls. Wasn't sure what you wanted, so I ordered a little bit of everything."

I looked at all the food and back to John. "How'd you have time?"

"I discovered Door Dash, an essential App in today's world. All you do is order what you want online, and they bring it right to your door." He walked over to the wine cabinet. "I don't know what goes well with Chinese."

"How about a beer?"

"Beer it is." He reached into the fridge and pulled out two bottles of Yuengling, popped off the caps and handed me one. We tapped the necks of the bottles together. "To the future," John said.

"To our future," I replied and took a mouthful. I looked in John's eyes, and saw what my life could be with him back in it.

"Let's eat," he said.

After dinner, we sat next to each other on the couch. Though it was late August, John picked up his remote and started the fire. Light from the flames danced across the walls. I pulled up my legs, curled them to the side, and rested my head on John's shoulder. We said nothing, but nothing needed to be said. We stared at the fire for over an hour, then headed upstairs to bed. The love making was slow and comfortable, each of us taking time, experimenting with what the other wanted. For the first time since we were married, our lives were no longer separate. John became a part of me and I a part of him.

John fell asleep while my head rested on his chest, his breathing slow and rhythmic. I felt safe and secure realizing there was nowhere else I wanted to be. I listened to the powerful beat of his heart, gradually slowing to a hypnotic pace. Sleep drifted over me like a soft poem.

In the morning, I put on my favorite pink fuzzy robe and sat in a chair, staring at John as he slept. The bed sheets only covered half of him, his light mocha skin a warm contrast to the white sheets. I must have been sitting there for a half hour before his eyes fluttered open. He smiled. "Good morning, sweetie." It was the second time he had called me that. Not sure where he came up with the name, but I liked it.

He propped up on his elbow. "Seeing you here is like waking up to an angel."

I groaned. "Did you read that in a Hallmark card somewhere?"

A sheepish grin spread across his face. "That bad, huh?"

"It's about the corniest thing I've ever heard you say — but I love it."

He threw a pillow at me and jumped out of bed. "I'm starving."

We went to the kitchen and I opened the fridge. "We still have a little bit of left-over Chinese, but I don't think I can handle that for breakfast. Not much else in here except milk, a carton of eggs, and a few vegetables."

"Just enough to make one of my famous omelets."

I raised an eyebrow. "Famous?"

He winked. "Soon to be. Start chopping those red peppers and onions while I get the eggs ready.

John was right. It was the best omelet I'd ever eaten. I was pouring him a second cup of coffee when my robe shifted, exposing one of my breasts.

John leered.

"Still not full?" I asked.

"Never." He put our plates in the sink. "We need to start christening each room of our new home, beginning with this one."

He swept me up into his arms and set me on the island. I wrapped my legs around his waist. It was exciting, like we were doing something naughty. I stared over his shoulder at the large bay window behind the breakfast table. "This is crazy, John. What about the neighbors? They might see us."

"Too many trees, but if they do, who cares? The possibility is what makes it fun."

Several minutes later, I looked again. There, barely visible, just within the edge of the trees, I thought I saw someone in jeans and a black hoodie. I couldn't make out his face. Was *Winston's protection detail around? Could someone get past them?*

"Somebody's watching," I screamed.

When John looked, the person was gone.

"It was your imagination," said John.

No, it wasn't.

<hr>

While John showered and dressed for work, I cleaned the kitchen and put the dishes in the washer, all the while rechecking the backyard every few minutes looking for the guy in the hoodie. When John came down the stairs, I hugged him. "Could you do me a little favor today?"

He stepped back. "For you, anything, especially after our breakfast surprise this morning."

I handed him a small clear plastic bag containing the cigarette butt I removed from Scott Matheson's ashtray yesterday. "Would you send this to Quantico for a DNA analysis and forward the report to a Dr. Fred Deutschle?"

"To whom?"

I repeated the name. "He's the coroner for Collier County, Florida."

"What for?" John's eyebrows furrowed together. "Lisa, what are you up to?" Then, his look softened and he smiled. "Makes no difference why you want it. If it's important to you, it's important to me. I'll take care of it."

"One more thing. I'm worried about what I saw in the woods this morning. It wasn't my imagination."

"Does this have anything to do with this DNA profile you want?"

"Yes. Please humor me on this, at least until you have the new alarm system installed."

He promised to keep a couple agents stationed in front of our house. Before leaving he reached into his pocket. "Forgot to give you the keys for the front and back doors." After handing them over, he smiled, kissed me, and left.

As I watched John's car disappear down the street, the image of the hooded man wormed its way through my mind. Maybe John was right. *Maybe it was only my imagination. Then again, it sure seemed real. Could it have been one of Winston's men? But wearing a hoodie? Unlikely.* Winston warned me there might be others out there making plans to get me.

After double checking all the doors to be sure they were locked, I retrieved my Sig from my purse and kept it at my side. The only thing on my schedule for the day was to head over to the Marriott, pack up my clothes, and check out. I planned to move in with John that evening.

FORTY-EIGHT

Washington, DC

The final member of the Client's list had been eliminated. Ishmael had already been in Philadelphia, waiting for his new identity papers when he received an urgent notice from Fedallah. The Client insisted on adding one more contract. Ishmael protested saying that he was finished.

"Refusal in not an option," said Fedallah. "It would not be in your best interest."

Ishmael headed for Washington.

———————————————

After following the woman and her husband across the National Mall, Ishmael had discovered her point of vulnerability. She was married and clearly smitten. Perhaps a marriage on the mend? Her husband was Deputy Director of the FBI. Assassinating her wouldn't be easy, but doable. A contingent of at least four guards maintained an umbrella of protection around her at all times. The perimeter wasn't entirely impenetrable, not for Ishmael. He managed to get within ten yards of her while she and her husband fed the ducks. She even smiled at him. *Beautiful day.* The contract terms could be satisfied but her protection detail needed to be circumvented, though they probably didn't watch over her after she was in the safety of her home.

There might be other problems though. Fifteen million was excessive for the woman. She was a nobody, and it was the same amount as for the Ohio Governor. Made no sense. Typically, half of his retainer would be forwarded to his account in advance and the balance transferred after confirmation of the kill. Ishmael found no evidence that the money had been deposited. Again, it made no sense unless the amount was simply bait, and the Client had no intention of ever paying.

Another problem was the second team shadowing Mrs. Crawford. They were good but not good enough, and they seemed as interested in Ishmael as the woman. The only explanation was they were there to ensure completion of the job and then to terminate him once he neutralized Mrs. Crawford. The Client was severing all ties to the other thirteen killings. It posed a dilemma. Failure to execute the woman meant an angry Client, a powerful man with limitless resources. Ishmael would be forced to spend the rest of his days on the run. On the other hand, if he eliminated the woman, he'd soon be taken out himself. Damned if he did and damned if he didn't. He'd need a quick escape. Even then, he had no guarantee the Client wouldn't eventually track him down.

He called Fedallah and explained the situation. Ishmael didn't trust the man, but using him was the only good option. "We're both in danger. The Client plans to betray us. I believe he intends to eliminate me — and you as well. Take the necessary precautions on your end. I will need at least a half dozen different identities with corresponding passports and credit cards. Please make the arrangements with your man in Philadelphia. After I terminate the woman, I'll contact you for further instructions. We must act quickly." He was disappointed his final work would be so inartistic and messy.

FORTY-NINE

Rockville, Maryland

The husband returned from work at six o'clock that evening. He unholstered his gun and set it on a table just inside the front door. When he turned around, Ishmael, wearing a black hoodie and jeans stepped forward, a silenced 9mm in his right hand. "Good evening, Director Crawford. Please have a seat."

John lunged for his gun and was rewarded with a shot to his right thigh.

"I was hoping to be more civilized about this, John, but you forced me to do that. I know it hurts but it's not a fatal wound. You'll survive as long as you cooperate."

Ishmael secured John to a chair with duct tape.

"You were the guy in our back yard this morning," said John.

Ishmael smiled. "You and your wife put on a pretty good show in the window. I know she saw me. Maybe she enjoyed having somebody watch. She kinda kinky that way?"

Anger contorted John's face, and he tried to lunge at Ishmael. "Asshole. How'd you know where we live?"

"Simple. Followed you here after you left the mall. Waited in the woods until you both left this morning. I'm surprised you didn't assign anyone to keep an eye on your house while you were gone. Surprisingly careless for an FBI man. You made it easy for me, John. Your alarm system is shot, and your locks are worthless. Even an amateur could've broken in."

"Fuck you."

Ishmael searched John's pockets, found his cell phone, and held it in front of John's face to unlock it. "Now, I want you to text your wife and ask her when she's coming home."

John knocked the phone away with his head. "Go fuck yourself."

"What's with the language, John? So much for civility." Pfft. A shot to the other leg. John howled in pain.

"Guess I'll have to do this myself." Ishmael sent a series of texts to Lisa.

Afterward, Ishmael pulled the drapes aside slightly and saw the car parked across the street. "You bring a few friends home with you tonight, Director? Should've had them standing guard this morning. Too little too late."

He sealed John's mouth shut with the duct tape. "Can't have you yelling out for help." Ishmael turned toward the door. "Now I have to take care of those men in the car. Their blood's on your hands, Director."

FIFTY

Clyde's of Georgetown
Washington, DC

I was at the Marriott packing up my belongings when Cassie called. She'd been going stir crazy after having been confined to Winston's mansion for the past two weeks.

"Don't get me wrong. Everyone treats me well, but I'm tired of seeing the same faces every day. Mr. Hamilton has a gourmet chef preparing some bizarre Indonesian meals and a God-awful coffee made from animal droppings. Think I've lost weight."

I laughed. "I know what you mean. Winston has some exotic tastes. What you need is some good old fashioned American comfort food. Brad's in custody, so it should be safe for us to go out."

"I'd love that, Lisa."

"How about we meet up at Clyde's in Georgetown? It's informal and only ten minutes from Winston's estate. I'm sure Kingsley will be happy to drop you off, and I can drive you back."

"Sounds great," she said. "Around seven? I'll make reservations."

"See you then." I thought about the hoodie and mentioned it to Cassie. "It's probably nothing but you might want to bring your Glock just in case."

"I'm always carrying. See you at seven."

Patrons packed themselves around Clyde's long poplar-wood bar. Pendant Tiffany lamps above and vintage posters on the walls behind set the ambiance. Opposite the bar, a row of wooden booths with burgundy-colored benches matched the ceiling color.

We each tried a dirty martini and ordered the hamburger special. We joked and laughed the way you can't when men are around.

"I have some great news," I said.

Cassie leaned closer and smiled. Excitement glowed in her eyes. "What?"

"John and I are getting back together. He bought a new home for us, and I'm moving in with him tonight."

The excitement faded and she leaned back in the booth. "That's wonderful, Lisa. I'm so happy for you." Her words didn't match her demeanor.

I reached over the table and took her hands in mine. "I want you to know you've become an important part of my life, and I don't ever want that to change. I won't let it."

Cassie smiled.

"One reason I had so many problems and felt the need to escape to Naples was because I didn't have a close friend like you, someone with whom I can share my innermost feelings, things a woman can't always share with her husband. I want to make sure our relationship continues. I love you too much to lose you."

A waiter dropped a tray of drinks and the glasses shattered on the floor. After all we'd been through, any sudden, loud noise sounded too much like a gunshot. We both jumped out of our seats, Cassie with her Glock in hand, my fingers on my Sig.

"Jesus," she said. "I might have shot someone."

We both laughed at the insanity of it. Other patrons stared at us as we slid back into our booth.

"I'm afraid it's going to be a while before either of us gets over our jitters," I said.

"I know," said Cassie. "I still look over my shoulder, even in Mr. Hamilton's mansion."

"Me too. I think the situation calls for another drink."

The waiter brought two more martinis and I started feeling pretty chatty. "I used to be part of a team that did some extremely dangerous things. We worked around the country and Europe protecting the world from terrorists. The job prevented me from having a normal life, something I yearned for even though I didn't know what a normal life was. I think maybe I fell in love with the idea of having a husband and children as much as I cared for John. A person in love puts the other person's needs above their own. I didn't do that. I put my feelings before John's. That's the reason I ran."

"From everything you've told me, I think John did the same. You're not the only one to blame."

"John and I never communicated very well. We tended to avoid discussing painful issues, but over the past few days, we've had a chance to spend time alone together, without outside distractions. We've discussed our problems, our fears, and our dreams for the future. We rediscovered why we fell in love in the first place. Yes, I still want my old career, but it's no longer as important to me. I'm willing to sacrifice it to have John in my life. That's my priority. I can tell John feels the same way. It took three years for us to realize it, but we're happier now than we've ever been. Life has given us another chance, and neither of us wants to squander it."

Our hamburger specials arrived, and we devoured them. They were as good as the Big Macs we had after the Florida governor's reception. We each ordered a Drambuie for dessert. Before the drinks arrived, my phone buzzed with a text from John.

Hi, Lisa. When are you coming home?

Lisa? Not L? Not even sweetie? I tightened my grip on the phone. Something was off.

> Me: **Just met Marsha for dinner at Clyde's. Headed home in a few hours.**
>
> John: **Tell her I said hi. See you soon.**
>
> Me: **Will do. She says hi back.**

I stared at the screen for a second. Something was terribly wrong. John was in danger.

I turned to Cassie. "I'm not sure what's happening but John's in serious trouble. I have to leave right now."

"Trouble? How do you know?"

"I told him I was with Marsha, and he said to tell you hi. He knows your name is Cassie." I patted the Sig in my purse. "Winston warned me that someone besides Brad might want me dead. Whoever he is, I believe he might be the one who tried to kill you. He's probably holding John hostage as bait to get me there."

"You think we should call the police?"

"No way. I don't know how many killers are with John. If the cops storm the house with guns pulled, John will be killed for sure. I need to do this myself. Whoever has him won't be expecting me for another couple hours. Gives me a chance to check on the house and figure out what to do."

"You're not going anywhere alone. I'm coming with you. Whoever's holding him hostage won't be expecting you to have backup."

I left a hundred dollars on the table, more than enough to settle our tab, including a generous tip. We rushed out, leaving the glasses of Drambuie untouched.

FIFTY-ONE

Rockville, Maryland

G oogle maps said it was a twenty-seven-minute drive to our home in Rockville. I made it in twenty and parked several blocks up the street. The situation called for stealth and surprise. I checked my watch. Still had an hour before the killer expected me, enough time to formulate a plan. We approached the house on foot, avoiding streetlamps, and remaining in the shadows. A dark sedan was parked across the street. *The bodyguards John promised this morning. Could be a problem.*

I was describing the layout of the house to Cassie when I saw a shadow through the kitchen bay window. Only one person and it definitely wasn't John. Too short. I turned to Cassie. "I'm going up the back deck to enter through the kitchen door. Maybe I can catch the guy off guard and take a shot. If not, I can distract him while you sneak in the front." I pulled the front door key from my keychain and handed it to her. "Give me fifteen minutes and then ease your way in."

I checked the sedan. "There are probably a couple of FBI guys in that car in front. Don't let them see you or they might try to storm the house and start shooting anything that moves."

"Copy that." Cassie racked the slide of her Glock and chambered a round.

I did the same with my Sig as she disappeared around the corner of the house.

I inched my way around to the back, tiptoed up the deck steps, and crawled over until I could peek through the corner of the bay window. To the left of the kitchen island sat John, secured to a wooden slatted chair with gray duct tape. "Oh my God." My heart stopped. Fresh blood stains spread across both his pant legs. A strip of the tape covered his mouth, and his eyes looked swollen like he'd been beaten. Anger replaced any feeling of fear. I eased my way toward the door and leaned my back against the brick. Reaching over, I slowly turned the knob. Locked. I fumbled with my key and inserted it into the lock, creating more noise than I wanted. *Shit! So much for catching the guy off guard.* Crouching low, I slowly pushed the door open with the tip of my Sig. *Pfft.* The doorframe next to my head splintered from the gunshot. I fired a couple rounds in the direction of the sound but couldn't see the killer. I rolled across the floor and took cover near the back of the island. John was ten feet to my left. I tried to get to him, but more gunfire pushed me back.

A voice arose from the hallway. "Very clever Mrs. Crawford, but not quite clever enough. You're not getting any help with those two agents parked in front. They've been incapacitated."

I reached over the island and fired two more shots toward the voice. Had to be careful. Didn't know where Cassie was. After the gunfire, she was sure to be coming in.

A man dressed in a black hoodie and jeans emerged from the shadows, pointing a silenced 9mm directly at John's head. It was the same guy I saw in the back yard. He made no effort to hide his face. Bad sign. He didn't care because John and I weren't going to be around long enough to identify him. He had me at a distinct disadvantage. If I didn't play this just right, John and I would both die. Hopefully he hadn't planned on me having backup. "Put your gun on the table, Mrs. Crawford, or my next shot will be into your husband's head."

Keeping my gun aimed on the intruder's chest, I slowly stood and turned sideways to decrease my target profile. "That's not going to happen. Shoot him and a milli-second later, you're a dead man."

He never blinked. Most killers, even professionals, looked a little jittery when faced with the possibility of being killed in a gunfight. Not this guy. He remained eerily calm.

"It appears what we have here, Mrs. Crawford is a Mexican standoff." He smiled as if detached from the reality of the situation, his demeanor aloof and calculating.

"No one has to die here tonight," I said.

"Of course, they do, Mrs. Crawford." His cold eyes fixated on John. "An irrevocable contract was placed on your life. Failure to execute the terms of that agreement will result in my own death. Then, someone else will come after you. You are going to die one way or the other. The only question is will you save the life of your husband?"

I needed to keep him talking and distracted so Cassie could enter. "But why me? I'm a nobody."

"You and your lady detective friend were never supposed to be a part of this. You weren't on the list of thirteen, but you both kept snooping around that murder in Naples and stumbled upon certain sensitive information. I was commissioned to terminate Detective Pierce to stop her investigation. Even with your friend dead, you kept turning over stones you should have left untouched. You started getting uncomfortably close to my client."

"Client? What client?"

"Don't know. I never do." His smile faded. "Makes no difference. Now step away from your husband. I have no issues with him. I don't kill people I'm not paid to eliminate."

An assassin with a code of conduct? Nonsense. I didn't believe him. The guy intended to kill us both regardless. John realized it. He struggled with his restraints and tried to yell from under the duct tape. A futile effort, but it served as the distraction I needed. The killer didn't hear Cassie in the hallway. *Keep him talking, Lisa. It's the only way to get John out of this.* I stared at the gunman. "Why Savannah Wellington? Why kill her?"

His eyebrows merged. "The Florida woman? I di —"

Boom. Cassie fired a single shot from the hallway, hitting him in the left shoulder. He spun and returned fire in her direction.

I charged him, firing repeatedly as I ran. Using my momentum, I drove him hard into the wall.

"I don't have a shot," yelled Cassie.

I grabbed his gun with my left hand.

He was too strong and twisted the barrel to my head.

I drove my Sig into his wounded left shoulder and fired.

He howled in pain, pulled free and fired twice before running past me and escaping out the kitchen door toward the deck.

Cassie tried to give chase but stopped when she saw John. "He's been hit!"

I dropped to my knees, my heart racing as a rosette of blood expanded across John's shirt. I ripped it open and found an entrance wound to the left of his sternum. Air sucked in through the bullet hole. "Call 911!"

I applied pressure to the wound with my left hand while pulling the duct tape from his mouth and using it to seal the hole in his chest. After I cut his restraints, I lowered John to the floor, resting his head in my lap.

His lips turned ashen gray.

"Look at me, John!"

His eyes fluttered shut. "No, JC. Keep looking into my eyes. I'm right here with you."

His breathing became shallow and labored. A deep gurgling sound percolated up from his throat.

"Don't leave me, JC. Please don't leave me," I sobbed.

He coughed up blood. His head rolled to the side.

"No. Stay with me. Open your eyes. Please open your eyes."

When the EMTs arrived, they huddled around me. "I'm fine. Take care of my husband."

"She's been shot," one of them said. Someone started an IV line in my left arm and another applied pressure to my abdomen. The room turned black.

FIFTY-TWO

Sibley Memorial Hospital
Washington, DC

In the ambulance, the siren screamed as I drifted into and out of consciousness. I saw brief snippets of scenes like watching a series of high-speed movie trailers. Overhead fluorescent lights flashed across my eyes as the EMTs rushed me down a hallway. IV tubing led to my arm. Blurred faces I didn't recognize hovered over me, poking and probing.

"Where's John?" I heard myself ask. "You've got to save him."

No one paid attention. Doctors and nurses in green scrubs scurried about yelling to one another. One put a catheter in my bladder. "She has blood in her urine."

Another placed a mask over my face while several others cut my clothes away.

"GSW of the left upper quadrant. Bleeding profusely." They rolled me over like a rag doll. "Exit wound in the back."

A cold metal disc pushed against my skin.

"Left lung's collapsed. Get me a chest tube."

A woman's voice yelled, "Abdomen's distended. She's bleeding internally." Another frantic voice on my right side. "Pulse thready. Pressure's dropping. We're losing her, people. Start another line. Get me two units of O-negative STAT. Type and cross for six more units."

"Call surgery."

I woke up to the sun streaming through the window, the room so bright, I thought I might have died and gone to heaven. I doubted dead people could feel pain, and my whole body hurt. A monitor behind me beeped regularly. Definitely not dead.

I turned to my right and saw a blurry image in a chair gradually come into focus. "Back to the land of the living, I see. Can I get you anything?"

Cassie! The chair she had been sitting in had a pillow and blanket tossed over it. From the looks of things, she had been there all night—perhaps several nights. My first words were, "John?"

Before she could answer, a young nurse walked in, a little too chirpy. "You're looking much better. You gave us quite a scare for a few days."

A few days? How long have I been out?

"The bullet tore the artery to your spleen and damaged part of your kidney. On its way, it nicked your lung and collapsed it, but you're going to be fine. Doctor said we can remove one of your IVs and the catheter today." She turned off the IV, pulled the needle out, and applied pressure to the site. A minute later, she lifted my gown, exposing things I preferred to keep hidden. That's when I saw my bandage, from my sternum down past my navel. She noticed me looking. "It'll look better in a year. You were crashing and there was no time to make it look pretty."

Without a word of warning, she deflated the balloon and removed the catheter from my bladder.

Absolutely no dignity in a hospital. If I had felt strong enough, I might have punched her in the nose.

She used a syringe to inject medicine into my remaining IV line. "You rest now. I'll be back in a little bit." I felt Cassie squeeze my hand before I fell back to sleep.

I had no idea exactly how long I'd been in the hospital, but Cassie still sat in the chair next to me. My overriding concern continued to be John. Did he make it? While serving on the team, I had seen many people die. I knew the look. I hoped against hope I was wrong. I dared not ask the question but had to. Casey still sat in the chair next to me.

"John?" I asked again.

She reached over and held my hand. "I'm sorry, Lisa. So sorry."

The words ripped through my heart, and my lungs refused to allow air in. I had left John for what I hoped would be a better life for me. In doing so, I had made the final months of his life miserable. It took leaving him for me to realize how much I loved him. Our last three days together had been the most exquisite in my life, our love for each other stronger than it had ever been. Now, he was gone, killed because someone wanted me dead. It should have been me. Had I stayed at his side in Washington, instead of running to Naples, I would have never known about Savannah or been involved in the search for her killer. John would still be alive. I was alone, falling back into the same dark pit I had just escaped, a place without hope, a place where I deserved to be. Painful irony. The grief devoured me, tearing apart the final fragments of my soul. Life held no promise. I hated that I was still alive. I hated a God who would allow an evil psychopath to slaughter a good man like John. I no longer cared about anything or anybody, least of all Savannah Wellington and her baby.

After my discharge from the ICU, Winston brought Norman and Carla to the hospital to see me. I had nothing to say to them. The same was true when other team members visited.

One the fourth day, Jacob arrived with his fiancé, Raphael at his side. Tears trickled down her cheeks. Jacob shook his head. "We're so sorry, Lisa. You should've told me what was happening. I should've been here for you. I should have protected you. I thought —"

I held up my hand. "Nothing you could have done, Jacob. Besides, I didn't want to ruin your wedding plans. I never expected anything like this to happen."

"We postponed the wedding. Neither of us want to go ahead until you've fully recovered and can be there. We both love you." Those last words caught in his throat. "I'm going to get this guy. I promise you."

I grabbed Jacob's hand. "We can do it together — for John."

For obvious reasons the FBI took over the investigation. Several agents arrived and cleared the room before questioning me. The senior agent took the lead. "Can you describe the assailant? Your friend tried but she only saw him briefly, from the side."

"Above average height, about six feet tall. Average build. Brown hair, combed and parted on the left. He looked like any man you might pass on the street. One thing strange was his eyes. They were dark, lacking any emotion. No fear. He smiled during the entire ordeal. It seemed to be a game for him." I replayed the minutes of that night in my mind. It happened so fast. "He wore gloves, purple latex."

"Your friend described them. We searched to see if he might have discarded them as he ran. Sometimes we can get a print from the inside, but we couldn't find any gloves. Our imprint analyst did find bloody footprints on the rear deck, made by a Nike size eleven, consistent with a male about six feet tall."

"Which we already know," I said.

"Yes, but if we find a suspect, we can match his shoes to the footprint. The soles leave characteristic markings similar to fingerprints."

"Won't happen," I said. "Those shoes are long gone by now." I looked at a bloody stain on my arm bandage from where the IV had been removed. "I shot him in the left shoulder, point blank."

The junior agent jotted a note in his phone. "We found a lot of blood in the hallway, some from you, but most of it was his. The trail of blood led out the back door and into the woods. Looks like he had a vehicle parked on a street behind yours. We canvassed the homes in the neighborhood. Nobody noticed anything suspicious, but one security camera in a house behind the wooded area picked up the image of an individual. It's dark and too grainy to run through the facial recognition database." He showed it to me. "Does he look familiar?"

"Same kind of hoodie. It might be the guy, but I can't say for sure."

"We're hoping you can work with one of our forensic artists so we can put together a composite sketch. That should help. We also have a DNA profile on him from all the blood he left behind at the scene."

Scene? The word sounded so distant and sterile. It was more than just a damn scene. It was our home, the place where John and I made love, where we planned to spend the rest of our lives together. Just as the place where Savannah was murdered was more than a mere scene. It was a place where a woman and mother-to-be had her life stolen.

I looked at the agent. "The blood will be a dead end. The guy was a pro. I doubt he's in the CODIS. Might find a match in the military databases, but I'm not optimistic. I suspect the guy doesn't exist—officially that is. He's a ghost whose identity was created out of nothing years ago by whoever handles him." I feared we might never find the killer.

Jacob came back into the room shortly after the two agents left. "Did they ask you about possible motives behind the shooting?"

"No, they didn't, but I'm sure they will eventually. It'll be complicated, and I don't want to answer any questions unless I have to. I think we should look into this using our own methods."

Jacob was of the same opinion. "The Bureau is committing a lot of assets to the case. John was one of theirs, and the two agents standing guard in front of your house were also killed. They're pissed, but I'm not optimistic about what they'll be able to accomplish. They're handcuffed by their own investigative protocols. I'm afraid this case is going to go cold very quickly. However, I have an idea. If the guy bled as much as they believe, he couldn't have gotten far without some treatment. I'm sure the Bureau has thought of this and will be checking all hospitals within a hundred-mile radius for any gunshot wound admissions. If John's killer is the professional you believe him to be, he has someone managing him, and that someone must have a stable of off-the-grid contacts to handle emergencies. I don't expect the Feds to find much, but, I have some ideas of my own. It's going to take a while, but I'll come up with something."

FIFTY-THREE

Rockville, Maryland

I shmael had always accepted the possibility that he could be shot or injured at some point in his career. The risk went with the territory, but the fact that he avoided firearms and up-close situations made it unlikely. The Crawford woman created a problem. Fedallah gave him little time to prepare and the Client insisted upon immediate results. That meant inadequate planning. That's why everything fell apart. *Had the situation under control but Mrs. Crawford distracted me enough that the other woman caught me off guard and made the shot. It was the Florida detective who was supposed to be dead. It was in the damn papers. How'd she get there?*

The shots hurt worse than he imagined. He fired twice in response and was convinced he hit the primary target, but couldn't tell if it was a kill shot. If not, the Client would be extremely unhappy, which meant Ishmael was a dead man walking.

First priority was to survive long enough to get far away. He removed his shirt and stuffed it into the shoulder wound to stop the bleeding. Worst pain imaginable. Almost impossible to drive with the injured left arm while applying pressure with the right hand. No time for the typical secure channels of communication. He needed help immediately, before he passed out. He called Fedallah directly with his cell phone, knowing the FBI might trace it. He had to take the chance if he hoped to see tomorrow. Fedallah gave an address and hung up.

Thirty miles away? Could he make it? He struggled to remain conscious. A quick jerk on the steering wheel avoided a ditch. Almost crashed into the small building when he finally arrived.

The doctor seemed competent enough. "Both bullets passed through your shoulder without injuring any major vessels, but there's been damage to some of the nerves that control your left arm." Before addressing the gunshot wound, the doctor gave him a tetanus shot and started an IV to administer fluids, antibiotics, and pain meds. Then, he cleaned and dressed the wound. "You were lucky, but you must stay in bed and remain quiet for at least forty-eight hours. If you don't rest, the wound might reopen, and you could bleed to death."

The room wasn't like any hospital Ishmael had ever seen. Absent was the presence of nurses and the cleanliness of the typical emergency room. Then there were the dogs. They hadn't stopped barking since he arrived. "I'm not going to die in this shithole," he promised himself. "Not in a veterinary hospital with these damn animals howling around me."

I'm leaving in the morning. If I'm going to die, it'll be on my terms. All he had to do was make it to Philadelphia where he'd pick up his new identity papers and hide until he healed. Then he'd drive to Dallas where he already had a flight booked for Buenos Aires where a plastic surgeon awaited.

FIFTY-FOUR

Congressional Cemetery
Washington, DC

Jacob visited me in the hospital for an hour every day and discussed progress on a plan he had devised with Winston. The methods used by Jacob and the team were not available to the FBI, clearly outside the accepted limits of the constitution. They were techniques exceptionally suited to dealing with international terrorists, intent on doing harm to the United States. The methods were also incredibly useful in tracking down paid assassins.

It was Cassie who remained at my side every hour of every day, sleeping in a chair by my bed, leaving only for an occasional shower and change of clothing. It was Cassie who helped me eat and steadied me with her arm, as I struggled to walk up and down the halls, pushing my IV stand in front of me. Initially, I could only take a few steps, but with Cassie's continued encouragement, I began ambulating fairly well. She was there for my first dressing change. A line of staples extended from below my navel to my sternum. I wasn't sure whether to laugh or cry. I tried to joke. "Well, guess I'll be throwing out all my new bikinis." Then I felt ashamed of myself for being so self-centered while my poor husband lay dead in a morgue somewhere. I rolled over, faced the wall, and cried.

A week after they removed my staples, the doctors discharged me so I could attend John's funeral. Winston and Cassie made all the arrangements. His memorial service was held at the grave site in the historic Congressional Cemetery. I sat in a chair, with Winston and Cassie on one side and Jacob and his fiancée on the other. I stared at John's coffin. *Life was a cruel joke, a winding path filled with nothing but ruts, potholes and pain, leading to nowhere. What's the purpose? Why did God design his creation this way? Why bestow the gift of life if His intent was to snatch it away? He betrayed me.*

Pewter gray skies threatened. Several agents and the acting director of the FBI gave eulogies thanking John for his exemplary career. They spoke of dedication and loyalty to the Bureau, but none described John the person, a man who was so much more than just his job. The real John was a gentle person, a devoted husband with an impeccable moral compass, a man who rose from the impoverished Letcher County, Kentucky to graduate cum laude from Cornell Law School. I didn't hear much else of what they said. I felt like an abandoned building, still standing but an empty shell, weakened to the point of being uninhabitable.

After the ceremony, the Director approached me and expressed his condolences. Hundreds of other people I didn't know did the same. The team members, including Carla and Norman hugged me, all offering to do whatever they could.

As the crowd began to disburse, Jacob pulled me aside and whispered. "This might help you feel a little better. We have a lead on the assassin. The hospital emergency rooms were a dead end, but I found a veterinarian in Marshall, Virginia. Carla and I paid the guy a visit and, after a short period of persuasion, he admitted to treating a man of the assassin's description for gunshot wounds to the left shoulder over a week ago. The good news is that he gave up the name of the patient. He's called Ishmael."

The name startled me. "You mean like the character from *Moby Dick*?"

"Yes. I assume it's a code name, but it's a start. The doctor claimed the man left a day later. He's probably working on a new identity to get out of the country. Carla and I will check on the usual forged document experts. Our best bet is in Philadelphia and that's our next step. We pressured the vet for the identity of the handler who arranged for the assassin to see him. After further enhanced interrogation, he mentioned the name Fedallah."

"The harbinger of death? Yet another *Moby Dick* character?"

"Might help lead us to the one who ordered the hits," said Jacob.

It started raining. *How cliché.* I stood under an umbrella and studied the chapel and all the religious symbols adorning the cemetery. Exercises in futility. I no longer believed in a benevolent creator. I doubted the existence of a God who would allow the slaughter of my family when I was a young child. What kind of a God would allow a soulless assassin like Ishmael to take the life of my wonderful John, a man who only sought to do what was right? Karl Marx was correct. Religion was the opiate of the masses, no more than a fantasy, promising eternal bliss as a reward for tolerating all the shit life threw at us. I needed something more concrete and immediate. I vowed to find Ishmael. When I did, my face would be the last thing he'd see in his miserable life.

The rain brought a drop in temperature. I shivered.

Winston placed his coat over my shoulders. "Where will you stay, my dear?"

I hadn't thought about it. I couldn't bring myself to live in the house where John was murdered. Too soon. Didn't know if I could ever return there. I once read that time healed all wounds, but I doubted it. The most I could possibly hope for was a softening of the pain, but I knew it would never be gone completely. It was a good thing. I needed the pain to keep me focused on what I had to do.

I couldn't exactly check back into the Marriott and remembered my clothes were still in my car. I had planned to take them to our new home the night that—I cried. Tears happened a lot these days. Out of nowhere, even without thinking about it, I'd start sobbing.

Winston put his arm around me. "You need to surround yourself with the comfort of friends." He insisted I stay in his home. "I have more rooms than I could ever use. Cassie, Norman, Kingsley, and Carla will be there to keep you company."

"I need to pick up my car. My clothes are in the trunk."

"Your car's already in my garage. I took the liberty of having it moved while you were in the hospital."

FIFTY-FIVE

Winston Hamilton Estate
McLean, Virginia

Kingsley drove me to the mansion. Cassie was right. It was huge, the entrance protected by a heavy wrought-iron gate with the letters W H emblazoned on the front. A long asphalt drive snaked its way up a gradual incline through acres of mature trees, manicured lawns, and flower beds. The limousine rolled around a grand motor court, anchored in the middle by a large Italian marble fountain. The car stopped in front of a series of stone steps that led under a portico.

A butler in a formal tuxedo opened an arched, heavy wooden door and welcomed me inside. The entrance foyer alone was as large as the home where John and I planned to — I began weeping again.

The butler distracted me. "On the left you'll see Mr. Hamilton's private library and smoking room. Feel free to use it at any time." Wood paneling on the walls and a marbleized fireplace dominated the room. Plush burgundy leather chairs completed the ambiance.

"Behind that is his master bedroom apartment. That's private." On the right, he pointed out a dining room with a table large enough to seat twenty people. I doubted it had ever been used. "Straight ahead is the reception area." The room was as big as a basketball court and decorated in a Great Gatsbyesque style. A curved wall of windows in the back held a series of tall glass doors leading to a flagstone veranda. It overlooked several acres of formal gardens and woods. I prayed there were no hooded strangers lurking back there at the edge of the trees. I'd probably worry about that for the rest of my life.

The butler led me up a set of cherrywood stairs that reminded me of ones Scarlet O'Hara had walked down in the movie, Gone With The Wind. Near the end of a long hallway, the butler opened a set of double doors. "This is your suite." It was a full apartment with its own kitchenette. "Miss Pierce has the room next to yours and Norman is across the hall. Carla and Kingsley's rooms sit at the other end. If there's anything you need, don't hesitate to call. I'll have Kingsley bring your bags up shortly."

He poured a pitcher of water into a crystal glass. "If you're hungry, I can have the chef make lunch for you."

"No, thank you. I think I'll just lie down and rest."

"As you wish, Mrs. Crawford."

For the next several weeks, everyone at Winston's treated me well. Kingsley kept me distracted trying to teach me chess strategies in the afternoons. Norman updated my computer and downloaded a dozen apps for my phone. I doubted I'd use most of them but appreciated his efforts. Even the chef spent time trying to teach me to cook, a wasted endeavor. I read a few books I found in Winston's library.

The evenings were the hardest. I wouldn't have made it through them without Cassie's help. Those were the times when I blamed myself the most. I 'd lost the love of my life—twice, both times because of my own actions. I'd left John without any explanation as to why. I should have stayed and tried to talk through our problems. Like a broken record running through my mind, over and over I relived the past several weeks. If I hadn't run away to Naples, I would have never become involved in Savannah Wellington's death. It would have been only one of the twenty-thousand or so other murders committed in the United States every year. I never would have uncovered the thirteen political assassinations. My relentless need to pursue the case ultimately led to John's death.

Cassie tried to console me. "You can't look at it in retrospect. You made a decision that made the most sense for you at the time. When a person decides to follow one path over another, they have no idea where the chosen path might lead, just as they can't be certain that the other path would have been any better. Countless stories and poems have been written about the path not chosen. Had you not traveled to Naples, there's no way of knowing what the future might have brought you or John. Staying in your old situation might have caused you to forever resent John. As it turned out, the two of you rediscovered each other and fell in love again. That was the result of what you did. There was no way you could predict what might happen to him. His death had nothing to do with you. Only the assassin, Ishmael can be held responsible."

In my mind, I knew Cassie was right, but not in my heart, and the heart always wins that argument.

Cassie went to the wine cabinet and grabbed a bottle. "We both need a drink." She checked the label. "I'm not familiar with the brand, but knowing Winston, it's probably very good and extremely expensive." She poured a glass for each of us, and we relived the night of Ishmael's attack. Talking about pain was often the best medicine.

"Fortunately, the bastard's gone," said Cassie.

That's when it hit me. Whoever hired him was still out there. "Eventually, they'll learn Ishmael failed to kill me and might even discover you're alive."

"That means they'll keep coming after us. We'll be in danger for the rest of our lives."

"I'll talk to Winston about increasing the security around the mansion."

"What good will that do?" Cassie asked. "Sure, it's a great place, but we can't live here forever."

"Then I'll have to find a way to stop them."

"How do we do that? They are powerful people with unlimited resources."

I didn't have an answer.

During most nights, horrible dreams plagued my sleep as I relived my failure to save John from the disaster. In last night's version, John was drowning in the middle of a lake. I struggled to swim out to save him, but the water transformed into a thick red glue. The harder I struggled to get to him, the more difficult it became. John disappeared below the surface. My screams smothered in my throat.

I bolted straight up in a sweat, causing spasms over my incision site. The pain wouldn't allow me to return to sleep. I decided to get up and take a Tylenol PM. When I went into the bathroom and turned on the light, roaches scurried under the counter. I stifled a scream. Really? In a mansion? Always hated bugs, especially those creepy things that crawled out as soon as the lights were off.

That's it! With my cell phone in hand, I ran down the hall to Cassie's room and woke her up. "I know what we need to do."

She blinked at the sudden bright light, and covered her eyes with her hand. "What? What are you talking about?"

"What happens when you have roaches and you turn the lights on?"

Cassie sat up on the edge of her bed, her eyes still unfocused. "They scatter and hide."

"Exactly." I punched a number into my cell phone. "We're going to turn the lights on."

"Lisa," she said. "It's three o'clock in the morning. Tell me you're not going to call someone at this hour."

"Believe me, she's going to be happy to hear from me." I dialed the number. A groggy voice answered on the fifth ring. "Maddie, it's Lisa. Remember that blockbuster story I promised you? I have it."

"Lisa? What? Give me a few minutes to shake the cobwebs from my brain. I'll call you right back."

"Sure, I'll be here along with Cassandra Pierce."

"We probably shouldn't mention her just yet," said Maddie. "Remember, she's supposed to be dead, and I don't think people in Naples are ready yet to hear about the specifics of her miraculous resurrection."

Maddie was back on the line in five minutes. "Just splashed cold water on my face, chugged down a cup of coffee, and dug a legal pad out of my desk drawer. Think I'm ready now. Before we get started, I want to let you know how sorry I was to hear of your husband's death."

"Thank you, and I appreciate the flowers." I told her about how John's death was related to an investigation that had been a spinoff of the Savannah Wellington case. "At least thirteen state politicians have been murdered over the past two years."

"What? Murdered? Are you shitting me?"

"Someone hired a professional assassin to eliminate them. Governor Robinson Murray was his last victim.

"The Governor of Ohio? For real? I thought he died from some kind of peanut allergy."

"Part of the pattern. All cases were reported as being due to freak accidents. That way, no suspicions were raised. However, our investigation revealed that many unusual deaths to be a statistical impossibility. Something big and sinister is underway, and it has to do with an organization called TBA.

"TBA?"

"Take Back America. They occupy an office in the Atlantic Building in DC." I gave her as much background information on them as I could. "Their primary mission is to enact Article V of the Constitution calling for a convention of the states. Their goal is to pass a balanced budget amendment and term limits. All thirteen victims were heavily involved with trying to pass resolutions in their individual states. Someone immensely powerful didn't want them to succeed."

"So, who is that someone?" she asked.

"I don't know, but the same assassin who killed the thirteen politicians killed John while trying to get me. He also tried to kill Detective Pierce. In addition, he's responsible for the murder of Savannah Wellington. His name is Ishmael. His handler is a person called Fedallah."

"Like the characters from *Moby Dick*?"

"Both code names. Whoever their client is, the man must be incredibly wealthy and doesn't care how many influential politicians he needs to eliminate to prevent the constitutional convention from happening. I'll send a complete list of the victims via email, and I'll include our statistical analysis.

"Hold on," Maddie said, sounding frantic. I heard her flipping pages on her notepad.

"This is a big story, Maddie, one that should catapult you into the limelight. I must admit that I'm sharing this not only because I owe you, but also because I'm trying to protect myself. The best way to do that is to expose the perpetrators of this conspiracy. They've been hiding behind a curtain of anonymity. I want you to pull that curtain back. I'm hoping they won't come after Cassie and me after your story runs, for fear it would lend too much credibility to the report."

After several seconds, Maddie said, "There's a ton of information here and I need to corroborate some of it. Do you mind if I handle this as a series? It would be best for me because the major news outlets will come knocking at my door for details."

"That's fine, but make sure you mention Ishmael and Fedallah. Float the conspiracy angle immediately. Otherwise, I might not be around long enough to read what you report."

"The first teaser will be out in the morning edition and on the wire services by the afternoon."

344

FIFTY-SIX

Von Hamburg Castle
Brussels, Belgium

The Baron squinted at the wide screen television affixed to the wall opposite his bed. The news coincided with the article he'd been reading in *The Wall Street Journal*. The worst of his fears were coming to fruition. He reached over into his nightstand for a cigarette, a habit he stopped two decades ago but he could never shake the need for the ceremony. He placed it between his lips and considered lighting up. On this, of all days, he deserved one. The only thing stopping him was the knowledge that any flame could explode his oxygen delivery system.

"LaTrane," he screamed, the weak effort making him even more short of breath than usual.

The door opened, and LaTrane slithered in, checking every corner of the room. "You're looking better today, sir."

"Cut the crap. I look like shit, and feel worse." He waved the newspaper toward LaTrane. "Have you seen this article in The Journal? It's written by some shiksa called ..." he stared at the paper, "Madeline something."

"Carmichael, sir. Her last name is Carmichael."

The Baron spit out the cigarette. "So, you read it?"

LaTrane stood with his hands behind his back. "I have."

"I told you I wanted that Lisa Crawford lady dead. Get her before she can talk to anyone else. Get rid of that damn reporter too."

LaTrane brushed the lapel of his suit coat. "With all due respect, sir, I believe that option is no longer advisable. As of now, this is an article written by a relatively unknown reporter and it's based purely upon speculation. There are few facts to support it. The story will soon die, as most do. We have a controlling interest in a substantial portion of the news media. We can divert the narrative in any direction we wish. If we kill the woman now, it will simply lend credence to the story and give it traction."

LaTrane leaned forward. "Don't you see, sir? We've already won the battle. The thirteen have been eliminated. With Ohio out of the picture, the issue of a constitutional convention is dead just as it died a decade ago. TBA's cheerleaders are gone, and their sources of funding are drying up. There will be no term limits. Your network of power will remain intact. American politicians are too preoccupied with the Russians and the Chinese. Their news media will continue to focus on distractions like immigration, gender, and race issues, ones that garner the greatest attention of the voters."

The nurse came in to inject the old man's next cycle of chemotherapy.

He scoffed. "Damn stuff is poison." After she left, he looked at LaTrane. "The article refers to Fedallah and his assassin by name. Are their activities traceable back to us?"

"We are fairly insulated from the entire process."

The Baron squinted his eyes. "Fairly?"

"One problem is that Fedallah's man killed the FBI's deputy director in charge of antiterrorism. The Bureau is sure to devote a huge number of resources to find him. That's the only way they can trace the assassinations back to us. If the Americans track down Fedallah, he could turn on us as part of a plea deal."

"Eliminated him then," said the Baron.

"It will take me time to uncover his true identity and whereabouts, but I'll handle the matter personally."

As LaTrane turned to leave the room, the Baron said, "And LaTrane?"

"Yes, sir."

"Find the whereabouts of Fedallah's assassin. What's his name?"

"Ishmael, sir."

"Terminate him also."

"Puta factum, sir. Consider it done."

FIFTY-SEVEN

National Mall
Washington, DC

Waiting for Maddie's article to hit the news was nerve-racking. I couldn't sit still so I rearranged the books in Winston's library, grouping them by category, and placing them in alphabetical order. That chore took Cassie and me an entire morning. Afterward, she got me involved in watching reruns of the TV series, *Yellowstone*. We shared a bottle of wine, and each time Rip appeared on the screen, Cassie would say, "That Rip is hot."

"I thought you didn't like men."

"In his case, I'd make an exception. That cowboy can ride my pony any time."

I spit out a mouthful of wine, and we laughed until tears ran down our cheeks — the happy kind.

***

Life settled down a week after the first installment of Maddie's report hit the wire services. It was on the front page of every major newspaper in the world. Winston's intelligence network reported that no groups were shadowing us anymore. He believed we could resume our normal lives but insisted that a pair of protection specialists continue to follow us.

Cassie hadn't seen the National Mall, so we asked Kingsley to drop us off in front of the Lincoln Memorial.

Summer had yielded to autumn, and the trees were displaying their fall foliage, the cherry trees transforming to shades of bronze and red, the willow oak leaves turning yellow. We tried to run the path around the reflecting pool, but my surgical incision protested. We switched to walking and slowed in front of the Lincoln Memorial, our protection detail in full view. An annoying necessity.

Cassie said, "Mr. Hamilton asked if I'd be interested in joining the team. What do you think?"

"It's a good idea. You'd fit in perfectly."

"I wouldn't have to return to Naples and explain why I faked my own death. It would get Dr. Deutschle and Maddie off the hook. More importantly, I can remain in Washington, with you."

"I'd like that, Cassie."

We walked up the steps to the memorial. "It looks like a temple," said Cassie.

"I think that's the whole idea, paying tribute to the man who saved the Union."

"Lincoln's statue is larger than I expected," Cassie said. "He almost looks alive sitting there."

We stood side by side in awe and read the Gettysburg address inscribed on the walls. I'd never given the speech much consideration other than the famous first sentence. The final words caught my attention. I read them aloud. "… that government of the people, by the people, and for the people shall not perish from this earth." The words reflected the sentiments of TBA, to return government control to the people. Noble goal.

We continued strolling around the water toward a sign that read, "Tidal Basin and Paddle Boat Rentals."

Cassie grabbed my hand. "Let's go. It'll be great fun. We can escape our babysitters."

We followed the path until we found the boat rental station and selected one. Our guards tried to follow along the water's edge but couldn't keep up. We made our way across the basin, toward the Jefferson Memorial, the paddles slapping against the water as a gentle breeze blew through our hair. We enjoyed the solitude and privacy with nobody chasing us or hovering nearby to protect us.

I leaned back and gazed up at the peaceful, clear blue skies and bathed in the life-giving rays of the sun. For the first time in weeks, I allowed myself to feel happy. I reached over and gave Cassie's hand a squeeze. "Thank you, Cassie. You saved my life when you shot Ishmael. Without you, I would have never been here to enjoy this perfect day. I love you for giving me that opportunity."

She turned to me, smiled, and said, "From the first time we met in that park, I knew we'd be good together. After all that's happened to me, I never thought I could feel this way again." She sat up and looked into my eyes. "I've fallen in love with you, Lisa."

It took a few seconds for her words to register. *Did I hear her correctly? In love?* I sat up straight. "Cassie, you misunderstood. When I say I love you, I mean as my dearest friend, not romantically. I'm not wired that way."

Her eyes widened. "Oh, my God. I'm so sorry. I don't know what I was thinking. I got caught up in the moment."

"No, I'm the one who's sorry. In my grief after John's death, I must have given you the wrong impression."

We said nothing further as we paddled back to the dock and called for an Uber.

FIFTY-EIGHT

Winston Hamilton Estate
McLean, Virginia

For the first few days after the incident at the tidal basin, Cassie and I had little contact. I figured she must have been too embarrassed, but she finally approached me and said we needed to talk. "There's a beautiful stone terrace in the back, overlooking an English garden and woods. Let's have coffee outside."

We sat at a round glass-top table and the maid brought out coffee and a plate of madeleines. "I could so get used to living like this," I said.

Cassie took a bite of the small cake. "I know what you mean. If it were up to Winston, I think he'd want you to stay. You're the daughter he never had."

We enjoyed the madeleines, sipped on our coffee, and gazed at a hummingbird flitting from flower to flower.

Cassie set her coffee cup down and met my eyes. "I want to apologize for what I said at the tidal basin a few days ago. It was presumptuous and completely inappropriate—not to mention embarrassing."

"You have nothing to apologize for. After John's death, I felt alone and was being needy. I sent out the wrong signals and I'm sorry for that. I don't want it to affect our friendship."

"Neither do I," she said. "Good friends are a rare gift, something to be cherished."

We clicked our cups together in a toast. "To our friendship."

Cassie looked lost in thought. "Do you think Carla and your brother will find the bastard who killed Savannah and John? He needs to be removed from the face of the earth."

"They will. Jacob has ways of finding the people he wants. It's only a matter of time before he tracks Ishmael down. I think he'll leave the punishment aspect up to me."

Something continued to crawl around the edges of my mind, bothersome feelings just beyond my reach. Thoughts of Savannah's death remained like the clouds of a thunderstorm lurking over the horizon. I wasn't convinced Ishmael was the one responsible, and I couldn't brush my concerns aside. Since the Florida convention resolution had been passed several years before her death, there was no reason for him to kill Savannah. And why kill Rachael? Their deaths made no sense. Something was wrong.

I replayed the night of John's murder over and over in my mind. Cassie and I had both shot Ishmael in the left shoulder, but he returned fire hitting me and killing John. *That's it!* Our shots had to have rendered Ishmael's left hand useless, but he kept firing his gun anyway. That meant he had to have used his right hand, but Dr. Deutschle's autopsy report stated Savannah's killer was left-handed.

Ishmael didn't kill her, but if not him, then who did, and why? The only remaining motive was the pregnancy. It posed enough of a problem for someone to commit murder. There was still one lead I had failed to follow through on. I stood. "I'm sorry Cassie, but I need to make a few calls."

"Is anything wrong?" she asked.

"No. I simply have to check on a few things. We'll talk later."

"I'd enjoy that."

I went into my bedroom, closed the door, and called John's secretary in the Hoover Building.

"Hello, Mrs. Crawford." *She called me Mrs. Crawford? That's a first. Up until now she'd only referred to me as "the wife."* Death had a way of creating friends out of enemies. She continued, "I'm so sorry my husband and I didn't get a chance to talk to you after the funeral. There were so many people."

"I understand completely. I couldn't even tell you who half of them were."

"Well, I'm sorry for your loss. He was a wonderful man."

"Thank you. That he was, and I miss him terribly."

"If there's anything we at the Bureau can do for you, just let us know."

"Now that you mention it, there is one thing."

A pause on the line, then she said, "Anything."

"John and I were working on a project together and sent a specimen to Quantico for DNA analysis. Could you please check John's computer files. I need to see if it was completed?"

"I don't know, Mrs. Crawford. That would be a violation of protocols."

"It's just reading a note he already had in there. It would mean a great deal to me and his memory."

I heard a deep sigh, then some clicking of a keyboard. "Yes. He submitted a cigarette butt, and a DNA profile was successfully obtained. He checked the results against the National CODIS and the individual had no prior record."

"Thank you so much. There's just one more little thing. Did he email the results to a man by the name of Dr. Fred Deutschle?"

More hesitation and deeper sighing. I was pushing her to her limits of cooperation. More typing. "Yes. Dr. Deutschle simply replied that it was a match."

"Thank you so much. You've been a great help. Don't worry. This conversation never happened." I disconnected the call.

FIFTY-NINE

TBA Offices
The Atlantic Building
Washington, DC

I had the father of Savannah's baby, and probably her killer. I called the TBA offices and told them I needed to meet with Scott Matheson. "Tell him it's urgent."

I showered, dressed, and headed out the door thirty minutes later.

When I arrived at the Atlantic Building, the lobby of TBA boiled over with dozens of reporters waiting to attend a press conference in response to Maddy Carmichael's article on the untimely death of Ohio Governor Robinson Murray and the suspicious deaths of people affiliated with the Constitutional Convention project. Absent was Penny, the lady in the black blazer with the pinched red lips. Scott Matheson squinted at the bright lights of the television cameras and delivered a brief statement about the loss of the Governor. "He was a great supporter of the citizens of Ohio and an American patriot. He'll be sorely missed. Our condolences to Mrs. Murray and her family."

One reporter asked, "Are you planning to attend the memorial service, Mr. Matheson?"

"Definitely. The Governor and I had become close friends over the past several years."

Another reporter from Fox News asked. "What about the other victims mentioned in *The Wall Street Journal* piece? Like Governor Murray, they all had a close relationship with TBA."

"That matter is in the hands of the FBI. We need to await the outcome of their investigation." When he saw me, he nodded toward his office. "Unfortunately, I must leave you for a critical meeting. Our Executive Assistant, Jeremy Mumford will answer any further questions. Thank you."

Jeremy stepped up to the makeshift podium and smiled for the cameras. "These tragic events are examples of the degree of corruption that infects our government. They serve as testimony to the urgent need for term limits." He was in full damage control mode, with the intense eyes of a cornered animal. He would do anything to protect the TBA organization and to shield his boss. I recalled his words from when I first met him. "My primary job is to put out brush fires, to make problems go away."

Did that include disposing of persons like Savannah who might pose a threat?

The receptionist escorted me past the gauntlet of reporters, all asking a flurry of questions. One was Maddie Carmichael, wearing a *Wall Street Journal* press credential around her neck. She was a different woman than the one I had seen at Buddy's Blue Line bar several months ago. Her once empty looking eyes now glowed with the enthusiasm of a new life. She smiled, mouthed "Thank you," and stepped aside. The others swarmed around me. "Excuse me. Who are you? Any comments on the death of Governor Murray and the others?" Blood thirsty sharks. Plowing through them took several minutes. Not answering, I lowered my head and covered my face, avoiding photographers.

By the time I walked into his office, Scott Matheson was already seated behind his desk, his top button undone and his tie pulled askew. He was sucking on a cigarette, but when I entered, he stood and took my hand. "It's a pleasure to see you again, Miss Hamilton. Before we start, I want to thank you again for the million-dollar donation from your father. I must admit, the loss of Governor Murray has been a severe setback, and we expect to see a decrease in financial support."

I sat opposite his desk and got to the point. "I must be honest with you, Mr. Matheson. My motives haven't been entirely pure. I'm not the daughter of Winston Hamilton."

Matheson's eyebrows scrunched together and he cocked his head to the side. "I'm not sure I understand, Miss?"

"Crawford. Mrs. Lisa Marie Crawford."

He leaned back in his chair and his eyes bore into mine. "So, what's going on and why all the intrigue?"

I turned and checked to be sure the door was closed. Of course, there were no assurances that the room wasn't bugged. "This meeting is off the record, just between you and me."

He leaned forward and crushed out his cigarette. "Are you another reporter?"

I locked my eyes onto his. "No, but I am affiliated with Winston Hamilton, and he intends to contribute another fifty-million to your cause, all contingent upon your cooperation with my questions."

Another cigarette. "I still don't understand."

"As part of a different murder investigation, several individuals and I have uncovered the information that led to the exposure of the attacks upon thirteen of your financial and legislative supporters. I'm the one who fed the information to the press. Those killings are somehow related to the death of Mrs. Savannah Wellington."

His face turned pasty. "Do you think Savannah was targeted by the same assassin?"

"I did at first, but now I'm not so sure. I know she was one of the earliest supporters of TBA and was instrumental in recruiting other state legislators around the country to support the Article V resolutions. Many of those individuals are now dead."

"Savannah was a special person to whom we are deeply indebted. She's been missed by everyone here at TBA."

"Especially by you, Mr. Matheson?"

He shifted in his seat, took another long drag on his cigarette, but said nothing.

"I know you and Savannah were romantically involved."

He lowered his head and took a deep breath before responding. Time for honesty. "It's true. We did have an affair, something we both deeply regretted. We had already known each other for several years and had worked closely together on multiple projects. The affair began when we both attended a CPAC convention in Atlanta last year. I was invited to give a TBA presentation about our Constitutional Convention efforts. Savannah was there as the legislative house speaker from Florida. We'd had a few too many drinks at a reception and wound up in her hotel room together." Another heavy drag on the cigarette, its tip glowing red. "The relationship continued for five months, but we both called it off. I know it's hard to understand, but I still loved my wife deeply and would never leave her. Savannah realized that and the decision to end the relationship was mutual."

His head dropped, as he stared at his hands folded together on his desk, clutching the cigarette. He looked up with my next question.

My eyes bore into his, searching for any signs of deception. "Did you know Savannah was pregnant when she was killed?"

His head jerked back like a jolt of electricity just surged through his body. His pupils dilated and his jaw dropped. "Pregnant? But how was that possible?"

I stared at him, tilted my head to the side, and said, "How do you think?"

He ran his hand through his hair. "She never told me. How far along was she?"

I noticed he didn't ask if the baby was his. It would have been a question asked by a weasel trying to wiggle his way out of the situation. He was being honest and accepting responsibility. "Five months. We did DNA testing, and it proves you were the father."

He sat in a near catatonic state. "I didn't know. She never told me."

I believed him. The man was devastated by the news and obviously had nothing to do with Savannah's death. He had no motive without the knowledge of the pregnancy. He was a good person who made a terrible mistake.

He shook his head. "I know Savannah had her faults, but she was a wonderful person."

Wonderful? That was the last word I'd use to describe Savannah. From what I knew about her, she wasn't a good person by any measure. A classic self-centered narcissist, but she didn't deserve to be murdered. I lied and said, "I'm sure she was."

He stopped talking for a minute as though another word would unleash tears he fought hard to control. "She would have been a good mother." His hands trembled.

I leaned in, closer to the desk. "I'm sure she would have." Another lie on my part. I waited a few seconds. "Any idea who might have done this to her?" My thoughts drifted to his assistant, Jeremy, the problem solver.

"Savannah had been involved in a serious relationship for over a year by the time we first got together. She broke it off, and apparently the guy took it pretty hard."

"Do you think he was capable of murder?"

"Never met him so I can't say. Savannah did mention he was controlling and extremely jealous. That's one reason why she stopped seeing him. She told me he begged her to take him back. He began stalking her and making threats.

"Do you have a name?" I thought about the video Spyder Tomlinson described.

"No. She was pretty secretive about it. Eventually I stopped asking."

I leaned back to think. This was new information to me. I knew she had a reputation for being promiscuous, but I wasn't aware of any serious long-term relationships. "What about her assistant, Rachael. She was also murdered. Do you think this guy had anything to do with it?"

"It's possible. Savannah and Rachael had been close friends since high school and confided in each other about everything, including their love lives. Rachael knew about me and even contacted me last month, threatening to blackmail our organization after Savannah was killed. She demanded several million dollars, or she would expose our affair to the public. I refused because the demand for more money never ends. I was going to confess to my wife, but Jeremy wanted to pay Rachael off. We argued about it, but he won. Just when we were about to transfer funds into her account, we found out she was dead."

"If she'd blackmail you, she could have blackmailed anyone, including Savannah's prior lover if he was married. That would be a strong motive to kill Rachael."

"I don't know." He stared into space., his eyes unfocused. "After we decided to end our affair, Savannah said she was going to try to get back with her husband. Guess she wanted a stable family home in which to raise the baby. She sounded so happy the last time we talked."

It was obvious he still loved Savannah. How a person could love two people at one time, I could never understand. The door to his office swung open and Jeremy poked his head in. "I'm sorry to bother you, but there are a few questions I can't answer out here."

Matheson jerked his head in Jeremy's direction. "What?"

"I need you for a few minutes."

Scott shook his head to clear it, his mind tilting on that precarious edge between composure and emotional collapse. "Excuse me, Mrs. Crawford. I'll right back." He stood, straightened his tie, forced a smile, and walked out to face the jackals. After the door closed, I explored his office. On the wall hung a copy of the same photograph I had seen in Preston Wellington's office, the one of Florida Governor Cartwright with his arm wrapped around Savannah's waist and Scott Matheson to the side. It was dated several years prior to her death. Another photograph was of Scott at the CPAC convention he just mentioned. Savannah stood next to him, looking beautiful and smiling, posing with a glass of wine, her large diamond wedding ring sparkling in the light. It was the night their affair began.

I leaned closer, squinted my eyes and studied the picture more closely. I blinked my eyes several times to be sure I was seeing what was before me. My heart skipped a beat. *What? Impossible.* But if true, it explained everything.

The door opened, and Scott returned, his face drawn and pale. "I'm sorry. I don't know where we go from here, Mrs. Crawford. Are you wanting me to resign? I'll do that for the sake of the movement."

"Absolutely not. You have an important mission, and the country needs what you are trying to accomplish."

"Might not make any difference," he said. "TBA is on the brink of folding, and we're just about broke. Prospects for additional funding died when *The Wall Street Journal* published that article."s

I leaned forward. "I might be able to help you. I have some influence with a reporter there. She might be willing to draft an article about how someone is trying to manipulate American politics. The public doesn't take kindly to the threat of foreign interference in our government. I can add the fact that Mr. Winston Hamilton is still committed to your cause and continues to promise fifty-million dollars."

"I don't —"

I held up my hand. "I'm the only one who knows of your affair and the DNA results. I'll make sure all records of that test are destroyed. Other than the financial pledge from Mr. Hamilton, this conversation never occurred. Everyone deserves a second chance, Mr. Matheson. That applied to Savannah, and I believe it's especially true for you."

I stood, shook his hand, and headed for the door. "By the way. You don't have to worry about assassins targeting any more of your supporters. I've seen to that."

I rushed out of Matheson's office and pulled my cell phone from my purse as I left the building. "Norman, it's Lisa. I have another project for you and that Looking Glass program of yours." I explained what I needed. "Can you get it?"

"Are you kidding? How soon do you need the info?"

"By tomorrow afternoon if you can. It's important."

SIXTY

Rockville, Maryland

As I left the Atlantic Building and wandered the streets of DC, my mind reverberated with a hundred different questions. I needed someone to talk to, someone I trusted, but Winston was busy in meetings at the NSA about a series of dirty bomb explosions in the African Congo. Jacob and Carla were in South America tracking down John's killer. I struggled to wrap my head around what I knew. I thought of the words of Sir Arthur Conan Doyle. *When you have eliminated all which is impossible, then whatever remains, however improbable, must be the truth.* My truth was not only improbable but completely unfathomable. Before arriving at any final conclusions, I needed more substantiation.

My most immediate concern was finding somewhere to rest so I could digest everything. Returning to the Marriott was out, as was Winston's mansion. My only option was the last place I wanted to visit. I walked over to the National Museum of Natural History, hailed a cab, and gave the driver my home address in Rockville, Maryland.

I opened the door to the house where John and I planned to spend the rest of our lives together. I feared the worst, expecting to be mercilessly assaulted by a flood of nightmarish sights. Fortunately, Winston had arranged for a professional cleaning company to remove all traces of that night. They had replaced the carpeting and much of the furniture. The walls and woodwork where the FBI had dug out several 9mm slugs had been repaired. Black smudges of fingerprint powder had been cleaned and the walls repainted. Despite their efforts, they couldn't wash away the memory of John dying in my arms. I stared at the site where he desperately gasped for air — until he couldn't any longer.

I sat on the couch where John and I had snuggled only weeks ago. I curled into a ball around a throw pillow and cried until I had no tears left. A part of me never wanted to stop crying. To do so seemed like a betrayal of John's memory. I found some Gray Goose vodka in the liquor cabinet. I opened it and drank straight from the bottle while remembering all the wonderful moments John and I shared. I drank until the world dissolved.

The following morning, the sound of my cell phone awakened me, each ring a jackhammer destroying the inside of my skull. I fished the phone from my purse and checked my watch: two-thirty in the afternoon.

Norman's excited voice slammed into my ear, but his words soon vanquished my hangover. "I don't know how you figured it out, but you're a genius, Lisa. I pulled all the Verizon cell phone records you requested. Rachael Morris made four calls two days before her murder. Only two responded. One was from the TBA offices, and I assume you're aware of that. The other came from a burner phone. I couldn't identify the caller, but the call definitely originated from somewhere around Naples. After that, there was no further activity."

I walked over to the Keurig and made a cup of coffee, strong and black as he continued.

"Then I checked on calls coming to Savannah. Someone called her regularly from a number that's been retired and I can't retrieve it. About six months ago a new number, another burner phone, began calling her a dozen times a day."

The rejected lover?

"The week before Savannah's murder, it was almost every fifteen minutes."

I gulped down the coffee and made another cup.

Deets continued. "Now, for the best part. Several weeks ago, you asked me to hack into some guy's computer. Spyder something."

"Spyder Tomlinson at Guardian Security."

"Yeah, that's it. Well, I downloaded all his files, including videos, but never bothered to review them after you had me researching the deaths of all those politicians. I watched them last night and found a video of Savannah in a romantic situation with someone other than her husband. I'm sending a snapshot of the video right now."

My screen came alive and my mind refused to fully accept what I was seeing. It confirmed my suspicions. Savannah was sitting at a breakfast table wearing a loosely fitting silk robe, her breasts spilling out from under the fabric. With her arm around Savannah's neck, Detective Cassandra Pierce stared directly at me with the eyes of a woman hopelessly in love. My friend, Cassie, the same person who set into motion the series of events that ultimately led to John's death, killed Savannah. She shot Ishmael, not so much to save me, but to stop Ishmael from denying involvement in Savannah's murder. She needed him dead. He was her scapegoat.

My stomach churned, not from the vodka or the coffee, but from the realization of being betrayed by a person I thought was my closest friend. Cassandra Pierce, murderer and baby killer. I didn't know where to go from here. The DC police had no official jurisdiction over a crime committed in Naples. I was certain Cassie wasn't aware that I knew yet, but by the time the Naples DA filed the extradition papers, she might find out and run. If Winston were available, I'd let him handle it the same way he did Brad.

I called Maddie. "Holy shit, Lisa. Are you kidding me? You're a source of endless surprises. It was her all along? Let me check with my sources at the Naples DA office. I'll call you back and let you know what to do."

I was still in yesterday's clothes. I ran upstairs to undress and shower hoping the hot water would wash away the effects of last night's alcohol and the unclean feeling of having trusted Cassie. I dried off and sat on my bed in a robe, waiting for Maddie to call me back.

My phone rang, but it wasn't her.

It was Norman, and he was terrified. "I'm sorry Lisa."

"Sorry? About what?"

"I screwed up. She knows."

"I don't understand."

"After I sent you the snapshot, I left my computer on while I wheeled myself to the bathroom. You know how nosey Cassie's been, always looking over my shoulder. She saw her picture with Savannah. Oh shit. Here she comes."

I heard a gunshot.

SIXTY-ONE

Winston Hamilton Estate
McLean, Virginia

I threw on a sweatsuit, picked up my Sig, and ran to my car. I called 911 and raced to Winston's, running redlights and swerving the wrong way down one-way streets. How could I have been so blind? Cassie had even admitted to a history of violence. She hit one of her foster parents over the head with a whiskey bottle. Deutschle's autopsy report estimated the killer to be about six feet tall and left-handed — like Cassie. I should've suspected something when Cassie said the expensive wine at Sands was Savannah's favorite. I missed it. She'd known Savannah all along. She was the obsessed lover who stalked her. It's why she was so shaken when she saw Savannah's hand. I thought it was the insulin, but it was the realization of what she'd done. That's the reason she took my original call from Seminole Park in the first place. She showed up rather than sending a beat op. She needed to control every aspect of the investigation. She kept insisting that if we found the father, we'd have the killer. That explained why she was so hellbent on Governor Cartwright being the killer. She believed he was the one who stole Savannah's heart and got her pregnant. She wanted revenge and diverted the investigation away from herself. It worked — until she was put out of commission when Ishmael tampered with her insulin.

I practically flew through the gates of Winston's estate and around the fountain to the front door. I found Kingsley, barely able to walk, bleeding from his thigh, and carrying Norman down the front stone steps. He set Norman down on the lawn and collapsed next to him. I slammed on the brakes and jumped out.

Norman yelled, "When Kingsley rushed in and found Cassie with a gun, he fired. She shot him in the leg and ran. Kingsley lifted me from my chair and carried me out here. He saved me."

"An ambulance is on the way." I said as I removed Kingsley's belt to use it as a tourniquet on his leg.

Norman's face turned pale. "Are you injured?" I asked.

"No, she said she'd never hurt me. I don't think she wanted to shoot Kingsley either, but when he fired on her, she shot him."

"Where is she now?"

Norman looked toward the door. "Inside somewhere. Kingsley must have hit her, though. I saw a lot of blood on the steps."

I heard the sirens in the distance and chambered a round into my Sig. It was a huge house, and Cassie could easily ambush me in a dozen different places. I didn't really believe she'd shoot me, but I also never imagined she was capable of murder. She had a dark side.

I followed two trails of blood up the stairs, cringing as each step creaked as I climbed. The blood led toward Norman's room. I slowly pushed his door open with the tip of my gun. I checked behind the door, inside all the closets and under the bed. The bathroom was the only area left. My heart pounded loudly in my ears as I stayed low and entered. I slammed back the shower curtain, ready to fire. She wasn't there.

I exhaled slowly and returned to the hallway. One blood trail led downstairs and across the massive living room, toward the glass doors leading to the veranda. They were open.

I pointed my gun forward and stepped into the darkness as sirens approached.

"Hello, Lisa." Cassie sat at the same table where we shared coffee yesterday morning. Her Glock was on the table in front of her. "Don't worry. I could never hurt you. Didn't want to shoot Kingsley. It was a reflex."

I lowered my Sig to my side, but kept my finger on the trigger. I sat opposite her. She looked up at the night sky. "Beautiful evening. The stars are unusually bright tonight." A blood stain expanded over the left side of her blouse. "How did you know?"

"Your bracelet, the silver one with the interlocking hearts you always wear. You told me you and your lover each wore the same one as a symbol of your devotion to each other. I always assumed it was Gail from Chicago. When I was in the TBA offices, I saw a photograph of Savannah and Scott Mathison at a CPAC convention. It was the night they first got together. She was wearing that same bracelet. You two were lovers."

Cassie looked down at the bracelet on her wrist. She shook it, then gazed into the darkness of the night. "Scott Matheson, huh? So, he was the father of her baby."

"I don't understand," I said. "Why did you have to kill her?"

"I wasn't planning on it. We were fine and then, out of the blue, she said she had fallen in love with someone else. I had no idea it was a man. After a year together, she cut me out of her life. Tossed me to the curb like a bag of garbage. I called and called, begging her to reconsider. She refused. Then she blocked my calls. I purchased several burner phones to hide the number, but she blocked those also."

Cassie gazed out over the back gardens, her breathing labored. "We often rode bikes together in the Seminole Lakes Park. We'd stop near one of the benches and share a bottle of wine. It was our special spot where we didn't have to worry about others seeing us together. I waited for her that morning, a bottle of wine and two glasses in hand, hoping the memories would rekindle her love. 'Please talk to me,' I begged."

Cassie inhaled a deep breath. Her chest rattled. "She talked to me all right. She told me she was pregnant, and the father was married. Pregnant? The word sucked the life out of me, but I told her it was okay. I understood. We could raise the baby together."

Cassie shook her head as though trying to erase a memory. Her demeanor broke, and tears ran down her cheeks. "Savannah's eyes turned dark, and she laughed. The woman I loved actually laughed at me and said, 'I'm not going to have my baby raised by some dyke.'"

Cassie lowered her head. "My mind exploded, and I hit her in the side of the head with the wine bottle. She tried to pedal away but ran her bike down the slope into the water. By the time I got there, her head had been under for too long, and she'd been attacked by a gator. I knew she was dead." She sobbed. "I... I just wanted us back together. I never wanted to kill her. I... I loved Savannah."

I heard the sirens just outside the gate and thought for a few seconds. "Cassie, you didn't plan to kill Savannah. It was temporary insanity. The police will be here soon. Turn yourself in and you'll only get convicted for manslaughter. You could be out in five to ten years."

She looked down at the ground. "Maybe, but Rachael's death was premeditated. She tried to blackmail me. I didn't have the kind of money she demanded, so I had to get rid of her. I feel bad about killing her boyfriend too, but I had no choice. If I surrender now, I'll get life, and you know what they do to cops in prison. I can't do the time. A lethal injection would be a blessing."

I stood and tucked my gun into my waistband. "What can I do for you?"

Tears pooled in her eyes as she looked up at me. "What I did eventually led to John's death. You have every right to shoot me."

"Like you once told me, when you choose any path of action, you have no idea what lies at the end of that path. You couldn't foresee what would happen to John."

"I want you to do it, Lisa. If I must die, I want it to be at the hand of someone I love."

I shook my head. "I can't, Cassie."

The blood stain on her blouse had doubled in size.

She looked up and pointed. "Look, a shooting star." She continued looking at the night sky. "Think I'll sit out here for a few minutes and enjoy the evening." She turned to me. "Would that be all right with you? Perhaps I'll see another."

I turned and left her alone on the terrace. By the time I made it back to the front door, the sound of the gunshot echoed through the house. I dropped to my knees.

EPILOGUE: SIX MONTHS LATER

Cote de Azure
Saint Mandrier, France

Ishmael parked his new Ferrari 812 GTS on the gravel drive in front of his villa in Saint Mandrier, a tiny town fifty miles east of Saint Tropez. His housekeeper was just leaving.

"Bonjour, Mr. Wilson. I'm headed to the grocery store but I left a cigar and a chilled glass of chardonnay for you out on the patio."

"Very thoughtful. Thank you, Camille."

She was young and beautiful. He hadn't tried to seduce her yet but promised himself it wouldn't be long. He turned on the outdoor stereo to Chopin, undressed, and opened the sliding doors onto his pool deck. On a table next to his favorite lounge chair sat the promised glass of wine, a cigar, and a pair of powerful binoculars. After swallowing a mouthful of the chardonnay, he lit the cigar and sat down to enjoy the magnificent view across the deep blue waters of the Mediterranean. Life was good. He had a perfect villa home and still had over forty-seven million euros in the bank, more than enough to live his life in luxury.

All he needed was a companion. He had grown weary of the local herd of high-end prostitutes who only pretended to care about him as long as the cash kept flowing. He thought of his neighbors, Mrs. Fenton and her daughter from Kentucky. Maybe he'd send for them.

His mother's voice screamed in his mind. *Are you kidding? You fool. What makes you think they'd spend their lives with the likes of you?*

It was a bad idea anyway. They could be followed. Sending them the occasional letter was a large enough risk. Maybe Camille? Perhaps he would start a family with her, even have a couple of kids. Just a fantasy. Problem was he missed his days as an assassin. He didn't need more money. He yearned for the excitement of the chase, the planning of the perfect hit.

A huge yacht idled a hundred yards offshore. Through the binoculars, Ishmael read the name, "Checkmate III." *Strange name for a boat.* On the aft deck, stood a hottie with a head of magenta-colored hair and wearing a skimpy bikini. Great body. She also had a pair of binoculars, and was looking in his direction. Behind her stood a short guy dressed in white slacks, a navy blazer, and a white fedora. The fingers of his right hand caressed a cigar. *Must be the owner. Lucky guy.*

Ishmael drained the rest of his wine and poured another glass. The woman on the yacht waved and he returned the gesture, but his arm felt heavy. Too much alcohol? He decided a dip in the pool would clear his head, but when he tried to stand, his legs didn't work.

So far, the plan was working beautifully. After pouring the tetrodotoxin solution into Ishmael's wine glass, Jacob rushed back to join me behind a cluster of bushes fifty feet away. When Ishmael walked out onto the deck, he didn't look like the man who had killed John, but reports were that he underwent extensive facial surgery. My phone buzzed with a text from Norman:

Carla just took a photograph. Ran his image against the ones from the airport in Brazil. He had surgery to change

his appearance, but my software package corrected for the changes. It's Ishmael.

I texted back: **How certain are you?**

He responded: **99.97%. Mr. Hamilton gave you a go ahead for the mission.**

Jacob and I stood and slowly walked over to where Ishmael struggled to move. The bullet hole scar in his left shoulder confirmed his identity beyond any doubt. I smiled. "Hello Ishmael."

His pupils dilated in terror.

"Surprised to see me? Don't try to answer. You've been drinking a deadly neurotoxin which is slowly paralyzing every muscle in your body. Comes from a puffer fish of all things. Soon, you'll stop breathing but will be mentally alert enough to experience your own slow suffocation."

His eyes widened further.

"Who is Fedallah? Tell us where to find him, and we might let you live."

His response gurgled in his throat. "Don't know."

"Too bad." I held up a syringe. "This is the antidote to the poison that's circulating through your body. Only a few drops will neutralize it and save your life." I held it in front of his face, so close it almost touched his skin.

The fingers of his right hand twitched. "I see you still have a little motor control, but you're losing it rapidly. What do you think, Ishmael? Should I be merciful? Should I save the life of the man who murdered my husband and killed dozens of others?" I placed the syringe in his right hand.

His eyes fixated on the life-saving injection. "I tell you what. I'm going to let God decide your fate. If He feels you deserve mercy, He'll give you the strength to use it." I turned and walked away.

Jacob climbed behind the wheel of the Ferrari. "Always wanted to drive one of these." He turned on the ignition, and the engine roared to life.

I picked up my phone and called Winston. "Mission accomplished. We'll be at the dinghy in five minutes." I opened the passenger door and hesitated a second.

"What's wrong?" Jacob asked.

"He kicked. Strong little guy, like his father. I think I'll call him Johnny." I looked up at the blue skies. "Would that be all right with you, John?" My baby kicked again, harder. I had my answer. I got into the car, and we drove away, the wind blowing through my hair. The world was now a safer place. We still didn't have the person who hired Ishmael, but that would come in time. I turned my face to the sun and rubbed my belly.

"Thank you."

OTHER BOOKS BY T. MILTON MAYER

The Immigrant
Scorpion Intrusion
Quantum

For more information about T. Milton Mayer, go to
Tmayerbooks.com

The story of Matthias Toebben begins as a tale of a young child growing up under the scourge of Nazi Germany. He was forced to witness things a boy of his age should never see. For Matthias and his family, every day was a struggle for survival in a time of overwhelming oppression.

At the age of twenty-one, he headed forth across the Atlantic Ocean to America. Although he was unable to speak a word of English and had only ten dollars in his pocket, he wasn't deterred. Those obstacles were offset by an abundance of ambition and determination. He found the United States to be a land of immense opportunity for anyone willing to work hard and make their visions a reality. He dedicated himself to the principles upon which his new country was founded: devotion to God, love of family, and dedication to the community. Through sheer determination, he succeeded, and with each success came another. Along the way, he faced multiple disasters, both professionally and personally. It was the way in which he overcame the setbacks that had defined him as one of the area's most respected and influential leaders.

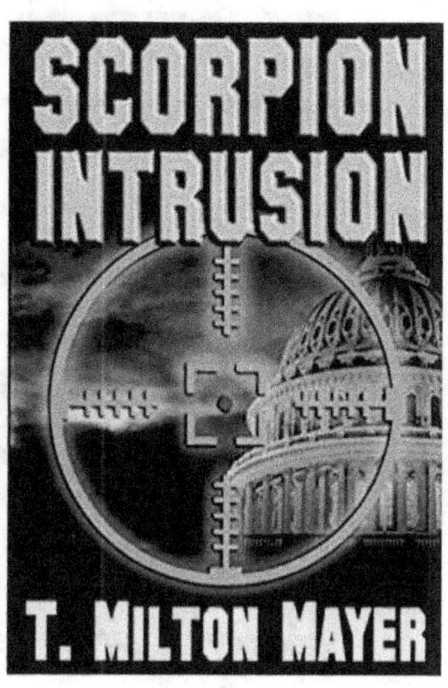

A high-tech machine is stolen from a research laboratory in Oslo, Norway. A Stanford University sophomore detonates a bomb, killing himself and a hundred other students during a pre-med chemistry lecture. The country's foremost aeronautical engineer and his family are kidnapped from their yacht while cruising to Bimini Island. The events are somehow related to a mysterious shipment being smuggled into the country from Canada. Something sinister is about to threaten the very foundation on the United States…an event more devastating than the 9/11 attacks.

Veteran CIA man Winston Hamilton, FBI Special Agent John Crawford, and Dr. Jacob Savich each possess unique skills. They combine their talents to become the country's only hope of avoiding the impending disaster. They follow a convoluted trail that begins in a tiny Afghan village thirty years ago and winds its way through present day corporate America. Can they stop the threat in time?

The United States faces a catastrophe far worse than the Wuhan pandemic of 2020. Like before, the threat originates in China, but this time it's not just another virus. It is a powerful device that is already embedded in cities throughout the civilized world. When activated, billions could die.

Jacob Savich is the only man capable of stopping whatever is planned. Though plagued by his own personal demons, he is commissioned by the President to assemble a clandestine team of warriors with the necessary backbone and moral flexibility to protect the country. Until now, they have been successful, but this new mission poses the most dangerous challenge Savich has ever faced. He must identify the nature of the attack, when it will occur, and who is responsible. His relentless pursuit of each clue takes him a step closer to stopping the elusive mastermind behind the plot, but it also leads him toward his own death. Despite the danger, Savich must hurry. Time is running out. The day of YAOGUAI is near. Modern civilization is about to end.

Quantum was a 2022 winner of the Royal Palm Literary Awards by Florida Writers Association.

www.ingramcontent.com/pod-product-compliance
Lightning Source LLC
Chambersburg PA
CBHW070555300726
48975CB00006B/1594